Praise for Sherryl Woods and the Sweet Magnolias

"Woods begins the Sweet Magnolias series with a focus on the unsettling effects of divorce and infidelity on the children of broken marriages, a theme that adds depth and emotional intensity to the romantic relationship."

—*Booklist* on *Stealing Home*

"Woods continues her Sweet Magnolias trilogy with this topical, interesting story. The characters are nicely layered, and the conflict is believable."

—*RT Book Reviews* on *A Slice of Heaven*

"Woods updates her readers on the continuing antics of the Sweet Magnolias in her holiday-themed, heartwarming contemporary romance, paving the way for even more stories set in this charming South Carolina town only a short drive from Charleston."

—*Booklist* on *Welcome to Serenity*

"Woods' readers will eagerly anticipate her trademark small-town setting, loyal friendships, and honorable mentors as they meet new characters and reconnect with familiar ones in this heartwarming tale."

—*Booklist* on *Home in Carolina*

"Woods never fails to come back to the romantic point."

—*Publishers Weekly* on *Sweet Tea at Sunrise*

For additional books by #1 *New York Times* bestselling author Sherryl Woods, visit her website, www.sherrylwoods.com, and click on the checklist.

SHERRYL WOODS

HOME IN CAROLINA

MIRA®

Recycling programs
for this product may
not exist in your area.

ISBN-13: 978-0-7783-1902-3

Home in Carolina

For questions and comments about the quality of this book, please contact us at
CustomerService@Harlequin.com.

www.MIRABooks.com

Printed in Italy by Grafica Veneta S.p.A.

First printing: July 2016
10 9 8 7 6 5 4 3 2 1

Dear Friends,

Welcome back to Serenity, South Carolina, and the world of the Sweet Magnolias. In *Home in Carolina*, not only will you get to catch up with old friends, but you'll be spending time with some of the younger generation.

Almost from the moment Ty Townsend and Annie Sullivan first appeared as a young teen couple in the pages of *A Slice of Heaven*, readers started begging for their story. My consistent reply for a very long time was that they were much too young to have a story of their own. They needed to go out into the world and learn a few life lessons. Boy, have they done that now!

Ty, the staunchest of friends when Annie was struggling with her eating disorder, has betrayed her terribly. When the now Major League pitcher returns to Serenity to recover from potentially career-ending shoulder surgery, not only does he need the help Annie can provide as a sports-injury therapist, he needs her forgiveness. If you remember anything about her mom, Dana Sue, forgiveness doesn't come easily to the Sullivan women.

I hope you'll enjoy Ty and Annie's path toward reconciliation, and spending time with the Sweet Magnolias once again. And be sure to check out *Sweet Tea at Sunrise*, which features Annie's best friend, Sarah, as she struggles to regain her self-esteem after a disastrous marriage. There's an absolutely wonderful sweet-talking guy on the scene to help with her recovery.

All best,

Sheryl Woods

HOME IN CAROLINA

CHAPTER ONE

Settled at her usual table near the kitchen of her mom's restaurant, Annie Sullivan ate the last of her omelet and opened the local paper to the sports section. Even though she and major league pitcher Tyler Townsend, a hometown boy, had been apart for a long time now, it was a habit she hadn't been able to break. She kept hoping that one day she'd see his name in print and it wouldn't hurt. So far, though, that hadn't happened.

Today, with the baseball season barely started in mid-April, she was expecting nothing more than a small jolt to her system from the local weekly. Instead, her jaw dropped at the headline at the top of the page: Star Braves Pitcher Ty Townsend on Injured Reserve. The article went on to report that after pitching just three games, the baseball sensation from Serenity would be out indefinitely following surgery two weeks ago for a potentially career-ending injury to his shoulder. He'd be doing rehab, possibly for months, and he'd be doing it right here in town. He was, in fact, already here.

Clutching the paper in a white-knuckled grip, Annie had to draw in several deep breaths before she could stand. Shouting for her mother, she headed straight for the restaurant kitchen, only to be intercepted by sous-chef Erik Whitney.

Regarding her with concern, Erik steadied her when she would have dashed right past him. "Hey, sweetheart, where's the fire?" he asked.

"I need to see my mother," she said, trying to wrench free of his grasp.

"She's in her office. What's wrong, Annie? You look as if you've seen a ghost."

Though she'd poured out her heart to Erik as a teenager, right this second she was incapable of speech. Instead, Annie simply handed him the paper.

Erik took one look at the headline and muttered a curse. "I knew this was going to happen," he said.

Annie stared at him, her sense of betrayal deepening. "You knew about this? You knew Ty was back in town?"

Erik nodded. "Since the day before yesterday."

"Mom, too?"

He nodded again.

Now it was Annie who uttered a curse, made a U-turn and headed back to the table to grab her purse. What had everyone been thinking, conspiring to keep something this huge from her? Especially her mom, who knew better than anyone the damage secrets, lies and betrayal could do.

Erik stuck with her. "Come on, Annie, don't blame your mother for this. Go to her office. Talk to her," he urged as she stormed past him through the kitchen. "She was just trying to protect you."

At the door, she turned and asked angrily, "So I could be blindsided, instead? Ty had surgery two weeks ago, Erik! He's been in town how long—a couple of days? A week? It's not as if this happened yesterday."

"I'm sure Dana Sue thought it wouldn't make the paper here before she had a chance to tell you."

"Forget the stupid newspaper. We're talking about Serenity in an age of cell phones and the Internet," Annie said incredulously. "Gossip spreads in minutes, and around here Ty's big news. Heck, even *you* knew, and you're not tapped into the grapevine. You all knew before one word of this hit the paper."

"Helen's tapped in and I'm married to her, to say nothing of working for your mom. Not much gets past the Sweet Magnolias. And in this case, they all knew what was going on the instant Maddie found out Ty had to have surgery."

"Which begs the question," Annie said bitterly. "Why didn't anyone think I had a right to know?" A thought suddenly struck her. "That's where Maddie went a couple of weeks ago, isn't it? She went to be with Ty when he had his surgery."

Erik nodded. "Look, it's not about you deserving to know," he said reasonably. "You've been pretty touchy about anything to do with Ty for quite a while now. Nobody's known quite how to handle it."

Okay, that was fair. In fact, Annie totally understood the dilemma. She and Ty had been together on a casual basis during her senior year in high school and for a couple of years after that. Since their mothers, Dana Sue and Maddie, were best friends, she and Ty had been friends forever, as well. The ties binding them had been tight on many levels.

And then it had all unraveled. Annie supposed the breakup had been as inevitable as the fact that they'd fallen in love in the first place. After all, a superstar professional athlete had beautiful women falling at his feet in every city. How was Annie, the quiet hometown girl struggling every day to beat an eating disorder, supposed to compete with that, especially when she was still in college?

The official disintegration of their relationship had dragged out over an entire year, partly because neither of them had known how to dash all those parental expectations that they'd marry and live happily ever after.

For months they'd seen the handwriting on the wall, but they'd both been in denial. When tensions had been running especially high, they'd tried to avoid coming back to Serenity at the same time. On the rare occasions when family get-togethers couldn't be avoided, they'd tried to deal with the awkwardness with carefully orchestrated polite indifference. They'd both understood how a bitter split could potentially damage the lifelong friendship between their mothers, and they'd wanted to avoid inflicting that kind of collateral damage. At least they'd agreed on that much.

Of course, all of that was before the real damage had been done, before Ty's infidelity had become public knowledge in the worst possible way. After that, all bets had been off. There'd been no more pretense that things had ended amicably.

Fortunately, neither her mom nor Ty's had asked too many questions once the facts were out there. It went beyond sensitivity. Annie suspected Dana Sue and Maddie had made a pact years earlier to leave the two of them alone. Goodness knew, the Sweet Magnolias, as Dana Sue and Maddie and Helen had been known since high school, meddled in everyone else's lives, but over the years they'd barely mentioned Ty in Annie's presence or her to him. More recently, the silence had been deafening.

Annie supposed their current avoidance of the subject was part of the same old pattern, though she was in no mood to cut them any slack this time. Didn't they think she'd care that

Ty had sustained a serious injury? Didn't they know what it would do to her for him to be right back here, in her face every single day? Couldn't they at least have warned her?

As she started out the door, Erik tried once more to stop her.

"Wait!" he commanded. "Come on, Annie. If you won't talk to your mother, talk to me. I swear I'll just listen. You can rant and rave all you want."

She regarded him with a bleak expression. "There's nothing to say." Ty had as much right to come home to Serenity as she did, even if it would turn her life upside down.

"Where are you going?"

She shook her head. She honestly didn't know. Not to work, that was for sure. She worked at The Corner Spa, owned by her mom, Helen and Ty's mom. Maddie, in fact, ran it. Annie didn't want to face her right now, either. Though they both tried, it had been awkward between them ever since the breakup. Now it would be a thousand times worse. She wasn't sure she could bear another of Maddie's pitying looks.

Ironically, Annie worked at the spa as a sports injury therapist and personal trainer. Armed with her degree as a physical therapist and two years of experience at a sports injury facility in Charleston, she'd had the idea to add a physical therapy component to the spa's services.

And while the spa was open only to women, there wasn't a doubt in her mind that Ty intended to do his rehab there in the off-hours when no one else was around. He could be counting on his stepfather and former coach, Cal Maddox, to oversee his rehab, or even the spa's other personal fitness instructor, Elliott Cruz, but Annie suspected that sooner or later someone was going to suggest she get involved. She was the one with the expertise in sports injuries, after all.

Just the thought of seeing Ty again was enough to make her want to throw up. It had been years since she'd won her battle with anorexia, and though she'd never been bulimic, right this second any thought of food made her nauseous. The little bit she'd already eaten churned in her stomach.

Even as the dark thoughts registered, Annie gasped. No way! she thought fiercely. She was not going to let Ty's return send her back into the kind of self-destructive eating pattern that had nearly killed her. She was stronger than that. And he was a pig. In fact, that might have to become her mantra, one she repeated at least a dozen times a day.

"I am strong, and Tyler Townsend is a pig!" she said aloud, testing it.

Yes, indeed, that ought to keep her from backsliding. And if she felt herself slipping on either front, well, she could always take an extended vacation somewhere far away from Serenity until Ty's shoulder had healed and he was back to his glamorous, self-indulgent lifestyle, the lifestyle he'd chosen over her.

Satisfied with her plan, she considered going to work, after all, but concluded it might be a bit too soon to test herself. Instead, she called the spa and asked Elliott to take any of her appointments he had time for and to cancel the rest.

"I'm taking a mental health day," she informed him, falling back on an excuse she hadn't used since high school.

"Ah, you heard about Ty," he said, sounding sympathetic. "Anything I can do?"

"Has he been sneaking in there after hours?" she asked, hating the fact that there were virtually no secrets in this town except those kept from her.

"Just a couple of times," he admitted. He hesitated, then added, "I've started working with him, but he'd do better with you."

"Hell will freeze over before that happens," she said heatedly.

"Think about it, Annie," Elliott urged. "His career's on the line, and he was once your friend."

"He was more than a friend and he blew it," she retorted, unyielding. "Will you deal with my appointments today or not?"

"Of course I will," he said. "I'm sorry you're hurting."

Annie sighed. "I just wish I knew if I'm more hurt because Ty's back or because everyone apparently conspired to keep it from me."

"A little of both, I suspect," Elliott said. "Do something totally spontaneous today, something a little crazy. Blow off some steam. You'll feel better."

Annie considered the suggestion, then dismissed it. The only thing that might make her feel marginally better would be having Elliott—or anyone else—agree to punch Ty's face in. She smiled at the thought and suddenly knew exactly where she needed to go—to the one person who might actually do that for her.

Ten minutes later, she was sitting on a stool behind the counter at her dad's hardware store on Main Street, while he waited on a customer. Ronnie Sullivan had a history of being quick-tempered and protective. This might work to her advantage today.

As soon as they were alone, her father surveyed her intently. "You don't look so good, kid."

"You could make me feel better," she suggested.

"By punching Ty's lights out?" he guessed, proving he, too, had been in on the town's worst-kept secret. "I don't think so."

She sighed. "Why not? He deserves it."

Ronnie laughed. "No question about it, but can you imagine the ruckus that would stir up between your mom and

Maddie? They'd be forced to take sides, and so would Cal and I. Then Helen and Erik would be drawn into it, and eventually the entire town would likely follow suit. Pretty soon, everybody would have to wear buttons or ribbons to declare which side they're on. Sorry, sweetie, it just wouldn't be good for business, and in the end, you'd be consumed by guilt for stirring it all up."

Despite herself, Annie chuckled at her dad's logic. It was true: Serenity did have a tendency to take sides, and there was no way this feud between her and Ty would stay quiet for long, even without her dad beating Ty up for her. And, damn her soft heart, she *would* feel guilty about it.

"I guess I'll just have to deal with this," she said morosely.

Her dad pulled a stool up next to hers and studied her with a frown. "Is there anything else I can do to help?"

"You can tell me why men are such idiots," she said. The question wasn't rhetorical. She really wanted to know.

"Hormones and a lack of common sense," Ronnie said at once. "Just look how I messed things up with your mom for no good reason. Weigh that against how long it took me to make things right. Idiocy definitely played a role in that." He slanted a look at her. "You want to talk about what happened? I know it's a touchy subject, but you've never said a word about how you felt when things blew up and all Ty's dirty laundry was spread all over the tabloids."

"I think my feelings are pretty obvious without dissecting them," she told him.

"Sometimes talking does help."

She shook her head. "Not likely."

"Sweetie, I know how badly he hurt you, and if I really thought it would help, I would punch him." He hesitated, then added, "I also know how important his friendship was to you for a long time before that. Do you really want to lose that, too?"

"I lost our friendship a long time ago," she said mournfully. That, as much as anything else, was what had broken her heart. "I just have to face it, Dad. It's over. Not just the relationship, but also the friendship. I'll never be able to trust Ty again."

"Your mom learned to trust me again," he reminded her gently.

"Not the same," she said.

Her dad was right about one thing, though. Cheating was something he and Ty had in common. The big difference was that Ronnie had recognized his mistake after one careless, irresponsible slip. Ty not only hadn't acknowledged it, he'd compounded it by cheating over and over until he'd finally gotten caught. He had a three-year-old son as proof of his infidelity.

Annie might have been able to get past the cheating with enough time, but that precious little boy? No way. Any babies Ty had were supposed to be with her, not some gold digger who'd slept with Ty a couple of times, then dumped her kid with him in exchange for a big payoff when he wouldn't marry her.

Oh, Annie knew all the gory details. Not because Ty had told her, but because they'd been tabloid fodder for weeks. Obviously if Ty was home, so was his little boy. Now everyone in Serenity who'd been living on Mars when the story first broke would know just how big a fool she'd been to give her heart to some hotshot sports superstar.

Worst of all, despite everything—the betrayal, the hurt, the humiliation—she still loved him. And that made her an even bigger idiot than he was.

* * *

"You need to call Annie," Maddie told Ty after seeing the headline about his return in the Serenity newspaper. "It was crazy to think we could keep your being back here quiet for long."

"Don't you think Dana Sue probably filled her in?" he said, torn between dread and anticipation at the thought of speaking to Annie. Their relationship had ended really badly, and it had been all his fault. "Besides, Annie doesn't want to talk to me. She made that plain three years ago."

"When Trevor was born," his mother guessed.

Ty nodded. He loved his son to pieces, but he knew that Annie would never in a million years get past the fact that he'd not only cheated, but fathered a child with someone else. There wasn't an explanation in the world good enough to make her see past that one huge mistake.

Claiming that they hadn't been exclusive certainly hadn't worked. Reminding her of the countless times they'd talked about how reasonable it was to date others while she was still in college and he was on the road with the team had only backfired.

"That didn't include getting another woman pregnant," she'd retorted, her eyes filled with the kind of hurt he hadn't seen since her mom had kicked her dad out for cheating when Annie was fourteen. "How am I supposed to forgive that?"

"I don't know," he'd told her, defeated. "I honestly don't know."

Truthfully, he still didn't. But when he'd been injured, the one bright spot had been the chance to come back to Serenity and maybe take a stab at making things right with Annie. He could have done the rehab anywhere, had the best trainers in the world working with him, but he'd refused every option the team had proposed, packed up Trevor and come home. He wasn't entirely sure why making amends to Annie was so important right now, but it was. One of the lessons he'd learned the hard way was that friendships were more valuable and lasting than casual sex. Too bad he'd had to lose his best friend before he'd figured it out.

Now that he was here, though, he had no idea what the next step should be. Maybe his mom was right. Maybe it just needed to start with a phone call.

"Does she ever mention me?" he asked, looking for some sign that Annie's attitude had mellowed.

Maddie shook her head. "Certainly not to me. Can you blame her?"

"I suppose not."

"I so wish things had turned out differently, Ty. You two—"

"Are over," he said flatly. "Her decision."

"If you honestly believe that, then why did you come back here?"

"I thought it would be good for Trevor to spend some time with his family." That, at least, was true. His son needed more stability than he could get even from the most doting nanny and a dad who was on the road for days—sometimes weeks—at a time.

His mother studied him skeptically. "Really? And that thought only occurred to you after I mentioned that Annie had moved back home?" Before he could respond, she continued, "Because it certainly didn't cross your mind during the off-season last year, or the year before that."

"Coincidence," he claimed.

"Oh, Ty," she chided. "At least be honest with yourself. You're here because of Annie. Why bother denying it, at least with me? Now, what are you going to do to make things right?"

He glanced across the table and saw the lingering disappointment in his mother's expression. That was as hard to take as losing Annie. After the way his dad had cheated on his mom and the way Ty had hated him for it, surely he should have behaved more responsibly. Instead, he was apparently a chip off the old block, after all.

"I have no idea what I can do," he admitted.

"Well, you need to come up with a plan. The two of you are bound to cross paths. Not only is this a very small town, but our families are connected. Dana Sue and I are friends. We're in business together. Annie works for me, for heaven's sake."

Ty winced at the complicated mess he'd managed to create. "I'm sorry, Mom. If this is going to become some big thing between you and Dana Sue, I can go somewhere else for rehab. There are plenty of facilities in Atlanta."

"No," she said, backing down at once. "Having you back home is such an unexpected joy for me and for your brothers and sisters. It's giving us a chance to spend time with Trevor, too."

She drew herself up. "Dana Sue and I will figure out a way to deal with this," she said confidently. "We've been friends a long time, and we've always known that something might come between you and Annie. That's why we tried so hard to stay out of it."

"How about you and Annie, though?" he asked worriedly, wishing he'd thought his decision through before disrupting everyone's lives. Coming back had been selfish, he could see that now. "She's been like another daughter to you, and you work together. It's going to freak her out knowing I'm around. What if she quits just to avoid me?"

"Annie's more mature than that," Maddie said with certainty. "She's a strong young woman. She'll cope."

"What if it, you know...?" He hesitated, then voiced his greatest fear, the one that had nagged at him since the day they'd parted. "What if she goes back to being anorexic?"

Maddie regarded him with dismay. "No, Ty! She won't do that."

"She could, Mom." He shook his head. "What the hell was I thinking? The stress of Ronnie taking off is part of what triggered her eating disorder in the first place. She felt like her life was a mess, and food was the only thing she could control. Now, having me in her face could do the same thing. I'd never forgive myself if that happened."

"It's not going to happen," Maddie said emphatically. "She was just a teenager when she got so sick. She's twenty-three now. It's been years. Believe me, Dana Sue and Ronnie know all the signs. Annie still sees Dr. McDaniels from time to time. They'll be all over her if there's even a hint that her anorexia is back. Besides, she didn't fall apart when you two split up, so there's no reason to think she will now just because you're here in Serenity."

"I suppose." Still, he couldn't help worrying about Annie. She'd never been half as tough as she'd wanted everyone to believe she was. He was one of the few who'd seen her vulnerability way before she'd been diagnosed with anorexia. She'd looked up to him, trusted him, talked to him...fallen in love with him.

Then he'd betrayed her. And for what? A string of casual flings that had meant nothing. He'd wanted to prove he was hot stuff. Hanging out with groupies had been a rite of passage into the big leagues. All the guys liked to unwind after the games. There were always eager women around.

Unfortunately, it had taken too long for him to realize just how empty and meaningless all that was. Compared to what he had with Annie—the real deal, he knew now—it was just sex and a few laughs with women who liked to brag they'd hooked up with a baseball player.

To his very deep regret, Trevor's mom had barely stood out from the crowd. When they'd met after a road game in Cincinnati, she'd struck him as shy, with her big brown eyes and corn silk hair. She was quieter than most of the others, less aggressive. She'd actually been able to hold up her end of a conversation. Ironically, he'd seen a vulnerability in her that had reminded him of Annie.

The next time he'd been in Cincinnati, Ty had seen Dee-Dee again, spent three nights with her. On his third trip to town, she'd told him she was pregnant.

The news had hit him like one of his own fastballs in the gut, left him slack-jawed and sputtering. He realized he didn't even know her last name.

Nor could he be sure the baby was his. He wanted proof, insisted on it, which set off their first huge fight. Dee-Dee, whose last name turned out to be Mitchell, was insulted he would even ask. He was appalled that she thought he was so stupid he wouldn't.

Struggling with years of conditioning to take responsibility for his own actions, Ty had turned to a buddy on the team for advice.

"You in love with her?" Jimmy Falco had asked.

"No," Ty admitted. "I barely know her."

"Then you wait. You get a paternity test. If the kid turns out to be yours, you go from there."

Dee-Dee had been furious when he'd told her the plan. She'd threatened to go to the tabloids if he didn't marry her immediately. Despite all the potential for very public ugliness, Ty held firm. That was when he should have gone to Annie and confessed everything, but he'd waited. And, of course, the news had leaked out.

By the time Trevor was born, any faint feelings he might have had for Dee-Dee were dead and buried. The positive paternity test didn't change that. In court, he acknowledged being the boy's father, relinquished custody to Dee-Dee with visitation rights for himself, arranged to pay child support, and even agreed to a generous lump-sum payment to get Dee-Dee her own place, a two-bedroom condo in a very nice building.

Two months later, he'd opened the door to his hotel room on a road trip to Denver to find Trevor in a basket on the doorstep, and Dee-Dee nowhere in sight. In an instant, he took on the role of single dad.

Because of the prior arrangement and Dee-Dee's disappearance, it had taken a year of wrangling in court to change their custody agreement so that he had sole custody. He'd struggled to balance parenthood with a physically demanding career that took him away from home too often. Finding a nanny he'd trusted had been a nightmare, but eventually he'd found Cassandra, an older woman who'd raised four children of her own and doted on Trevor as if he were one of her own grandchildren. To Ty's amusement, she treated him as a son who'd gone astray and needed firm moral guidance. Cassandra had been a godsend for both of them.

In the meantime, the whole thing had played out in the tabloids. He imagined that Dee-Dee had gotten a pretty penny for the inside scoop, to say nothing of what she must have gotten for tipping off a photographer before she left the baby outside his hotel room.

And it had all hit the fan before he'd been able to work up the nerve to tell Annie about any of it. He'd been the worst kind of coward.

What Annie thought of him—what he thought of himself—didn't matter, though, not as long as she didn't fall back into her old anorexic eating pattern. He didn't think he could handle that. Hurting her was bad enough. He'd never be able to live with destroying all the progress she'd made, the normal, healthy life she was leading.

Then, again, maybe he was exaggerating the pain he'd caused her. Maybe she'd made peace with what had happened, considered herself lucky to be rid of him. She could have moved on by now. It was certainly what he deserved, but the thought depressed him just the same.

Because Annie Sullivan had slipped into his heart about a million years ago, and she was still there...despite everything he'd done to show her otherwise.

CHAPTER TWO

Helen Decatur-Whitney left the courtroom feeling triumphant. She barely resisted an urge to pump her fist in the air on the courthouse steps. Such gloating, she thought, might have been a bit unseemly.

Still, she couldn't help savoring today's victory. Her client had gotten everything she deserved from her weasel of an ex-husband. Helen had enjoyed the man's shell-shocked expression as the judge had handed down his ruling.

A few years ago such a verdict wouldn't have been worthy of note, because just about all her clients won, no matter how bitterly contested the divorce. Lately, though, ever since her marriage to Erik and the birth of her daughter, Sarah Beth, Helen had taken fewer and fewer cases. Her standing as the barracuda attorney of choice in the entire state of South Carolina was no longer assured, so today's triumph was especially sweet. She was back!

As she had for years, she wanted to celebrate with her best friends, the Sweet Magnolias, with one of their margarita nights. This victory had been a long time in coming. For quite a while, Helen had feared she'd lost her edge to the complacency of marriage and motherhood. After today, she almost believed she could have it all.

First she punched in Dana Sue's number on her cell phone. "My place, tonight at eight," she announced. "We're celebrating my courtroom comeback."

"Eight o'clock on a Friday night?" Dana Sue asked incredulously. "Haven't you heard? I run a very successful restaurant. We're packed at that hour."

"And my husband, your outstanding sous-chef, is perfectly capable of handling the last couple of hours on his own and closing up," Helen reminded her. "When was the last time we all cut loose?"

"It's been a while," Dana Sue conceded. She paused, then asked, "Have you spoken to Maddie?"

There was a cautious note in Dana Sue's voice Helen couldn't quite read. "Not yet, why?"

"She might be avoiding me."

Helen drew a blank. "Why? Did you two have words about something?" Over the years, there had been spats among the three of them, but they'd been healed almost before they'd begun.

"Ty and Annie," Dana Sue said succinctly. "It all hit the wall today. Annie found out that Ty's home. Erik saw her right after she found out, and he says she's livid because none of us warned her. I called the spa earlier, and Elliott told me she called and took the day off. Now I can't find her."

Helen muttered an expletive she rarely used. "Ty and Annie's issues have nothing to do with you and Maddie," she said. Then amended, "Well, of course they do, because they're your kids, but didn't you resolve years ago to let them work out their own problems?"

"It's harder to stick to that now that they so obviously have big-time issues," Dana Sue said. "Ty came back here with a little boy, for goodness' sake! How's that for rubbing it in my daughter's face that he cheated on her?"

"It stinks," Helen agreed. "And if you want to torture Ty, I'll help, but please, please don't let it come between you and Maddie. You two are my best friends in the world. I don't want to have to start tiptoeing around or seeing you separately because the two of you aren't speaking."

"Look, I know this isn't Maddie's fault," Dana Sue acknowledged, then added with real heat in her voice, "but how are we supposed to pretend that her son didn't rip out my daughter's heart? Am I supposed to ignore that?"

"Don't you think Maddie's as upset about that as you are?" Helen suggested. "She loves Annie, too." She thought about it for a minute, then said, "How about this? We'll just declare the topic off limits. Or else I'll negotiate a truce. I'm very good at negotiating things, in case you've forgotten."

Dana Sue laughed at last, cutting through the tension. "As if you'd let us forget."

Helen seized on the tiny opening. "Come on, sweetie, don't say no. I want you there. It won't be a celebration without you."

"Okay, fine, but if things get tense, I'll leave."

"Let's just cross that bridge when we come to it. I'll see you at eight," Helen said, determined to make sure her friends made peace before the night was out.

"I'll bring the food," Dana Sue said. "I'll make a fresh batch of guacamole and steal some appetizers from the freezer here."

"Can't have margaritas without that killer guacamole," Helen agreed.

After she'd disconnected the call, she dialed Maddie and repeated the invitation. When Maddie hesitated, Helen jumped in. "Dana Sue's coming. The subject of Ty and Annie is off limits. We're only going to talk about me."

Like Dana Sue, Maddie laughed. "Not much new about that. Okay. I'm not convinced you can keep us from veering off onto the subject of our children, but I don't want to miss out on watching you try. Should I tell Jeanette?"

"Absolutely," Helen said. Jeanette, who was in charge of the day spa services at their business, had become an honorary Sweet Magnolia. Though she'd only been around for a few years now, she was definitely one of their own. "If you'll invite her and maybe pick up some chips and cut veggies for Dana Sue's guacamole, that'll give me time to buy the biggest bottle of tequila at the liquor store and to spend time with my daughter before she goes to bed."

"By the way, what are we celebrating?" Maddie asked.

"I took Henry Porter to the cleaners in court today, pun intended." Porter ran a chain of dry cleaners in the region. He'd hoped to leave his wife of thirty years with next to nothing, even though she'd worked right alongside him building that chain from one little neighborhood shop to the dozen outlets they had now. Helen had seen it differently, as had the judge, especially after the testimony of the Porter children about how involved their mother had been in the business.

"Good for you," Maddie said. "I hate men who minimize their wives' contributions to their success."

Maddie knew more than some about that, since she'd had just such a husband before divorcing physician Bill Townsend and winding up with the high school baseball coach, Cal Maddox, who was ten years younger. In Helen's opinion, that particular revenge had been especially sweet.

"Well, we can toast to all the women who've been mistreated like that and emerged victorious," Helen said.

"Sounds like fun to me," Maddie said, then hesitated. "Helen, how did Dana Sue sound really? Is she very upset that Ty's back? I know it's awkward, and I feel awful for Annie, but I'm so happy to have him and Trevor here for a while."

"I know you are, and I don't think Dana Sue begrudges you this time with them. It's just hard for her to see Annie so upset."

Maddie sighed. "You should probably know that Annie didn't show up for work today."

"So I heard," Helen admitted.

"Elliott said she'd just found out about Ty," Maddie continued, her tone sympathetic. "She read it in the paper, of all things. I probably should have told her myself, but I thought Dana Sue would. This is so damn complicated. I have no idea what my son was thinking."

"I doubt thinking was involved in this mess," Helen said dryly. "If you want my advice, you need to enjoy having Ty around and stay out of his relationship with Annie. They're adults now. And in case you're wondering, I said pretty much the same thing to Dana Sue."

"It's just that I was so sure..." Maddie's voice trailed off.

"They were so sweet together, I think we all thought they'd be together forever," Helen admitted. "But it was never up to us."

"I know. See you tonight."

Helen hung up, relieved that her desire to celebrate her courtroom victory might give Maddie and Dana Sue the chance they needed to meet on neutral turf. For the first time in several years—since Sarah Beth's birth, in fact—she felt like her old self again...in control and on top.

Helen's feeling of euphoria lasted for just under two hours. She'd barely walked in the door and set down the tequila and other supplies she'd bought for tonight's gathering, when a hospital in Florida called to let her know that her mother had been admitted with a broken hip. Clutching the phone, Helen sat down hard.

"She broke her hip," she repeated, her tone dull. How many times had she heard of seniors whose health went on a downward spiral after an accident like this? Not that her mom was that old. Flo Decater was barely into her seventies and still active, so maybe this wasn't so bad.

"How serious is it?" she asked with surprising hesitation for a woman who prided herself on being quick, knowledgeable and decisive in any emergency.

"The surgery went well," the nurse said, her tone chipper. "But she is asking for you, and you should know she won't be able to be on her own for a while once she's released from the hospital. That means a rehab facility or nursing home or at-home care. You can discuss that when you see her."

"But I…" Helen began, then stopped herself before she said that she didn't have time to fly to Florida. She and her mother might not be close, but she owed her.

After her husband's death when Helen was only ten, Flo had worked two jobs to see that Helen had everything she needed growing up. Flo had scrimped and saved to make college possible, hounded Helen to keep her grades up so she could win scholarships.

Now it was up to Helen to see that her mother was well cared for. In her mind, a condo by the water in Florida and monthly checks were adequate compensation, but clearly her mother now needed more. Helen couldn't abandon her to figure all this out for herself.

"Tell her I'll be there tomorrow," she said eventually. After all, she was an expert at juggling. Her decisiveness kicked in. How long could it possibly take to make arrangements for her mother's care? A day or two at most. The nanny could cover Sarah Beth's needs, and Erik would be here to take up the slack. Helen's secretary could reschedule her appointments. Even as the thoughts crossed her mind, Helen began making lists of what needed to be done. She had an entire page of notes, including the nurse's recommendations of local rehab facilities, before she'd hung up the phone.

By the time the first of the Sweet Magnolias walked in the door, Helen had all of the arrangements made for a quick overnight trip to South Florida. Handling all the details kept her from actually thinking about what she'd find when she got there.

Thank heaven for margarita night, she thought, taking her first deep swallow of a very large, very tart drink. She was going to need alcohol and good friends to face what lay ahead, because she and her mother could fight over nothing faster than two cars going sixty could collide head-on.

Still upset by his conversation with his mother about Annie, Ty found himself heading for Cal's office at the high school on Friday afternoon. Even before Cal had become his stepfather, he'd been Ty's coach and mentor. Ty could talk to him about things he'd never say to his mom or even to his father. As a former big league player himself, Cal understood that world in ways that no one else around here could.

Ty was slouched down in a chair, idly rubbing his aching shoulder, when Cal eventually came in.

"Well, this is a surprise! What brings you by?" Cal asked, studying him intently. "You having trouble figuring out what to do with all this time on your hands?"

"Something like that," Ty said.

"You could hang around here this afternoon, help me coach the pitchers."

Ty shook his head. "I'd need to show 'em what I'm talking about, and right now I throw balls like a girl."

Cal gave him a commiserating look. "Rehab's just started, Ty. It'll get better."

"It never did for you," Ty said, referring to the fact that Cal's own major league career had been ended by an injury.

"And my life turned out just fine," Cal pointed out. "I love teaching. I love your mom and our family. I don't have a single regret."

"Oh, come on, Cal," Ty scoffed. "You can't tell me you weren't depressed when you realized you were never going to play ball again."

"True enough," his stepfather admitted. "I was in a self-pitying funk, as a matter of fact, but then a very wise man came to visit me and told me that there were still plenty of worthwhile things I could do. He steered me toward teaching and coaching. In fact, he's the one who brought me to Serenity." He grinned. "Fortunately for you, you have me to tell you the same thing."

"Gee, how reassuring," Ty grumbled sourly.

Cal gave him a long, hard look. "You really are having a pity party for yourself today, aren't you? Look, here's the truth, Ty. There's no reason to think our situations are alike. I had complications. You're healing well. It's just going to take time and determination. You lose the rest of this season, so what? You'll be back stronger than ever next year."

"Is that your medical opinion?" Ty inquired.

Cal came around his desk and perched on the corner. "Okay, what's really got you down today? It's got nothing to do with pitching, because we both know your prognosis looks good. What put you in this mood?" Cal gave him a knowing look when Ty remained silent. "Why did I even ask? This is about Annie. You came home thinking everything would fall into place just the way it was in the old days, and now you're figuring out that if you want her back, you're going to have to work for it."

"I never expected it to be easy," Ty insisted. "I know she hates my guts."

"If she does, that's probably a good thing," Cal said.

"In what universe?"

"Hate's the opposite of love, or so they say. If she had no feelings for you at all, that's when you'd really need to worry. Have you called her?"

Ty shook his head.

"Stopped by the spa while she's there?"

"No."

"Dropped in over at Ronnie and Dana Sue's?"

Ty regarded him incredulously. "You have to be kidding me! Dana Sue'd probably slap me silly with a cast-iron skillet. You weren't here for the scene she made when she found out Ronnie had cheated on her. That is one scary woman."

Cal chuckled. "She is feisty, no question about that. So, what, then? You're waiting for Annie to make the first move? Good luck with that."

"Yeah, I know," Ty said glumly.

"Then what is your plan?"

"I don't actually have a plan." He thought about it, then murmured, "Flowers? I could send over a ton of daisies. Annie always loved daisies."

"It would break the ice, at least. But I don't think you can count on flowers doing the hard work for you. When it comes to courting a woman, you have to put yourself out there, take a few risks. Flowers are too easy."

"In other words, she's going to want to see me bleed."

Cal bit back a smile. "In a manner of speaking. I think you owe her a little public groveling, don't you?"

"Just for starters," Ty conceded. Truthfully, he owed Annie that and a whole lot more. He stood up, feeling marginally better. "Thanks."

"You coming by the field tonight? Ronnie and I could use some help coaching Little League. We have too many kids and too few coaches."

"And give Ronnie a chance to beat me to a pulp? No, thanks."

Cal chuckled. "You could always hold your little sister or your baby brother. Ronnie would never throw a punch at a man holding a kid."

"I am not hiding behind a toddler who's still in diapers," Ty said, referring to Cole. "Or Trevor or Jessica Lynn, either, for that matter. That would be pathetic."

"So is hiding out from Annie," Cal said, clapping him on the shoulder. "Deal with her, Ty. At least you'll know where you stand."

Unfortunately, he already knew where he stood with Annie. And Cal was right about one things: flowers—even entire vanloads of them—weren't going to fix things.

Annie shoved the plate of food aside, untouched. But a pointed glance from her mother had her pulling it back.

"I'm just not hungry right this second," she grumbled, even as she ate several bites of Sullivan's pot roast special only to wipe the look of concern from her mother's face.

"You're upset about Ty," Dana Sue said. "I get that. And I'm really sorry I kept quiet about him being back here. I was just trying to find the right time to tell you."

"I understand," Annie said. Once she'd cooled down, she'd realized how impossible the whole situation was, especially for her mom and Maddie.

Her mother regarded her worriedly. "I just don't want you to…"

"Stop eating," Annie said, completing the unspoken thought. "Mom, it's okay. Really. I ate breakfast this morning—ask Erik. I'd almost finished before I saw the article in the paper about Ty being back. I even had a bowl of soup at Wharton's for lunch. You can ask Grace, if you want to."

"I'm not going to spy on you," Dana Sue said with a self-righteous display of indignation.

Annie raised a brow. "It wouldn't be the first time."

"That was a long time ago," her mother replied. "When you first got out of the hospital, yes, your dad and I kept a close eye on your eating habits. We had to." Unspoken was the fact that Annie had lied so often, they hadn't dared to trust anything she told them.

"You had your spies when I was away at college, too," Annie reminded her without rancor. She'd understood why they'd done that, too, and since she'd had no intention of reverting to her old ways, she'd never voiced any objections to the frequent calls to the dorm counselors. Lately, though, she'd thought they were beyond all that. She'd worked hard, not only to stay healthy but also to regain her parents' trust. It hurt to see that distrust back in her mother's eyes, but on some level she understood it.

"I'm a mom. Sue me," Dana Sue said blithely, not so much as blinking at the charge that she'd spied. "Let's drop this for now. I have something important I need to ask you, and I want you to be totally honest. If this bothers you, you have to say so."

Annie regarded her curiously, surprised by her somber tone. "What are you talking about?"

"I'm supposed to go to Helen's tonight."

"A Sweet Magnolias night," Annie guessed. "What does that have to do with me?"

"Will it bother you if I hang out with Maddie?"

There was a tiny little twinge, but Annie stomped on it. Her mother was *not* being disloyal. "Mom, don't be absurd," she said, meaning it. "You guys have been friends forever. Just because Ty and I aren't speaking doesn't mean you and Maddie shouldn't."

"You're sure?"

"Of course I am. Go."

"You and I could do something instead, especially if you want to talk about all this. Or we could drive over to Charleston and see a movie. I've already cleared it with Erik to leave him in charge here at the restaurant, so I can take off now."

"The last thing I want to talk about is Ty. That subject is dead. Over. Kaput."

"Really?" her mom asked skeptically.

"Yes, really."

"Then how about the movie?"

"So I can sit there for two hours and feel guilty for keeping you from spending the evening with your friends? No way."

"Then what will you do tonight?"

Annie shrugged. She didn't want to go home and sit in an empty house. Who knew what time her mother would get home, and her dad would probably stay late at the hardware store. "Maybe I'll see if Dad wants to go to a movie or something. We haven't hung out in a while."

"Your dad's planning to go to Little League batting practice, then go for pizza with Cal and the kids." Dana Sue's expression brightened. "You could go with him. He'll have to help Katie keep an eye on Jessica Lynn and Cole while Cal's coaching. I'm sure he'd love an extra pair of hands."

Rather than dismissing the idea outright and giving her

mother more to worry about, Annie said, "I'll think about it. Maybe."

Dana Sue clearly wasn't fooled by the evasive answer. "Are you concerned you'll run into Ty there?"

"Mom!"

"I'm just saying you don't need to be. The past couple of nights he's gone to the spa to work with Elliott. The way I hear it, he's been there for hours. I'm sure that's where he'll be tonight, too."

Rather than reassuring her as her mom had clearly intended, Dana Sue's words only solidified Annie's resolve to avoid the ball field at all costs. "Which means his son will probably be at the ball field with Cal," Annie said. "No, thanks."

Dana Sue looked crestfallen. "Oh, sweetie, I'm sorry. I didn't think about that. I still haven't gotten used to the idea that Ty even has a son."

"Yeah, well, it's all I think about." Despite her resolve not to let anyone see how much she still cared, Annie felt the sting of tears in her eyes. She stood up and announced, "I'm going for a walk."

Seeing the immediate worry in Dana Sue's eyes, she bent down and kissed her mother's cheek. "Don't start fretting, Mom. I'll be fine. Have fun and watch those margaritas. Helen's are lethal."

Dana Sue laughed. "Don't I know it."

Annie left before her mom decided to suggest she tag along, as she had the last time the Sweet Magnolias had gotten together. She knew she'd be welcome, but it would be way too awkward being there with Maddie with the one subject on everyone's mind suddenly taboo because of her presence.

It really was too bad, though, because a lethal margarita and the oblivion that was bound to follow sounded really good about now.

CHAPTER THREE

The last place in all of Serenity—in all of the universe, for that matter—that Annie wanted to be was the local ball field by the high school. And yet, here she was, walking along the perimeter of the parking lot, far enough from the field itself not to be spotted by her dad or Cal, but close enough to maybe catch a glimpse of Ty's little boy.

Though she'd seen plenty of images in the tabloids, Annie had never seen Trevor in person. She hadn't wanted to, because then he'd be real, a flesh-and-blood preschooler, whose mere existence had torn her life apart. Tonight, though, after leaving Sullivan's, she hadn't been able to shake off the sudden yearning to see the little boy who might have been hers. Yes, she might have been the mother of a three-year-old, if things had turned out the way she'd always thought they would.

At first, as she skirted the field, Annie thought the trip was probably wasted. The area was crowded with kids of all ages. The sidelines and bleachers were jammed with families. She could smell hot dogs and popcorn, even from where she was standing on the opposite side of the street. The noise of all that cheering was deafening, but it wasn't loud enough to drown out Cal's shout to his pitcher or her dad's startled cry when a dark-haired boy darted away from him and headed straight for the street, apparently chasing one of the ducks from a nearby park. The loudly quacking duck was trying to get away from all the frenzy and back to his more peaceful habitat.

Seeing the child toddling straight toward danger, Annie's protective instincts kicked in without a single thought, she made a mad dash into the street and gathered the boy up before he could get a half foot away from the curb.

"Duck!" he cried mournfully, pointing to his rapidly fleeing target.

"The duck's going to find his family," Annie assured him. "Ducks need their families just like we do."

When she finally looked into the boy's startled gaze, she saw Ty's eyes. No question about it. Stunned, she set the child on his feet and hunkered down in front of him, suddenly shaking over how quickly the incident might have turned into a tragedy.

Before she could utter a word, her father was beside them, kneeling down. "You okay?" he murmured, the comment meant for her, since it was obvious that the boy was just fine beyond being startled to have been plucked up out of the street by a stranger.

Tears stung Annie's eyes. "It's him, isn't it?" she asked her dad, her voice barely more than a choked whisper. "This is Trevor."

The boy's eyes brightened. "Me Trevor," he confirmed. "Who are you?"

Completely captivated now and unable to look away, she said, "I'm Annie."

"Annie's my daughter," Ronnie told him.

"And I know your daddy," Annie said before she could stop herself.

"Daddy plays ball," Trevor said with obvious pride. "But not now. He hurt."

"That's what I hear," Annie said. Suddenly unable to bear it another minute, she stood up. "I have to go. Bye, Trevor. See you, Dad."

"Annie!"

The worry in her father's voice stopped her. She forced a smile. "It's okay. Really." She turned her gaze to Trevor. "No more running into the street, okay? You need to be very, very careful."

"Trust me, he won't get away from me again," Ronnie said grimly. "I'd forgotten how fast these little guys could move. I blinked and he was gone. I thought he was fascinated by the ducks."

"He was, so much so that he followed one when it tried to leave."

Her dad flinched. "Maybe we should stick to playing on the swings, buddy. What do you think?"

"Swings go high, 'kay?" Trevor said excitedly.

Ronnie looked a little sickened by that, but he nodded gamely. "We'll see," he promised.

"Dad, are you sure you have this under control?" Annie asked worriedly. It had been a long time since he'd had anyone Trevor's age left in his care.

"Not a problem," Ronnie insisted. "Katie and Kyle are around somewhere. They're supposed to be babysitting their younger siblings and Trevor, but they have their hands full just with Jessica Lynn and Cole, so I said I'd watch Trevor. You go on. Enjoy your evening."

"Yeah, sure," Annie said, walking away.

She just wished she had the slightest idea how she was supposed to enjoy anything after that bittersweet moment with Ty's son. Worse, how was she supposed to get that little boy out of her head now that she'd held him in her arms?

The mood at margarita night was way too somber. It was getting on Helen's nerves. Everybody was walking on eggshells, trying too hard not to say the wrong thing. And no matter how innocuous the topic, Dana Sue and Maddie couldn't see eye to eye. They'd argued over everything from the weather to the amount of tequila that was supposed to be in the margaritas. Jeanette and Helen had been left to referee.

"Okay, this isn't working," Helen announced after an hour. "Let's just get it all out there. What are we going to do about Ty and Annie?"

"Nothing," Maddie and Dana Sue said simultaneously.

"Well, that's progress," Helen said. "It's the first thing the two of you have agreed on all night."

"We're not going to meddle in their lives," Dana Sue added for good measure. "That's final."

"Are you sure about that?" Jeanette asked hesitantly. Although both Dana Sue and Maddie scowled at her, she refused to back down. "I mean, I know I haven't been around all that long, but those two were so much in love. It's just a shame to have them both back home and not even speaking to each other."

"I agree," Helen said. "Worse is what it's doing to the two of you. I haven't been to a party that felt this awkward since the first boy-girl party we had back in junior high."

Maddie flushed guiltily. "I'm sorry. I'll try harder."

"Me, too," Dana Sue promised. "I just get so darn mad when I think about what happened."

"Do you think I don't?" Maddie erupted with feeling. "I wanted to shake my son when I heard what he'd done, but what am I supposed to do? He's my son, and that little boy is my grandson. I love them."

"And you should have been able to celebrate having your first grandchild with us, your best friends," Helen said. "Instead, we've all acted as if Trevor doesn't exist. That's just wrong. None of this is his fault, and it's certainly not yours."

"I agree," Dana Sue said. "If I leave Annie out of it for just a minute, I can actually be happy for you, Maddie. Having a grandchild must be so amazing."

Maddie reached out and squeezed her hand. "Do you think I don't understand how you must feel? We were going to have grandkids together, you and me, because my son and your daughter were supposed to give them to us. I know we always vowed not to pressure them like that. Heck, we tried our best not to talk about it ourselves. We didn't want them to know how much we were counting on it, but we were."

"And now it will never happen," Dana Sue said, her expression bleak.

"That is just so sad," Jeanette commiserated. "I still think—"

"No," Maddie said. "We cannot meddle. It will get even more complicated if we do."

Dana Sue stood up, grabbed the pitcher of margaritas and poured herself another one. "Anyone else?"

Maddie held out her glass. "What the hell," she murmured.

Dana Sue poured, then grinned. "Helen?"

"Make mine a double. I have to go see my mama tomorrow."

"Oh, boy," Dana Sue murmured, exchanging a look with Maddie. "You didn't say anything about that earlier."

"Because I didn't even want to think about it," Helen said, explaining about the call from the hospital.

"Maybe we should go down there with you," Maddie said. "At least one of us."

"Don't be ridiculous," Helen said. "I can handle this. I'll make a few calls, look at a couple of rehab places and get her settled. No big deal."

"I don't question your ability to cope with the details," Maddie said gently. "It's the compassion that concerns me. You tend to be the tiniest bit impatient, and Flo's probably in pain and not at her best, either."

Helen scowled at the too-accurate assessment. "Thanks for the vote of confidence." Her frown deepened when she noted her still-empty glass. Dana Sue still hadn't poured her another drink. "I'll take that margarita now."

"Don't you need to go down there tomorrow with a clear head?" Dana Sue asked.

"I'd rather not," Helen said, lifting the glass in a gesture that commanded Dana Sue to fill it to the brim.

"Flo's going to be just fine," Maddie said. "A broken hip will heal in no time."

"At her age?" Helen asked skeptically. "What if it doesn't? What if she can't be on her own anymore?"

"Then you'll deal with it," Dana Sue said. "You can handle anything. We're all in awe of you."

"That was the old me," Helen bemoaned. "The current me is still trying to figure out how to get a few more hours into the day. Way too many of them vanish without my having a clue where they went."

Jeanette had been listening to the exchange in silence. She'd only recently resolved some of her own family issues. "What about bringing your mom back here to recuperate?" she asked eventually.

Helen stared at her in horror. "Bite your tongue."

"Well, it just seems like it would be easier to keep an eye

on things if she were right here in Serenity," Jeanette persisted.

"Not going to happen," Helen said sharply. "Her life's in Florida now, and that's where it's going to stay."

Maddie gave Jeanette a commiserating look. "Don't mind Helen. She and her mother have issues. They get along best when there's some distance between them."

Unfortunately, since her reconciliation with her own parents, Jeanette wanted all of the world to follow suit. "If there are issues, what better way to fix them than to be right here together while she's getting back on her feet?"

"Fortunately, my mother will side with me on this," Helen said with confidence. "She was glad to see the last of Serenity."

"But it's her home," Jeanette stressed.

"It's the place where she nearly worked herself into an early grave," Helen contradicted. "Now she's living in style with every comfort she could possibly want."

"You and her granddaughter aren't there," Jeanette replied, then frowned when Maddie scowled at her. "I'm just saying..." She sat back, looking chagrined. "Oh, never mind. It's none of my business."

She looked so upset by the possibility that she'd overstepped that Helen patted her hand. "It's okay. You are not the first to think the Decatur women should be reunited in blissful harmony. I get the same thing from Erik all the time." She grinned. "I also tell him to butt out."

Jeanette laughed. "Well, in that case, I don't feel so bad."

"Have another margarita," Dana Sue encouraged. "Then you won't feel anything. I haven't felt my feet for the past ten minutes."

Maddie blinked. "Me, neither, come to think of it."

Helen stared at the two of them. "Oh, sweet heaven, am

I going to have your husbands over here yelling at me for sending you home damaged? I'd better make coffee."

"I think it'll take more than coffee to fix this," Dana Sue said direly. "I'm going to take a little nap. Somebody call Ronnie and tell him we're having a sleepover."

"I can't sleep over," Maddie grumbled. "I have children."

"Who probably shouldn't see you in your current state," Helen said. "I'll call Cal, too. Jeanette, are you staying? Should I call Tom?"

"Well, I'm certainly not going to leave you three here to have all the fun," Jeanette said. "But I'll call Tom myself." She fumbled in her purse, but apparently couldn't find her phone. "I know I have a cell phone." She stared at her purse accusingly. "Where's it hiding?"

"Never mind. I'll call," Helen said.

It had been a long time since she'd thrown a party that no one left before dawn. After a shaky start, this was starting to show signs of being one of the best margarita nights ever.

Ty's workout at The Corner Spa had only lasted an hour tonight. Every move he'd made, every weight he'd tried to lift, had sent pain radiating down his arm and across his shoulder and back. He knew he'd been pressing it by starting rehab so soon after the surgery and trying to do more than the doctors had recommended. It was just so blasted frustrating to be barely weeks into what had promised to be the best season of his career, only to be sidelined by an injury.

Eventually Elliott had called a halt. "You need to ease up on yourself before you do more harm than good."

"One more set," Ty pleaded.

Elliott blocked his way when he would have picked up the weights. "Not tonight. Listen to me, Ty. I know you're anxious to get back on the field, but if you try to do too much, you'll have a setback. You've done an okay job of trying to hide the fact that you're in pain, but it's not working, pal."

Ty knew he was right, but it grated. "Okay, whatever."

"Have you given any more thought to asking Annie for help?" Elliott asked.

"We both know I can't do that. She wouldn't even consider it, anyway."

"She might," Elliott said.

Ty regarded him curiously. "Have you discussed it with her?"

"As a matter of fact, I mentioned it to her earlier today."

For a moment Ty felt something akin to hope. "Did she say she'd do it?"

"Actually she said no," Elliott admitted. "But I think that's because I was the one asking. If you talked to her..." He met Ty's gaze. "The two of you were close once. I honestly don't think she could turn you down. It goes against everything she believes about helping people recover from injuries. She thinks of it as a mission. She'd never turn her back on you, not if you explain what the stakes are for you."

Ty shook his head. "I won't put her in that position," he said. "It's not fair." No matter how quickly he wanted to get back on the ball field, he wouldn't use the kind of manipulation Elliott was suggesting to speed up the process of his recovery. Besides, realistically, what could Annie do that Elliott wasn't already doing? If there came a time when he needed more skilled help with his rehab, he could always bring in another trainer. The team would send someone the instant he asked.

"Let's just keep things the way they are," he told Elliott. "Unless I'm cutting into too much of your free time."

"Absolutely not. I'm happy to help. After everything your mother did to help Karen when her life was a mess, helping you out is the least I can do. Karen and I found each other back then."

"Same time tomorrow, then?" Ty asked, relieved.

"You got it. Meantime, cut yourself some slack. Relax, okay? Take the rest of the night off."

Unfortunately Ty was too edgy to relax. And since his workout had been curtailed and Trevor was with Ty's siblings and Cal at the ball field or the town's favorite pizza place, he decided to burn off some of his energy and his frustrations by running. At least he could stay in shape that way.

He debated heading for the track at the high school, but he didn't want to take a chance that Little League practice might still be going on. The kids treated him like some kind of hero. That made him feel like such a fraud. He might be an excellent ballplayer, but he'd failed at the one thing that really mattered...being a good man.

Instead, to avoid an uncomfortable encounter with some pint-size fans, Ty drove over to the path around the lake. In early spring the park was filled with huge bushes of pink, purple and white azaleas in full bloom. The riot of color and balmy evenings drew quite a few people, but it was late enough now that most people had finished their evening strolls, and he could be alone with his thoughts.

He was on his second lap, panting hard and testing his limits, when he saw her. Annie was sitting by herself on a bench, mostly in the shadows. If a breeze hadn't stirred the leaves, allowing a shaft of moonlight to fall on her, he might not have noticed her.

The fact that she was out here alone in a secluded area infuriated him. She ought to know better. Serenity might be comparatively safe, but a woman out unaccompanied after dark was still putting herself into the position of becoming a target for some predator.

He crossed the grass to stand over her. "What the hell do you think you're doing?"

At the sound of his voice, Annie blinked hard and stared up at him with unmistakable dismay. "Go away, Ty."

He stood his ground. "Not a chance. Are you crazy, sitting out here all alone at this hour, practically asking some nutcase to assault you?"

"It's not the middle of the night, for heaven's sake. It's barely nine o'clock. And this is Serenity. I'm perfectly safe."

"Really? Did you even hear me coming? Did you notice you weren't alone? Geez, Annie, I could have attacked you and you wouldn't have seen it coming."

She scowled at him. "You don't get to worry about me."

"Well, I do, especially when I see you doing something stupid."

That brought her immediately to her feet, her cheeks flushed with anger. He knew her well enough to guess she was mostly furious because she knew he was right. She seemed to be having a hard time finding the right words to tell him off, again because she knew she was the one in the wrong.

Out of the shadows now, he could see the tracks of dried tears on her cheeks. Before he could ask about that, she pulled herself together and—right or wrong—got right up in his face.

"Stupid! You're calling me stupid?" she said, poking a finger into his stomach. "Boy, that takes some gall. Then, again, you know all about stupid, don't you, Tyler Townsend? You mastered it several years ago. Too bad there wasn't anyone around to save *you* from yourself."

In some ways, her fury was better than the anguish in her eyes when he'd told her about the baby. He'd known back then not only how he'd disappointed her, but how much he'd hurt her. He'd rather have her fighting mad any day. At least she was displaying some real spirit, instead of staring at him with the defeated expression he'd seen on her face when he'd first approached.

"I wish there had been," he said softly. "I wish someone had sat me down and told me I was behaving like a jerk."

"Well, maybe it's three years too late, but I'm happy to help out," she said. "You're a jerk, Ty. An idiot. A pig."

"There's nothing you can call me that I haven't called myself."

"Good, then it's unanimous."

"I don't suppose it would help if I said again that I'm sorry."

"It didn't help then and it doesn't help now," she retorted without hesitation.

Ignoring her temper and her dismissal of his apology, he drank in the sight of her. To his eyes she looked too thin, but not in that awful way she had when she'd been anorexic. Her hair, which had been dull and brittle back then, shone now. Her eyes sparkled, though that was probably because she was angry with him. Her mouth…well, it was probably better if he didn't focus on her mouth. He might make the mistake of trying to kiss her.

"I've missed you," he said quietly.

She stared at him for a heartbeat, and for one tiny instant he felt hopeful. There was no mistaking the emotion in her eyes, the hint of longing, but then her expression hardened and her voice turned cold.

"I met your son tonight," she said. "He looks just like you."

Ty had no idea how to respond. Obviously encountering Trevor had upset her. How could it not? Maybe that explained the tears. Guilt washed over him for about the millionth time.

"I'm sorry," he said again. It was all he could think of to say.

"For what? You weren't there. It's a small town. I was bound to see him sooner or later. I have to tell you, I'd hoped it would be later. Maybe in some other lifetime."

Ty raked his fingers through his hair. "I knew this was a mistake. I never should have come back here. It wasn't fair to you. I guess I'd just hoped..." He cut himself off when he caught the faint flicker of guilt in her eyes. "Don't you dare feel guilty," he said. "I'm the one who messed things up. It's my fault you're bumping into my son. Hell, it's my fault that I *have* a son."

She met his gaze. "It shouldn't matter," she said wistfully. "I don't want it to matter."

He ached to take her in his arms, to tell her what she wanted to hear, that he would go, but he couldn't do any of that. She wouldn't thank him for the touch, the sympathy or the offer.

Instead, he asked, "What can I do to make things easier for you?"

"Nothing," she said immediately. "I need to go." She tried to brush past him.

"Annie, no," he protested, reaching for her hand. "Can't you stay here a few minutes, maybe talk things out? We used to be able to deal with anything that came our way. Nobody understood me better than you. The reverse was true, too. I always got you in ways nobody else did."

"Not anymore," she said fiercely, jerking her hand free. She gave him a look that would have wilted a man with a lesser ego. "Besides, haven't you heard?" she said wryly. "The lake's no place for a woman at this time of night. The only people around are nutcases."

With that, she turned and walked away, spine rigid, shoulders stiff.

This time he didn't try to stop her. He waited until she was out of sight, then released a pent-up sigh. That certainly hadn't gone the way he'd wished his first encounter with her would go.

Then, again, he thought optimistically, she hadn't hit him with anything or walked off without saying a word, so maybe there was hope for the future, after all.

CHAPTER FOUR

Annie had a jam-packed schedule of clients on Saturdays. Most were regulars, but one or two new people showed up each week. As tempted as she was to take another day off, she knew it would be unfair to all of them. It would also be cowardly.

Sooner or later she was going to have to face people, even knowing that a lot of those people were going to bring up Ty's return to Serenity just to gauge her reaction. As for facing Maddie, she couldn't put that off forever, either. At least on Saturday Maddie didn't hang around as long. She popped in to check on things, then spent the rest of the day with her family. Chances were, if Annie was careful she could avoid bumping into Maddie until at least Monday.

Despite giving herself a stern pep talk, Annie got her first taste of how bad the day was likely to be when she stopped by Wharton's for breakfast. She rarely ate her morning meal in the old-fashioned drugstore on Main Street with its booths and soda fountain, because it was always crowded and the coffee was better at her mom's restaurant. Today, however, the doors at Sullivan's had been locked tight, and there'd been no sign of her mom or Erik. She'd have to find out what that was about later.

In Wharton's, where half the town hung out at some point during the day, she slid into a booth and buried her face in a menu. Unfortunately that wasn't enough to discourage the locals from staring and whispering or to prevent Grace Wharton from squeezing her ample body onto the seat opposite Annie.

"I know you probably don't want to talk about Ty," the older woman said, then went right ahead and did it, anyway. "I thought you ought to know that everyone in town is on your side in this. The way that boy treated you is a crying shame. His mama taught him better than that. Of course, his daddy's example…" Her voice trailed off in obvious embarrassment at the mention of Bill Townsend's sleazy affair with his nurse and its resulting pregnancy.

Despite the slip about Ty's father, the genuine sympathy Annie heard in Grace's voice, to say nothing of her indignation on Annie's behalf, brought tears to Annie's eyes. "Thanks, Grace," she murmured, not looking up. "But could we not talk about this, please?"

"Of course," Grace said, immediately apologetic. "I know the whole situation is upsetting, but I wanted you to know how people around here feel. You're a strong young woman. You'll get through this."

"Thanks."

"And with a little time, maybe the two of you will be able to work things out," Grace added, regarding her hopefully.

"Not a chance," Annie said flatly.

Grace seemed taken aback by Annie's fierce declaration. "Well, then, just so you know, he's been coming in here around this time of the morning for breakfast, and he usually has his son with him."

Annie fought a sudden desire to bolt. Before she could weigh her options, though, Grace added, "If he comes while you're here this morning, I'll send him away. It's the least I can do."

Annie bit back a groan at the thought of the gossip that would stir up. "No, don't do that, please, Grace. Just bring me a bowl of oatmeal with some milk and honey. With any luck, I can eat and be gone before he gets here."

Grace looked vaguely smug, though Annie had no idea why.

"Are you sure?" Grace continued, her tone solicitous. "I'll be happy to stop him at the door."

Annie knew she meant it, too, but then word would be all over town by lunchtime that Ty had been banished from Wharton's because of her. She thought back to what her dad had said about the town taking sides. Here was the first taste of what that would be like.

"No, just hurry with the oatmeal, okay?"

Grace patted her hand. "Whatever you say, dear."

She scurried away and returned in less than a minute with Annie's food. "Now, you take your time. I'll be on the lookout. I'll let you know if Ty's heading this way. You can even scoot out the back door, if you want."

"Thanks, Grace. Leave my check, okay?"

"It's by the register. I'll get it for you in a sec," Grace promised. "Or you can just pay me next time you come in."

Despite Grace's offer of a warning, Annie practically gulped down the piping-hot oatmeal, burning her tongue in the process. Just one more thing she could blame on Ty, she thought bitterly.

Just then she looked up to find him standing beside her table, wearing snug, faded jeans and an old Duke T-shirt that fit him like a glove, emphasizing every muscle in his well-toned body. His dark hair was rumpled, and he held Trevor in his arms, the boy still wearing his pj's from the looks of it.

So much for the early warning system, Annie thought in despair. Where the devil was Grace now? And why did Ty and Trevor's sudden appearance, looking as if they'd rushed over here, immediately stir her suspicions?

"Hi, Annie," Trevor said, his tone chipper. "Are me and Daddy gonna eat with you?"

She looked around desperately for Grace, but the woman was suddenly nowhere to be found. Nor was Annie's check.

"It's okay," Ty said, his expression somber. "No need to make up excuses. We just stopped to say hello. We won't interrupt you."

For the second time in less than twenty-four hours, he'd innocently managed to put her on the defensive. Annie was sure he was trying to make things easier, but instead he made her feel guilty because she was incapable of pretending things between them were fine. If they'd been nothing more than old friends, an invitation to join her would have come naturally. Instead, the expected polite words lodged in her throat.

"I was just leaving," she finally managed to say, scrambling to dig money out of her purse. She found herself rambling on, to Ty's obvious amusement. "I usually don't eat here, but no one's around at Sullivan's to feed me. I suppose I should have just grabbed a muffin at the spa."

Ty grinned, reminding her of the boy he'd been when she'd first fallen wildly in love with him. Back then she would have done just about anything to coax that beguiling smile out of him.

"Apparently margarita night got out of hand," he explained. "Your mom and mine spent the night at Helen's. The way I heard it from Cal, Erik's trying to cope with a whole houseful of women with hangovers."

Despite herself, Annie chuckled. "I'm not surprised. Have you ever had one of Helen's margaritas? They could knock a linebacker down for the count."

"They've never offered me one. It sounds as if you have personal experience, though."

She nodded and surprised herself by continuing to exchange small talk rather than bolting for the door as she'd planned. "They invited me to a margarita night right after I got back to town. They said it was time the next generation of Sweet Magnolias was indoctrinated into one of their rituals. It took me at least a day to recover, and I was careful. I only had two."

"But you stayed away last night," he said, studying her. "Was that because of me, because you thought it would be more awkward between your mom and mine if you were there as a reminder that I messed things up between us?"

"Not everything is about you," she said, because she didn't want him to get the idea that he had that much influence over her life, her moods or anything else these days. To reveal that he did after all this time would be pathetic.

"Dammit, that *is* why," he said as Trevor's eyes widened.

"Bad word, Daddy," his son announced.

Ty winced. "Yes, it was. Pretend you didn't hear that, buddy, and whatever you do, don't tell your grandma."

Annie had to hide her amusement over Ty's obvious fear that his son would tattle on him. She was in no mood to let him think she'd enjoyed anything about this encounter.

"I have to go to work. Bye, Trevor," she said, pointedly excluding his father as she left without trying to track down her check. She'd pay Grace when she picked up her lunch later.

"Bye-bye," Trevor called after her.

Ty merely watched her go. She could feel his knowing

gaze on her all the way out the door, and sure enough, when she glanced back once she was on the street, he was still watching her. What bothered her the most, though, wasn't that he couldn't seem to tear his gaze away, but that his expression was so undeniably sad. That was something she understood all too well.

"Well, that went better than I'd expected," Grace Wharton said to Ty after Annie had gone. Miraculously, she'd emerged from the kitchen the second Annie was out of sight. He suspected Annie wouldn't be pleased about that sudden reappearance after Grace's timely absence.

"Thanks for calling to let me know she was here," Ty told Grace. "I know everybody in town is on her side, you included, but all I want is a chance to make things right. The only way that's going to happen is if we keep running into each other. Sooner or later I'll chip away at all that anger. For a minute there, we had an actual conversation."

"If you ask me, I think you're being overly optimistic," Grace told him. "I think it's going to take a grand gesture, not two minutes in public with the two of you trying to be civil with each other."

Ty shrugged. "I have to start somewhere." He met Grace's gaze. "You'll let me know next time she's in here?"

"As long as I don't see any evidence that you're making her miserable. If Annie's upset, our deal is off. Like you said, much as I like you, I'm on her side."

Ty nodded. "Fair enough."

"Now, shall I bring this young man a pancake? And scrambled eggs with bacon and whole-wheat toast for you?" she asked.

"Thanks, Grace."

She started away from the table, then came back. "Don't

you hurt that girl again," she warned. "If this is just some game to occupy you while you're doing rehab, stop it right now or, at the very least, leave me out of it."

He couldn't blame her for thinking the worst. Ty held her gaze. "It's no game, Grace. I swear it."

She studied him intently, then finally nodded. "Okay, then."

Grace had barely walked away when Ronnie Sullivan slid into the booth opposite him. "What are you and Grace in cahoots about?" Ronnie demanded, even as Trevor scrambled into Ronnie's lap, rubbed a hand over his shaved head, then gave it a little pat. "Did I hear right? Does it have something to do with my daughter?"

Ty groaned. "Where'd you come from?"

"I was grabbing a cup of coffee at the counter when I over-heard just enough to send a chill down my spine." He sipped from his take-out cup and said slowly, "Now, I'm not likely to take Grace apart limb by limb, but I can't say the same where you're concerned." He leveled a threatening look into Ty's eyes. "Clear enough?"

"Ronnie, I'm not the enemy," Ty swore. "I'm trying to fix things with Annie. I miss her. You know how it was when you were trying to make things right with Dana Sue and nobody wanted to cut you any slack? Well, that's how it is with me right now. I screwed up, and thanks to the tab-loids, the whole world knows about it. I can't change that, but maybe with time I can prove to Annie that it will never happen again."

Ronnie's gaze narrowed. "And that really matters to you? You care what Annie thinks of you?"

"Always have," Ty declared.

"You had a damn strange way of showing it," Ronnie said. "Nobody knows that better than I do."

Ronnie studied him intently, clearly trying to gauge whether or not Ty could be trusted. Eventually, like Grace, he seemed to like what he saw. He nodded. "Okay, then, I'll give you a break for the time being. But if you make that girl cry or upset her in any way, all bets are off."

"Seems perfectly reasonable to me," Ty said, swallowing hard as he considered the certainty that Ronnie meant exactly what he'd said.

Ronnie's gaze didn't waver. "However, I can't speak for Dana Sue. You understand that, right? She may not be inclined to be as generous."

"Which is one reason I'm not stepping foot inside Sullivan's until Annie and I make peace. I've seen your wife handle the knives in that kitchen, to say nothing of all those skillets," Ty said with a shudder.

Ronnie chuckled. "Yeah, who knew a skillet could be used as a weapon of feminine destruction? I learned that one the hard way."

Ty barely contained a grin. "I remember."

Ronnie stood up with Trevor still in his arms, then set the boy back down in the booth. "For what it's worth, if you really are the man you used to be, then I hope this works out. I'll never forget the way you looked out for Annie when she was sick. You stood up to her then, got through to her in a way no one else had been able to. You were there for her when a lot of kids your age would have turned their backs. You banked a lot of points with me for doing that. *That* man is someone I'd trust with my daughter."

Ty felt a knot form in his throat. "Thanks, Ronnie."

"Doesn't mean I won't beat the crap out of you if it turns out you're not that man," Ronnie said, then walked away as the warning hung in the air.

Grace returned and set their plates on the table. Based on

her timing, it was evident she'd been waiting nearby for the confrontation to end.

Ty gave her a hopeful look. "I know you heard all that," he said. "Do you think you could keep it to yourself? It won't help my cause if Annie knows her father's tried to put the fear of God into me. She'll think that's the only reason I'm on my best behavior around her."

"Or maybe it'll stir up her sympathy," Grace said.

"I think we'd better go with my theory," Ty told her. "Can we forget this scene ever happened?"

"I can keep my mouth shut," Grace said indignantly, then shrugged. "Of course, there are other customers in here, and what they couldn't hear, they're likely to make up."

Ty groaned at the accuracy of her assessment. "Just do whatever you can to keep this quiet, okay?"

He had an uphill battle ahead of him as it was. Proving to Annie that he could be trusted was going to be tricky enough without her wondering if he was being nice only because he was scared of her daddy.

Unlike her mom, who was still best friends with the women she'd grown up with, Annie hadn't stayed in touch with the two girls she'd been closest to in high school. Because of the anorexia, she'd wanted to put those tough times, those awful memories, completely behind her. And since she, Sarah and Raylene had gone to different colleges, it hadn't been all that difficult to break the ties without anyone's feelings being hurt. That didn't mean she didn't remember them fondly. Like Ty, they'd stuck with her during her difficult recovery from her eating disorder.

The last Annie had heard, Raylene was married to a bright young orthopedic surgeon and living in Charleston. It was exactly the match her very socially connected grandparents in Charleston had hoped for when they'd arranged for her to attend a debutante ball. Annie had met Raylene's husband, Paul Hammond, at a couple of professional gatherings, and he'd even recommended her to a few of his patients, but she and Raylene had rarely crossed paths during the brief time Annie had spent in Charleston after college. When they had, she'd noted that Raylene had looked every bit the young socialite, a role she'd come to late but adapted to nicely.

Sarah had been engaged by her junior year in college, and after graduation had moved to Alabama to be near her fiancé's family. To Annie's surprise, no wedding invitation had ever arrived in the mail. Nor did anyone in town seem to know if Sarah had actually gotten married. Her parents had moved away a few months ago, just before Annie's return to Serenity.

When Elliott called from the front desk at the spa to tell Annie that her next client had arrived, she was stunned to find Sarah waiting for her. She was even more startled by the amount of weight her friend had gained and, even more shocking, her dull eyes and unkempt appearance.

"I'll bet I'm the last person you expected to see," Sarah said, forcing a smile that never reached her eyes.

Annie tried to hide her initial reaction. She held out her arms and embraced her. "You definitely are, but it's a wonderful surprise. How are you?"

"How do I look?" Sarah asked, her tone bitter, then waved off her own question. "No, don't tell me. I can't take brutal honesty right now."

Annie heard a note of near hysteria in Sarah's voice that cut right through her. "Let's grab a glass of tea," she suggested. "It's a beautiful morning. We can sit on the patio and catch up."

"Given the shape I'm in, maybe we should start right in with the exercise. It's going to take a while to fix me."

"You don't need to be fixed," Annie said fiercely, trying to combat the note of defeat. "Maybe just a little fine-tuning."

"You're a liar, but thanks."

"Just so you know, I always start out spending time with a client to see what her goals are, so this is just routine," Annie assured her. Unsure what her old friend's financial situation might be, she added, "You don't pay for this session, okay?"

"Money's not an issue," Sarah assured her. "I just don't have time to waste."

Again, there was a note of hysteria that set off alarm bells.

"We can talk about why that is, too," Annie told her, leading the way into the spa's small café, which sold a variety of drinks, smoothies, salads and pastries. The food was supplied by Sullivan's.

Annie ordered two iced teas, then ushered Sarah out to the patio, choosing a table in the shade of an old oak tree. Two other tables were occupied, but they had relative privacy to talk. "So, you're obviously married now, since I didn't recognize the last name when you made the appointment."

"For the moment," Sarah said, her expression grim. "Walter says if I don't get a grip on my weight, he's through with me."

Annie stared at her with shock. "Your husband threatened to leave you if you don't lose weight?"

Sarah nodded, tears gathering in her eyes. "He meant it, too. He's already seen a lawyer. To tell you the truth, I think he's been looking for an excuse, and I handed it to him when I gained weight during my pregnancies with our two kids. I kept an extra twenty pounds after each of them."

Annie was startled. "You have two kids already? When did you get married?"

"The week after we graduated. I was already pregnant with our first. That's Tommy. That's why you didn't get a wedding invitation—his family thought it would be best if we didn't make a fuss. We had a very small ceremony."

Annie felt awful for her. She remembered how they used to talk about their weddings. Of all of them—even including Raylene's social ambitions—Sarah's dream had been the most lavish.

"You'd hardly be the first bride to be pregnant when she walked down the aisle," she said, indignant for Sarah.

"Not in their town," Sarah said. "At least that's what you'd think to hear them tell it. Me, I think the whole place is a hotbed of people sleeping with anyone they can get their hands on. The Prices think they own the whole stupid town, which I suppose they do, if you consider they own the cotton mill that keeps a lot of folks employed." She waved her hand. "Never mind. I don't want to talk about them. They're hateful people."

"Have you moved back here, then?"

"I'm staying at Mama and Daddy's place for a few months, while I 'get a grip,' as Walter says. It's akin to hiding me in a closet. Thank heaven, Mama and Daddy had the foresight to see something like this coming and kept the house just in case I ever needed a place to come home to."

"And your kids?"

"Tommy and Libby are here with me, at least for now. If Walter really does divorce me, it's going to get ugly. He's going to fight to keep Tommy with him."

Annie regarded her with shock, certain she'd misunderstood. "Only your son?"

"Have to have an heir, don't you know," Sarah said angrily. "The family barely acknowledges that Libby exists. Seems my second pregnancy was a worse embarrassment than the first, coming so quickly on the heels of Tommy's birth." She leaned close and confided in an exaggerated undertone, "It suggests we had s-e-x."

Annie had contained herself as long as she could. "Somebody needs to tell Walter what he can do to himself. I recommend Helen."

For the first time, Sarah's smile appeared genuine. "I was hoping you'd say that. I want to get fit, but I'm doing it for me, not Walter, no matter what he thinks. Then I intend to hire a lawyer like Helen, stand up for myself and teach him a thing or two," she said with more spirit. "I can't do that when I feel like such a failure."

"You're not a failure. And if you're as determined as it sounds, you'll be back in shape in no time. I'll see to it," Annie promised.

Sarah leaned forward. "So, how do we start?"

"Any health problems I should know about? You've seen a doctor?"

"The only thing wrong with me is the extra weight I'm carrying."

"Have you been doing any exercise at all?"

"Nothing beyond chasing a couple of kids night and day. Does that count?"

"It's definitely a start," Annie told her, thinking of how worn-out her dad had been after his brief babysitting stint.

"What's next, then?" Sarah asked eagerly, her expression more animated than it had been since she'd first hugged Annie.

"We'll take it one step at a time," Annie told her, "literally. Let's get inside and get you on the treadmill."

At the doorway, Sarah paused and gave her an impish grin. "Who ever thought things would turn out like this? Me having an eating problem and you being the one who's going to help me conquer it. Talk about the tables being turned."

"I know," Annie said. "But you know the best part? Every time you have the slightest doubt, all you have to do is look at me and remember the mess I was. That's all the proof you'll need that anything is possible."

Sarah pulled her into an embrace. "It is so good to see you, Annie. I've missed you. I've missed having a friend who knows all my secrets going clear back to preschool."

Ironically it was having Sarah know *her* secrets that had made Annie want to forget the old friendship, but right this second she regretted having let it slip away.

"Do you ever hear from Raylene?" she asked Sarah. The three of them had once been as inseparable as the Sweet Magnolias.

"You mean the hoity-toity princess?" Sarah said with a chuckle. "Not so much. She sends out fancy Christmas cards and even scrawls a note on them about how fabulous her life is, but we haven't talked in years. You?"

"I ran into her a couple of times in Charleston, but we definitely weren't traveling in the same social circles. I had some business contact with her husband, who seemed like an okay guy."

"Was he gorgeous?" Sarah asked.

"Ordinary, actually, but he had a terrific sense of humor."

"And he's rich, of course, and has that pedigree her family wanted," Sarah assessed. She grinned. "I've missed this so much, Annie. When I heard you were back in town, it made the prospect of being banished here a whole lot easier."

To her surprise, Annie realized she understood just what Sarah meant. It was as if a piece of herself had just clicked back into place this morning. "I know, sweetie. I know just what you mean."

For the first time in her life, she understood why her mom, Maddie and Helen had stayed so close over all these years. Friends like these, who stuck together through thick and thin, were worth their weight in gold. It was about time she appreciated that for the blessing it was.

CHAPTER FIVE

It had been nearly a year since Helen had seen her mother, and she was shocked by the changes. Flo Decatur looked old and frail, asleep in her hospital bed, her complexion ashen, her gray hair badly in need of a perm. She was only seventy-two, but years of hard work and smoking had clearly taken a toll.

She moaned softly, then opened her eyes. Her expression brightened when she saw Helen.

"You came," she said in a way that suggested she hadn't believed Helen would take the time.

"Of course I came," Helen said briskly, giving her mother a kiss on the cheek. "I had to see for myself just how much trouble you've gotten yourself into. How did it happen, Mom? How'd you break your hip?"

"Believe it or not, I was taking a class in line dancing at the community center," Flo said, then added wryly, "I thought it would be good exercise. At my age you'll try anything to keep your parts working." She patted her hip. "I guess this one was already shot."

Helen smiled at the image of her mother taking any kind of dance class, much less one involving country music. She'd always claimed to hate all those love-gone-wrong songs. She said she'd lived it, and it wasn't worth glorifying. She'd also always had two left feet, or so she'd said. It appeared she might have been right.

"So, what happened?"

"Tripped over my own feet, if you must know," Flo said, her expression chagrined at the admission of clumsiness. "Down I went. Took two other people with me."

"Were they hurt, too?"

"Nope. They both had a few extra pounds on them. They bounced," she joked, then coughed so hard, Helen handed her a cup of water. When she'd taken a sip, Flo regarded Helen intently. "Did they tell you?"

"Tell me what?"

"I can't go back to my apartment."

She didn't sound as dismayed by that as Helen had expected. Still, Helen sought to reassure her. "The nurse mentioned you'd need some rehab, then maybe some help at home. Don't worry about that. We'll work it out, Mom. The nurse has already suggested a couple of places, and I'll talk to the social worker and get some more recommendations. I'll make sure you're set up someplace really nice."

Flo was shaking her head before the words were out of Helen's mouth. "I'm not going into a nursing home," she said flatly. "That'll be the beginning of the end, and you know it."

"I didn't say anything about a nursing home," Helen argued. "I'm sure there are some great rehabilitation centers around, places dedicated to getting you back on your feet and back home. The minute they say it's okay for you to be back in your condo, I'll arrange for someone to come in and help you."

Her mother's jaw set. "No."

"Well, what then?" Helen asked, trying to hang on to her patience. "You can't go directly back to your place. There's no way you can manage on your own right now. The doctors won't allow it, anyway."

Her mother's gaze locked with hers. "I want to come home with you."

Helen regarded Flo with alarm. That was out of the question. They'd kill each other in a week. Besides, she was barely coping with a husband, a toddler and a nanny in the house. Adding her mother to the mix simply couldn't happen, not when she was finally getting back some real balance between family and career. Just the thought of it made her palms sweat.

And yet, if this was what Flo really wanted, did she have a choice?

"Wouldn't you be happier right here? You have friends here," Helen said, a desperate note in her voice. "I'm sure they're all anxious to have you back on your feet."

"I have friends here, but I have *family* in Serenity," her mother declared, her gaze not wavering, her tone stubborn.

Her argument mirrored so closely what Jeanette had said that it gave Helen pause. "Why?" she asked, bewildered by the sudden change in attitude from the time when Flo had been eager to leave Serenity.

"I want to spend some time with my granddaughter," Flo said, her expression wistful. "She's growing up so fast, and I'm missing it."

"That doesn't solve the problem of rehab, Mom. Maybe once you're back on your feet, you could come for a visit."

Her mother shook her head. "I want to come home permanently." She frowned at Helen. "Oh, don't look at me as if I've invited myself to stay with you forever. As soon as I'm back on my feet, I'll get my own place."

Helen was still bewildered by her mother's determination. "I thought you loved your apartment here," she said. Helen had spent a fortune buying and furnishing the place for her mother, trying to make her golden years easier than the early years of her life had been. Helen had spared no expense, either with the location or the furnishings. Her monthly checks to help out with expenses were generous, as well.

"It's a lovely apartment and I appreciate you wanting me to have it, but I miss home, Helen. This accident was the final straw. If it had happened in Serenity, you wouldn't have had to disrupt your life to fly all the way down here. I've made up my mind—I'm coming home. If you don't want me underfoot at your place or you don't have the room, then find a rehab facility up there. What was that one place called? Sunset Manor?"

Helen stared at her in horror. "Mom, you can't go there, even temporarily. That place was a dump ten years ago when we visited your coworker there."

"Surely by now there's another alternative," Flo said. There was no mistaking the intractable note in her voice or the determined glint in her eyes.

"I'll have to discuss this with Erik," Helen said, more to buy time than out of any conviction that he'd say no. In fact, he'd seemed to get along with her mother better than she did on the few occasions when they'd met.

"Of course," her mother said, sounding meek now that she was well on her way to victory.

"And it would just be until you're back on your feet and we've found you your own place." Helen wanted to be very sure they were on the same page about that.

"Absolutely."

"Maybe we shouldn't sell your condo just yet, though. You could change your mind."

"Sell it," her mother said emphatically. "In fact, hand me my purse. It's in that cabinet."

Helen retrieved it for her. Her mother reached inside and whipped out a business card.

"Here's the Realtor I've been talking to. Call her. Tell her to get the ball rolling."

Helen regarded her with dismay. "You were already planning to sell and move home? Without even discussing it with me?"

"I knew you'd try to talk me out of it," her mother replied succinctly. Her expression brightened and even her color improved. "Now you can see how it's all working out for the best."

Helen merely stared at her. If the idea hadn't been so completely crazy, she might actually wonder if her mother weren't happy about her broken hip. The next thing she knew Flo would be calling it a blessing in disguise.

Resigned, she sighed. "I guess I'd better start making calls. I'll be back a little later."

"Take your time," Flo said cheerily. "I'm not going anywhere, at least not until you take me."

Outside her mother's room, Helen leaned against the wall and drew in several deep, calming breaths. She, the barracuda attorney, the master negotiator, had just been outmaneuvered by a wisp of a woman who couldn't even get out of bed.

As Helen had anticipated, when she called home later that day, Erik was no help at all. If he'd voiced even one objection, she could have seized on it and told her mother no, then gone on a hunt for a rehab facility even if it turned out to be miles and miles from Serenity. In fact, Charleston would have been ideal.

Instead, Erik thought it was a great idea to have Flo living with them for a while. "It'll be wonderful for our daughter to get to spend some real quality time with her grandmother. Extended family is important for kids."

"Why don't we just have your family move in, too?" Helen grumbled under her breath.

Erik chuckled. "Careful what you wish for," he warned. "You'll start giving me ideas."

"Erik, you have no idea what Flo is like. She's disorganized and unreliable."

"All I know is that she raised an amazing daughter all on her own, so she can't be all bad. Besides, she raves about my cooking."

"How much adulation can you possibly need?" Helen inquired testily. "Your cooking gets rave reviews in magazines and newspapers all over the state. Why on earth do you need to bask in a few words of praise from my mother?"

Erik hesitated, then said, "Look, if you really don't want to do this, why don't you find a good facility for her."

"Thank you!"

"Hold on," he said. "Let me finish. You can do that, but it seems ridiculous to spend that kind of money when we have room for her here, and this is where she wants to be. It's not going to be forever."

Helen tried another approach. "She'll need help, Erik. I can't stay home from work now when I'm just getting back on track with my law practice."

"We'll hire a caregiver, a physical therapist, whatever she needs. I'll make some calls today, get some people lined up."

"What about moving her back to Serenity? I can't spend days down here packing up her apartment."

"It's not likely to sell overnight, and she won't need her furniture until we've found her a house or apartment here. Leave everything there. When the time comes, we'll get

movers to do the packing. I'll even go down to supervise.
You won't have to lift a finger."

"You have an answer for everything," she groused.

"The same answers you would have if you weren't so re-
sistant to this whole idea."

"Well, when our house is chaotic, don't say I didn't warn
you," she said.

"Nope, I definitely won't be able to say that," he replied
so cheerfully Helen wanted to throttle him. "I love you.
Talk to you later."

"Hold it," she commanded before he could hang up. "How
am I supposed to get her up there? I doubt she's able to ma-
neuver well enough to fly."

"Rent a car and let her rest in the backseat while you
drive."

The thought of listening to Flo criticize her driving for
hours on end set Helen's teeth on edge, but it was a reasonable alternative.

"Okay, fine," she said glumly. "I'll see you tomorrow
night unless I deliberately drive off the road and drown us
both in a swamp en route."

"You won't do that," Erik said confidently.

"Don't be too sure. She can get on my last nerve faster
than a flea can pester a dog."

"You have me and our baby girl to get home to," he reminded her. "Put our picture up on the visor and glance at
it whenever you're trying to recall why you need to live."

She smiled despite her sour mood. "That ought to do it,"
she conceded. "I do love you, you know."

"I know."

"Even if you are a pain."

"I prefer to think of myself as sane and reasonable."

"And I'm not?"

"No comment, Counselor. See you tomorrow. Let me know what you need me to do on this end."

Helen sighed and hung up. Obviously this move of her mother's was going to happen whether she liked it or not. She might as well get with the program and make the best of it.

Ty was icing down his shoulder after his workout at The Corner Spa, when his cell phone rang. It was nearly ten at night. At this hour, a call was never good. He glanced at caller ID and saw it was his attorney, Jay Wrigley. That was even worse.

"Hey, Jay, what's up?" he asked.

"We've got a problem, Ty," he said.

Since his tone was ominous and Jay never overreacted, Ty braced himself. "Is it my contract? Is the team balking at paying my salary because of my being on injured reserve?"

"No, those terms in the contract are airtight. It's nothing like that."

"What, then?"

"I had a call tonight from Dee-Dee."

Ty sank down on a bench at the mention of Trevor's mother. "What the hell did she want?"

It was the first time Dee-Dee had made contact since they'd finalized the custody agreement nearly two years ago. Even then, she'd sent the notarized papers by courier. She'd claimed that seeing Ty or Trevor would shake her resolve to do the right thing and let Ty raise their son.

"I'm not a hundred percent sure," Jay said. "But I thought you ought to know."

"What do you mean, you don't know what she wanted? She didn't call just to chat, I'm sure of that."

"I'm telling you, she never said. She rambled on about thinking about Trevor and missing him, but she didn't ask about locating you. Look, I wouldn't even have bothered you about this, but it was just so out of the blue after all this time, I thought you should know."

"Was she drunk?"

"I don't know her well enough to say. Actually, she sounded kind of sad, like a mom who was missing her little boy."

Ty closed his eyes against the tide of fear washing over him. "Is there something we need to do?"

"She didn't ask for anything. She didn't make any threats or demands. There's nothing to do. You might want to give Tom Bristol a heads-up about the call," he said, referring to the family court lawyer who'd handled the custody case for Ty. "What do you want me to do if she asks to get in touch with you or to see Trevor?"

"Tell her no way," Ty said fiercely, knowing he probably sounded hardhearted, but he was protecting his son. Trevor rarely asked about his mother. So far, when he had, he'd seemed satisfied with Ty's explanation that she was living in another state. If Dee-Dee suddenly appeared, who knew what the emotional impact would be? He wasn't ready to find out, especially if this was just some whim on her part.

To be sure Jay knew he'd meant what he said, he added, "After the way she abandoned him, I don't want Dee-Dee anywhere near Trevor, not unless there's proof that she's changed. I can't have her waltzing back into his life, playing mommy while it suits her and then taking off again. If the time comes that it seems like it's in Trevor's best interests for them to have a relationship, I'll consider it. In the meantime, though, everybody needs to keep in mind that she abandoned that little baby on my doorstep, Jay. Maybe it was an act of kindness or one of desperation, I don't know.

But I do know I don't want anybody to ever forget that she was capable of something so reckless."

"Got it," Jay said. "I'll keep you posted if I hear from her again."

"Yeah, do that," Ty said. He clicked the phone shut and barely resisted the urge to throw it across the room, which was a good thing because it might well have hit Annie, who'd just walked in the door. She caught sight of him and stopped in her tracks, her expression immediately wary, either because of his expression or merely his presence.

"I thought you'd be gone by now," she murmured, already backing toward the door. "I saw the lights on and thought you and Elliott had just forgotten to turn them off."

"I was getting ready to leave when I got a call I had to take."

She started to turn to leave. "Good night, then. You can cut off the lights on your way out."

Jay's call had left Ty feeling restless and out of sorts. He didn't want to be left alone with his thoughts in turmoil. "Annie, don't go," he pleaded.

She regarded him with a torn expression. Though she was obviously still poised to flee, she'd clearly heard something in his voice that had stopped her.

"The call, was it bad news?" she asked hesitantly. Years ago she would have pestered him till he told her the problem, but now it was clear she wasn't sure if she wanted to get involved.

Ty knew better than to tell her about Dee-Dee's sudden, unexplained reappearance. "My attorney just wanted to alert me to a potential problem."

"Then why did you want me to stay?"

He quickly came up with an excuse that would ring true. "Because most of my conversations these days are either about which superhero T-shirt Trevor wants to put on or how badly I've screwed things up with you. Since I doubt you'll want to discuss either of those topics, I was hoping we could talk about…oh, anything else." He met her gaze. "Maybe the weather," he suggested hopefully.

"It's South Carolina in the spring. It's already hot and humid," she said wryly. "Can I go now?"

"You can, but I hope you won't."

She hesitated for what felt like an eternity, then sat down on the bench of a weight machine halfway across the room. "How does it feel being home again?" she asked eventually.

"Weird," he admitted. "How about you?"

"Definitely weird. My parents don't quite know how to treat me. I'm too old for rules and curfews, yet I'm under their roof. I can hardly wait to save enough to buy my own place."

He took heart from the fact that she'd willingly strung more than a couple of sentences together. "Then you're planning to stay here?"

"Of course. Why else would I move back?"

He shrugged. "I wasn't sure."

"It certainly wasn't because you're here," she said, bristling.

Ty grinned. "I know that, Annie," he said with exaggerated patience. "You got here months before I did, so unless you had some premonition that I was going to injure my shoulder, the two of us being here at the same time is coincidence." Okay, maybe on his part it had been calculated to take advantage of a situation, but she didn't need to know that. He held her gaze, then added, "By the way, if you did have a premonition, I wish you'd warned me about it. This hurts like hell." He removed the ice pack and rubbed his shoulder.

"Try the hot tub," she said grudgingly.

"Only if you'll join me," he taunted, just to see if he could put a blush of pink in her cheeks. It worked.

She stood up at once, her face flushed. "Only after hell's frozen over," she said. "I have to go."

"Plans for the rest of the evening?" he inquired innocently. Annie had never been a late-night person, and it was now going on eleven o'clock. There was no place she needed to be except away from him.

"Yes," she said, looking directly into his eyes and lying through her teeth. "Big plans, as a matter of fact."

Ty laughed. "Sleep well, Annie."

"I'm not going home to sleep," she insisted indignantly. "I'm—"

Before she could utter a blatant lie, Ty crossed the room and touched a finger to her lips. "Don't," he said quietly. "Whatever happens between us from here on out, let's keep things honest and real."

She swallowed hard, proving to him that she was affected by his nearness, but then that stubborn chin of hers jutted up.

"That would be a refreshing change," she said, then whirled on her heel and left him standing there.

Even though Annie had just put him squarely in his place, Ty laughed. From where he stood, it seemed as if she was working her way back to the feisty, indomitable woman he'd loved and lost. Getting her back again was going to be an absolutely fascinating challenge.

Of all the nerve! How dare Tyler Townsend stand right there in *her* workplace and taunt her like that? How dare he touch her, even if it had been nothing more than a faint brush of a finger across her lips?

A little voice in her head suggested she was lucky he hadn't kissed her instead, and made a liar out of all of her declarations that he meant nothing to her.

It was hours later, after a sleepless night, and she was still seething as she slammed pots and pans around in the kitchen at Sullivan's. At all the noise, her mother came dashing in.

"What on earth are you doing in here? You're not trying to cook, are you?"

Annie scowled at her. "I can cook."

"Not in the restaurant kitchen, you can't. If you want to burn things or ruin pots and pans, do it at home."

"If I'd done that, Dad would have wanted to know why I was making such a racket."

"Believe me, *I* want to know why you're making such a racket," Dana Sue said, studying her expectantly.

Warned away from the expensive and satisfyingly noisy pots and pans, Annie grabbed a stool and sat on it. "Ty," she said succinctly.

Her mom froze in midstride on her way to the walk-in pantry. "What did Ty do?"

Annie thought back to the incident in the spa and sighed. "Nothing, really. His mere existence is a thorn in my side."

Her mother chuckled. "I see."

"Do not laugh at me. None of this is even remotely amusing."

Dana Sue sobered at once. "I know that." She went into the pantry and emerged with various ingredients that looked promising. Annie's mouth watered at the prospect of her mother's justifiably famous French toast.

"You could take some time off, maybe get away for a while, if having Ty around is going to be too hard for you," her mom continued. "Maddie wouldn't object."

Indignant and alarmed, Annie stared at her mother. "And

you know that how? Have the two of you been discussing how to be supportive of poor little Annie?"

"Absolutely not," Dana Sue claimed, breaking eggs in a bowl and adding cinnamon, nutmeg, barely a whiff of almond extract and a dash of cream before slipping thick slices of French bread into it to soak. "I just know that she would understand if you need a break. She's sensitive to the situation."

"Which means you did discuss it," Annie said in disgust. "Margarita night must have been a real blast."

"To be honest, I don't remember that much about it," her mom admitted, looking chagrined. "Helen apparently overdid it with the tequila. She was a little stressed out."

"Helen was stressed out? Why?" Annie regarded her mother with dismay, distracted for the moment from her own turmoil. "She and Erik aren't in trouble, are they?"

Dana Sue forked the bread slices into a skillet in which butter sizzled. "No way. This was about her mom. Flo broke her hip. Helen's in Florida now. I had a call from Erik last night that she's driving her mother back up here today."

"Flo's coming home with Helen?" Annie asked, stunned. "Oh, brother, how'd that happen?"

"Flo asked, then Erik encouraged it. I gather she wants to move home. For now, that means into Helen's place."

"Yikes!"

"That was pretty much my reaction," Dana Sue said, setting two plates with golden slices of French toast in front of them, along with a pot of strawberry jam and a small pitcher of warm maple syrup. "Something tells me if things don't go well, Erik is going to spend the next few weeks hiding out right here."

"He'd be better off in another state."

"Enough of that. Let's get back to Ty," Dana Sue said.

"I'd rather not," Annie said. She concentrated on her favorite comfort food, hoping if she didn't make eye contact, her mother would drop the subject.

Dana Sue persisted. "Is there anything I can do?"

"Not unless you know how to deaden the pain in my heart every time I see him," Annie said wistfully.

"Afraid not, kiddo. There's never been a cure invented for that particular kind of pain."

"What about margaritas?"

"Based on recent experience, I can tell you for certain that whatever temporary escape they might provide is nothing compared to the pain they leave behind."

"Too bad," Annie said. "Maybe you should put the Sweet Magnolias to work on a cure for the lovesick blues. You guys could make a fortune."

"I'll mention it next time we get together. We are pretty inventive."

They ate in silence for a few minutes. Eventually Annie faced her mother. "I still love him," she admitted. "I don't want to, but I do."

"I know, sweetie."

"Am I supposed to forgive him and give him another chance after what he did?"

"Only you can decide that," Dana Sue said.

"How did you decide it was time to take Dad back?"

"He convinced me I could trust him again."

"Just by coming back when I was in the hospital, and then not giving up even after you kept pushing him away?"

Dana Sue's expression turned thoughtful. "That was part of it, but mostly I took a leap of faith. I think that's all any of us can do once we've been betrayed. It's a question of looking at the evidence that someone's changed, evaluating whether you're happier with them than without them, then taking that leap."

"Sounds scary."

"It is."

Annie sighed. "I don't think I'm there yet."

"You don't need to be. You'll get there when it feels right."

"What if Ty's healed and gone by then? What if he's given up on me?"

"If you believe with everything in you that you're meant to be, then you go after him."

Annie stared at her. "Pride be damned?"

Dana Sue nodded. "Pride be damned. Look at your dad. Once he came back to town, remember how hard he fought to get back into my life, back into both our lives? I kept pushing him away, but he never gave up. You've got our stubborn genes. You're strong enough to get whatever you really want."

She covered Annie's hand and gave it a squeeze. "Meantime, make sure Ty does his fair share of groveling. You'll feel better for that, no matter what."

Annie chuckled. "You know, I think I will."

CHAPTER SIX

When Ty got up on Saturday morning, he pulled on a pair of cutoff jeans and wandered toward the kitchen in search of his son. Usually by now Trevor had crawled into bed with him to wake him for the trip to Wharton's for breakfast. Ty made it as far as the living room before stopping in his tracks.

There, lined up on the sofa, were his fourteen-year-old sister, Katie, and four of her friends. Judging from their rapt, slack-jawed gazes and sudden silence when they saw him, they'd been waiting for him.

"Good morning, girls," he said, regretting that he hadn't grabbed a T-shirt and maybe a decent pair of pants. "Katie, I didn't know you had company."

"Mom said I could invite some friends over," she said with a touch of defiance.

"Any particular occasion?"

The girls giggled, their cheeks turning bright pink. Katie frowned at them. "You're acting crazy," she scolded them. "I told you it was okay to come over, but only if you didn't act all weird. He's just my brother."

"He's *Ty Townsend!*" one girl corrected in an awestruck voice. "And he's right here, *and* he's not wearing a shirt!"

Ty bit back a groan. "Katie, I think maybe you should offer your friends something to drink. They seem a little overheated. Where's Trevor, by the way?"

"Cal took him, Jessica Lynn and Cole for a walk. He said for you to meet them at Wharton's."

"Okay, then. Nice meeting you, girls," he said. He left to a chorus of more giggles as he went back to his room to shower and dress.

When he emerged, the girls were gone, except for Katie, who hurriedly stuffed something behind her. He regarded her suspiciously. "What was that?"

"What?" she asked, all innocence.

"You put something behind the cushion," he said, crossing the room in a few quick strides and yanking away the cushion before she could stop him. Five-dollar bills scattered. Ty stared at the money in shock. "You charged them to meet me?" he asked incredulously. "What? Five dollars apiece?"

Katie's face flamed. "Ten, because you weren't wearing a shirt. We'd agreed they'd pay extra if you weren't."

"I'm surprised you didn't let them peek in my room while I was sleeping. They might have gotten quite an eyeful."

"That would have been rude and an invasion of your privacy," Katie said indignantly. "I would never do that."

Ty wanted to be furious with her, but she sounded so solemn about the boundaries she'd set, he couldn't seem to muster the energy to yell. "You do know that even this was wrong?"

"Why?"

"Because I'm your brother, not a sideshow at the circus. And what if one of those girls had snapped a picture with a cell phone and sold it to a tabloid or something?"

Katie rolled her eyes. "They don't know people who work at tabloids."

"I think you're missing the point. You don't let people into the house to ogle your brother. It's inappropriate."

"People pay to see you pitch," she argued.

"This is hardly the same thing."

"You're famous. I'm your sister. I should be able to cash in on that."

"If you're that desperate for money, I'll find some chores you can do. You can mail pictures to my fans for me."

"That's no fun. This makes me kinda famous, too. The kids like me better 'cause I'm your sister."

She sounded so woebegone that Ty sank down beside her on the sofa. "I can't believe you don't have plenty of friends without doing something like this. You're pretty and smart and funny."

"I have braces and I'm too smart," she countered.

"The braces will only be on a few more months, and there's no such thing as too smart," Ty told her.

"There is if you like Dougie Johnson. He calls me Brainiac—and he doesn't mean it in a good way."

"Then Dougie Johnson is an idiot and not good enough for you," Ty declared emphatically.

"But he's sooo cute," Katie said plaintively. "I've liked him since second grade."

Ty hid a smile. "Then it's time you met someone new. Why don't you come with me to the ball field today? I'll bet there's someone on one of the teams who's cuter and smarter than Dougie Johnson and who'll think you're awesome."

She hesitated, her expression thoughtful. Eventually, she said, "There is this one guy who plays on Tom's team. He's at least fifteen and way cuter than Dougie. I asked Jeanette at the spa—she's married to Tom now—if she could find out if he had a girlfriend, and she told me he doesn't. I'll bet if he finds out I'm your sister, he'll pay attention to me."

At last, a way to use his fame for good, Ty thought with amusement. He'd be his little sister's teenage boy magnet. Of course, if one of the little punks even looked at her cross-eyed, Ty would be forced to beat the daylights out of him, but he'd cross that bridge later.

"Let's go hook up with Cal and the little guys," he said. "Then we'll put this operation into action."

Katie grinned at him. "You're the best big brother ever."

He waved the fistful of money under her nose. "Let's not tell Mom why you think so," he warned. "You need to give this money back, okay? Promise me."

"Do I have to?"

"If you want me to find you a cool guy, you do."

"Okay," she said grudgingly. "But this guy better be worth it. I was saving up for a new iPod. I lost my old one, and Mom says I have to replace it myself so I'll learn to be more responsible."

Ty draped an arm across her shoulders. "Growing up and being responsible sucks, doesn't it?"

Katie sighed dramatically. "You're telling me."

Annie was working with one of her regulars when Sarah came in, twenty minutes early for her appointment.

"You must be really eager to get started," Annie said, surprised not just by the early arrival, but also by the spark of excitement in Sarah's eyes.

"Forget the workout. I heard something this morning, and I couldn't wait to get in here to tell you. It's going to make your day." She grinned at Annie's client. "I'm sorry to interrupt your session, but could I borrow her for just one minute?"

"If it means I can stop this torture while she's gone, take your time," Marijo Butler said.

Annie gave her a stern look. "Just for that, do ten more reps while I'm gone."

She walked to the side of the room with Sarah. "What's this about?"

"Ty," Sarah said, then held up her hand when Annie would have turned right around and walked away. "I know he's bound to be a sore subject with you, but this will cheer you up. It was the hot news at Wharton's this morning."

She described how Katie had been selling admission to her friends to catch a glimpse of Ty. "So the word is already all over Wharton's, and then he and Katie walk in to join Cal Maddox. The whole place erupts with wolf whistles and catcalls. Ty about died right on the spot."

Despite herself, Annie couldn't help chuckling. Served him right.

"I swear I don't think I've ever seen anybody so embarrassed in my whole life, except maybe you after you passed out in his arms while you were dancing at his mom's wedding to Coach Maddox."

Annie flinched. "I'd really rather not think about that," she said. It was a memory she'd tried to bury, though Dr. McDaniels dragged it out every once in a while as a reminder of when she should have realized just how bad her eating disorder had gotten.

Sarah regarded her intently. "But the story was worth it, wasn't it? You're not mad at me for mentioning Ty?"

"I'm not mad."

"One of these days we're going to have to sit down so you can tell me how things between the two of you got to be such a mess. I saw the tabloids in the supermarket a few years back and couldn't believe my eyes. What on earth was that man thinking?"

"We'll have to wait till I figure that out myself," Annie

said. "Now, since you're here early, there's no point in wasting time. Go spend the extra few minutes on the treadmill until I can get to you."

Sarah looked distraught. "You are mad at me, aren't you?"

"No, I'm being a good friend by making you do what you came to me for. You did hire me to see that you had a hard workout, right?"

"Something I could come to regret," Sarah grumbled, but she dutifully went off and climbed onto a treadmill, leaving Annie to gloat quietly to herself over the scene Sarah had described in Wharton's.

Then she thought of sweet little Katie doing such a thing in the first place and her smile spread. Maybe she wasn't going to have to do a thing to humiliate Ty and have her revenge for the pain he'd caused her. At this rate, his family might make him suffer quite nicely without her help.

Because she couldn't help herself, Annie lingered at the spa after closing to see if Ty would show up for his workout. She was still in her office when Elliott walked in.

"You know Ty's going to be here soon, right?"

She grinned. "I'm counting on it."

Elliott looked taken aback for an instant, then chuckled. "Oh, you heard about the teen version of show-and-tell, didn't you?"

Annie nodded. "I hear it's the talk of the town."

"And you intend to rub it in," he guessed.

"Just a little."

"As long as you're hanging out, anyway, you could take over his session and I could get home to Karen," Elliott suggested slyly. "I hate having a wife I hardly ever see."

"Don't pull that pitiful act with me. I happen to know that

Karen works at the restaurant on Saturday nights, anyway, so you're not missing out on alone time with her."

Elliott sighed dramatically. "What was I thinking, trying to put one over on her boss's daughter?"

"I think you were just trying to throw me together with Ty," she told him. "And it's not going to work. All I want is a few minutes of gloating time, and then I'm out of here."

Just then Ty appeared in the doorway. Clearly he'd overheard her remark, because there was a telltale blush on his cheeks. "I gather you heard."

"I did. You're now the poster boy for the young teen girls in Serenity. How does it feel?"

"Ridiculous," he muttered.

"How much older do they need to be before it feels terrific?" she asked, unable to keep the bitter note out of her voice. "How old is the average major league groupie, anyway?"

Elliott backed out of the room. "That's my cue to leave. Ty, I'm ready when you are."

"Five minutes," Ty replied tightly, his gaze never leaving Annie.

When Elliott was gone, he shut the door, then locked it for good measure. Annie began to get the idea that she might have pushed him too far.

"A lock won't keep Elliott out if I scream," she warned.

Ty just stared at her and shook his head, looking hurt and bemused. "What is wrong with you? You know that the women I was involved with were just that, women. You also know I would never lay a hand on you in anger. I get that you're mad at me, but you're crossing a line, Annie."

She knew she was on shaky ground, but she stood up and stared him down, anyway. "You're the one who crossed a line. You don't get to act all self-righteous now."

"I do if you're going to hint around that there was anything improper in what I did. I betrayed you, Annie. I cheated on you. I have no defense for that, but it wasn't ugly and you know it. You know *me* better than that."

She flinched under his furious gaze. "Yes, I do," she admitted, deflated. "I'm sorry. That was a low blow. I could hear the words coming out of my mouth, but I couldn't seem to stop them."

"How about this? How about I blow off my workout with Elliott and you and I go someplace and have this out once and for all. You can yell at me, call me names, make all the outrageous accusations that will make you feel better, and maybe then we can finally move on."

She was shaking her head before he finished. "I won't let it be that easy for you."

"You want me to pay?"

She nodded. "I'm not sure what that says about me, but I do. I want you to hurt the way I hurt."

He met her gaze, his expression weary. "Believe me, Annie, not a day goes by when I don't feel that kind of pain. I know what I cost you, what I cost us. And I know there's nobody to blame but myself. I'll have to live with that the rest of my life."

He was close enough to touch her cheek, a quick brush of his fingertip that left a trail of fire and a sea of longing. "Let me know if you ever change your mind and want to have that talk."

Then, before she could respond, he walked out, not just out of her office, but out of the spa.

Elliott walked in and found her still standing there, tears tracking down her cheeks.

"What the hell did he do to you?"

"Nothing."

"It wasn't nothing. You're crying."

"Because I didn't think it was possible for things to get any worse between us," she whispered. "And now they are."

And for the life of her, she couldn't imagine how they'd ever be right again.

"Helen, I'm not made of spun glass. You can drive a little faster," Flo commented from the backseat of the rental car as they crossed the Florida-Georgia border. "Otherwise it'll be midsummer by the time we get home."

"Mother, I'm driving the speed limit," Helen replied, gritting her teeth against the desire to say a whole lot more.

"Nobody drives the speed limit," Flo scoffed. "There's a five-mile-an-hour cushion before the cops will stop you."

"Not in Georgia. These cops have a reputation for strictly enforcing the law. Why are we even arguing about this? I'm the one behind the wheel."

"I just thought you'd be more anxious to get home," Flo retorted.

"I am anxious, but I'd like to get there in one piece. Why don't you rest for a while? Close your eyes. I'll wake you when it's time to stop for lunch."

"We'll have to do a drive-through," her mother said. "I don't know if I can get out of the car."

"Sooner or later, you're going to need to use a restroom. We'll have to go inside then, so we might as well go to a regular restaurant."

"Then how about Cracker Barrel?" Flo suggested at once. "I like that place. I can do a little shopping, maybe find something for Sarah Beth. They have real cute things in the gift shop."

"I'll watch for a sign," Helen conceded. Maybe she could

rent a book on tape and play it loudly enough to drown out her mother's complaints about her driving.

Getting ready for the trip had taken a day longer than she'd originally planned. Her mother had insisted on going home at least overnight, so she could supervise the packing of the things she'd need right away in Serenity. A friend had helped Flo pack up clothes, while Helen had made sure all the bills and business papers were boxed up for the trip. The back of their small SUV rental was jammed with suitcases and cartons.

Loading the car had been a breeze compared to getting Flo herself settled comfortably. In the backseat, she was surrounded by pillows and covered with a blanket, since she claimed Helen kept the car much too cold. By the time they'd gone twenty miles, she'd grumbled about the temperature, the speed, the bumpiness of the highway, the boring scenery and Helen's refusal to stay in the left lane.

For a moment, though, there was blessed silence from the back. Helen dared to hope that they could cover another hundred miles before her mother woke and started in again. She'd like to have lunch north of Savannah. From there it would only be another couple of hours before she'd be in Serenity. Erik, with his seemingly endless amount of patience, could take over.

"I keep thinking I've left something important behind," her mother said, destroying the rare moment of quiet.

"Such as?"

"Well, if I knew that, it wouldn't keep nagging at me," Flo said. "It's not as if I can make a quick trip around the corner to get it."

"If you left anything important behind, you can send your friend Betty over to get it. She has the key."

"True," Flo said, "but I don't know as I want her digging around in my things."

Helen rolled her eyes. "Then why'd you give her a key?"

"Someone needed to have one for emergencies, and she lives closest."

"She seemed nice to me. I'm sure she's perfectly trustworthy."

"Of course she is," Flo said. "She's just nosy. She'll use any excuse to go poking around in things that are none of her business."

"Mom, we have all of your important papers with us. We have your jewelry, most of your clothes and personal things, even a bunch of knickknacks. What could she possibly discover, a box of condoms in your nightstand?"

"Helen Decatur-Whitney, that is not amusing."

Helen bit the inside of her lip. She thought it had been at least a little bit funny.

"My relationship with Frank Rogers is not a laughing matter," Flo added for good measure, which pretty much wiped the beginnings of a smile right off Helen's face.

"Frank Rogers?" she repeated in a choked voice. Her mother had been having an affair? Why hadn't she known about that? "You were involved with a man down there?"

"I don't know why you sound so shocked," Flo said. "It wasn't serious, for goodness' sake. If it had been, would I be moving back home?"

Condoms? A fling with a man named Frank? Helen could barely concentrate on the highway. She now had way too much information about her mother's life, to say nothing of images that no daughter ought to have of her seventy-two-year-old mother. She needed to get off I-95 and go somewhere she could scream.

Thankfully there was a sign for a Cracker Barrel at the

next exit. Even though she'd hoped to drive a little farther before stopping, she took the exit ramp, followed the signs and found a parking spot that wasn't too far from the front door.

"Come on, Mother, let's have lunch."

"I'm not hungry yet."

"Well, I am. You can have a cup of coffee and use the restroom."

"I don't need to," her mother protested.

"Fine, then just wait for me in the car," Helen said. She was about to slam the door and walk away, when her mother heaved a sigh and emerged from the car, then wrestled with the walker she'd been told to use.

Helen assisted her inside, got her settled at a table, gave the waitress an order for a huge breakfast she'd never be able to eat, then excused herself and practically ran back to the parking lot with her cell phone in hand.

She considered calling Erik, but given his recent tendency to support her mother, she opted for calling Maddie instead.

"My mother was having a fling with some man named Frank," she announced the second Maddie answered.

"Okay," Maddie said slowly. "Did I need to know that?"

"*I* didn't need to know that," Helen said. "I'm in hell."

"Where are you actually?"

"Somewhere south of Savannah and north of Jacksonville. We stopped for lunch."

"At eleven in the morning?"

"I had to get out of that car," Helen said.

"Where's Flo now?"

"Inside. I have to get back before our food comes, but I needed moral support."

"Always," Maddie said, though she didn't seem to be doing

a very good job of hiding her amusement. "Having Flo back home may turn out to be more interesting than any of us thought. Is Frank going to be your new daddy?"

"You are *so* not funny," Helen said.

Maddie tried unsuccessfully to choke back a laugh. "Sorry," she murmured. "You might want to prepare yourself, though. Your mother seems to be full of surprises."

"I knew this was going to be hard. I didn't expect anything like this," Helen said. "Maddie, what am I going to do?"

"I don't think there's anything you can do. She's a grown woman." Maddie hesitated, then added, "I know you don't want to hear this, but I think it's kind of sweet."

"Having a boyfriend is kind of sweet," Helen corrected. "Having condoms beside her bed, not so sweet! That image will be burned into my brain through eternity."

"Sweetie, Frank is in Florida. He's been left behind. Once she's here, she won't even be able to leave the house for a while, so I doubt you'll have to worry about her meeting anyone new. No one will be heating up the sheets in your guest room."

Helen considered that. A sigh of relief washed over her. "True. Thank you. I'd better get back inside."

"It's going to be fine, you know. It really is."

"Tell me you'd feel that way if Paula suddenly announced she was moving in with you and Cal," Helen challenged, referring to Maddie's artist mother whose eccentricities drove Maddie mad.

"Point taken. Drive safely. I'll stop by tomorrow unless you want help tonight getting your mom settled."

"No, tomorrow's good. Thanks again for dragging me off the ledge."

"Anytime," Maddie said.

Feeling marginally better, Helen went back inside to find that her eggs, bacon, biscuits, potatoes and sausage gravy had all been served. She stuffed down every bite, along with her feelings.

CHAPTER SEVEN

Annie stood outside Sarah's house—a small white bunga-
low with a lawn that needed tending—and suddenly felt
like she was a kid again. She was just blocks from her own
home, where she'd been living with her parents since coming back to Serenity.

How many times had she hung out here, listening to
music, giggling over boys, crying when her mom had kicked
her dad out and he'd left town? This was where she'd first
voiced her dreams of a future with Ty. She'd been so crazy
about him. Still was, if she were to be totally honest.

She sighed, then continued up the walk and rang the bell.

When Sarah opened the door, Annie's jaw went slack.
Inside a house that had always been in perfect order, all was
now chaos.

"I know," Sarah said, following the direction of Annie's
gaze. "It's a disaster. The kids leave toys everywhere, and
I'm so exhausted from chasing after them and fighting to
get them into bed, I can't make myself tackle the straight-
ening up that needs to be done. Let's go in the kitchen. It's
not quite as bad."

But it was. The remains of what must have been the kids'

dinner of mac and cheese, peas and carrots, was not only all over the table, but on the floor. Sarah blinked with dismay as she took it in, then tears slid down her cheeks.

"I swear," she began, but her voice trailed off and she sat down at the table and buried her face in her hands. "I'm sorry. I am so, so sorry. I thought I'd have this all cleaned up. I guess in my mind I saw it the way I wanted it to be the first time you came over, but it's awful. No wonder my husband is fed up with me. It was this way back home, too. No matter how hard I tried, I just couldn't keep up with things."

After her initial shock, Annie focused on making things better for her friend. "Hey, I've seen worse," she said briskly, reaching for the dishes and moving them to the sink. "You should have seen Maddie's place right after she had Jessica Lynn and then Cole barely a year later. Cal's a saint, and he did everything he could to help. Even Kyle and Katie pitched in, but it was always a mess. There's only so much you can do when kids are really little. Debris seems to follow in their wake."

Sarah's obvious misery didn't lessen. "You're so sweet to say that, but come on, Annie, this is ridiculous. There must be something wrong with me that I can't take care of my kids and my house."

"Is that something else your husband planted in your head, that you're an incompetent wife and mother?" Annie asked heatedly. "I know I haven't even met him, but I really dislike this guy. What did you ever see in him? He sounds like a bully."

Sarah looked shocked by the accusation. "Oh, no, he's nothing like that. He just likes things a certain way."

"Spotless house, perfect kids, skinny wife," Annie said, unable to keep a sarcastic note from her voice. "That way?"

"He works hard and makes a good living for our family," Sarah said, defending him. "The rest is the least I can do."

Annie had her doubts about how hard Walter worked. "Doesn't he work for the family company?" she asked as she began rinsing the dishes and putting them into the dishwasher. "Did he have to scramble to get the job? Is his father going to fire him if he makes a mistake? Don't talk to me about *him* being under pressure. Let him spend a few days at home with two young kids and see how he handles it."

"His father's a perfectionist," Sarah said, still defending him.

"So, like father, like son. He needs to get over himself," Annie declared, turning on the dishwasher, then wiping off the countertop.

Sarah's mood remained gloomy. "Look at what just happened here. You had those dishes cleaned up and in the dishwasher while we were talking. I've had all day and couldn't get it done."

"I didn't have those two children underfoot," Annie reminded her.

"No, it's me. I just can't do anything right."

Annie was dismayed by the fact that Sarah sounded as if she'd heard that lecture frequently enough to have learned it by rote. Rather than expressing any more criticism of Walter, whom she'd never even met, she simply began sorting and folding the laundry piled atop the dryer.

Sarah started to get up. "I should be doing that," she protested.

"Sit there and relax," Annie ordered. "This won't take long. How about some sweet tea? I know I could use a glass. Do you have any made?"

"There's a pitcher in the fridge," Sarah said. "And I'd love some. It's funny how we never kept that in my house. I got hooked on it because your mama always had it."

"Not anymore. She said it doesn't taste the same with artificial sweetener, and since she's trying to be careful so she doesn't wind up with type two diabetes like her mother, she stopped making it. It about killed Daddy and me when she did, though to be honest we're probably better off without it."

Sarah's expression brightened. "How is your daddy? I hear that business he started on Main Street is thriving."

"To tell the truth, the hardware store is no better than it was before he took over, but he's supplying a lot of the contractors around here now, and that side of the business has really taken off," Annie said as she poured the tea over ice and handed one glass to Sarah, then sipped from the other. "Even with the downturn in the housing market everywhere else, Serenity's doing okay, at least for now."

Sarah nodded. "I couldn't believe it when I drove into town and saw two new developments west of town and a brand-new elementary school." Her expression turned sad. "I loved growing up here. I wish my kids were going to be here longer than a few months. There's just something about this town that no place else can match."

"I know," Annie said. "I loved Charleston, I really did, but this is home."

Sarah grinned. "I always thought you, me and Raylene, we'd be raising our kids right here, and that they'd be best friends just like us and the same way your mother, Helen and Maddie are. You'd be married to Ty, of course. I have no idea who I'd planned on marrying, and of course nobody around here would have been good enough for Raylene. But it was a nice dream."

"Indeed, it was," Annie agreed. She folded the last of the

pint-size T-shirts and set the basket aside, ready to be carried into the back of the house. "There you go. Everything's done in here."

"I swear I didn't invite you over here to clean and fold laundry for me."

"It didn't take but a minute, and we got to do a little more catching up," Annie said. "Now I'm going to go and let you get some rest while those kids of yours are quiet."

"I'd promise you can meet 'em next time, but it's probably better this way. They're little hellions, especially by the end of the day."

Annie lifted a brow at her harsh assessment. "Another of Walter's opinions?"

Sarah laughed. "No, that one is all mine. Sometimes even I can't deny the truth. How two kids under three years old can cause so much commotion is beyond me."

"It's because they're under three," Annie told her. "At that age, they have nonstop energy, right up till the second they crash. One night next week we'll hire Katie to babysit, and you and I will go out for a quiet, civilized dinner at Sullivan's and let Mom pamper us."

"You're not going to count my calories, are you?" Sarah asked suspiciously.

"No way. For one night only that diet I gave you is suspended. Everybody deserves to splurge once in a while."

Sarah patted her hip. "I might have taken that concept to extremes."

Annie had the feeling Sarah's self-deprecating humor had become a defense mechanism against whatever criticisms her husband doled out. She really hoped she never crossed paths with the man.

She gave Sarah a fierce hug. "I don't care how many pounds you've put on, you're beautiful. Remember that."

As she walked home, she resolved to teach Sarah the hardest lesson she'd ever had to learn…that body image and self-image were two different things. What Sarah needed more than anything these days was to get her self-esteem back, to start believing in herself again. And Annie intended to see that she did.

Distracted by Trevor, who was trying to climb up the slide on the playground, Ty answered his cell phone without glancing at the caller ID. At the sound of his father's voice, he nearly groaned.

Though Ty and Bill Townsend had eventually made peace after the divorce, it was an uneasy truce. They'd gotten together a few times in Atlanta, when Bill had come to town to see Ty pitch, but the truth was, in some ways Ty considered Cal more like a father to him.

"Hey, Dad, what's up?" he said, keeping a close eye on Trevor as he talked. The colorful playground equipment was kid-friendly, but it had plenty of hazards when a rambunctious boy like Trevor had no idea of his own limits. Ty's respect for Trevor's nanny had tripled the first time he'd tried to keep up with his son on a playground. She must have nerves of steel.

"Why'd I have to find out you were in town from the local paper?" his father asked.

"I'm sorry about that. The news got out before I could call. I've been pretty preoccupied with rehab." He didn't bother noting that the item had been in the paper days ago, and his father was just getting around to calling. His dad's standards for behavior were flexible. He'd had plenty to say when he'd found out about Dee-Dee, despite his own past infidelity and an unplanned pregnancy.

"And that's another thing," his father said. "Why didn't you discuss your treatment plans with me? I'm a doctor, Ty. I may be a pediatrician, but I have a halfway decent network of colleagues. I could have made sure you were getting the best care."

"The team has excellent doctors, Dad." He caught a glimpse of Trevor trying to stand at the top of the slide. "Hold on. I need to grab Trevor before he falls."

He caught his son around the waist to steady him. "Okay, now sit," he instructed. "Feet in front of you. Ready?"

Trevor nodded, his eyes alight with excitement. Ty released him, and he slid down the metal surface and landed in the dirt at the bottom, squealing with delight.

"Again," he commanded.

"In a minute," Ty said, returning to his phone call. "Dad, I'm with Trevor at the park. I need to watch him to make sure he doesn't break his neck."

"Sure. How about dinner one night this week? We can catch up."

Ty resigned himself to a couple of hours of being interrogated about his surgery, his treatment and the qualifications of his doctors. "Tomorrow's good for me."

"You staying with your mother?"

"Yes."

"Then I'll pick you up there. Seven okay?"

"That'll work. Bye, Dad."

He glanced at his son, saw the adoration in Trevor's eyes as Ty looked up at him, and knew he'd once regarded his dad the same way. Then Bill Townsend had cheated on his mom, gotten one of his nurses pregnant, and the whole family had been rocked.

Though his dad had initially planned to marry the younger

woman carrying his child, instead she'd had the wisdom and maturity to call off the wedding. Convinced Bill was still in love with Ty's mother, she'd moved out of state to be with her family. Ty now had a half brother he'd never even met. He wasn't entirely sure if his father spent much time with the boy, who was only a couple of years older than Trevor. It wasn't something he'd dared to ask his mother, and his father never volunteered much about his child.

As crazy as it was trying to raise a son and juggle a major league baseball career, Ty was glad he'd handled things differently, even if it hadn't been by design. Despite the way Trevor had been conceived and the mess his existence had made of Ty's relationship with Annie, he loved being a dad. He wouldn't have wanted to miss a moment of this time with Trevor. He hoisted his bright-eyed, exuberant son into the air until the boy giggled.

"I might have started off on shaky ground," he told Trevor, "but I promise I will never let you down, buddy."

He intended to do everything in his power to keep that promise, because he knew all too well what it felt like to be betrayed by the man you looked up to.

Though Annie had been back at work for a few days now, she'd managed to steer clear of Maddie. She'd done it by tightly scheduling her clients, dashing out the door when she was free and hiding out the rest of the time. Unfortunately, there was no way to keep that up forever. Besides, Maddie liked to confront issues head-on, so eventually she managed to waylay Annie.

"Let's have tea on the patio," she suggested at midmorning before Annie could make a dash for her office.

"I have an appointment," Annie said, avoiding her gaze.

"Elliott's free. He'll take it."

"I can't ask him to cover for me again."

"You didn't. I did," Maddie said, then gestured toward the spa's shaded patio. "Let's go."

Annie sighed and followed her outside. For so many years Maddie had been like a second mother to her. Annie loved her to pieces. Right this second, though, Maddie felt like the enemy. Or at least the mother of the enemy.

Annie sat down and sipped her tea, waiting.

"I'm sorry," Maddie said, her tone filled with sympathy.

At the simple, heartfelt words, tears welled up in Annie's eyes. Sympathy was the last thing she needed. She was barely holding herself together as it was.

"Not your fault," she said in a choked voice. "I really don't want to talk about Ty, not with you of all people."

"I know my son better than anyone," Maddie reminded her. "If it helps, he's just as miserable as you are."

Annie regarded her incredulously. "I doubt that."

"He is. Have you seen him? He's lost weight. There's no sparkle in his eyes."

"I imagine he's upset over his career."

"Of course that's part of it, but it's about you, too. He's worried sick about you."

"That's not the impression I have. The first night I ran into him, all he did was insult me."

Maddie looked surprised by that. "You've seen him?"

"A few times, as a matter of fact. It hasn't gone well on any of the occasions when our paths have crossed." She didn't admit that she might have been responsible for some of the bitter exchanges.

Maddie regarded her intently. "You know what makes me saddest about all of this?"

Annie shook her head.

"You two were always so close. You were the best of friends. You counted on each other."

"I really thought we were friends," Annie agreed. "It turns out I was wrong. Best friends don't betray each other, not like Ty betrayed me."

"He made a mistake, Annie. A huge one, but it would be just as big a mistake to let it destroy what you once had. Good friends, especially friends who've been together practically forever, are hard to come by. Look at your mom, Helen and me. Look at the connection the three of us have because of all that history."

Annie frowned. "What are you asking me to do? Tell him all is forgiven?" she asked bitterly. "And then what?"

"Put the past behind you, not just for Ty's sake, but for your own."

"Sorry, not going to happen."

Maddie looked saddened by her response. "Are you really so cold, Annie? When did you become so unforgiving?"

"When my best friend, the man I loved, told me he was having a baby with some groupie he hardly even knew." Before she could stop herself, she added, "You should know how that feels."

For a moment, Maddie looked shocked, but instead of getting angry, she merely nodded. "I do. It hurts like hell."

"You didn't forgive Bill," Annie reminded her.

"That's not entirely true," Maddie corrected. "I didn't take him back, but I did forgive him, and I did move on with my life. Whatever you decide about Ty, you need to move on. I get the feeling you haven't done that. You're still too caught up in the anger. It isn't healthy, Annie. Take that from someone who's been through that, too. When I found out about Bill and the baby his girlfriend was expecting, I was furious. Worse, I was humiliated. Everyone in town knew that he'd cheated on me. I wanted to stay in the house and hide." Her lips curved slightly. "At least when I didn't want to hunt him down and destroy him. Sound familiar?"

"Absolutely, which means you should understand exactly how hard it is having Ty back here," Annie said.

"Of course, I do, but you have to know that Ty regrets what he did. He wants to make amends."

There was no doubting Maddie believed what she was saying, but Annie didn't buy it. Not entirely. She studied Maddie with a narrowed gaze. "Is this really about me forgiving Ty and getting on with my life?" she asked.

"Of course it is."

"You sure it isn't about me helping Ty with his rehab?"

Maddie looked genuinely shocked by the suggestion. "I wouldn't try to manipulate you like that. Annie. I have too much love and respect for you to do such a thing."

Annie sighed. "I'm sorry. I suppose I wouldn't have blamed you if you had. He is your son."

"And I am concerned about him, but I'm just as concerned about you."

Annie couldn't deny the sincerity in her voice. "Thanks, Maddie. I do appreciate that you're in an awkward position, that you feel as if you're caught between me and Ty and even my mom. Take care of your son. Don't worry about me. I'll be fine."

Maddie still looked worried. "Do you want some time off?"

"Absolutely not. I'm not letting him run me out of town."

"I wasn't suggesting—"

Annie cut her off before she could finish. "I need to get back to work."

"Just one more thing," Maddie said, halting her when she would have gone back inside. "I'm sure this will make you question everything I've just said, but there is one thing I want you to think about. When you were really sick, Ty was there for you. He never hesitated, not even when he cut school to see you in the hospital, even though that could have gotten him thrown off the baseball team. It was an act that could have changed his entire future." She caught Annie's gaze and held it. "And that's all I'm going to say about it."

She stood and walked past Annie, pausing to give her hand a squeeze. "I do love you, you know."

After Maddie was gone, Annie sat back down and let the tears flow. It was true what Maddie had said—Ty had been there for Annie during the darkest hours of her life, when she'd been in the hospital and scared to death that she'd never get past her eating disorder. Ty might not be in danger of dying the way she had been, but his career could go up in smoke if his rehab wasn't handled properly. Maybe she did owe him to oversee that.

Not that he'd asked, but Maddie had. In her own subtle, maternal way, she'd chided Annie for not being big enough to put her personal feelings aside, at least for this one thing.

Annie sighed heavily. Sometimes being the bigger person really sucked. And right at this moment, she wasn't a hundred percent sure she could pull it off.

When his dad pulled into the parking lot at Sullivan's, Ty winced. He'd never given a thought to where they might be going for dinner, but naturally his father would choose the fanciest restaurant in town, even if it was run by his ex-wife's best friend and the mother of the woman Ty had betrayed.

"Dad, maybe we should go someplace else," Ty suggested.

"Why? I thought you loved the food here."

"It's the best in town, but I don't think I'm too popular with Dana Sue these days."

His father looked blank.

"Because of Annie," Ty explained with exaggerated patience. "I hurt her."

His father still looked bewildered. "I thought that was just some teenage crush she had on you."

Leave it to his father to be so self-absorbed he'd missed the obvious. "We dated all through college. We were planning a future," Ty told him.

"Officially? Was there a ring on her finger?"

"You can't be that insensitive," Ty said, regarding him with dismay. "Then again, you didn't even let the ring on mom's finger stop you from cheating."

His father frowned at that. "I thought we'd put that behind us a long time ago."

"I thought so, too. Maybe this dinner is a bad idea. We seem to be operating on different wavelengths tonight."

There was no mistaking the disappointment in his father's expression. "Look, I'm sorry if I sounded insensitive. I guess I just hadn't realized how serious things had gotten between you and Annie. Let's just go in, have something to eat, and you can fill me in on that or we can stick to your rehab."

Ty nodded slowly. "Let's stick to baseball," he said eventually. "Just promise to get between me and Dana Sue if she comes charging out of the kitchen."

Bill chuckled. "I can do that much for you. Dana Sue doesn't scare me."

"She probably should," Ty said dryly.

Inside Sullivan's, it was crowded, but his dad had made a reservation and they were immediately led to a table. Silence seemed to fall in their wake. When the waitress arrived, she greeted Bill cheerfully, then faltered as she recognized Ty.

"I didn't expect to see you in here," she said, then flushed.

Her tone turned stiffly polite. "Sorry. Can I get you something to drink?"

"Iced tea is fine," Ty said.

"Nothing stronger?" his dad asked.

"I'm still taking painkillers," Ty told him.

Bill frowned. "Shouldn't you be off those by now?"

"I *was* off, but once I started rehab, I needed them again. I've been pushing myself hard."

"Maybe you should slow down. You want to let that shoulder heal properly. Pain's an indicator that something's not right. Does your surgeon know you're working out as much as you are?"

"It's all good, Dad. Everybody and their brother has chimed in on this plan, including the team doctors and trainers." Of course, some of them agreed with his dad that he needed to slow down, but Ty wasn't about to mention that.

"Okay, then. I just don't want you to have a setback."

"Believe me, that's the last thing I want, either. That's one reason I could meet you tonight. I took a night off from working out."

For the next couple of minutes, they studied the menu, then ordered the catfish special. After that, they stuck to chit-chat about the Atlanta Braves and how the team was doing without Ty in the pitching rotation. Years ago, Bill had been his biggest booster, coaching him, playing catch with him in the evenings, cheering him on at the games, at least until Ty had balked at Bill bringing his pregnant girlfriend to the games with him. He figured now it was good that they still had baseball in common.

"How's your mother?" Bill asked eventually.

"She's great," Ty said, noting the wistful expression on his dad's face. "I know you regret the way things turned out."

Bill nodded. "My own stupid fault."

"What about you? Are you seeing anyone?" Ty asked.

"I go out, but the truth is no one holds a candle to your mother. I wish I'd known that sooner."

"That's how I feel about Annie," Ty admitted. "I loved her, but I threw it away for no good reason."

"You still in love with her?" Bill asked after the waitress brought their meals. "Because if you are, don't wait too long to fight for her. I did and look what happened. Your mom wound up with Cal."

Ty asked something he'd often wondered about. "If it hadn't been for Cal, do you think you and Mom would have tried again?"

"Maybe," Bill said. "But *what-ifs* and *maybes* are pointless. That's why you need to go after what you want when it counts."

"Interesting advice coming from you," Dana Sue commented, arriving at their table in time to overhear Bill.

"How are you?" Bill asked her. "The food was excellent, as always."

"It was fantastic," Ty confirmed. "Better than anything I've ever had anywhere else."

Dana Sue turned her gaze on him. "And you have gotten around, haven't you?"

Ty winced at the bite in her voice. He opened his mouth to apologize, but to his surprise, she leaned down and kissed his cheek. "I'm glad you're home, Ty."

He regarded her with surprise. "You are?"

"For your mother's sake, of course." She leveled a less friendly look at him. "Just watch your step with my daughter," she said in that same sweet tone. "Otherwise, that injury to your shoulder will seem painless compared to what I'll do to you."

She sounded so serious, so vicious, despite that syrupy tone, Ty couldn't help it. He chuckled.

She gave him a chiding look. "How long have you known me?"

"My whole life."

"Have I ever lied to you?"

"Not that I'm aware of," he said.

She patted his cheek. "Keep that in mind."

And then she walked away.

Ty glanced at his father, who looked vaguely shaken. "Told you she was scary."

"You messed with her kid's heart," Bill said. "I guess if I'm being honest, I don't blame her."

"Did you ever worry that Grandma Paula was going to tear into you?"

Bill chuckled. "All the time, son. All the time."

For the first time, Ty felt the faintest hint of sympathy for his father.

CHAPTER EIGHT

Rather than going to lunch, Annie stopped by her father's store on her midday break. She found Ronnie in the back room, unpacking a shipment of tools. He looked up, grinned when he saw her, then immediately sobered, probably because of her grim expression.

"Something tells me you're not here because you need a hammer or a paintbrush," he said. "What's on your mind?"

She shoved aside a stack of catalogs on his disorganized desk and perched on the corner. "How's business?"

To his credit, her dad actually managed to keep a smile from forming at the too-casual inquiry. "You looking for a career change?"

"No, I'm making conversation," she replied, her tone grumpy.

"Okay, then, I'll play along. Business on the construction side is real good. Hardware sales are slow." His gaze narrowed. "Didn't we talk about this the other day?"

"I'm trying to show an interest in your work," she claimed. "Things could have changed since then."

Ronnie set aside the box he'd been unpacking and pulled

up a chair. "Let's skip the small talk. What's really on your mind?"

She considered more evasion but decided it would be a waste of time. They both knew why her mood was so sour. "Ty," she said succinctly, grabbing a paper clip off the counter and twisting it out of shape until it finally snapped. She tossed it into the trash can and picked up another. "Isn't it always about Ty these days?"

Her dad's gaze narrowed. "Has he been bothering you? If he has—"

Annie cut him off with a shake of her head before he could offer to have a talk with Ty. That wasn't what she wanted. At least, she didn't think it was. She'd already heard a few rumors about Ronnie confronting Ty in Wharton's, though no one seemed to know for sure what had been said.

"He exists," she said bleakly. "That's pretty much all it takes to bother me." She reached for another paper clip, but her dad hurriedly moved it out of reach.

"Your mom told me Maddie was going to offer you some time off."

"She did. I turned her down."

"Maybe you should reconsider."

She shook her head. "What's the point of going someplace else? I'll still be thinking about him day and night, wondering if Elliott's doing the right rehab stuff."

Her dad looked surprised by that. "This is about the rehab for his shoulder? Are you saying you want to step in?"

"I don't want to," she insisted.

"You think you should?"

She met her dad's gaze and nodded. "I feel like I owe him. Do you remember the day he skipped school and risked Cal's wrath so he could come to the hospital and talk to me? Cal could have kicked him off the team for that. Back then, baseball was all Ty cared about and he took the chance, anyway. Maddie reminded me of that today, not that I needed to be reminded."

"Listen, kid, we all owe him for how determined he was to help you beat your eating disorder, but I don't want you making yourself miserable to pay back an old debt. I doubt Ty expects that, either. He hasn't said that, has he?"

"No, but Maddie has. She made me feel so guilty, Dad, and she wasn't even mean about it. You know how she is. She sort of dropped the idea out there, and now I can't shake it."

"You know I love Madelyn, but she's wrong this time. Once Ty cheated on you and broke your heart, I think that old debt was pretty much wiped out."

"On the flip side," she began, thinking aloud, "if I help him, he might get better faster and leave town."

Ronnie gave her a knowing look. "Is that what you want? Do you really want him gone?"

Annie frowned at him. "Of course. Why would you even ask such a thing?"

"Because sometimes being miserable is all we have left of what used to be. When I first got back to town, you were sick and your mom and I were barely speaking, but I knew I had to be here. It was better to be right here, even with her hating me, than to be away and alone."

Annie thought about what he was saying. In a way, her dad was right. Having Ty home was a constant reminder of everything awful that had happened between them, but in some ways it was better than not seeing him at all. Then she spent way too much time wondering what he was up to, who he was with. At least here, she'd know almost immediately if he was out with anyone else. The fact that she still cared about that really was annoying.

She regarded her dad wistfully. "How can I still be in love with him? Am I a total idiot?"

"No more than your mother was for taking another chance on me." His expression turned wry. "There are some who'd say she was nuts for doing that. Helen comes to mind, though I think we've finally made peace. What I know for a fact is that real love can survive almost anything, even a betrayal as deep as what Ty did to you. Don't worry about what anyone else thinks, not your mom and me, not Maddie, not the whole nosy town. Listen to your heart and do what's best for you. If you love Ty, then find some way to forgive him."

She nodded. It made perfect sense. She knew what her heart was saying. What she didn't know was whether or not it could be trusted. Even more important, she didn't know if Ty could be trusted.

Ty walked into The Corner Spa and looked around for some sign of Annie. He couldn't seem to help himself.

"She's gone," Elliott said, joining him and guessing what his survey was all about.

Ty didn't even try to hide his disappointment. "I keep thinking she'll mellow."

"If you want her to take over your workouts, you're going to have to grovel," Elliott said.

"It's not even about that. You know what you're doing. We're making progress."

"Not fast enough to suit you," Elliott said. "I know my limitations, Ty. Annie could get you where you need to be faster."

"Well, that's not going to happen. I'd settle for just bumping into her more frequently and having a few civilized conversations." He met Elliott's sympathetic gaze. "Pitiful, huh? A man willing to accept a few crumbs from a woman."

"Hey, I've been there. When I first met Karen, she wouldn't give me the time of day. Her attitude had nothing to do with me specifically, but her ex had been a disaster. She wasn't about to take a chance on another relationship, not with two kids to worry about. I made up any excuse I could to spend time with her. Fortunately there are a lot of matchmakers in this town." He grinned. "They helped."

"Unfortunately all those inveterate matchmakers are almost as mad at me as Annie is," Ty lamented. He shook off his mood. "Let's get to work. Maybe if you make me sweat enough, I'll get her out of my head, at least for a couple of hours."

"I'm a tough taskmaster, not a miracle worker," Elliott replied.

Ty knew exactly what he was saying, because it was definitely going to take a minor miracle to fix this mess he'd created. And with every day that passed, his confidence that he could win Annie back slipped a little more.

Helen couldn't remember ever feeling more exhausted and frazzled. She'd taken on too many cases as a defense mechanism to prove to herself that Flo's arrival wasn't going to disrupt her life. As a result, she was worn-out at the end of the workday and in no mood for her mother's endless complaints, accumulated during a day of boredom.

Each night, Helen barely made it inside before her mother wanted to know what they were having for dinner.

"I normally don't eat this late," she told Helen when they eventually sat down at TV trays in her mother's room. "In Florida, my friends and I always took advantage of the early-bird specials."

"Well, I don't get home until six. After I spend some time with Sarah Beth and get her settled for the night, it's usually seven-thirty by the time I can grab something to eat. Since Erik's working, it never seemed to matter much. But since you prefer to eat early, I'll ask Mrs. Lowell to fix a meal for you before she leaves."

Flo looked dismayed by the suggestion. "I don't want to eat alone. Besides, Letitia can barely fix a sandwich. Heaven knows what she'd do to a whole meal."

Helen regarded her impatiently. "Then what do you want?"

Her mother pushed her food around on her plate, then finally met Helen's gaze. "Maybe Erik could send a little something over from the restaurant," she suggested hesitantly. She pressed the idea, proving she'd been thinking about it for some time. "Then you wouldn't have to cook, and we could eat the minute you walk in the door. You'd still have time with Sarah Beth before her bedtime. You know she doesn't have to be in bed so early, anyway. It's not as if she has to go to school in the morning."

Helen bristled at the criticism of her child-rearing skills. "Routines are important for a child," she said, recalling how seldom they'd kept to one when she was young. She'd been determined to make sure Sarah Beth always knew she could count on consistency in her life.

Of course, when she'd kept Karen's two children briefly a couple of years ago when Karen had nearly fallen apart under stress, she'd quickly discovered that routines and schedules often went right out the window when faced with the reality of active kids. Erik had actually been the one to teach her to loosen up a little, though even he hadn't been able to break her entirely of her need for organization and schedules.

Flo met her gaze. "Do you really think your life would have been so much better if I'd been a stickler for rules and timetables?"

"I thought so then," Helen admitted. "And the books say that kids need to know they can count on things."

"I did the best I could," Flo said defensively. "Call me crazy, but I thought paying the rent and putting food on the table, and maybe saving a little for college, was doing right by you."

Helen sighed. "It was, Mom. I know you worked way too hard to do all of that and I appreciate it, but sometimes I wished that things could have been different. I needed you, I guess."

Flo looked taken aback by her declaration. "You had me. You were all I thought about."

"But you weren't around, and I knew that was my fault. I think maybe I felt guilty, seeing you so tired from trying to make sure I had everything the other kids had."

"It wasn't your fault. It was the way things had to be," Flo corrected. "You were my world, and I wanted your life to be so much better than mine had been." She gestured around at the lovely guest room filled with expensive furniture, luxurious bed linens, a large flat-screen TV. "Look at all this. You're able to have a home I could only dream about. I'm so proud of everything you've accomplished. I just worry sometimes that you've let it become more important than it should be."

"My priorities are in order," Helen replied defensively, even though she knew that hadn't always been true.

"If you say so," Flo said doubtfully.

Helen tried to look back at the past from her mother's perspective and realized that Flo truly had done what she thought was best for the two of them. If they hadn't been the same choices Helen might have made, that didn't make them wrong. In fact, as her mother had just pointed out, many of the blessings in her life now were due to the sacrifices back then. The least she could do was make a few changes to her precious routine to accommodate her mother for a few weeks.

"I'll talk to Erik," she promised. "I can stop by Sullivan's on my way home from now on and pick up dinner. We'll eat when I get here."

Flo nodded. "Thank you. I wouldn't have made such a fuss, except if I eat so late, I wind up with indigestion, and I can't get a wink of sleep. You'll see what I mean someday."

"Actually, that probably explains why I'm up half the night," Helen conceded grudgingly. "An earlier meal will be good for me, too."

When Helen would have picked up the trays and headed for the kitchen, her mother gestured for her to stay. "Sit for a few minutes longer and tell me what you did today. Any interesting cases?"

"Are you sure you want to listen to me go on and on about all this boring legal stuff?"

"Of course I do. It's not boring. *Divorce Court* was always one of my favorite shows. Nowadays, it seems as if every station has some judge or another with a show. I have to say, I can't imagine dragging all my dirty laundry onto TV in front of millions of people, but I get a kick out of watching others do it."

Helen chuckled as she recalled the TV tuned into *Divorce Court* years ago. Day in, day out, it was what Flo watched while she did the ironing she took in for a few extra dollars. "Do you suppose that's why I wound up specializing in divorce cases?"

Flo seemed intrigued with the idea. "I do believe it could be," she said. "You always picked the side of the person you thought wasn't getting a fair shake. I swear, by the time you were ten, you could argue their cases as well as any lawyer or judge on the TV could."

"I'd forgotten that. I guess I owe you even more than I realized."

"You don't owe me a thing," Flo insisted. "Seeing you so successful and happy, being here with you, Erik and Sarah Beth—that's all the thanks I'll ever need." She hesitated, then added, "Of course, I wouldn't mind a cocktail, if it's not too much trouble."

For the first time since her mother's arrival, Helen laughed, rather than letting the request immediately get under her skin.

"Coming right up," she said. "And I believe I'll join you."

Who knew, maybe rather than her going insane while her mother was underfoot, the two of them would wind up bonding.

"Don't make mine too strong," Flo called after her. "And hold the ice. I like it neat. Use one of those little tumblers. It always seems like more when you use those."

Then again, Helen thought as the orders followed her down the hall, maybe bonding was a little unrealistic. Surviving with her sanity intact might be the best she could hope for.

Ever since she'd started working as a personal trainer and therapist, Annie hadn't felt the need to schedule additional workouts. She got plenty of exercise during the day. Lately, though, she felt the need to go out running early in the morning before the heat and humidity kicked in. It helped to clear her head, and she had a lot of thoughts tumbling around in there these days.

She'd been following her new routine for a week, when her mother called her on it.

"You haven't stopped by Sullivan's for breakfast lately,"

Dana Sue noted casually, though there was a worried glint in her eyes that immediately put Annie on the defensive.

"I've been out running in the morning," she told her mother. "Then I grab a quick shower and head in to work."

"When are you eating breakfast?"

Annie bristled at the direct question. "Mom!"

"I'm just asking. You *are* eating, right? Your dad hasn't seen you eating at home, either."

"I don't like to eat right after I run," Annie said, her annoyance growing that they were obviously comparing notes on her eating habits again.

"Then you're eating at the spa when you get there?" Dana Sue persisted.

"Why are you pushing this?" Annie asked, though of course she knew.

"You know exactly why," Dana Sue said without even a hint of apology. "I'm not going to ignore it when I think you're in trouble, Annie. Not this time."

"I'm not in trouble," Annie said furiously. "Get off my case, okay? I'm an adult."

"Then act like one and answer a simple question. Are you eating at the spa?"

"Yes," Annie said. "Of course I am."

Despite the adamant response, Dana Sue looked as if she'd been slapped. "You're lying. I can see it in your eyes. You're saying what you think I want to hear."

"Well, why wouldn't I, if it will stop this interrogation?" Annie shouted, then whirled and left the house.

She'd walked the few blocks to Sarah's before she even realized what she was doing. When she rang the bell, Sarah answered, looking frazzled.

"I wasn't expecting you," Sarah said, greeting her with a halfhearted smile.

"Is this a bad time?"

Sarah rolled her eyes. "It's always a bad time around here. I thought you saw that for yourself the other night."

"Well, it has to be better than my house," Annie declared. "Mind if I visit for a little while, at least until I calm down?"

"Sure," Sarah said at once, stepping aside and kicking a toy truck out of her path. "Watch where you're going, though. Walking in here is like traipsing through a minefield."

Annie headed directly for the kitchen and, without waiting for an invitation, poured two glasses of sweet tea. She leaned against the counter, her gaze taking in the fact that the room looked cleaner and more organized than it had on her last visit.

"Looks as if you're getting things under control in here," she observed.

Sarah gave a wry chuckle. "Looks can be deceiving. I had a cleaning lady come in yesterday and give the whole house a thorough once-over. You saw how long that lasted in the living room. The only reason the kitchen's still looking good is that I banned the kids from setting foot in here and ordered pizza for dinner last night. I want one room in this house that I can walk into and not feel like crying."

She sipped her tea and studied Annie over the rim of her glass. "You looked upset when you got here. More problems with Ty?"

Annie shook her head.

"What, then?"

Annie wasn't sure she wanted to talk about her mom's suspicions. She also knew why. There had been a faint whisper of truth to Dana Sue's assessment that Annie was inching precariously close to reverting to her old eating habits.

When she remained silent for too long, Sarah's expression turned dismayed. "Oh, Annie, no! Don't tell me you're not eating again."

Shocked that Sarah's first guess had hit the nail on the head, she demanded, "Why would you even say that?"

"Because you've lost weight just since I got back to town. It's not like it was back in high school, but you've definitely shed a few pounds. And you haven't mentioned that dinner the two of us were going to have at Sullivan's again. When I reminded you the other day, you blew me off."

"I had a tough schedule this week."

"And yet here you are, apparently at loose ends," Sarah said, calling her on it.

Annie pulled out a chair and sat down slowly, trying to absorb the idea that her parents and her friend were all worrying about her, all seeing the same signs that she was in trouble.

"When did you eat last?" Sarah asked, her tone gentle.

"Not that long ago," Annie said automatically.

"What did you have?"

When she thought about it, she honestly couldn't remember. Was it possible she was skipping meals that often and not even aware of it? If so, even she could recognize that it wasn't a good sign. Maybe she needed to pay attention to what everyone was telling her.

"I don't remember," she admitted eventually.

"Then how about I make you a sandwich? Ham and cheese with tomato? Tuna salad? Peanut butter and jelly?"

Annie's stomach churned at the thought, which in itself gave her pause. Determined not to give in to the reaction, she said, "Tuna salad sounds fine."

Sarah made the sandwich for Annie and put a scoop of tuna on a plate for herself. Annie picked up half a sandwich, took a couple of bites, then almost pushed it aside. The knowing look on Sarah's face forced her to finish.

"Do you still see Dr. McDaniels?" Sarah asked. "That's the shrink you saw back then, right?"

Annie nodded. "Once in a while, but it's been a few months now."

"Maybe it wouldn't hurt to make an appointment, you know, just in case."

"I'm not anorexic," Annie said fiercely, even though her struggle to choke down that sandwich suggested otherwise.

"I'm not saying you are, but it didn't happen overnight last time, either. Your dad left, and slowly but surely you stopped eating. Now Ty's here, and you're obviously stressed out about it. Maybe it's just a normal loss of appetite because of the stress, but maybe not. Are you willing to take a chance?"

Annie recalled the horror of what she'd gone through, of fading away to the point where she'd wound up in the hospital with major heart problems. She shuddered to think of it happening again.

"No, of course not," she said emphatically. "I think you're all overreacting, but I'll make an appointment to see Dr. McDaniels."

"Soon?" Sarah pressed.

"I'll call tomorrow," Annie promised. "I guess I should go home and apologize to my mother. I know why she worries, but I act like she's nagging for no reason at all."

"We're quite a pair, aren't we?" Sarah said as she walked Annie to the door. "I'd like nothing more right this second than a huge hot fudge sundae, and I can barely get you to eat some tuna salad."

Annie gave her a hug. "But the good news is, I *did* eat the sandwich and you *aren't* eating the sundae."

Sarah grinned. "The night's not over."

"Don't you dare fix that sundae," Annie said. "You've already lost a few pounds. No backsliding, okay?"

Sarah's expression fell. "It's just that sometimes I wonder why I'm working this hard, when I know what the end result is going to be."

"You being healthy?" Annie said.

"No, me getting a divorce, anyway." She held Annie's gaze. "That is what's going to happen, you know. I'm just putting off the inevitable."

"But you will be healthy and energized and you will kick his sorry butt in court," Annie told her. "And when you walk out looking like a million bucks with a boatload of his money in your pocket, the little weasel will eat his heart out."

The look of discouragement on Sarah's face faded and her eyes sparkled. "Now, there's a plan I can get behind."

"Call Helen tomorrow," Annie suggested. "Take the initiative on this, unless you believe there's a chance you can save the marriage and that's what you want."

Sarah shook her head. "My marriage is over. I've made peace with that. I'll call Helen, if you'll make that call to your shrink."

"Deal," Annie said at once.

Despite the commitment she'd made, as she walked back home, she couldn't help wondering if she really needed to see Dr. McDaniels. Wasn't it enough that she'd recognized the potential problem on her own? It would be better if she could prove to herself and everyone else that she had her life under control. Wasn't that the goal of counseling? Weren't you supposed to reach a point where you could handle things without asking for help?

By the time she reached her house, she'd convinced herself that everyone was worked up over nothing. She'd tell them that, too, if the subject came up again.

Not that she was quite ready to test her newfound conviction against her mom's concern. She slipped past the living room, where Dana Sue was watching the Food Channel, and headed straight for her room. Denial, she'd discovered long ago, was a whole lot easier in private.

CHAPTER NINE

Thoroughly frustrated by his inability to make any progress at all with Annie and by the slow progress of his recovery, Ty decided to make a quick trip to Atlanta to see the team doctors and tie up a few loose ends. He could see Jay while he was there and make sure there was no news from Dee-Dee, since he was the one she'd chosen to contact. He also needed to set up a meeting with Tom Bristol, who'd represented him in family court. They needed to have a strategy in place in case Dee-Dee did decide she wanted to be a part of Trevor's life, after all.

He'd debated taking Trevor along with him, if only so he could spend a little time with the nanny he asked about every day. Though Cassandra had initially come with them to Serenity, she'd stayed only a couple of days since there was plenty of family around, including Ty himself, to take up the slack with Trevor.

After several days of tear-filled requests for his beloved Cassie, Trevor had finally settled in with the family. Maddie and Cal had convinced Ty that it didn't make sense to disrupt his son's schedule for a couple of days when Ty was going to be tied up most of the time.

"He'll start missing Cassandra all over again when you come back," his mother warned him.

Ty had seen the logic and eventually agreed, despite his desire to give his mom and Cal a break. "You're sure leaving him here is okay?" he asked Maddie one last time when he stopped by the spa on his way out of town. "It's not too late for me to take him along with me. Cassandra's eager to see him."

"Don't be silly. With Jessica Lynn and Cole already creating chaos around the house, one more hardly makes a difference. He'll be fine."

"I'll be back tomorrow night," Ty promised. "It could be late, so don't wait up."

Maddie's face took on her worried mom frown. "If it's going to be late, I'd rather you drive back the next morning. I don't want you on the road late at night. You never know what might happen."

Ty bent down and kissed her furrowed brow. "When are you going to stop worrying about me?"

"Never," she said at once. "It's part of the job description for a mother."

Ty grimaced. "I was afraid of that. If I'm not going to make it back, I'll call."

He turned to go and saw Annie in the doorway, her expression frozen.

"You're leaving?" she said.

He had the feeling if he'd turned just a second sooner, he'd have seen genuine dismay in her eyes. He held her gaze. "You gonna miss me?" he taunted.

"Of course not," she denied too quickly.

Ty fought the desire to chuckle. "Not to worry. I'm just going for a couple of days. I have some business to take care of in Atlanta. I need to check in with the doctors there."

This time she didn't even attempt to hide her alarm. "Your shoulder's worse?"

"No," he said. "It's just that they paid a lot of money for my pitching skills. They like to check on their investment."

"And I imagine you have other people to see, people who've been missing you," she said, her more familiar reserve firmly back in place, along with that edgy tone she used when referring to his past history with other women.

"You'd be surprised by how few people genuinely care where I am," he said. "Trevor's here, and he's the only one who counts."

"Yeah, right," she murmured. She started to turn away, but Maddie called her back.

"Annie, were you looking for me for a reason?"

Obviously flustered, she shook her head. "It can wait."

"Don't leave on my account," Ty told her. "I'm on my way out."

Annie's gaze met his, and for a minute, he saw the old Annie in her eyes, the one who'd believed in him, who'd always wished him well. "Drive safely," she said, then looked away as if she regretted saying even that much.

"Thanks. I will," he told her. He hesitated a moment, then added, "Annie, when I get back…" He couldn't decide how to finish that thought. He didn't want simply to talk, at least not the sort of stilted conversation they had these days. He wanted to spend time with her the way he used to, sharing their dreams, talking about stuff that mattered.

She studied him quizzically. "Yes?" she said when he still hadn't spoken.

"Maybe we could get together or something," he said finally, knowing even before the words were out that the response would be no.

She didn't fail him. "I don't think so," she said at once.

Then she must have caught Maddie's disappointed expression, because she added, "Thanks, anyway."

The words were so polite, so emotionless, he had to fight the urge to drag her into his arms and kiss her until she admitted that the old feelings were still there, that the old passion could still be sparked.

Of course, that wasn't something he would ever do in front of his mom, and it was probably best if he didn't do it at all. He settled for waving to Maddie and nodding in Annie's direction.

But as he left the building, he couldn't help wondering if he hadn't just missed an important opportunity.

Annie turned to find a scowl on Maddie's face. She sensed a lecture coming even before her boss opened her mouth.

"I know I was rude. I don't know how else to be," she told Maddie.

"*Not* rude would be a good start," Maddie said. "He's reaching out to you, Annie. One of these days he's going to get tired of being slapped down."

"I hardly slapped him down. I said no." She shrugged. "Of course, it's little wonder he looked so shocked. I doubt that's a word Ty hears too much these days."

Color flooded Maddie's cheeks. "That's not fair, Annie. Do you have any idea what the past three years have been like for him? He made a terrible mistake, and the person he counted on for most of his life got hurt. That's you, in case you have any doubt. So, not only has he been filled with guilt, he has a little boy who needs love and attention. Raising a son isn't easy for a man who's all alone. Ty had to grow up fast. He learned to put someone else first."

She drew in a deep breath, then added pointedly, "Of course, I think he already had a pretty good handle on that concept, because that's what he did with you. For years, he put you first."

Annie flushed with guilt at Maddie's criticism, but she still couldn't stop herself from retorting, "And then he stopped. Let's not forget that, Maddie. He didn't have some one-night stand with one woman. He was having flings with women in every city with a National League team. It just so happened that Trevor's mama got pregnant. Ty stopped worrying about me and my feelings a long time before that happened."

Maddie's burst of anger fizzled out. "Okay, okay," she said wearily. "I know you're right. What he did to you was lousy. I just can't help thinking about the way it used to be. Every time I turned around, the two of you had your heads together. Even when you were little, when Ty thought most girls were an annoyance, he had a soft spot in his heart for you. As for you, you always thought he hung the moon. I remember my heart aching for you because you were so obviously crazy about him, long before he started thinking of you as having girlfriend potential. When you two finally got together, it was as if my prayers had been answered. I knew things were the way they were supposed to be."

She sounded so nostalgic, Annie sat down and regarded her with sympathy. "I wish it were the way it used to be, too, but I can't change what happened, Maddie. I can't forget it, either."

Maddie shook her head sorrowfully. "You two apart, it's such a waste." When Annie remained silent, Maddie sat up straighter. "Okay, obviously you didn't come in here to talk about my son. What did you need?"

Annie hesitated, afraid her reason would be too telling, especially after the conversation they'd just had. Still, it was important. "I've been doing some research," she began, phrasing her words very carefully.

"On?"

"Some equipment that might be helpful for people with shoulder injuries."

Maddie's expression brightened, but she was wise enough not to connect Annie's idea directly to Ty. "You have the information with you?"

Annie reached in her back pocket and pulled out the pages she'd printed off the computer over the past few days. She handed them to Maddie. "I know this stuff is expensive, but we could start with just one piece, see how much use it gets." She pointed to the page on top. "I think this one, which helps with range of motion, should be the first one we consider. We don't have anything comparable."

Maddie gave her a knowing look. "How many clients do you have at the moment who might benefit from this?"

Annie swallowed hard. "I don't have any right now, but we both know that Elliott does."

Maddie nodded. "That's what I thought. It's for Ty."

"He won't be the only person who'll ever need it," Annie argued. "Women hurt their shoulders playing tennis or lifting kids all the time."

Maddie grinned. "Nice save. How about this? I'll consider the equipment, if you'll reconsider working with Ty. I might even make him buy the machine, since he'll be the primary beneficiary for the time being. That way I won't have to try to squeeze the money out of the budget and explain it to your mom and Helen."

"You're trying to manipulate me," Annie accused.

Maddie didn't flinch. "Yes, this time I am," she admitted. "He's my son and he needs you."

The outright request wasn't unexpected, but still, Annie sighed heavily. "I'll think about it," she said eventually. "I'll give you an answer in a couple of days."

"Perfect. We can discuss it again as soon as Ty's back in town."

Annie would have left then, probably *should* have left then, but she stayed. "Would you tell me something?"

"If I can."

"Why did he come here for rehab when he could have had a whole team of top-notch doctors and therapists in Atlanta, along with every piece of top-of-the-line machinery on the market?"

Maddie smiled at the question. "Do you really need me to answer that?"

"He wanted to be home," Annie said, half hoping that was all it had been.

"He wanted to see you," Maddie corrected. "There's not a doubt in my mind about that. The rest of us, we're just the icing on the cake."

Annie wanted so badly to believe her, but doing that, having hope…she wasn't sure she dared.

Helen walked to the door with her client, then turned to find her longtime secretary regarding her wearily, a fan of pink message slips in her hand.

"Your mother," Barb said succinctly.

Helen took the half dozen or so pieces of paper and asked, "What on earth did she want that was so important? I'm sure she talked your ear off about it, whatever it was."

"I believe she'd like you to pick up some shampoo. She doesn't like the brand you use. And then there's the soap. It's too harsh for her skin. And since you're going to the store, anyway, it would be nice to have some chocolate-dipped macaroons. They're her favorite."

"Did you tell her shopping lists aren't in your job description?"

"I thought maybe the parameters of my job were changing," Barb said tartly, though her expression was filled with amusement.

Helen sighed. "I'll tell her she can't call here all day long."

"Hold on a minute. I didn't say I minded chatting with her," Barb protested. "I'm sure she's bored to tears cooped up in that house all day long. Has she been in touch with any of her old friends?"

"Not that I'm aware of," Helen said. "I'm not sure how many old friends she still has around town. She had coworkers, but she didn't have a lot of spare time to spend with other people."

"Well, she needs some distractions, and trust me, Letitia Lowell is not going to provide them. I know I told Erik she's a good caregiver and she is, but she has the personality of a tortoise...slow, steady and dull."

"We didn't hire her to provide entertainment," Helen said.

Barb gave her an impatient look. "I know that, but try to imagine being stuck in the house all day long with nothing to do and no way to get away from the tedium. You'd be calling Erik every ten minutes."

"True," Helen admitted. It had been hard enough in the first weeks after Sarah Beth's birth, when she'd taken time off from work. Even though she'd been able to pack up the baby and visit friends, she'd almost gone stir-crazy before she'd finally been able to come back to work at least part-time.

"Did she belong to a church here in town?" Barb asked. "A lot of them have people who visit members of the congregation when they're confined to home."

Helen's expression brightened. "Actually, she did go to the Methodist Church. Right before she left she mentioned something about joining their seniors group. I think she might have gone to a few of their activities."

"Well, find out and call some people. In the meantime, if you'll let me take a break, I'll go pick up those things she wanted and drop them by."

"You are not her personal shopper," Helen protested.

"I know that, but I could use some things, too, so I can kill two birds with one stone." She grinned. "And I can do it on your time."

"If you're sure you don't mind, go," Helen told her. "I'll answer the phones."

On her way back to her office, she checked her schedule and saw that Sarah Price was due in for a two o'clock appointment. It was after that now. Helen thought about the fact that a couple of years ago, a client who wasn't prompt might have had to wait weeks for another appointment. These days she was determined to maintain a more rational pace. That didn't mean that having a few unexpectedly free minutes didn't make her antsy. Apparently, she and her mom were more alike than she'd thought. Neither of them knew how to fill free time.

When Sarah finally arrived, Helen tried to reconcile the harried young woman who rushed in filled with apologies with Annie's stalwart friend from high school. Obviously her life had taken a stressful detour.

"Sarah, how are you?" she asked, giving her a hug.

"Believe it or not, I'm a whole lot better than I was when I got back to town a few weeks ago," Sarah said with a half-hearted grin.

"Come on into my office and tell me why you're here," Helen said.

"Actually, I was thinking maybe I should reschedule," Sarah told her. "I found a sitter at the last minute, but I don't really know her. I probably shouldn't stay."

"Sounds like cold feet," Helen said.

Sarah stared at her blankly. "What do you mean?"

"Just that you came in here with an excuse all ready for not going through with whatever made you set up the appointment in the first place."

For an instant it seemed Sarah might argue, but eventually she sighed. "You caught me. Annie kind of talked me into coming to see you, and then I had second thoughts."

"Is this about a divorce?" Helen asked, her tone a lot more gentle than it might have been a couple of years ago. Since marrying Erik, she'd discovered the dynamics of a marriage could be incredibly complex, and the prospect of ending it was never as cut-and-dried as she'd previously assumed.

Sarah nodded.

"Do you want the divorce or is it your husband's idea?"

"That's the thing. Nobody's mentioned it yet, but I just know it's coming. I'm pretty sure Walter's already seen a lawyer. I guess what we're doing right now is a trial separation, though nobody called it that, either. I want to be prepared."

"Do you want to fight it?"

"I did. When I first came home for this break to get myself together, I wanted to do whatever it took to save my marriage." She lifted her chin and met Helen's gaze. "Now I want to do what's best for me and the kids. I don't think that's going back to Alabama and my marriage."

"Do you want to initiate proceedings?"

Sarah looked startled by the question. "I don't know. I guess I've been so busy worrying about what would happen when Walter—he's my husband—filed and insisted on full custody of Tommy that I never for one minute thought about taking charge and going after what I want."

"Which is?"

"I want to stay in Serenity and raise my kids right here, *both* of my kids," she stressed.

Helen jotted down some notes. "Are you saying that you think your husband's only going to try to get full custody of your son?"

Sarah nodded. "Pretty archaic, isn't it? His whole family just wants to be sure there's a son to inherit the family business."

Helen was appalled. "You're kidding me! He would split the children up, basically reject your daughter?"

"I can't swear to it, but that's what he's been hinting at for months now. It's like he wants to divvy up the kids the same way he'd split the china and silver between us."

"Not going to happen," Helen said direly. "I'll see to that. In fact, as far as I'm concerned, the fact that he would even consider such a request is grounds to declare him an unfit parent."

Sarah's expression turned hopeful. "Then we could fight him? We'd have a good case?"

"Absolutely." She met Sarah's worried gaze. "Sweetie, I do not want to push you into doing anything you're not ready to do, but if you're certain that a divorce is the next step, I would encourage you to establish residency back here again as quickly as possible, make sure all the utilities are in your name, register to vote, get the house in your name, if you can. Get a job, even if it's part-time. Then file here, before he can file over in Alabama. You want this fight on your turf, if at all possible."

Sarah looked a little overwhelmed by the lengthy list of instructions.

"Thank you so much, Ms. Decatur," Sarah said. "I'll think about everything you said. I'll be back as soon as I've made a decision."

"It's Helen. And don't wait too long, Sarah. Think about what you want, about what's best. If you decide you want to fight for your marriage, there are some counselors I can recommend."

Sarah gave her a rueful look. "As if Walter would ever agree to see anyone. He thinks I'm the only one who needs to change."

Helen cringed. How often had she heard those exact words? And ninety percent of the time, the assessment came from the men most in need of help.

"How long is he expecting you to be away?"

"Until I'm fixed," Sarah said, her tone wry.

"Excuse me?"

"I'm supposed to lose weight, learn how to manage the kids and figure out how to run a household to the high standards of the Price family. I'm not sure there's a time frame long enough for me to accomplish all that to his satisfaction."

"Which makes divorce a near-certainty, then, doesn't it?" Helen said.

Sarah sighed. "I suppose it does." She shook off the hesitancy, then said, "I *know* it does."

"Then make sure it's on your terms," Helen told her. "And I'll be honest with you, from the very little bit you've already told me, I'd say you'll be well rid of him."

"Annie says the same thing."

Helen seized on that. "Has she ever met him?"

"No, she's just going by what I've said."

"Too bad. It would be nice to have her as a witness."

"The only people who know Walter well are in Alabama and they'll all take his side," Sarah said. "His family practically owns the town we live in."

"Then all the more reason to file here."

"I know you're right. It's just such a huge step, you know."

"I do know, and only you can make the decision. Just

think about the consequences of waiting around until he acts."

Sarah stood a little taller then and a hint of resolve stole over her face. "I'll be back tomorrow, if that's okay."

"Call me first thing in the morning and I'll see that we fit you into the schedule," Helen said, relieved that she'd apparently gotten through to her.

Over the years she'd discovered that there was an early balancing act to be done with a prospective new client. She never wanted to tip the scales in favor of divorce if there was any chance at all of reconciliation, but she was experienced at recognizing the signs when divorce was inevitable. This was one of those times.

"It's going to be okay, Sarah. I promise you. When I go into court, I fight to win."

Sarah didn't look entirely convinced, but she did look more at peace than she had when she'd first arrived.

After she'd gone, Helen sat back and thought about the conversation. For years the women—and sometimes men—she'd fought for had been her own age or older. They were, more often than not, divorces that hit as part of a midlife crisis, when one person or the other suddenly decided they needed to make a dramatic change. She'd dealt with cheaters and abusers, as well.

Sarah was the first client she'd handled from the next generation, someone still at the age when the future should have been at its brightest, the glow of marriage still incandescent.

Saddened by the meeting, she reached for her phone and dialed Erik's cell.

"Hey you," he said, the warmth in his tone immediately cheering her. "What's up?"

"I just needed to hear your voice," she admitted.

"Tough case?"

"One of Annie's friends," she told him. "She's much too young to be a married mother of two, it seems to me, much less already talking about divorce."

"Not everybody waits around till they hit forty to think about getting married the way you did," he reminded her.

"Well, they should. I'm not sure it's possible to understand just how rare and wonderful a good relationship is until you're at least that old."

"So you appreciate me," he teased, his voice dropping. "Does that mean what I think it does?"

Helen laughed at the hopeful note in his voice. "I'll fix Flo an extra cocktail tonight so she'll sleep soundly. She should be out for the night by the time you get home."

"Should I bring home some champagne?"

"No need," she told him. "All I need is you."

"Then isn't it a good thing that you have me," he said. "Always."

Helen sighed happily. "It's a very good thing."

In fact, right this second she couldn't imagine anything better.

CHAPTER TEN

Ty paced back and forth in Jay's office waiting for the attorney to get off the phone. Just before the call had come in, he'd informed Ty that Dee-Dee had surfaced again, but they'd been interrupted before he could fill in the details.

By the time Jay eventually hung up, Ty had worked up a full head of steam.

"What did she want?" he demanded.

Jay regarded him blankly. "*She?* I was talking to Gus Davis," Jay said.

"Not Gus, dammit. Dee-Dee. You said she'd been in touch again."

"Settle down, Ty. I know this will upset you, but you have to think about what's best for Trevor."

"In other words, she wants to see him again," Ty said, his heart sinking. It was exactly as he'd feared. Out of the blue, she suddenly wanted to be part of their son's life again. If she could be counted on, maybe, just maybe, that would be okay. His greatest fear, though, was that she'd breeze in, Trevor would get attached to his mom, and Dee-Dee would lose interest. He had to prevent that at all costs.

He fought against the tide of dismay washing over him. "Why now?"

"She claims her life is more settled now. She's engaged and expects to marry this fall. She wants a relationship with her son, and her fiancé…" He glanced down at his notes. "The fiancé's a guy named Jim Foster and he's backing her on this. I don't know anything about him, but she made him sound like a pillar of the community."

"I don't care if he's a candidate for sainthood—it's too little and way too late," Ty said heatedly. "She can't just waltz in and turn my son's life upside down." He heard the hardhearted way he sounded and tried to calm down and focus on Trevor and whether or not it was time to let his mom into his life. He knew he simply couldn't do that until he knew more.

Reining in his temper, he said, "Okay, what else? Your expression tells me there's more."

Jay nodded. "Look, I'm no family court lawyer, so you need to tell Tom Bristol everything I've told you. He'll know best whether a judge is likely to give her the benefit of the doubt."

"But you think that's likely, don't you?" Ty said, the churning in his gut worsening.

"She made a compelling case to me," Jay told him. "She says she wasn't even twenty when she had Trevor, that she had no job and she panicked at the thought of raising him all on her own, so she gave him to you because she knew you'd be able to provide for him. Now with her life stable and a marriage coming up in a few months, she's ready to handle the responsibilities of motherhood in a way she couldn't back then."

Jay met his gaze and said quietly, "I think you'd better sit down before I tell you the rest."

Ty gave him an incredulous look and kept pacing. "Just spit it out," he ordered, his heart thudding dully in his chest.

"She says because she's going to be in a steady, permanent relationship and you're not, she should be considered for full custody."

Ty stopped in his tracks. "Over my dead body," he said, his fury so overwhelming he could barely get the words out.

"Calm down," Jay said. "Again, you need to go over all of this with Tom. Personally, I don't think any judge will agree to full custody after what she did three years ago, but there's certainly every chance she'll be granted generous visitation rights."

Ty tried to imagine his son slowly but surely being wooed away from him by a woman on a mission to reclaim him. It simply couldn't happen. He loved Trevor. He'd raised him. No way was he going to allow his son to be stolen away from him. That Dee-Dee would even suggest going after full custody simply proved how selfish she was.

Of course, a voice in his head nagged, perhaps he was being no better, trying to keep his son to himself.

"Good God, what a mess," he muttered, raking a hand through his hair. "What am I supposed to do, Jay? Take my son and leave the country? I can't let someone as irresponsible as Dee-Dee take him away from me. Visitations—preferably supervised—I suppose I can work that out, but that's it. That's as far as I'll go, at least until Dee-Dee's proved she's trustworthy."

"Okay, you need to focus here. A kid needs a relationship with his mother. Agreed?"

"If the circumstances are right, yes," Ty conceded reluctantly.

"Then it won't help anyone if you go running off and do something crazy. Right now, you have a strong case. You've been Trevor's sole parent for most of his life, but if you do anything to make a judge question your parenting or your maturity, things could change in a hurry. Tom will tell you the same thing when you talk to him. I know that much."

Ty stuck to his guns. "There's no way I'm going to calm down until someone proves to me that Dee-Dee has changed. Then we'll have something to talk about."

"I'm sure Tom has investigators who'll be able to get you proof one way or the other. Let them do their job, Ty." He regarded Ty with sympathy. "Look, I know how much you adore that little boy and that, in the end, you'll do the right thing, whatever it turns out to be."

Jay seemed to be giving him more credit than he deserved. Right now anger and fear were all twined together.

"I want to win," Ty corrected. "I want to protect Trevor from a woman who'd abandon a tiny, defenseless baby in front of my hotel-room door." It was an image he doubted he would ever get out of his head, no matter how much Dee-Dee had changed from the reckless, selfish woman she'd been back then.

"I have to get out of here," he told Jay. "I need to speak to Tom and get him on this." He stood up, ready to bolt, then turned back. "Look, I appreciate you being an intermediary with Dee-Dee. I have no idea why she called you. More than likely, it was because she knew you'd always know how to get in touch with me, but I appreciate that you're caught in the middle now. I'll try to take over from here on out."

"No big deal," Jay said. "Part of my job is to have your back, no matter what comes along. This is going to be okay, Ty."

As he left the office, Ty wished he had Jay's confidence. It wasn't until he was in the elevator of the high-rise on his way down that he leaned back, closed his eyes and drew in a deep breath.

This couldn't be happening. Trevor was *his* son. Dee-Dee had given up her claim to him. She'd given up any right to call herself his mother. She might have carried him for nine months, but the second she'd realized that he didn't come with Ty as a bonus, she'd lost interest. Surely any judge would see this sudden turnaround for the joke it was.

As soon as the elevator stopped, Ty emerged and crossed the building's fancy marble lobby, anxious to get outside into the fresh air and sunshine. He pulled out his cell phone and dialed before he thought about what he was doing.

At the sound of Annie's voice, he sucked in a sharp breath. He knew this call should have been to his family law attorney, but it was Annie's voice he'd needed to hear.

"Hello?" she said again with a touch more impatience.

"Annie, it's Ty."

"Oh." Her voice had gone flat.

He knew then that he couldn't dump all of this on her. They'd barely exchanged a few dozen civilized words in weeks now. How could he suddenly tell her about Dee-Dee and a looming custody battle? What did he expect her to do? Listen? Sympathize? Offer advice?

At his silence, she asked, "Did you need something?"

"I just came out of a meeting and you were on my mind," he said. "I shouldn't have called."

There was a faint hesitation, but then she said, "It's okay. Didn't the meeting go well?"

"It was a disaster," he said.

"So naturally you thought of me," she said wryly.

He chuckled. "I guess because you're usually so good at putting things into perspective."

"I suppose I could do that, if you want to tell me what happened."

Surprised by her willingness, he suddenly didn't want to spoil the rare moment of peace between them by bringing up a topic that was bound to ruin it. He backed up to the meeting he'd had earlier in the day at team headquarters.

"The team trainer was on my case about the progress I'm making, or more specifically, not making. He thinks I'd be better off doing rehab back here." All of which was true. He'd just dismissed the idea.

"Maybe you would be," she said.

Ty couldn't quite tell if that was relief or disappointment he heard in her voice. She'd grown too good at hiding her emotions, at least from him.

"Come on, you know you'd miss me if I left," he teased, keeping his tone light.

"Your mom certainly would," she said, evading his point.

"Nice dodge," he said. "One of these days, you're going to let down your guard and admit you still care about me."

"Don't count on it," she said.

It seemed to Ty there was less venom in her voice than usual. He took heart from that.

"I need to go," she told him. "I have a client waiting."

"Okay. I'll probably see you tomorrow."

"Bye."

Before she could hang up, he called out to her.

"Yes?" she said.

"Thanks for taking my call." Oddly enough, even though he'd never even mentioned why he'd originally made it, he felt better just for having heard her voice. He just wished he could count on her being by his side for this custody battle that was looming on the horizon.

★ ★ ★

Thoroughly flustered by her conversation with Ty and the unexpected lack of hostility on her part, she turned to find Maddie regarding her with curiosity.

"Was that Ty?" Maddie asked.

Annie nodded.

"I haven't heard from him since he left town yesterday and yet he called you? Why is that?"

"I have no idea," Annie said. "Take it up with him if he's not checking in the way you think he should."

Maddie chuckled. "Do you really think I care about that? I just want to know when you two started speaking again. This time yesterday you barely exchanged two words."

"Don't make too much of this. I have no idea why he called me. He said something about a tough meeting with the team trainer, who wants him to go back to Atlanta for rehab."

Maddie stared at her incredulously. "Well, that's obviously why. In his own roundabout way he was trying to get you to offer to take over his rehab. Did you agree to do it?"

"He didn't ask."

"Of course he didn't ask directly," Maddie said impatiently. "He thought you'd volunteer, or at least he hoped you would."

"Well, I didn't. I told him maybe he would do better in Atlanta."

Maddie looked horrified by that. "Annie, what were you thinking? He belongs here."

"Hold on a second, Maddie," Annie said quietly. "I understand why you'd want that, but the resources he needs are in Atlanta. Keeping him here is selfish. We should all be thinking about what's best for Ty and his shoulder, isn't that right?"

For a moment, Maddie looked stunned by Annie's reasoning. "Yes, of course," she said at last, but there were tears in her eyes.

Annie felt awful when those tears spilled down Maddie's cheeks. Awkwardly she gave her a hug. "I'm sorry. I should have kept my big mouth shut, especially when it doesn't matter what I think. Ty's determined to stay right here."

"Really?" Maddie asked, her expression brightening.

Annie grinned and gave her a tissue. "See, you didn't need to get all worked up. He never listens to me, anyway."

"Oh, sweetie, that's not true. Your opinion is probably the only one that matters."

Annie doubted that, but she felt better for having reassured Maddie.

"Now even you can see why it's more important than ever for you to take over his rehab," Maddie told her. "No more excuses, Annie. Ty's counting on you and so am I."

Gee, pile on the guilt, Annie thought, but deep down she knew she'd put off this decision for just about as long as she possibly could.

Rather than dwelling on the decision she needed to make, Annie opted once again to spend the evening at Sarah's. Despite the frequently chaotic conditions, Annie had taken to hiding out there. It prevented cross-examinations by her mother and, for the most part, kept mentions of Ty to a minimum. Sarah had enough problems of her own without worrying too much about Annie and Ty.

And somehow they seemed to balance out each other's issues with food. Annie kept Sarah on her diet and Sarah made sure Annie did more than simply push her meal around on her plate. Somehow she did it in a way that didn't stir up Annie's defenses the way nudging from Dana Sue would.

Annie had even grown used to having one or the other of

the kids scrambling into her lap, smelling of talcum powder or, in Tommy's case, the little-boy scent of sweat and grass from playing hard outside. Whenever she held Tommy and read him a bedtime story, she couldn't help thinking of another little boy who was just a little older and wondering what it would be like to read to him, even to be a mom to him. She tried really hard not to let herself go there.

Tonight, though, it was Libby who'd reached out to her for cuddling. The pink bow in her silky blond hair was dangling askew and there was ketchup on her cheeks and on her clothes, but Annie scooped her up, anyway, as Sarah went to answer the phone.

Though they'd just been laughing, Sarah's expression sobered at once.

"Of course your son is here," she said. "Where else would he be? He's two. It's not as if he'd be out partying on his own."

She stood there, stoically silent while her husband apparently ranted about something.

"You're being ridiculous," she said eventually. Whatever he said in response to that had her cheeks flaming. "Don't you dare speak to me that way, Walter Price. I am still your wife and the mother of your children, and you will show me some respect." Then she slammed down the phone and stood there, trembling.

Alarmed, Annie set the baby down on the floor and went to her. "Are you okay?"

"He had the audacity to suggest that his mother should come over here and take the children home with her, since they're too much for me." She met Annie's gaze. "You know what he's doing, don't you? He's setting the stage for the custody battle. I just know it."

Annie knew Sarah had seen Helen earlier, but Annie

hadn't wanted to ask questions. She'd left it to Sarah to reveal whatever she wanted Annie to know. Now, though, she couldn't stop herself from saying, "You need to call Helen and tell her about this."

"I'm supposed to see her tomorrow," Sarah said.

Annie shook her head. "Don't wait. If you want me to, I'll call. She won't mind."

"I hate to interrupt her evening."

"She'd want to know what he's up to."

"I suppose," Sarah said, then shook off her uncertainty. "Go ahead. Call her."

Annie made the call, filled Helen in on the little bit she knew, then handed the phone to Sarah, who explained the rest.

Silence fell, but Sarah didn't hang up. She just stood there, staring at her kids, then off into the distance. "Okay," she said at last. "Get the papers ready to file first thing in the morning. I'll be in to sign them." Again, she hesitated, then said, "Yes, I'm sure."

After she'd hung up, she turned to Annie, her expression bleak, and said, "I guess that's it, then. I'm going to end my marriage."

Annie gave her a fierce hug. "You know it's for the best, don't you? You're going to be better off in the long run."

Sarah didn't look as if she believed that. "Sure. I'm unemployed. I haven't held a job since college. My kids are a handful. Everything's going to be just peachy."

"Thanks to your parents, you have a roof over your head," Annie reminded her. "Helen will see that you get alimony and child support. You have friends here. You have a college degree that you can finally use. And you won't have to put up with all that demeaning garbage anymore. The way I see it, it's all good."

Sarah shook her head in denial. "I know it's not supposed to be this way, but I'm used to having a man around to take care of stuff." She flushed with embarrassment at the admission. "Walter even dealt with paying the bills. I have no idea where we stand financially."

Annie regarded her incredulously. "Good grief, the man was a total control freak. Don't you see that? That's its own kind of abuse."

"He said it was easier that way," Sarah confessed. "I honestly thought he was being considerate."

"Okay, let's give him the benefit of the doubt. Maybe he was. That doesn't mean you're incapable of running this household or your life. You are a perfectly competent woman," she said indignantly. "There's not a thing that man did for you that you can't learn how to do yourself."

Sarah's brow shot up. "Well, there is *one* thing," she said, a wicked glint in her eyes as her sense of humor kicked in.

Annie chuckled. "You'll find some other man, a much better one for that," she promised.

Sarah looked skeptical. "You've been back in town how long?"

"Not quite a year."

"And you've met how many men?"

Annie knew the point she was trying to make, but she merely shrugged. "Don't go by me. I haven't been looking."

"Because you're still in love with Ty," Sarah suggested, her tone cautious.

"Let's not go there," Annie replied. "Let's stay focused on *your* pitiful life, not mine. I'm telling you, this time next year you're going to have a new life, a new man and every bit of the happiness you deserve."

"You're assuming I won't still be jumping through hoops

in a courtroom. The Prices are not going to take any of this lying down."

"But you have Helen on your side. They're not going to know what hit them," Annie assured her. "Helen didn't earn her reputation as a barracuda lawyer by playing nice in the courtroom."

"I sure do hope you're right about that," Sarah said, but her expression was doubtful.

"Trust me," Annie said. "No, I take that back. Trust Helen. If I were in a situation like this, she's the one I'd want in my corner."

Of course, with Sarah's assessment of her nonexistent social life still ringing in her ears, it didn't seem likely she'd be married, much less in need of Helen's matrimonial legal services anytime soon.

The minute Ty walked into his mother's house, Trevor came running toward him and hurled himself into Ty's arms. To Ty's way of thinking, there was no sweeter moment in his day. After road trips with the team, these reunions had been the best part of his return home. Tonight, though, he hugged Trevor even more tightly than usual and held him just a moment longer, until Trevor squealed to be put down.

Cal stood in the doorway watching, a smile on his face. "Better than pitching a no-hitter, isn't it?"

"Pretty much," Ty said, then watched as Trevor ran back to whatever game he, Jessica Lynn and Cole had been playing. It seemed to involve stacking blocks, then toppling them over. Jessica Lynn, her brow knit in concentration, did the methodical stacking, while Trevor and Cole energetically destroyed all her efforts.

"You look beat," Cal observed. "Everything okay?"

"It was a tough trip," Ty admitted, then glanced around. "Where's Mom?"

"Still at the spa. I was in charge of dinner and cleanup. There's pizza left if you're interested."

"Maybe later," Ty said. "Can we talk before Mom gets home?"

Cal frowned. "Something you don't want her to know?"

Ty nodded. "Not yet. I don't want her worrying."

"You realize she's going to take one look at your face and know something's up."

Ty laughed, though without much humor. "Yeah, I'll have to work on that."

In the kitchen, Cal pulled out a couple of beers, handed one to Ty, then gestured toward the dining room, so they could sit and still keep an eye on the kids.

"Tell me," he said, once they were seated.

Ty filled him in.

"Son of a gun," Cal said, looking shocked. "And your attorney thinks Dee-Dee has a shot at getting what she wants?"

"At least some of it," Ty said, hating the fact that Tom had pretty much confirmed everything Jay had told him.

"Then talk to Helen," Cal said at once. "See if she agrees. She's the expert. This Wrigley, he's a sports lawyer. He may be top-notch when it comes to your contracts, but he could be out of his element with this kind of stuff."

"He's not the only one I spoke to," Ty admitted. "The family law attorney who handled the original custody agreement said pretty much the same thing, but I will see Helen tomorrow."

Of course, the minute he went to see Helen, there was a good chance that he wouldn't be able to keep any of this quiet. Not that she would ever blab confidential information, but his mom and Dana Sue could read her like a book.

The mere fact that he'd seen her would spell trouble in their eyes, and the pestering would begin. Sooner or later Annie would know, too. How could he hope to win her back if this whole mess from his past was about to blow up again?

"You worrying about Annie's reaction if this mess is suddenly front and center in the Serenity gossip mill?" Cal guessed.

Ty nodded. "This is just going to rub her face in the situation one more time."

"She'll be on your side," Cal said confidently.

"I hope so," Ty said quietly, because the truth was, he had no choice. He had to fight to make sure that whatever happened, it would be what was best for Trevor.

CHAPTER ELEVEN

These days Annie only saw Dr. McDaniels, the psychologist who'd treated her for her anorexia, on rare occasions. Right after making the decision to help Ty with his rehab, she made an appointment. She wanted to be sure that putting herself into the position of seeing him on a regular basis wouldn't precipitate a setback with her eating disorder. She needed to be sure she was strong enough for the emotional stress she'd be under.

"You're looking well, Annie," Dr. McDaniels said. "It's been a while since you've been in. Is everything okay?"

Annie drew in a deep breath and blurted, "I'm afraid I'm going to stop eating. In fact, I already have a couple of times. I've gone whole days without eating more than a mouthful or two."

To her relief the older woman didn't looked shocked or dismayed. Instead, she remained calm. "It's been a long time. Has something happened recently to make you feel as if you're losing control?"

Annie nodded and explained about Ty. "I've decided I need to help him, but I'm not sure I'm strong enough to see him every single day."

"If you really believe that, then don't do it. Recommend another therapist."

"There isn't another sports injury therapist with my qualifications in Serenity," she countered. "He'd have to go to Charleston or Columbia, more than likely. Or else he'd go back to Atlanta, which will break his mom's heart. She loves having him and her grandson here."

"Don't you imagine he can afford to bring in a skilled therapist, if staying here is what he wants to do?" Dr. McDaniels asked reasonably. "Why are you so sure it has to be you?"

"Because everyone keeps reminding me that I owe him, and I do," she said.

"Has he been pressuring you to do this?"

Annie shook her head. "No. He's made it clear he'd like to spend time with me, even that he wants to make amends for what happened, but he hasn't pushed me to help him at all. It's everyone else—well, really, just his mom and Elliott, who's been working with him."

"I don't know about Elliott, but I can tell you want to please Maddie. I remember that she means a lot to you."

"She's been like a second mom," Annie confirmed. "It bothers me to have her so disappointed in me."

"She's piling on the guilt?"

"Pretty much. She won't let me forget how Ty stuck by me."

"Your lives were very different then," Dr. McDaniels reminded her. "He was a wonderful friend, no question about it, but since then, he's broken your heart. You have to weigh that against whatever you think you owe him."

Annie continued to wrestle with her guilt. A part of her wanted so badly to just say no and be done with this quandary, to be done with Ty. Another part, she was forced to admit, wanted the sweet torture of being around him. What she supposed she was looking for here was absolution if she eventually decided not to help Ty.

"Then it wouldn't be awful of me not to do this?" she asked, hoping the psychologist would let her off the hook.

"Not if it's going to put your health at risk," Dr. McDaniels told her, filling Annie with relief.

Unfortunately, then she went and ruined it by studying Annie intently and asking, "Do you really believe it will? Think about that before you answer me. Do you really have so little faith in all the progress you've made? Or is it that Ty still has that much power to hurt you?"

"Probably the latter," Annie admitted. "I feel completely out of control when I see him or even think about seeing him. I haven't felt that way since my dad left town. We both know how I dealt with that."

"But you know the dangers and the symptoms of an eating disorder now. You also know that anorexia doesn't solve anything," Dr. McDaniels said. "I think you're a lot stronger and more equipped to handle this than you realize."

"Then you're saying I'd be okay, even if I have to see Ty every day?"

The psychologist regarded her with amusement. "I don't get to make the decision. You have to do that. Let me ask you this, though. When you and Ty broke up, did you stop eating?"

"Only for a day because I was feeling so miserable," she confessed.

"And I imagine you've known a lot of people who stop eating for a day or two when they suffer a traumatic loss or breakup," the psychologist said. "They simply lose their appetite for a bit. You know that's normal and acceptable, right?"

"I suppose."

"Okay, then, what happened next?"

"I realized what I was doing and made myself eat."

"And those couple of days recently when you didn't eat, what happened?"

"My mom and a friend jumped right on my case."

"And?"

"At first I lied, just the way I used to do, but then I saw that they were right, that I was trying to control food because I couldn't control the situation with Ty."

"Then you weren't in denial?"

She shook her head. "No," she said, then amended, "Okay, maybe for a minute, but I recognized the signs and I made myself eat. I remembered everything you and the nutritionist taught me."

"So what's different about this situation? What has you so worried? It sounds to me as if you're alert to the potential for problems and that you can handle them."

"When Ty and I split up, he was out of my life. I hated that, but it wasn't like I had to see him all the time. Even now, I've been pretty much able to keep all contact to a minimum. But if I agree to help him with his rehab, he'll be right there every day, reminding me of what we used to be to each other."

"Used to be?" Dr. McDaniels said, seizing on her words. "It sounds to me as if you *still* love him."

Annie moaned at the accurate assessment. "You're right. How pathetic is that?"

"Not pathetic. Just human. Do you remember something I told you a long time ago, that the best relationships are built on a foundation of friendship?"

Annie nodded.

"Maybe you should concentrate on that. See if Ty is still the kind of friend he once was. It sounds as if he wants to be. And be the kind of friend you once were. Anything else will take care of itself."

"Can we be friends if I can't forgive him for what he did to me?"

"Maybe not from day one, but it could be he deserves a chance to earn your trust again."

Annie was still skeptical, but she supposed it made sense. Maybe, in fact, they didn't even need to worry about being friends. This could be a simple business arrangement. He'd be contracting for her professional services, not that she'd ever charge him, but the principle was the same. She'd always been cool and businesslike with other clients. Even with Sarah, she tried not to let their longtime friendship get in the way of making her do what she needed to do during her workouts. It shouldn't be too much of a stretch to pull that off with Ty.

"Thank you," she said when she realized her time was up. "I know what I need to do."

"Just remember, I'm right here if you need me."

"I'm counting on that," Annie told her.

Outside, she pulled out her cell phone and dialed Ty's number. The familiar sound of his voice sent an unwelcome jolt through her, almost making her second-guess herself. She realized the odds of keeping her emotional distance were pretty much zero.

"It's me," she said eventually.

"I know. What's up?"

"I'll do it," she told him.

"Do what?" he asked blankly.

She realized then that he wasn't the one who'd been pushing her to do this. "I'll take over your rehab program. You'll make more progress with me than you will with Elliott."

He didn't try to deny it. "Annie, are you sure?" he asked,

sounding genuinely concerned for her. "I don't want this to be awkward for you."

"Do you want my help or not?" she asked testily, annoyed that he wasn't seizing the opportunity, even if his hesitation was out of consideration for her.

"Of course I do."

"Okay, then," she said briskly. "This is strictly business. You do exactly what I tell you to do and we won't have a problem."

He had the audacity to chuckle at that. "Wasn't that the way it always was?"

"Ty!"

"Okay, I agree. When do you want to start?"

"The spa's open till eight tonight. Be there at five after."

"Yes, ma'am."

"And leave the attitude at home."

"I'll do my best," he said in a meek tone she didn't trust for a second.

She was about to hang up, when he said, "Annie, just one thing."

"What?"

"Maybe you could do the same."

He hung up before she could tell him what she thought of his taunt. She stood there staring at her phone. "What the hell did I just do?" she murmured.

Despite her reservations, a little zip of anticipation raced over her. And that scared her to death.

The unexpected call from Annie improved Ty's outlook considerably. At least one thing was going his way. He had no idea what had finally changed her mind, but he was relieved. He'd had a tough time explaining to the trainers in Atlanta why he didn't want to come back there and begin a tougher regimen, when his progress in Serenity was slower than anticipated. They thought he ought to be chomping at the bit to get back into the pitching rotation.

In the meantime, though, he had to settle on a plan of action to deal with Dee-Dee. He was on the doorstep at Helen's office when she arrived there a full hour before her office was scheduled to open. Fortunately he was familiar enough with her workaholic tendencies to anticipate the early arrival.

"Ty! I certainly wasn't expecting to see you here," she said. "Do we have an appointment?"

"No. I was hoping you could fit me in before your first client."

Helen paused, her key in the lock. "Are you in some kind of trouble?"

"I'll explain inside," he said. "It's not something I want to discuss where anyone can overhear."

She regarded him with amusement. "We don't usually have spies lurking in the shrubbery around here."

"Don't be too sure," he said bitterly. "You'd be amazed where those tabloid photographers turn up."

"Okay, then, we'll go inside." She led the way into her office, flipping on lights en route. She plugged in her coffee machine, which was apparently already filled and ready to go, then turned it on. "That should be ready in a minute. Now, what's on your mind?"

He told her about his conversations with Jay Wrigley and Tom Bristol the day before. "Cal thought I ought to come to you to see if their perceptions are right. Is there a chance that Dee-Dee can take Trevor from me?"

Her expression was so grim, he was sure she was going to confirm Jay's assessment, but instead, she muttered a curse. "There ought to be a law against attorneys like Jay meddling in the kind of cases they don't usually handle. I'm sure Mr.

Bristol is perfectly competent, and he does have the background since he handled the original custody case." She gave Ty the kind of smug look he'd often seen when she was heading off to court to do battle. "But he's not me. I'm happy to work with him, if that's what you'd prefer, or I can take over. As for Mr. Wrigley, tell him the next time Dee-Dee calls, he's to advise her that all her dealings from here on out are to be with me. Once I've spoken to her, I'll have a better sense of what she's really after. This whole thing could just be a ploy to get some kind of payoff from you so she'll go away. Or she could be entirely serious about wanting to exercise her rights as Trevor's mother."

"Can she just do that?" Ty asked, not even trying to hide his frustration. "She signed papers, Helen. She gave me custody." He'd brought the papers back from his safety deposit box in Atlanta and handed them now to Helen.

"Thanks. I'll look these over later," Helen said, putting them into a new file folder. "What you need to know now is that she certainly has the legal right to try to reestablish her parental rights. A sympathetic judge may grant her some contact."

Before Ty could say what he thought about that, she regarded him with sympathy. "I know how that grates with you, but concentrate on Trevor. Does he ask about his mom?"

"Once in a while," Ty admitted.

"It will probably happen more and more," Helen advised him. "The more he's around other kids, the more he'll see that a key person is missing from his life. What have you told him?"

"That she had to move away."

"Well, that won't be enough to satisfy him as time goes on."

Ty sighed. "I suppose."

"Let's concentrate on the big picture and figure out how to bring Dee-Dee back into his life in a way that works for everyone."

"Even if she's still reckless and irresponsible?" Ty asked wearily.

"We'll make sure she's not before we do anything else," Helen promised him.

"How?"

"I'll put an investigator on it. Do you have any idea where she is? I don't like leaving the ball in her court. I'd like to take the initiative and contact her. I'll send a letter reminding her of the custody agreement she signed and pointing out all the weaknesses in her case. Maybe that will be enough to get her to back down."

Ty was doubtful about that. "When I was seeing her, she was living in Cincinnati, but she took off from there. When we finally tracked her down to sign the original custody papers, she was in Wyoming. She could still be there, or she could have moved on."

"She didn't tell your attorney?"

He shook his head. "She's been contacting him."

Helen nodded. "Then finding her will be step one." She glanced up from her notes. "It's going to be okay, Ty," she assured him. "We may have to make a concession or two, but nobody's going to take that little boy away from you. You've got a nanny who's been with Trevor from the beginning, plus family and friends, all of whom can testify to the fact that you're a devoted father who's been raising that boy on his own practically from day one."

Despite the uncertainties, Ty felt better. "Thanks, Helen. I need to ask you to keep this as quiet as possible for now, okay? I don't want my mom or anyone else to find out about it."

Helen frowned. "Anyone else being Annie?"

He nodded. "She and I, well, I feel as if we might finally be making a little bit of progress. She's agreed to help me with my rehab. I don't want to ruin that by rubbing her face in all this. I'm sure you know that it's the main reason we split up. If she hears that Dee-Dee is going to be making a nuisance of herself..." He shook his head. "Annie shouldn't have to deal with any of this."

"She won't hear it from me," Helen promised. "But I really think you need to fill her in. Sooner or later, word will get out. You said it yourself a minute ago when you were worrying about paparazzi in the bushes. You're a high-profile guy these days, and if Dee-Dee files any papers in court, it's going to go public. You don't want Annie to find out that way. Or your mother, for that matter. She'll be furious with both of us, especially when she finds out you've told Cal, too."

"I'll deal with Mom," he promised. "As for Annie, I hate the possibility that it's just going to prove to her that I'm a bad risk."

"And what will keeping it from her prove?" Helen asked quietly. "Tell her, Ty. She might be upset, but it's better than having her find out some other way."

He knew Helen was right. His relationship with Annie couldn't take a lie or even an omission right now. If he was ever going to win her back, he had to be totally honest with her. Luckily for him, he was already scheduled to see her tonight. It would be the perfect opportunity to fill her in.

And then pray that their first workout together didn't turn out to be their last.

Annie picked at the chicken salad that Sarah had prepared for their dinner.

"You don't like the recipe?" Sarah asked eventually. "I thought you loved chicken salad with walnuts and apples."

"I do," Annie said distractedly. "I just can't get my mind off this session I have with Ty at eight."

Sarah's eyes widened. "Then you decided to do it?"

Annie nodded.

"Good for you. I think it was the right decision."

"For him or me?"

"For both of you. He'll get the help he needs and you'll discover whether or not there are any of the old feelings left."

"Oh, I know the feelings are there," Annie said wryly. "That's not the problem. Now I'm going to have to figure out if I'm going to do anything about them."

"Well, speaking as a woman who has very recently set the wheels of a divorce in motion, I say you ought to grab on to real love and hang on for dear life. I don't care how complicated it is."

Annie met her gaze. "I forgot you were going to sign papers today. How do you feel about it?"

"Surprisingly relieved," Sarah admitted. "I thought it would make me feel awful, but it didn't. I suppose I'll feel sad when the final decree happens, but right now I actually feel a little bit excited. I can start planning my own future, think about what I really want for the rest of my life."

"Good for you," Annie said.

Sarah shrugged. "Not that I expect everything to go smoothly. This is Walter we're talking about. If he doesn't pitch a royal conniption, then his parents will."

"You can handle them," Annie assured her.

"Or Helen can," Sarah corrected. "By the way, I forgot to tell you that I saw Ty at her office this morning."

Annie's gaze snapped up. "Ty had a meeting with Helen?"

"I guess so. He was coming out of her office when I got there. Whatever they'd been talking about, he looked upset.

He walked right past me without even seeing me. I spoke to him, but I don't think he heard me."

"I wonder what that was about," Annie said. He could have dropped by for a visit, but then why would he look upset on his way out?

"You're going to see him in a half hour," Sarah reminded her. "You can always ask him."

"It's none of my business," Annie said, though it annoyed her to admit it. "I suppose he'll mention something about it if he wants me to know. I thought he told me his lawyer was in Atlanta, though."

"You never know what could have come up," Sarah said. "Maybe he wanted Helen to set up a trust fund for Trevor or something."

"We could speculate all night and never get it right," Annie said eventually. She glanced at her watch. "I'd better get over to the spa. Since I told him to be there promptly at five after eight, I'd better be there waiting for him."

Sarah regarded her knowingly. "Annie, don't let this thing with Helen bug you. Just ask him, okay? It's probably nothing."

Annie nodded. "We'll see how it goes."

After all, if she stuck to her promise to herself to keep things between them strictly professional, then his meeting with Helen really was absolutely none of her concern.

Annie was halfway down the block on her way to the spa when a big SUV went racing past her, then squealed to a stop in front of Sarah's. In her rearview mirror she saw a man bolt from the SUV, leaving it parked so that it blocked the driveway. Walter, she concluded, had gotten the divorce papers.

At the end of the street she hesitated, then made a U-turn. Something about his bat-out-of-hell arrival alarmed her. She didn't know much about the man. Sarah had certainly never mentioned any violent tendencies, but Annie wasn't willing to take chances.

Even as she pulled to a stop in front of Sarah's, she could hear raised voices coming from inside. Pausing only long enough to call Ty at the spa and her dad, Annie raced across the lawn and rang the doorbell. When no one answered, either because they were shouting too loudly to hear it or because they didn't want visitors, Annie pushed open the door and went inside.

Keeping a determinedly cheery expression on her face, she headed directly toward the kitchen where the confrontation was going on.

"Hi there," she said, stepping inside. "I guess you didn't hear me ring the bell."

Walter whirled on her, his cheeks flushed, his eyes filled with fury. "Who the hell are you?"

He was a big man, tall and muscular, though he reminded Annie a bit of a football player starting to lose his well-toned physique. He clearly was used to using his size to intimidate. She didn't intend to allow that. Rather than backing away, she took a step closer. "I'm Annie, a friend of Sarah's. Who are you?"

"I'm her husband. Now, get out!"

"Not just yet," Annie said, her gaze on Sarah, who looked dazed. "Sarah, sweetie, why don't you pour us all some sweet tea so we can sit and get acquainted?"

"This is not some damn tea party," Walter blustered. "I asked you to leave."

"No, you *told* me to leave, and not very politely, I might add. Since it's not your house, I think I'll just wait till Sarah tells me she wants me to go." She sat down at the table to emphasize her determination to stay.

"Maybe you should..." Sarah began, sounding frantic and near tears when the kids started to cry, obviously having been awakened by all the commotion.

"Go check on Tommy and Libby," Annie suggested gently. "Walter and I will be fine."

Sarah looked torn.

"It's okay," Annie assured her. "Don't worry about a thing. Ty and my dad will be here any second."

With perfect timing, Ronnie strolled into the kitchen, followed by Ty. The two men paused, clearly sizing up Sarah's husband.

Ty glanced at Annie. "Everything okay?"

"I think it's getting there," she said. "Sarah, check on the kids, okay?"

"What the hell is this?" Walter demanded, though a little of the fire had gone out of his voice now that his wife and Annie weren't the only ones on the receiving end of his bullying. He gave Annie a disgusted look. "Did you call in the cavalry? For what? To keep a man away from his own wife and kids?"

"It seemed prudent," Annie said. She turned to her dad. "Sarah filed for divorce today. That's what brought Walter here roaring over from Alabama."

Ronnie managed a commiserating look. He draped an arm over Walter's broad shoulders and guided him from the room. "Been there, done that," Ronnie told him. "But this isn't the way to handle it, okay? You can't come in here and try to terrorize your wife and scare your kids half to death."

Walter's response was lost as Ronnie steered him straight outside.

Ty sat down across from Annie, his gaze filled with concern. "You okay? You sounded completely freaked out when you called me. I don't think I've ever heard you like that."

Annie shuddered. "It's just that you read these stories about some guy going nuts when his wife leaves him. When I saw this car tearing down the street and realized it was Walter, I guess I did panic. Thanks for coming. You didn't have to. I called Dad, too. He was closer. I just wanted you to know I was going to be late. I didn't want you thinking I'd backed out of our first session."

His lips tilted slightly. "Worrying about me in the middle of a crisis was very considerate of you," he said. "And here I thought you wanted a hero to come to the rescue. Instead, I never even got to land a punch."

She grinned at his exaggerated disappointment. "I'm sure you would have if it had been necessary. And I do appreciate you coming right over." She met his gaze. "Is it okay if we postpone till tomorrow night? I think I should probably stay here with Sarah in case that idiot tries to come back."

"I think we should all stay here, at least for a while," Ty said. "Walter doesn't strike me as the kind of guy with sufficient good sense to go back where he came from."

"From what I hear, good sense doesn't run in his family. Do you know they intended to try to get custody of Tommy from Sarah, because he'd be the heir to the family business? Not both kids, just Tommy."

Color rose in Ty's cheeks at the mention of a custody fight. "And what? Sarah wants both kids here with her?"

"Well, of course she does! She's their mama. At their age, that's who they need."

"Not necessarily," Ty said, his temper stirring in a way Annie hadn't seen in years. "Sometimes it's the dad who's the better parent. Sometimes the mother is incapable of providing what the child really needs."

Startled by his vehemence, Annie stared at him. "Why are you getting so angry?"

"Because whoever said the mother should automatically get preference? That's ridiculous." He stood up. "I have to get out of here."

Annie regarded him with confusion. "Ty, what's going on? You're obviously upset, and I don't think it has anything to do with Sarah and Walter."

"Gee, you think?" he said. "I'll see you tomorrow. I'm glad everything's okay here."

Annie started to follow him to the door, but he was gone before she could get any farther than the dining room. Her dad walked into the room, looking back over his shoulder. Walter was right behind him, his expression calmer and definitely contrite.

"I'm going to check on Sarah and the kids," Walter said. When Annie started to object, he held up a hand. "I'm not going to yell. I just want to see my kids."

"It's okay," Ronnie said. "Walter understands how important it is not to upset anybody."

Walter nodded. "I just lost it when I got those papers," he explained to Annie. "I swear I'm usually not like that."

Annie trusted her dad more than she did Walter's words, so she dropped her objections.

"Why did Ty go racing out of here?" Ronnie asked as soon as Walter had left the room.

"I have no idea," Annie said. "Obviously something I said upset him, but I can't imagine what it was. One minute we were talking about the situation here, and the next Ty was furious and on his way out."

"Maybe you touched a nerve," Ronnie suggested.

Annie didn't get it. "About what?"

"Trevor," her dad suggested.

"But Ty has custody of his son. That was settled a long time ago."

Then she recalled what Sarah had said earlier about Ty being in Helen's office this morning and looking upset as he left. Maybe his custody arrangement with Trevor's mom wasn't as resolved as she'd assumed it was. If something had just happened to throw their arrangement into question, no wonder he'd reacted to her comment that Tommy and Libby belonged with their mom.

"Dad, can you hang out here with Sarah for a while? Or maybe ask Mom to come over? I think I need to track Ty down."

"I'm happy to stay here, but from what I saw, I don't think this is a good time for you to go after Ty. He doesn't seem to be in a mood to talk."

"Which is exactly why he needs to," Annie said. "Please."

Ronnie looked uncertain, but eventually he nodded. "I'll be right here and I'll get your mom to come over, too, in case Sarah needs to talk. Don't worry about things here. I really do think Walter's calmer now. He doesn't seem like such a bad guy, just a man who's scared of losing his family."

She stood on tiptoe and gave her father a kiss. "Thank you. You're the best."

"Always nice to hear. Now, go. Make things right with Ty."

"That might be a tall order, but at least maybe I can fix whatever went wrong tonight."

CHAPTER TWELVE

Ever since he was a kid, when Ty got upset, he headed for the ball field, whether here in Serenity or even the stadium in Atlanta. Here at home, he'd done a lot of late-night thinking sitting in the stands with moonlight filtering through the surrounding trees. It was ironic that the place that came alive during a game, that energized him with the shouts of the crowd and his teammates, could be so calming with no one around. Even this small-town ball field where he'd pitched his first games had that effect on him.

In fact, this was the place he'd come when he'd been struggling with his parents' divorce. He didn't miss the irony that it was where he'd chosen to come tonight with Annie's words about a child needing its mother still ringing in his ears.

True, she hadn't known that would be a sore subject with him these days. She'd been reacting to Sarah's circumstances, not his, but the remark had hit a nerve just the same.

Was that how everyone was going to feel? Would the court automatically assume because Trevor was still a preschooler, he'd need his mom more than his dad? That struck Ty as totally bogus and unfair. These circumstances weren't typical. Shouldn't the rule of law ride on the realities of a specific situation and not some archaic rule of thumb from the past? Trevor didn't even know his mom. He'd been with Ty practically from birth.

Ty heard a car drive up and stop. He knew instinctively that it was Annie. He hadn't expected her to come looking for him, but he wasn't surprised that she had. Naturally his uncharacteristic explosion of temper had stirred her curiosity, if not her understanding.

"It didn't take you long," he said without turning around.

She scrambled up the bleachers and sat down sideways on the bench in front of him so she could look up at him. "Come on, Ty, get real. You're not that good at hiding out. I can count on one hand the places you go when you're upset. This one's on the top of the list."

"Why'd you come after me?"

"You were angry. I wanted to know why," she told him, confirming his guess as her gaze held his. "Then I figured it out for myself. At least, I think I did."

"Do tell."

"Trevor's mom wants back in his life."

He regarded her with astonishment. "How'd you come up with that?"

"Your reaction when I said Sarah's kids needed their mom, plus the fact that she saw you at Helen's office this morning," she said, ticking the reasons off on her fingers as she went through them. "How am I doing so far?"

"Not bad," he conceded.

She smiled at the grudging concession. "And on the way over here, I remembered you told me that you had just come out of a meeting in Atlanta that had been a disaster, but then you didn't want to talk about it. I figured that had been about Trevor, too, but after you called me, you decided you couldn't talk to me about it because of…" She shrugged and looked away. "Well, you know why."

He shook his head. She'd leaped to a lot of conclusions, but she hadn't missed the mark. "You know me too darn well." He couldn't decide if that was a blessing or a curse.

Annie sighed. "I do, don't I?" Eventually she lifted her gaze again till it met his. "You going to fill me in?"

Ty struggled against an overwhelming desire to do just that, to pour out all of the rage and conflicting emotions warring within him right now. Annie'd opened a door and he wanted to walk through it, to use her as a sounding board as he always had in the past.

"No," he said eventually, decency winning out over his own longing.

"Is that because you don't need someone to talk to, or because you don't want it to be me?"

"Neither. I'd like your perspective, but I just don't think it's right to dump my problems in your lap, particularly this one."

"I appreciate the sentiment. I really do, but let's face it—sooner or later I'll hear it all, anyway."

He chuckled at the truth behind her words. "There aren't many secrets in this town, are there?"

"Never have been," she agreed.

Ty debated trying to keep this one buried inside, at least a little longer, but she was right, as Helen had been earlier. Annie was bound to hear the whole story. It might as well be from him, especially since she'd already guessed the gist of it.

Ty stood up and moved down to sit on the bleacher next to her, then leaned back, his elbows resting on the bench above. Despite the relaxed pose, every muscle in his body was tense. Talking about Dee-Dee to Annie wasn't going to be as easy as some of the other problems he'd poured out to her over the years.

"When I called you from Atlanta, I had just left my attorney's office," he began, trying to keep the fury he'd felt at that moment out of his voice.

"Not the trainer's," she said, reminding him of the lie he'd uttered.

"That was earlier."

"So you lied."

"Not about what the trainer had said, but about why I'd called." He gave her a wry look. "I was trying to be considerate."

"I think we're probably way past playing polite games with each other, Ty. I'd rather just hear the truth. If I'm ever going to trust you again, there can't be any more lies, not even little ones to protect my feelings."

He nodded. "You're right. I'm sorry. Jay—that's my attorney—had just told me that Dee-Dee, Trevor's mom, had been in touch with him about wanting to be a part of Trevor's life."

Haltingly he filled her in on the arrangement he and Dee-Dee had which wasn't quite the way it had been portrayed in the tabloids. No money had changed hands, beyond a court-approved settlement so she could start her life over. It had never been the kind of ugly deal described in the tabloids to make her go away.

He met Annie's gaze, trying to make her understand. "I was so sure that would be the end of it with Dee-Dee, that I could focus on my son and move on. My life had just changed dramatically. I was suddenly this single dad with big-time responsibilities, but I was determined to make it work, because nothing on earth matters more to me than that little boy. As for Dee-Dee, she had the freedom she claimed she wanted, the time she needed to grow up and get her life in order. When she surfaced a few weeks ago, I was stunned."

"I wonder what changed?" Annie said, her expression thoughtful.

"Apparently she's engaged and ready to settle down herself. I don't know if it was her idea or her fiancé's to get Trevor back in her life, but suddenly she wants to be a mom again."

"Maybe for her part of proving that she's matured is dealing with one very big loose end," Annie said.

"Seeing Trevor, making peace with how she handled things, I could understand that," Ty said. "But she's after more, Annie. This isn't a one-time thing."

"How do you know that if she hasn't actually contacted you directly?" Annie asked.

"I told you she called Jay—twice, in fact. The first time, she just asked about Trevor, how he was, that kind of thing. That was disturbing enough, but the other day she indicated she wanted more contact, maybe even custody."

Annie regarded him skeptically. "Do you believe that she's really settling down, that she's no longer a baseball groupie?"

"Last I heard she was in Wyoming. There aren't any teams real close by, unless you head down to Denver, so maybe she has settled down the way she said." He hated admitting that she might have changed even that much.

"And she told your lawyer she's engaged?"

Ty nodded. "To some pillar of the community, according to her."

Annie gave him a worried look. "Did you mention that to Helen?"

"No, why?"

"I just wondered if that will help her case. If she can portray herself as happily married and settled, how would that weigh against a single dad who's on the road all the time?"

Ty muttered a curse at the reasonable question. He should have thought of that. "I've been managing for three years. Anyone who knows me knows that Trevor has a stable environment with excellent care. Nobody could take better care of Trevor than Cassandra does when I'm away."

"But she's not his mother," Annie said.

"And Dee-Dee's shown no signs that she's capable of being a good mom, so where does that leave us?" he said, thinking that if Annie had been the one asking for custody, no matter what the circumstances, he wouldn't have hesitated. He knew with soul-deep certainty that she'd be the best mom ever, that she *should* have been the mother of his son.

"Still, I think Helen needs to know," Annie persisted.

"I'll tell her in the morning." He hesitated, studying Annie. She was turned away so he couldn't read her eyes, but her posture was rigid. She was obviously upset. "I'm sorry."

"For what?"

"Hitting you with all this. I knew it was a bad idea."

"I'm only upset at the thought that someone like her is trying to take away your son," she told him. She turned and met his gaze, her expression filled with compassion. "It really is lousy, Ty. I wouldn't wish something this painful on my worst enemy."

He smiled at that. "Am I your worst enemy?"

She hesitated, then shook her head. "Not even close," she said so softly he could barely hear her.

His eyes stung with tears. "Oh, Annie," he whispered, his own voice ragged. He hadn't felt this close to her since this whole mess had started. He reached out, only to touch her cheek, but alarm flared in her eyes and she inched away from him.

"Don't," she said. "Please, Ty, just don't."

He sighed. "I get it. It's too soon."

"I don't know that the time will ever be right," she said.

"It will be," he said. "I believe that with everything in me. Just give me another chance, Annie, that's all I ask. In all my life, the only time things made sense was when I was with you. I want that back." There it was. He'd actually put it out there for her to accept or reject.

He had his answer when she stood up without responding and started down the bleachers. "I'll see you tomorrow night just after eight," she said, her tone brisk.

"I'll be there," he promised.

At least she hadn't canceled the session. It might not be the opening he wanted, but it was an opening. He intended to do everything in his power not to screw it up.

Annie left the ball field with her emotions in turmoil. Sitting there with Ty in the moonlight, talking about things that really mattered instead of all the inconsequential words they'd been exchanging, had felt good. Right, in fact, just as he'd said. But she simply wasn't ready to go there yet.

What she wanted to do most was go home, crawl into bed and savor that instant when she'd thought he might kiss her. Even though she'd backed away, her pulse had raced with anticipation. She'd known then with absolute certainty how dangerous it was going to be to spend time with Ty. She'd made a promise, though, and she intended to honor it.

Right now, however, she needed to go and check on Sarah. She trusted her dad's judgment that Walter had himself under control, and she knew Ronnie and her mom would stick around just in case, but she didn't feel right leaving the task of watching over Sarah to them.

When she arrived at Sarah's, the house was still lit up, even though it was nearly eleven. Walter's fancy SUV continued to block the driveway, and her mom's car was parked at the curb, which meant she and Ronnie were still inside.

Rather than ring the bell and wake the kids, Annie walked around to the kitchen door and tapped lightly. She knew they'd all be gathered in there.

"It's open," Sarah called out.

As Annie opened the door, she saw Walter regarding his wife with dismay.

"Do you just leave the door open for any crazy person who wanders by?"

"Annie's not any crazy person," Sarah argued. "Who else would it be at this hour?"

Walter shook his head and turned to Ronnie for support. "Is Serenity that safe? Do you all lock your doors?"

"I do," Dana Sue said. "Ever since that rash of burglaries a few months back, I've been more careful."

"There you go," Walter said triumphantly. "Will you listen to Dana Sue, please? I can't be back in Alabama worrying about whether you and the kids are safe."

Annie regarded him with surprise. It actually sounded as if he was making peace with the idea of Sarah staying here. She looked around the table. "What did I miss?"

"I'm going to stop the divorce proceedings," Sarah told her.

Annie's surprise turned to shock. "Really?"

"Instead, we're going to try to figure out how things got so far off track," Sarah said, looking amazingly content with her decision.

"And you're going to do that with you staying on here and Walter back in Alabama?" Annie said, trying to imagine how a marriage could be mended long-distance.

"I'll be over here on weekends," Walter explained. "I

think we can make more progress without my parents butting in every time we turn around."

"Amen to that," Sarah said.

Walter actually smiled, and when he did, Annie was able to see a hint of the man Sarah had fallen in love with. That dimpled smile gave him a certain roguish charm.

"Is Helen on board with all this?" Annie asked, then held up a hand. "Sorry, this really is none of my business. If you all have reached a solution you can agree on, I'm very happy for you."

"I did speak to Helen, though," Sarah said. "And I also spoke to Dr. McDaniels." She studied Annie worriedly. "I hope you don't mind. Your mom suggested it. She's agreed to meet with us every Saturday for the next few weeks."

"Why would I mind?" Annie said. "She's a terrific psychologist."

Walter regarded her curiously. "You've seen her?"

"She's the one who's helped me during my battle with anorexia. I still meet with her from time to time."

He nodded slowly. "Oh, yeah, Sarah told me something about that a long time ago. It must have been tough."

Annie nodded. "There are times it still is."

Dana Sue reached over and squeezed her hand, then stood up. "It's late, folks. I think we need to get home. Ronnie, you ready?"

He stood up at once and wrapped an arm around her shoulders, then gave her a kiss on the cheek. "I'm always ready to be alone with you, sugar."

Annie rolled her eyes at the open display of affection. Though she loved that her parents were close again, sometimes their demonstrativeness made her feel very alone. She wanted what they had, what she'd thought she had with Ty.

"Well, then, it's too bad I'm coming home, too, isn't it?" she teased. "You two are going to have to behave yourselves."

Her dad ruffled her hair. "Thank goodness you're not the boss of us," he said.

Annie held back, giving them a head start. Walter excused himself to check on the children, leaving Sarah to walk to the door with her.

"I just love your parents," Sarah said. "Your dad's talk with Walter really made a difference, I think. Who knows if it'll last, but I want to try, at least. We owe it to ourselves, and especially to the kids."

"Earlier tonight I wouldn't have given you two cents for things turning out this way," Annie told her.

"Me, neither, to be honest with you. I know it looked real bad the way Walter came busting in here, but when he's scared, he gets mad. I think when he got those papers and he realized it really could be over with us and that I'd fight for the kids, it scared the dickens out of him. I'm sure he expected me to just go along with whatever he wanted."

Annie gave her a fierce hug. "I hope things work out exactly the way you want them to."

When she would have started out, Sarah held on to her arm. "What about Ty? Did you find him?"

"I did, but we can talk about that another time."

Sarah frowned. "Didn't it go well?"

"Actually it was a good conversation. We were more open and honest than we've been in a long time, but things are more complicated than ever. I'll tell you next time I see you, I promise."

"Then you'd better come by tomorrow," Sarah said. "Walter's going back home first thing in the morning."

"And after that you'll be at the spa to do your workout, right?" Annie said pointedly.

"Right on time," Sarah vowed. "But you know we can't talk there, so dinner tomorrow night. Let's go to Sullivan's. I'll see if Katie can babysit."

Annie shook her head. "I have to work with Ty tomorrow night. Maybe the day after. I'll have to see if he's going to need to work out every day or every other day. Then I'll let you know about dinner."

Sarah regarded her with concern. "Can I offer you one piece of advice?"

"Of course."

"Don't you dare start building your life around him, Annie, not till you know where things are headed. I don't want to see you get all caught up with Ty and his problems only to have him take off and leave you behind."

"Good point," Annie said. It wasn't as if she hadn't worried about the same thing herself. She just hadn't wanted to admit that it was a very real possibility that things would go exactly that way. "I'll be careful."

Of course, that was her head talking. Her heart seemed to have a will of its own.

Helen was still troubled by her conversation with Sarah on the phone the night before and earlier in the day in person. She seemed to suddenly be wearing rose-colored glasses where her marriage was concerned. Call her cynical, but Helen had never seen a turnaround that fast that actually lasted. She almost had whiplash from the speed of Sarah's change of heart.

Since Sarah had claimed that Dana Sue and Ronnie had witnessed Walter's transformation, Helen decided to ask them about it. Fortunately Ronnie could usually be found at Sullivan's early in the evening on the nights when Dana Sue was working. He'd even been known to pitch in as a waiter when they were short on staff. Mostly, though, he was just there to catch the occasional glimpse of his wife. Helen had to admit, it was kind of sweet.

"Hey, Counselor, how's it going?" Ronnie asked when Helen found him in his usual booth near the kitchen. "You here to sneak in a visit with your husband?"

"Actually I was looking for you and your wife." She glanced around the busy restaurant. "Probably not the best time to try to drag Dana Sue out of the kitchen, is it?"

"Let's just say when I stuck my head in to say hello, I was nearly run down. She, Erik and Karen are operating at top speed tonight. Not only that, some delivery they were expecting didn't come in, so they had to change specials at the last second. There are some pretty sour moods in there."

Helen sighed and slid in across from Ronnie. "Then I'll settle for you."

"I'm honored."

"You probably shouldn't be. I just want to pump you for information. I gather you were around when Sarah's husband showed up last night."

Ronnie nodded. "Well, a few minutes after the fact, but I saw enough."

"What did you think? Bad guy? Good guy? Out-of-control guy?"

"He has quite a mouth on him, I'll give you that," Ronnie said. "And he was shouting at top volume when I turned up, but he dropped the belligerent tone pretty quickly when I got him outside. In my opinion, he was scared witless and reacting the only way he knew how to the threat of his marriage ending."

"Sarah told me both you and Ty showed up, so he must have alarmed Annie for her to call both of you."

"She only called Ty because she was supposed to be meeting him at the spa. He decided on his own to come over."

Helen's brow rose at that. "Interesting."

Ronnie sighed. "That's one word to describe it. I'm worried about those two. Or really about Annie, I should say. Ty can take care of himself."

Helen thought of the looming custody battle. "She needs to watch her step," she said. "Ty's life is pretty complicated right now."

Ronnie studied her intently. "Because?"

"I can't say any more than that. Lawyer-client confidentiality."

"Well, damn," Ronnie said. "Is your taking him on as a client because of something that's going to wind up with Annie getting her heart broken?"

"Not necessarily," Helen hedged. "Just tell her to be cautious, okay? She needs to talk to Ty. Maybe she already has."

Ronnie's expression turned thoughtful. "Well, she did go chasing off after him last night, and I do think they had a talk."

"Then maybe I'm worrying for nothing," Helen said. "Getting back to Sarah, do you trust Walter?"

"If you mean do I think they can work things out, I have no idea. If you're asking if he's violent, I honestly don't think so."

"Then giving the situation time and space could be okay," she said, relieved.

"It could be," Ronnie concurred.

"Thanks," Helen said, standing up and dropping a quick kiss on his cheek just in time for Dana Sue to emerge from the kitchen and catch her.

"Hey, keep your hands off my husband," Dana Sue told

her. "The last woman who tried that still worries about what might be in her food when she comes in here."

"You wouldn't poison Mary Vaughn," Helen said.

"Not now that she's back with Sonny, no, but a couple of years back? Hard to say what I might have done." She slid in next to Ronnie and leaned her head briefly on his shoulder.

"Tired?" he asked.

"Dead on my feet and it's still a madhouse in here," Dana Sue said. "I need to get back."

"Well, I'm going to risk my husband's wrath and slip in there long enough to steal a kiss from him," Helen said. "And maybe some apple pie for my mother. It'll be penance for not getting home on time tonight."

"I'll go with you and protect you," Dana Sue offered after giving Ronnie a quick kiss. "How are things with Flo?"

"She's still impossible," Helen said, "but I have *almost* learned to let all the complaints roll off my back. I know she's in pain and that she's not one bit happier about these circumstances than I am, so that makes it easier."

Dana Sue grinned at her. "You sounded very mature just then."

Helen laughed. "I did, didn't I? Don't believe it. That woman can reduce me to behaving like a petulant two-year-old in ten seconds flat. Ask Erik."

"No need," Dana Sue said. "He's told me."

Helen sighed. "The rat fink," she said, though without animosity. In fact, just the sight of his eyes lighting up when he spotted her walking into the kitchen made every bad thing that had happened all day fade.

"Hey, you," he said. "You're late."

"She's been out front schmoozing with my husband," Dana Sue said. "Keep an eye on her."

"Always," Erik said. "Dinner's ready to take home for you and your mom. Since you're late, I added extra apple pie."

"You anticipate my every need, don't you?"

"I certainly try." He winked at her. "I'd try to fulfill another one, but it's crazy in here right now."

"Later, then," she said, picking up the take-out containers he'd set aside. "Love you."

"Ditto," he replied, but he was already distracted, his attention focused on the plates lined up in front of him and the meat and fish cooking on the stove.

Helen watched him for another minute, enjoying the brisk efficiency with which he worked, the little frown of concentration that knit his very handsome brow and his excellent backside in a pair of snug-fitting, well-worn jeans. Yes, indeed, an excellent antidote to a bad day!

CHAPTER THIRTEEN

When Ty arrived at the spa for his first session with Annie, he was surprised and somewhat dismayed to find his mother still in her office.

"You're working late," he said, standing in the doorway. "You can't do this, Mom. You're going to wear yourself out. You need to leave here on time, get home and spend time with Jessica Lynn, Cole and your husband."

Unsaid was the reminder that she wasn't some young kid. She'd been in her early forties when she'd had Jessica Lynn and Cole. If Trevor could wear him out, there was no telling how exhausting those two must be for his mom. Not that he dared to say any of that. As tactless as he could sometimes be, even he knew that suggesting she was old was not smart.

"You've taken up handing out marital advice?" Maddie queried, looking amused.

"Sure," he said, grinning. "It's a lot easier when you have no real experience, I think."

He studied her, genuinely worried by the exhaustion in her eyes. Maybe he needed to have a talk with Cal. Perhaps Cal could get her to ease up. "Why are you here so late, anyway?"

"Going over the books," she admitted with a sigh. "It's been a tough couple of months."

Ty frowned. "Is the spa in financial trouble? I thought it was a roaring success."

"It has been until recently, but you know how things have been with the economy. For a long time it's been really tough out there. Women aren't treating themselves to facials, massages and manicures the way they did when we first opened. The trainers aren't as booked up, either. I think a lot of businesses are going to be slow to recover."

"What do Helen and Dana Sue say?"

"That we'll weather this. It's not as if we've had to lay anyone off yet, but I'm feeling the pressure to be creative with how we allocate our money. And we decided not to expand and open another spa the way we'd been talking about. It's just not the right time."

"I could invest, if what you need is an infusion of cash," he offered. "I'm still making more than I know what to do with."

"I don't want an investment, but there is one thing you could consider." She handed him a computer printout. "Annie says this piece of equipment would be a help to you, but I can't squeeze it out of our budget, not when we don't have that many clients who need it."

Ty barely glanced at the page. If Annie said it would help him, that was all he needed to hear. "Order it," he told his mother. "Give me the bill when it comes in."

"You sure? Just like that?"

He grinned at her caution. Ever since she and his dad had divorced, she'd been prudent about money. It was one of the reasons she'd made such an excellent manager for this business venture she'd gone into with Helen and Dana Sue. His mom could squeeze a dollar till it squealed. It was also why she and Cal did well, despite Cal's modest salary as a teacher and coach.

"Just like that," he assured her.

The response didn't seem to please her. "You need to be investing your money for your future and Trevor's."

"I've done that," Ty assured her. "I learned money management from you, didn't I? And this equipment is an investment in my future, if you think about it."

"How so?"

"The sooner I'm healthy and pitching again, the brighter my financial future will look. Jay says if I can get the Cy Young Award, maybe get some all-star attention, I'll be a natural for commercial endorsements." Of course, an all-out custody battle for his son might cut into his image and value, which was yet another reason to get things settled with Dee-Dee as quickly and amicably as possible.

"Good point," his mom admitted. "I'll call about the equipment in the morning."

"Now, go home," he ordered. "Put your feet up and let Cal wait on you."

"My husband knows how to take care of me. He doesn't need advice from you." She did shut down her computer, though, and grabbed her purse from a drawer in her desk. "You're working out with Annie tonight?"

He nodded.

"Good," she said, and for a minute he thought she was going to leave it at that, but then she turned back. "Be careful with her, Ty. No matter how tough she seems, she's still fragile."

"I know that. I was the one who told you she was more vulnerable than she'd ever let on."

"I guess now that I have what I want, the two of you spending time together, I'm worried about her."

"Not about me?" he teased. "I'm your son."

She came back and kissed his forehead. "Nah, no worries about you. I know *you're* tough."

Ty let her assessment pass, though the truth was, when it came to Annie, he was every bit as vulnerable as she was.

Annie's heart climbed into her throat when she saw Maddie leave her office. She knew Ty had been in there chatting with her. Any second now he'd come looking for her. *Am I really ready for this?* she wondered. There was only one way she could think of to find out.

She drew in a deep breath, then crossed the spa toward Maddie's office and met Ty as he emerged. A slow smile lit his eyes when he saw her. She almost succumbed to the lure of that smile, but then she steeled herself against its power.

"Let's get to it," she said, deliberately keeping her tone cool and professional as she'd planned.

Ty's smile instantly faded, but he gave her a quick nod. "Yes, let's not waste time."

His attitude immediately put her on the defensive. "I was just saying—"

"I know what you meant, Annie. It's late and I'm imposing on your time."

Guilt stirred. "I'm sorry if that's how it sounded," Annie said. "I really didn't mean it that way." She dared to meet his gaze. "Are we always going to have to be so careful what we say to each other and how we say it?"

"I hope not." His gaze locked with hers. "Maybe if we got this out of the way..."

Before she realized what he had in mind, he stepped closer and sealed his mouth over hers. The first tentative touch of lips against lips was a shock, her first reaction dismay. Before she could push him away, though, he deepened the kiss and

Annie was lost in a sea of familiar sensations. The scent of Ty—part pure masculinity, part some citrus aftershave. The feel of rock-hard muscles against her soft curves. The faint scrape of lightly stubbled cheeks against her own smooth complexion. The low groan in his throat when his tongue found hers. It was heaven!

No, no, she reminded herself. It was dangerous. It was hell, and she really, really didn't want to drop into that abyss.

Belatedly, she mustered up the strength to pull away.

"Bad idea," she told him. "I can't do this…" She gestured vaguely around the workout room. "Not if you're going to do *that*."

His lips curved ever so slightly. "Sorry," he said unconvincingly. "I can't swear that I won't kiss you again."

"Tyler!" she protested.

"Okay, how about this? I promise I won't kiss you again in here. At the spa, I'll be strictly business. Will that do?"

It would as long as this room was the only place the two of them ever crossed paths. She could see to that. She held out her hand. "Deal," she said, then snatched her hand back before he could take it. "Your word will do."

He regarded her solemnly. "You have my word."

Later, after she was home alone in bed and thinking about that bone-melting kiss, she remembered that she had every reason to know that his word wasn't worth much.

Aching from his workout during which Annie had shown him no mercy, Ty retreated to the hot tub upstairs at the spa and settled in for a good soak. He hoped it would not only ease his muscles, but maybe take away the searing memory of that kiss he was supposed to forget about repeating.

Unfortunately, no sooner had he turned on the jets and eased down into the soothing water, than his cell phone rang. Tempted to ignore it, he decided against it when the ringing abruptly ended, then immediately started up again.

Getting out of the hot tub, he grabbed the phone from the pocket of his shirt. He glanced at the caller ID but didn't recognize the number.

"Yes, hello," he said impatiently.

"Ty?"

His heart sank as he recognized the voice. "Hello, Dee-Dee."

"Jay told me how to get in touch with you. He says you're back home in South Carolina doing rehab, something about your shoulder. Is it okay?"

To his surprise, she sounded genuinely concerned. "It's getting there," he said. He wanted to start ranting and raving at her, but a voice in his head that sounded a lot like Helen's told him to calm down. "What's up with you?"

"I'm getting married," she said happily. "Did Jay tell you?"

"He mentioned it," Ty said, keeping his own tone neutral. Then, recalling Helen's need to know how to reach Dee-Dee, he asked, "Where are you living these days, Dee-Dee? Still in Wyoming?"

"No, I moved back home to Cincinnati, but I'm not there now."

"Oh?"

"I'm in Atlanta, Ty. I knew the team had a series of home games, so I came down to see Trevor. I wanted to do that when you were here, so you wouldn't think I was sneaking around behind your back."

Ty bit back the desire to yell that there was no way she was getting within a mile of his son. Instead, he merely said, "I'm sorry you wasted a trip. You should have talked to Jay before you came all that way. He would have told you not to come."

"Actually, that's exactly what he did," Dee-Dee admitted.

"But I'm not taking no for an answer, Ty. I want to see my son. Tomorrow I'm going to drive up to Serenity. I'm just giving you a heads-up."

She sounded so blasted sure of herself, so convinced she had every right to charge into her little boy's life after an absence of three years. Ty's annoyance kicked up a notch, but he kept his temper in check.

"Not going to happen," he said quietly. "Not without a court order. I mean it, Dee-Dee. If you come over here, if you get near Trevor without my permission, I'll find a way to have you thrown in jail."

The threat seemed to silence her. "Why are you being so mean about this?" she asked eventually.

"Do you really have to ask? You abandoned him on my hotel-room doorstep, Dee-Dee. You left a defenseless little baby outside, as if he were nothing more than the morning newspaper. Have you forgotten about that?"

"I knew you were inside that room, and I made sure you opened the door and saw him before I left," she said, trying to defend the indefensible. "I was half out of my mind back then, you know that. I was way too young to be a good mother. I didn't think I could take care of him, and I knew you had the money to see he had a good life. Can't you see that I was trying to do the right thing?"

"Maybe so," he conceded, trying to see it from her perspective. "But as far as I can tell, nothing about that's changed. It's still all about you."

"*I* have changed," she insisted. "I've got my life together now, Ty. I swear it, and the man I'm marrying, he's a really good guy. We want kids."

"Then have all of them you want," Ty told her, still not relenting. Because she sounded so blasted sincere and reasonable, it scared him worse than if she'd been yelling and making outrageous demands. *That* Dee-Dee, he could have fought with a clear conscience. It was much harder to keep this one at arm's length and away from Trevor.

"Trevor's my firstborn," she argued. "We want him to be a part of our lives. Jim's being real sweet about it. He'll be a good stepdaddy."

Ty lost patience with the rosy picture she seemed to have of her future with Trevor at the heart of her new family. "Over my dead body," he said flatly. "This is not going to play out that way, Dee-Dee. Don't come over here. Don't call me again. Next time you want to talk about Trevor, call my attorney. Her name's Helen Decatur-Whitney." He reeled off Helen's phone number, then added, "She'll set you straight."

The flighty young woman Dee-Dee had once been would have taken that seriously and given up. The new, apparently stronger, more mature Dee-Dee merely said, "I'll be in touch, Ty. Count on it. And tell your attorney to be expecting a call from mine."

When the call ended, Ty was shaking. It could have been from the air-conditioning blowing on his damp skin, but he knew that wasn't it. He'd heard something in Dee-Dee's voice that terrified him—real, rock-solid determination.

Helen had taken a shower, put on her favorite ratty old robe, which would have shocked those who knew her as the local fashionista, and settled down with a glass of wine and a couple of case files when the doorbell rang. She opened it to find Ty on her porch, looking haggard.

"What's happened?" she asked at once, standing aside to let him in.

He hesitated, despite the implied invitation. "Are you sure it's okay to come in? I know it's late, but I've been walking around and I saw your light on."

"Of course it's okay. You know you're always welcome here, no matter what time it is. Can I get you a glass of wine? Something stronger?"

He shook his head. "Not with the painkillers."

"Of course. I forgot. How about a soda?"

Ty shook his head and Helen gestured toward a chair. "Then have a seat and tell me what's going on."

Instead of the comfortable chair she'd indicated, Ty sat on the edge of a dainty antique chair. His tall, loose-limbed body looked so incongruous there that Helen had to hide a smile. He was obviously upset, so she doubted he'd appreciate her amusement.

"Dee-Dee called," he announced eventually. "She was in Atlanta to see Trevor. Jay told her we were here, and she told me she intends to come here in the morning."

Helen winced. This was clearly going to come to a head sooner rather than later. "What did you tell her?"

"Not to come and to call you."

"Do you think she'll listen?"

"To the part about calling you, probably. As for not coming, I doubt it. She's hell-bent on seeing Trevor." He looked everywhere in the room except at her.

"Okay, Ty, what aren't you telling me?"

He regarded her with surprise. "How'd you figure out I was holding something back?"

"I've been at this a long time, and I know you," Helen said. "So, what is it?"

"I didn't mention this the other day, because I didn't think it was that important. Annie told me I needed to fill you in, but I didn't do it." He drew in a deep breath, then blurted, "Dee-Dee's engaged. She seems to think Trevor will make the perfect addition to her new little family."

Ty finally met her gaze. "That's really bad, isn't it? That she's getting married and I'm not?"

Helen bit back a curse. "I'm not going to lie to you. It could complicate the situation, especially if there's no question that she's able to provide a stable, loving home for Trevor. It'll make it a lot easier for the judge to require more extensive, unsupervised visitation."

"What do we do?"

"You could always get married," she said, only half joking. "How are things with Annie?"

Ty reacted with shock, evidently taking her seriously. "Come on, Helen. I can't do that to Annie. If I asked her to marry me now, she'd know why and hate me more than ever."

Helen sighed. "I know. I was only a little bit serious. We'll figure this out, Ty." She tapped a pen on the pad in front of her, gazing off as she tried to formulate a strategy. "Do you know how to get in touch with Dee-Dee now?"

Ty shrugged. "I guess her number's in my cell phone memory."

"Then call her. Not tonight. You'll seem too anxious. Call in the morning. Bite the bullet and get her over here tomorrow if possible. Let's have a face-to-face with her in my office. I need to understand her motives, get a read on her for myself."

"What about Trevor? I'm not ready for her to see him, not till we know how this is going to play out. Helen, I need to know if she's really serious or if this is just some game before I shake up my son's life."

"Tell your mom about what's going on. She can take the day off from the spa tomorrow and take Trevor on an outing. It'll be good for her, too. She needs a break from that place. She looked exhausted the last time I saw her."

"And you think spending the day with Trevor will relax her?" Ty asked incredulously. "Knowing her, she'll insist on taking Jessie and Cole along, too."

"Then she can take the nanny with them. The point is to take Trevor out of town for the day." She met Ty's gaze. "At the end of the day, though, it might be best to let Dee-Dee spend at least a few minutes with him. Supervised, of course. It'll show the court you're willing to be reasonable."

Ty scowled. "I'm not feeling very reasonable."

"Believe me, I understand that. Trust me, though. I know what I'm doing."

"I know that," Ty said. "That's why I'm here." He stood up. "Thanks, Helen. I'll get out of your hair now. Where's Erik, by the way?"

"He should be home from the restaurant any second now. They were swamped over there tonight. I'm sure he stuck around with Dana Sue and Karen to unwind. You provided the perfect distraction to keep me awake till he gets here."

She walked him to the door, then reached up to pat his cheek. "I know I'm wasting my breath, but stop worrying. We're going to solve this. In the end, we'll make sure whatever happens is what's best for Trevor."

Ty gave her a wry look. "That's all I care about. I'm just not sure I'm going to be able to live with the solution."

"My goal is to create a win-win for everyone, I promise you that," she assured him. "You and Trevor are too important to me for me to let you down." She grinned. "To say nothing of the fact that your mother would break my neck if I failed you."

Ty smiled for the first time since his arrival. "Nice to know someone else finds her as scary and formidable as I do."

"Maybe we should send *her* after Dee-Dee," Helen suggested.

"Now, that's a confrontation I'd like to see," he said, chuckling.

After he'd gone, Helen sat back down and rubbed her temples where she could feel the first faint throb of a headache coming on. Being upbeat for Ty's sake had taken a toll.

Just then, Flo walked in, leaning heavily on her new cane. "You were good with that boy," she said to Helen. "I suppose I never thought about how much of your work involved listening and counseling."

Helen regarded her mother with surprise. "You were eavesdropping?"

"I'd just made my way downstairs when he arrived." She grinned. "I didn't have it in me to try to go back up, so I stayed out of sight. Tyler's grown into quite a handsome man, hasn't he?"

"He has," Helen confirmed. "And he's already paid a heavy price for this mess he's in."

"You mean losing Dana Sue's daughter?"

Flo had once again surprised her. "Had I mentioned that?" Helen asked.

"Never had to. From the time those two were in their teens, I could see which way the wind was blowing. It's a shame it didn't work out."

"It still could," Helen said, not sure why she was feeling relatively optimistic about the possibility. Maybe it was being married so happily to Erik. It had rubbed the edges of her natural cynicism until they were all smoothed out. She saw possibilities she hadn't believed in a few short years ago.

She looked at her mother and realized that Flo was looking a little pale from her jaunt down the stairs. "Mom, did you come down for something in particular?"

"Just some company," Flo said. "There was nothing on TV worth watching."

"Would you like a little wine?"

"Maybe just a sip or two of yours," she said. "I do have to get back up those stairs."

"I'll get you your own glass. Erik can carry you up, if need be."

"Just like a knight in shining armor," Flo said, her expression filled with unmistakable longing. "I always wondered what that would be like."

"Me, too," Helen confided, then grinned. "And now I know."

Flo touched her hand as she headed for the kitchen for another wineglass. "I'm so happy you two found each other," she said sincerely. "I really am."

"Thanks, Mom."

When Helen came back with the wine for her mother, Flo had drifted off to sleep. Feeling oddly maternal toward the woman who had given birth to *her,* Helen draped a light throw across Flo's legs, then closed her own eyes.

Neither one of them woke when Erik came in and carried them, one at a time, up to their beds. In fact, Helen didn't wake until he slid into bed beside her. She snuggled against all that wonderfully familiar heat and strength.

"Knight in shining armor," she murmured.

"What?" Erik asked.

"You're mine."

Though he still sounded faintly bemused, Erik pulled her close. "Indeed I am," he whispered. "All yours."

Content for the first time in her very long day, Helen went back to sleep.

CHAPTER FOURTEEN

Annie had skipped too many breakfasts at Sullivan's lately. For once she'd been avoiding the unspoken questions about Ty, rather than food, but that didn't stop her mother from making subtle remarks expressing her concern. To prove there was no reason to worry, she headed to the restaurant on her lunch break, planning to grab one of Erik's excellent grilled sandwiches and eat in the kitchen while he, Karen and her mom worked.

When she arrived, though, she spotted Ty's car in the parking lot. Entering through the front door, rather than going around back to the kitchen, she glanced around the dining room and spotted him in a booth with Helen and a young woman she didn't recognize. The conversation appeared to be heated.

Any thought she might have had about stopping by the table died when she realized that the woman might very well be Trevor's mother.

Lingering in the shadows, she took a closer look. Dee-Dee, if it was her, looked to be in her early twenties with professionally highlighted blond hair, flawless makeup and an engagement ring so huge she could barely lift her hand.

Her clothes were trendy but sedate. Annie regarded her with surprise. This woman looked more like a young socialite than some impetuous wild child who'd abandon her own baby. Had she really made such an amazing transformation, or had Annie's jaded impression been wrong from the beginning?

She saw Helen glance her way and froze, praying that she wouldn't mention Annie's presence. When Helen turned back without acknowledging her, Annie took that as a sign that an interruption definitely wouldn't be welcome, and slipped into the kitchen. Her mom looked up and gave her a distracted smile, then took another look at Annie and frowned.

"What's wrong?" Dana Sue asked at once.

"Ty's out there," Annie admitted. "With Helen and someone else. I think it might be Trevor's mom."

Dana Sue winced. "Damn. I forgot about that. I would have called and warned you, but I had no idea you were stopping by. You haven't been around much lately."

"I decided to come for lunch," Annie said. "I had a craving for one of Erik's grilled Italian sandwich specials."

He acknowledged her with a wave. "Coming right up," he told her, and continued arranging the day's catfish special on a row of plates that were ready to be served.

Annie turned her attention back to her mom. "So that's Dee-Dee?"

Her mother nodded. "Helen introduced us when they came in. I have to say she's not what I envisioned."

"Me, neither," Annie said glumly. "You know she wants to be involved in Trevor's life. I suppose that's why she's here. Ty's furious about it, and scared, I think."

"Believe me, Helen will protect his interests," Dana Sue said. "You know what a pit bull she is when anyone tries to harm one of her own. As far as she's concerned, Ty's family."

Annie recalled how vehemently Helen had fought for

Dana Sue when Annie's dad had cheated on her. She'd even convinced Ronnie that Annie and Dana Sue would be better off if he left Serenity. Instead, that had been a disaster and a key trigger for Annie's anorexia. It had also been proof that Helen wasn't infallible.

Still, despite how that situation had turned out, Annie was reassured for Ty. Having Helen in his corner was definitely a good thing.

She had to admit, though, that seeing Dee-Dee in person and not in some hideous tabloid photo had thrown her. She'd always told herself Ty was an idiot for getting involved with someone so far beneath him. In some ways, that thought had consoled her. Now she had to question if that was true. For all she'd been able to tell by seeing the self-possessed young woman just now, Dee-Dee could have better breeding than anyone Annie knew. Not that social standing was what mattered. It certainly couldn't change what she'd done.

Annie barely noticed when Erik slid a plate onto the counter in front of her. Even so, the aroma of Italian salami, prosciutto, cheese and tomato, grilled to gooey perfection, tempted her. She bit into the thick sandwich. "Delicious," she called out, her mouth full. "When are you going to put this on the menu all the time?"

"It doesn't fit in with your mother's Southern cuisine ideas," Erik said. "I have to sneak it on when I can."

"Because it's an Italian sandwich," Dana Sue retorted, in what had clearly become a familiar argument.

"Oh, for goodness' sake, just call it a grilled cheese special and be done with it," Annie said. "Those are universal. Isn't that what you do, interesting spins on Southern comfort food?"

"She has a point," Erik said, clearly delighting in Annie's take on the controversy.

Dana Sue frowned at Annie for taking Erik's side. "Okay, I'll think about it," she conceded grumpily.

Just then the kitchen door swung open and Ty walked in. Dana Sue turned her frown on him. "You're not supposed to be back here," she told him.

Ty didn't appear to be daunted by her tone. "Neither is she," he said, pointing at Annie.

"She's my daughter," Dana Sue reminded him. "That gives her special privileges."

Ty crossed the kitchen and snuggled up to Dana Sue's side, stealing a sliver of carrot while he was at it. "And you're one of my moms," he said, giving her his most roguish smile. "You know you love me."

Annie lifted her glass of tea in a silent toast, congratulating him for his smooth move.

Dana Sue gave him a considering look. "Some days not so much," she told him. "And why are you in here, anyway, when you have a guest out there?"

Ty pulled out the stool next to Annie's and sat down, stealing the other half of her sandwich and taking a bite. Annie scowled at him. "Were they not serving in the dining room?"

"Sitting there with Dee-Dee pretty much killed my appetite. I needed a break before I said something that might ruin Helen's delicate negotiations. The meeting started off well enough in Helen's office, but then she suggested continuing over lunch. I argued against it and especially against coming here, but Dee-Dee said she'd read something about this place online and she wanted to see for herself if the food was as great as the article had said."

"How are the negotiations going?" Annie asked.

Ty shrugged. "Early stages. Right now they're just trying to work out a very quick meeting between Dee-Dee and

Trevor today. I'm all for her driving by and waving. She and Helen are negotiating for something slightly longer."

"She's not what I expected," Annie blurted before she could stop herself.

"Trust me, she's not exactly the woman I remember, either. I don't think I ever saw her wearing anything besides tank tops and shorts."

"Which one do you think is the real Dee-Dee?"

"Either. Both." He shrugged. "Maybe people really can change." He finished off the half sandwich he'd taken from her plate and stood up. "I guess I should go back. With any luck, I'll be able to keep my temper in check a little longer. I just have to keep telling myself I don't want Trevor to miss out on knowing his mom, as long as she'll be a good influence in his life."

"Good luck," Annie said.

"Thanks. See you at the gym tonight?"

"You'll still be able to get there?" she asked, wondering if Dee-Dee's visit would be dragging on.

"That's my plan," he said, "but if anything changes due to circumstances beyond my control, I'll call you." He started away, turned back and planted a kiss on her cheek, then winked. "For luck, and before you say anything, we're not at the gym."

After he'd gone, her mother immediately took his place on the stool next to Annie's. "Mind telling me what he meant by that?"

"He kissed me the other night," she admitted. "We agreed he wouldn't do it again."

A smile spread slowly across her mom's face. "But this agreement only applied at the spa?"

Annie nodded. "That was the loophole," she confirmed.

Dana Sue chuckled. "I know another man who's sneaky like that."

Annie met her gaze. "Dad?"

"Exactly."

For some reason the comparison improved Annie's mood considerably. Knowing her mom hadn't been able to resist a scoundrel like Ronnie Sullivan made her feel a whole lot better about her weakening resolve where Ty was concerned.

Ty was just about at his wit's end. Dee-Dee had managed to convince Helen that an hour-long visit with Trevor was not unreasonable. It was to take place in a neutral setting, such as the park, and Ty would be present throughout. There would be no alone time between Dee-Dee and their son. Even so, Ty was on edge about the ramifications. Once Dee-Dee had a toehold in Trevor's life, would things ever be the same again?

To top it off, because they'd sent Trevor away for the day with Maddie, they could only meet in the early evening. Since Ty had no idea how Trevor was likely to react to spending time with his mom, Ty had to stick around afterward to answer any questions he might have. That meant canceling his workout.

Worse, if all went well, Helen had suggested another meeting in the morning—breakfast at Wharton's—before Dee-Dee left town.

After Dee-Dee had gone back to her room at the Serenity Inn to await the scheduled meeting time with Trevor, Ty had expressed his dismay to Helen. Once again she'd reminded him of the importance of appearing reasonable and cooperative.

"Besides, if the judge does grant Dee-Dee some rights to spend time with Trevor, you want them to be acquainted.

You don't want it to be traumatic for him, like going off with a stranger."

Ty scowled at the implication. "Trevor isn't going off with anybody," he reiterated. "I draw the line at that." He met Helen's gaze, then sighed. "Okay, I know it may come to that, but not for a long, long time, not till we're absolutely sure that this transformation of Dee-Dee's is real."

"She definitely makes a good impression now," Helen reminded him.

"She may have a little more class on the outside, but the reckless, irresponsible Dee-Dee I knew is still in there," he said, unwilling to believe she'd changed so much.

"Well, I think you're going to have to face that this isn't a ploy to get money from you, Ty. Judging from the size of that ring she's wearing and her designer clothes, she has all the money she needs."

"Everyone wants more money," Ty said cynically. "Even people who have plenty."

"Well, she's going to have to be the one to ask for it," Helen warned. "Don't you dare even hint that you're willing to pay her off to get rid of her. She'll use it to destroy you, especially if I'm right that she only wants to have her son back in her life."

"Okay, okay," he said, regretting that the situation couldn't be resolved that easily.

After Helen left, he walked over to The Corner Spa and found Annie with a client. "Can you meet me on the patio when you have a break?"

Annie glanced at her watch. "It'll be about fifteen minutes," she told him. "And I won't have long."

"That's okay. I'll grab a couple of glasses of tea."

He stopped to speak to Elliott, then got the tea in the café and went outside. It was blessedly deserted. Though the temperature had climbed along with the humidity, a breeze made it bearable in the shade. He settled down to wait. It was only a minute or two before Annie slipped into the chair next to his. He lifted a brow questioningly.

"You looked upset," she explained. "My client told me to come on out. She'll finish up on her own."

"Sorry."

"It's not a problem. What's up?"

"I have to cancel tonight."

"Dee-Dee's staying," she guessed right away.

"Yes, and I have to take Trevor to the park to meet her." He shook his head. "It sounds weird just to say it. Kids shouldn't have to be introduced to their own mothers."

"This is an unusual circumstance," Annie said. "I can't even imagine how you must feel. Or even Dee-Dee, for that matter. She's probably scared out of her wits."

"Don't waste any sympathy on her. She looked pretty together when she insisted on this," Ty said.

"Sure, but come on, Ty, you know she must wonder what's going to happen when they meet. What if Trevor hates her on sight and screams his head off?"

"Trevor doesn't take an instant dislike to anyone," Ty said.

Annie gave him a knowing look. "And that's what really scares you, isn't it? You don't really want them to get along."

Ty flushed guiltily. "That's awful of me, isn't it? When I'm being rational, even I can see that."

"I'd say it's human." Annie started to cover his hand with hers, then withdrew. "I'm really sorry you're going through this. I wish I could help."

Ty met her gaze. "You mean that?"

"Of course."

"You could come along."

Annie stared at him incredulously. "Are you crazy? I've

only been around Trevor twice, and for about two seconds each time. You don't want him dealing with two strangers."

"Is it really that, or do you not want to get drawn into my drama?"

"That, too," she said candidly. "I'm on your side, that's a given, but I can't be in the middle of this fight, Ty. I just can't be."

Ty was disappointed, but he understood. He'd been asking too much. Still, it would have been nice to have Annie in his corner, not just figuratively but literally.

"I guess I'll just have to deal with this like a grown-up," he said grimly.

Annie smiled. "Guess so." This time when she reached for his hand, he turned his over and clasped hers. She didn't pull away. "You're a great dad, Ty. You're going to do what's best for Trevor. It'll be fine."

As scared as he was about how the whole situation was going to play out, her words comforted him. "Thanks. I'd better get going. Too bad about those painkillers, because I sure wouldn't mind a drink."

"Before taking your son to the park? Wouldn't that be pretty?" she chided.

"What would I do if I didn't have you to be my conscience?"

Annie regarded him with absolute confidence. "The right thing," she said softly. "Always."

Ty wished he were half as certain about that as she seemed to be. Her faith in him, despite the way he'd failed her, left him humbled.

After two hours of commiserating with Sarah about the time Ty was off spending with Trevor's mom, and drinking three margaritas, Annie giggled, her bad mood lost in a sea of tequila.

"What?" Sarah demanded, looking a little dazed herself.

"Do you suppose it was like this all those times my mom got together with Helen and Maddie?" Annie asked. "Why am I even asking? Of course it was. They let me come to one of their Sweet Magnolia margarita nights not long ago. Did I tell you that?"

"Several times," Sarah said, leaning back against the sofa, her eyes half closed. "You and me, we're kind of like the Sweet Magnolias. We've known each other since grade school, just like they did."

"That's right. We're the new generation of Sweet Magnolias," Annie said, lifting her glass and waving it around precariously. Amazingly, only a few drops of her drink sloshed out. "You know what? I think we should call Raylene. She can be a new Sweet Magnolia, too."

Sarah squinted at the clock. "It's nearly midnight. Are you sure?"

"Just think of all the people who wish they had friends who'd call 'em at this hour," Annie said. "Lots of people have no one."

"I'm just thinking that maybe the first time she hears from us after all this time, it ought to be at a civilized hour and maybe we ought to be sober," Sarah argued.

"Stick in the mud," Annie accused. "Besides, I want to hear her take on Ty. You're obviously totally biased where he's concerned. He says a few sweet things to you and you get all softhearted and sympathetic. I can't trust your opinion."

"That's a lousy thing to say," Sarah protested. "But he does seem to be trying. You have to admit that."

"Don't have to admit anything," Annie said staunchly,

digging in her purse until she found her cell phone. "Here it is," she announced triumphantly.

"You found your phone. Other than proving that you still have limited eye-hand coordination, what's the big deal?" Sarah scoffed.

"Not the phone. Raylene's number." She was dialing before Sarah could stop her. When she finally heard the sound of her friend's sleepy voice, she suffered a momentary pang of guilt. Still, she spoke cheerfully, "Hey, girlfriend, guess who this is?"

"Annie," Raylene said at once, sounding shocked. "Are you drunk?"

Annie paused thoughtfully. "Could be," she admitted. "Sarah, too. Want to say hi to her?" She shoved the phone toward her friend.

"Hey, Raylene. I tried to stop her," Sarah said. "I hope we didn't wake up everyone in your house."

Annie watched as Sarah's eyes widened. "Really? Emergency surgery? Does that happen a lot? Yeah, I'm sure it's one of the trials of being a doctor's wife."

Annie grabbed the phone back. "So, Raylene, how about getting together one of these days? Sarah and I would love to see you. We've been talking about the old days, when the three of us hung out together all the time."

"I really, really don't have any desire to set foot in Serenity again," Raylene said flatly.

"That's okay," Annie said, not even trying to defend the town. Raylene's family had never felt at home here. Her mother had come from an old Charleston family and had always thought she was better than most everyone in town. It wasn't surprising that Raylene eventually had picked up her attitude. It had started when she'd attended a debutante ball and had her first real taste of the life her mom had once been accustomed to.

"Sarah and I will come to you," Annie offered. "How about lunch one day next week?"

"I don't know," Raylene said at once. "My schedule's pretty full. I'm on half a dozen fundraising committees and we're planning for the fall social season right now. It's worse than having a full-time job. My time's just not my own. Why don't I check my calendar and get back to you?" The excuses tripped off her tongue.

Even with her faculties impaired by margaritas, Annie knew a dismissal when she heard it. "Yeah, you just let us know. Good to hear your voice, though."

"Yours, too," Raylene said, sounding relieved that Annie hadn't pressed her.

Annie hung up and regarded Sarah with puzzlement. "She completely blew us off."

"Her life's moved on, that's all," Sarah said, defending her. "And it's not as if either of us have done much to stay in touch with her before now. We all went our own separate ways."

Annie considered that, but she wasn't totally satisfied with the explanation. It was something she'd heard in Raylene's voice. Behind the too-quick dismissal, there'd been a note of something that sounded almost like fear. She replayed the conversation in her head. Yes, that was definitely what she'd heard. Not condescension, but fear.

"Maybe her life's a mess and she doesn't want us to know," she suggested slowly. "I'll bet that's it. Here it is a Friday night, and her husband's in surgery after midnight. Come on. That can't be good."

"I'm sure a lot of accidents happen on the weekend," Sarah replied. "People need to have bones set."

"I suppose," Annie said. In fact, she knew for a fact it

was possible, but something had sounded off to her, as off as Sarah's voice had sounded when she first got to town, as off as Annie's own voice no doubt sounded when she talked about Ty.

But she and Sarah talked openly about their problems. Annie found it worrisome that Raylene might not. Then, again, it was practically the middle of the night.

"I think we need to stay in touch with her," she said eventually.

Sarah blinked. "You're seriously worried. Why?"

"Instinct, I guess."

"After three margaritas, I'm not sure you can trust what you think you see, much less your instincts."

"Still, it won't hurt to call again in a couple of weeks. Isn't that what real friends do, hang in there even when the other person claims to be just fine? You two certainly did that for me back in high school. This is me trying to return the favor."

With any luck, maybe it was just the tequila clouding her judgment, but she didn't think so. Whatever the reason, she had a feeling their friend was in some kind of trouble, trouble she didn't want them to discover.

CHAPTER FIFTEEN

Annie felt as if she'd been run over by a truck. She was sitting at the kitchen table at home in the morning, trying to decide whether to live or die, when her dad walked in. He started toward the coffeemaker, then came back and took a closer look at her.

"What happened to you?" he asked, his expression troubled.

Annie had seen that look far too often. She'd learned to ignore it from her mom, but Ronnie was another story. He knew a little too much about lies and evasions to buy them from her. Straightforward honesty was the only way to go.

"Sarah and I had delusions about being Sweet Magnolias," she said. "We had a margarita night."

The crease in his forehead eased. "Yeah, I recognize the signs. I've seen your mom look this bad on one or two occasions."

"Did she live?" Annie inquired.

"You know she did, though I'm sure there were times when she didn't much want to. Come on, kiddo. You need more than coffee. Let's go to Wharton's."

"Food?" Annie questioned, gagging at the thought. "I don't think so."

"Grace has all the ingredients for my guaranteed hangover concoction."

"Mom runs an entire restaurant. Don't we have the ingredients here? I don't think I can actually move, much less walk."

"Yes, you can. The fresh air will do you good," he said. He tucked a hand under her elbow and pulled her to her feet. "There you go. See. That wasn't so bad."

"My head is spinning," she warned him.

"Stand there a second. It'll stop."

"You know way too much about this."

"I've had my moments, though in the very distant past," he assured her, his tone virtuous. "What time are you due at work today, by the way?"

"Noon, thank goodness."

"Okay, then, we have time to get you whipped back into shape. We'll walk to Wharton's. You'll sweat some of the alcohol out of your system. Walking this time of year is better than going to a steam room."

Annie stared at him incredulously. "My clients think I have a sadistic streak," she muttered. "Now I know where I got it."

"All this is for your own good," Ronnie assured her.

"That's what I tell them," she said, resigned to going along with her father's wishes, just as her clients usually caved in to hers.

The walk to Wharton's was torture. Her dad kept up a running pep talk, which was almost as annoying as the fact that he wouldn't slow down. Amazingly, though, by the time they reached Wharton's, Annie was miserably hot, but she felt almost human again. She doubted she looked it.

That made it doubly bad that the first people they encountered when they walked into the old-fashioned drugstore with its soda fountain and booths were Ty, Trevor and Dee-Dee, who looked as if she'd just stepped out of the pages of *Town & Country.*

Ty glanced up, caught sight of Annie and did a double take. "What the hell?" he murmured.

Annie didn't pause long enough to satisfy his curiosity. Her father, however, did stop. Whatever he said had Ty looking over his shoulder and shaking his head.

"What did you tell him?" Annie demanded when Ronnie joined her.

"That you and Sarah had a margarita night."

"Because of him?" Annie asked. "Please tell me you did not say it was because of him."

Ronnie looked bewildered. "I didn't know Ty had anything to do with it. I thought you girls were just trying to follow in your mom's footsteps with the Sweet Magnolias' tradition. What did Ty do?"

Annie considered the question, probably for longer than it deserved. "Nothing, when you get right down to it. I mean not recently, anyway. It's that woman."

Understanding finally dawned on her father's face. "Trevor's mother?"

Annie nodded. "I didn't expect her to be so, I don't know, put together, beautiful."

Ronnie glanced in Dee-Dee's direction. "Superficial," he said, dismissing her. "Anybody can achieve that look with the right clothes and makeup."

"I expected a floozy," Annie said disconsolately.

Ronnie gave her a knowing look. "Would that really have made this situation any better?"

She gave the question the thought it deserved. "No," she

admitted eventually. "Especially if she's going to get her way and be a part of Trevor's life. He should have a good mom."

"Exactly," Ronnie said, apparently proud that she'd grasped the importance of that.

"I don't want to like her," Annie grumbled.

Her dad smiled. "You don't have to."

Grace appeared just then with two cups of strong coffee and a glass of what looked innocently enough like tomato juice. Annie suspected it wasn't. "What's that?" she inquired suspiciously.

"Trust me," her dad said.

"It's good for what ails you," Grace concurred.

Annie took a tentative sip that burned all the way down. "Good grief! What is in that?" she asked, after swallowing a huge gulp of water as an ineffective chaser.

"A little of this, a little of that," Grace said. "Probably best if I don't tell you right now."

"Oh, sweet heaven," Annie moaned. "I can't drink a whole glass of that stuff. My entire esophagus will rot."

No sooner had she said that than Ty slid into the booth next to her, blocking her exit. Trevor climbed up beside Ronnie.

"Come on now," Ty coaxed, regarding her with sympathy and a hint of amusement that he was trying unsuccessfully to hide. "You'll feel better once you've chugged that down."

"You've had this awful stuff before?"

"On occasion," he said, trying to maintain an innocent expression.

"How many occasions?" she asked.

"The first couple of times your dad, Cal and Erik let me hang out with them."

"The man can't hold his beer," Ronnie said with a sigh. "It's a pitiful thing."

"Not when it's interspersed with shots of liquor, that's for sure," Ty said with a shudder. "Learned my lesson."

"Really? Then why did you ever have a second occasion to need this vile drink?" Annie asked. "Are you a slow learner?"

Ty laughed. "Could be."

Annie wanted to ask him a million questions about how things had gone between Dee-Dee and Trevor, but she couldn't with Trevor right there. As if he knew what was on her mind, her dad picked up Trevor and slid from the booth.

"Looks like my work here is done," he said. "I'm going across the street to open the store. Mind if my pal here goes along with me? I'll teach him how to use tools."

"He's three," Ty reminded him. "Tools may not be the best things to let him play with."

"I put your first hammer in your hand when you were about this age," Ronnie reminded him. "But not to worry. I have plastic sets for kids that'll be just right."

"Okay, then," Ty said. He looked at his son. "You want to go with Ronnie for a little while?"

Trevor nodded and patted Ronnie's cheek. "We buddies, right?"

"We are definitely buddies," Ronnie agreed.

Annie's eyes filled with tears at the sweetness of the moment. She turned away so none of them would see how sad it made her to see Ronnie with Ty's son in his arms, a child she had no claim to, a child that should have been Ronnie's grandson but wasn't.

"We gonna build things," Trevor announced enthusiastically.

"Absolutely," Ronnie replied.

"Then by all means, go and enjoy yourselves," Ty said. "I'll be by in a few minutes to pick him up."

"Take your time," Ronnie told them. "See if you can get our girl to eat something."

As soon as her father had walked away, Annie shot a daunting look at Ty. "Don't even try. My stomach's not up to it."

"Toast," he contradicted, waving to get Grace's attention and then placing the order.

"You're as bossy as ever, I see."

"Comes from having to remind a three-year-old who's in charge," he claimed.

Annie took a sip of her coffee, decided it was worth the risk, then took another before asking, "How'd it go with Dee-Dee and Trevor?"

Ty regarded her with concern. "You sure you want to talk about this?"

"Why not? Otherwise, it'll just be one of those huge elephants in the living room that everyone pretends to ignore."

"In that case, it went okay," he conceded. "She was really good with him. She didn't press too hard or expect too much."

Though it was a great answer for Trevor's sake, Annie had a hunch Ty hated admitting it as much as she disliked hearing it. "That's good, I guess," she said.

Ty nodded, though he looked miserable. "I could see how this could work. I just don't like it. I don't trust that it's going to last, and then where will Trevor be?"

"That may be one reason, but I'll bet I know another," Annie said.

"Oh?"

"Because you've had him all to yourself for three years." She nudged him in the ribs. "You never did like sharing. I remember back when we were kids when your mom had Kyle and then Katie, you didn't want to share anything with them. You were the worst."

A grin slowly spread across his face. "I was, wasn't I? I guess that hasn't changed."

"This must be a thousand times harder, because Trevor's your son. You want the best for him, but up until now *you* were what was best."

"That all makes perfect sense, and I know you're right about why I feel the way I do, but what am I supposed to do about it?" Ty asked. "I'm afraid I don't have any control over the situation."

"Letting go, even a little, must seem scary as hell," Annie said. "Keep in mind, though, that you have Helen. She knows more about controlling things than you or I will learn in a lifetime."

"I'm counting on that," he said.

He looked so sad, Annie wanted to put her arms around him, but she resisted the urge. She did put her hand over his. "You're going to figure this out, and it will be fine."

"I just wish I knew why this suddenly matters so much to Dee-Dee. For three years she didn't send Trevor so much as a card for his birthday or Christmas. She never called me or even Jay to find out how he was. Now this? I just don't get it."

"Maybe it's as simple as what she told you," Annie suggested. "She's turned her life around, is settling down and needs to make peace with the past and get to know her little boy. She must have a thousand regrets over how she handled things."

"Hogwash!" Ty said succinctly. "More likely, she decided on a whim that she wants something and is reaching out and grabbing for it, without giving one single thought to the consequences. When the whim passes, she'll disappear again."

"Does Helen think this is a whim?"

He shook his head.

"She's pretty good at reading people, especially in circumstances like this," Annie reminded him. "How about your mom? Has she met Dee-Dee yet?"

Ty shook his head. "She still seems a little too eager to rip out Dee-Dee's heart for everything she did, ruining my relationship with you and abandoning Trevor. I think it's best to keep them apart for the time being."

Annie gave him a penetrating look. "You might want to remind her that Dee-Dee did not make that baby alone."

Ty grimaced. "Believe me, I've heard my share of lectures on the topic. There's definitely plenty of blame to go around."

"But you are Maddie's precious firstborn," Annie teased.

Ty grinned. "It does give me a slight edge in the forgiveness department," he agreed, then sighed. "I really did make a mess of things, didn't I?"

"But you took on your responsibilities and have tried to learn from your mistakes," Annie said, surprising herself by giving him credit for that much.

Ty studied her. "Does that mean you could maybe start trusting me again?"

She hesitated, knowing what she wanted, what he needed to hear, but scared silly of the risk of saying it aloud. She and Ty were a lot alike when it came to facing the uncertainties of the future.

He gave her a weary smile. "Your silence speaks volumes," he said.

Annie considered correcting him, telling him he'd gotten it all wrong, but maybe it was better this way. His interpretation might keep her heart safe just a little longer.

Ty showed up at the high school ball field just as practice was ending. Cal had sent the players to the locker room, then lingered to help the team's equipment managers collect the bats, balls and gloves. When he caught sight of Ty, he re-garded him with surprise.

"I thought you'd vowed not to come around here until you were back to a hundred percent," he said to Ty.

"I was hoping for a favor," Ty admitted.

"Name it," Cal said at once.

"How about tossing a few balls with me?" He nodded to-ward the two boys who were gathering the equipment and sending surreptitious glances in their direction. "Once they're gone, that is. I don't want any spectators around."

Cal frowned at the request. "Are you sure you're ready for that?"

Ty shrugged. "There's only one way to find out."

Cal gestured toward the bleachers. Side by side, they crossed the field. Cal took a seat next to Ty. "I know how impatient you are," he said. "But do you really want to risk a setback?"

Ty gave him a bleak look. "I need to know."

"But you're not going to know anything, really. You'll be throwing hurt." He gave Ty a commiserating look. "Look, you know I've been exactly where you are. I had the same fears."

"And what? You played by the book? Did every step of rehab exactly the way they told you to? How'd that turn out?" Ty demanded, already aware of the answer. Cal had never played in a major league game again. Ty needed to know if that was his fate, as well. If his playing days were over, it was going to require a huge adjustment, not just fi-nancially, but in the way he thought about himself and what he wanted.

"It wouldn't have changed anything if I'd rushed things," Cal said.

"You'd have known that much sooner," Ty corrected.

"No," Cal told him. "I'd have known that the pain was making it impossible for me to get a decent fastball over homeplate. I wouldn't have known if I could do it once my shoulder had healed."

Ty sighed, his frustration mounting. "I hate this. All of it. The waiting around to see if I still have a career. Dealing with Dee-Dee. Being scared spitless that I could lose my son."

"You're not going to lose Trevor," Cal said forcefully. "You might have to share custody, but that's the worst that's going to happen. Frankly, I don't think it will even go that far."

"I don't want to think so, either, but I need to face facts. If Dee-Dee marries some nice, respectable guy and can provide Trevor with everything I can, who's the judge going to choose?"

"The man who's been in that little boy's life practically from day one, raising Trevor on his own," Cal said without hesitation. He glanced sideways at Ty. "You're not going to let me cheer you up, are you?"

Ty shook his head. "I don't know why it started getting to me so bad today. It could have been seeing Dee-Dee with Trevor this morning at Wharton's. He was giggling and crawling into her lap as if they'd never been apart. And then there was Annie, the woman who should have been the mother of my kids, a couple of booths away, looking miserable." His lips curved slightly. "Of course, some of that was due to overindulgence in margaritas last night, but still, I feel this huge rush of guilt every time I see her."

Cal gave him a knowing look. "How badly do you want Annie back?" he asked.

"As much as I want to keep my son with me," Ty admitted.

"Then fight for her, Ty. Don't sit around giving her space or waiting for her forgiveness. Be in her face every chance you get, prove to her that she's the only woman who matters to you, and don't stop trying until she believes you."

"I don't know..." Ty began, but Cal interrupted.

"Ty, now's not the time to hesitate. Once Dee-Dee starts hanging around more, or if she does, it'll be a constant reminder to Annie of what happened. When that day comes, make sure Annie already knows with absolute certainty that it will not happen again. Not with Dee-Dee, not with anyone else."

"Annie can't be rushed," Ty argued. "She likes to do things at her own pace."

"Every woman likes to be courted, Ty. If I'd sat back and given your mom too much time to think, too many chances to talk herself out of marrying me, where do you think we'd be today?"

Ty considered Cal's advice and realized he was right, at least when it had come to his courtship of Ty's mom. Maddie'd had plenty of excuses for turning her back on the relationship, including the fact that initially Ty had freaked over the thought of his mom dating his much-younger baseball coach.

Of course, Cal hadn't come into Maddie's life with the baggage Ty had with Annie. That was a huge hurdle to overcome. Maybe, though, it was time he dedicated himself to really trying and stopped being put off by Annie's protests.

He glanced at Cal. "You sure we can't toss the ball around for a while?"

"Go find Annie," Cal advised.

"I'm seeing her later at the spa."

"Any reason you can't surprise her now? Maybe take her some flowers. Nothing too elaborate. Maybe daisies, since you said she liked them." Cal grinned. "Your mom says that's a sweet gesture. I'm here to tell you it works like a damn charm."

Ty looked skeptical. "Daisies?"

"Pick 'em yourself, if you can find some in bloom. That's always a nice touch."

Ty recalled the frequent bouquets of flowers popping up at home and in Maddie's office. Cal obviously followed his own advice. "Did you pass along all this touchy-feely stuff when you were playing ball?" Ty asked. "If so, maybe that's why your career ended up down the tubes. Your sensitive side was freaking out your macho teammates."

Cal didn't looked particularly embarrassed by the suggestion. "I wound up with your mom, didn't I? The advice can't be all bad."

"Good point," Ty conceded, then grinned. "And I know exactly where to find some daisies."

Fifteen minutes later Ty was at his grandma Paula's house. His mom's mother, Paula Vreeland, was a renowned artist whose botanical prints were hung in galleries all over the country, but were especially popular in Charleston and the surrounding area. These days arthritis had taken a toll on her hands, so she was painting less, but she continued to garden. Her backyard was a colorful masterpiece in its own right.

When she opened the door to Ty, surprise and delight lit her eyes. "It's about time you came to see me, young man. Where's Trevor?"

"He's at home. I had an impulse while I was out and came straight over here."

"Uh-oh," she said. "Don't tell me you're here for some of my lemonade and cookies. I haven't baked in weeks."

Ty put an arm around her shoulders and noticed that the once tall, vibrant force of nature that she had been seemed to have shrunk since the last time he'd seen her. "How about the lemonade?" he teased. "Have any of that?"

"I think I could find a pitcher in the fridge," she said. "Now, tell me why you're really here."

"I was thinking about your garden earlier."

She studied him. "Oh? Why the sudden interest? You always hated it when I made you go out and weed for me."

"Still would," he admitted without hesitation. "But I was hoping maybe your daisies are in bloom and you wouldn't mind if I stole a few."

An immediate twinkle lit her eyes. "You've been talking to Cal," she guessed. "I swear, there are times I can't keep that man out of my garden. Your mother said one thing about liking daisies and he was over here all the time." Her expression turned dreamy. "Women love a man with a romantic streak."

"Was Grandpa like that?" Ty asked. His memories of the man were dim. All he recalled were long, dry discussions and constant admonitions about making too much noise. He'd seemed an odd contrast to his grandmother's free spirit.

"Heavens no," she said at once. "I'm not even sure he knew we had a garden. I was lucky if he poked his head out of the library long enough to have dinner with me. That's what I get for marrying a stuffy professor."

"Mom says you all would take off on a whim all the time," Ty recalled. "That must have been romantic."

"I suppose it was," she said. "We certainly saw the world over the years. I doubt there's a major art museum anywhere we didn't visit at one time or another."

She poured two glasses of lemonade as she talked, then led the way into the garden, which was filled with so many colors and fragrances it took a minute to absorb the beauty of it. She grabbed a pair of clippers from a workbench and handed them to Ty, then pointed across the path to a huge display of white daisies.

"Don't destroy the plant," she instructed. "Leave some blooms for me to enjoy."

Ty recalled how many times he'd gotten in trouble for not doing things exactly as she'd told him to. "Maybe you should cut them," he said.

"Do you want to tell Annie that I put her bouquet together, instead of you? It is for Annie, isn't it?"

Ty nodded.

"About time," Paula said. "You've been dragging your feet too long, instead of making things right with her. Cal was certainly on the money to give you a push."

Ty stared at her. "Do the two of you sit around over here and discuss matchmaking strategies?"

"You'd be surprised what Cal and I have discussed over the years," his grandmother said. "It's a wise man who knows to listen to the advice of someone older. Besides, I owe him a little free advice for helping to bridge the gap between your mother and me. For too many years I neglected her, and we both knew I disapproved of her marriage to your father. It wasn't until Bill was out of her life and Cal was hanging around that we began to see eye to eye about anything."

She gestured toward the daisies. "Get over there and start snipping. You'll want a large bouquet if you're going to get Annie's attention. And it's too hot for me to be sitting around out here all afternoon supervising."

Ty cut the flowers under her watchful eye until he had more than enough. His grandmother found some blue-and-yellow plaid ribbon in the house and showed him how to tie a bow around the stems. She insisted he do that himself, as well. It was a little lopsided, but the effect, he supposed, was charming. Despite his earlier doubts, he could imagine Annie's delighted reaction.

"Thanks, Grandma Paula."

"Anytime. Now, bring that great-grandson of mine over here the next time you come or don't bother showing up."

"I'll do that," he promised.

"And don't wait too much longer, either. I'm not getting any younger."

"You'll always be young," he said, kissing her cheek. "Thanks for the flowers."

"No problem," she said. "And, Ty, don't fret too much about Trevor's mom. Something tells me that's all going to work out."

He opened his mouth to ask how she knew about Dee-Dee, but closed it again. This was, after all, Serenity, where news—good and bad—traveled at warp speed.

CHAPTER SIXTEEN

Every single client Annie had worked with today had been difficult, including Sarah. Or maybe it was simply that she still felt lousy, so she took every comment about her tough regimens to heart. When Sarah moaned that Annie was torturing her, Annie lost it.

"Do you want to get this weight off and get healthy or not?" she asked. "It's not going to disappear just by wishing it away."

Sarah's eyes widened at her sharp tone and insensitivity. But rather than snapping back, she asked, "Are you okay?"

The genuine concern in Sarah's voice fueled Annie's guilt over her thoughtless words. "I'm sorry, Sarah, and no, I am not okay. Not only do I have a raging headache and look awful, but who do I see first thing this morning but Ty, with Trevor's mom, the beauty queen."

Sarah blinked. "Was she really a beauty queen?"

"I have no idea," Annie said, still unable to keep her impatience in check. "I just meant she looked a thousand times better than I did."

Obviously battling her own hangover—and without the benefit of Ronnie's special cure—Sarah struggled to keep up. "You're jealous of a woman Ty has absolutely zero interest in?" she asked incredulously.

"Of course not," Annie retorted, then sighed. "Okay, probably. She *is* Trevor's mother. That gives them a connection Ty and I will never have."

"Unless you get married and have kids of your own," Sarah suggested.

"Not going to happen," Annie said with certainty.

"Because he's not interested or because you're too scared?"

Sometimes it sucked having a friend who knew how easy it was to cave in to your own fears. Annie scowled at her. "Yes, I'm scared. Can you blame me? Just when I'm starting to admit to myself that I still have feelings for Ty, along comes this Dee-Dee person to remind me of why we broke up."

"Forget about Dee-Dee," Sarah advised. "I really don't think she's an issue. Ty loves you."

Annie wanted to believe her, but how could she? The existence of Trevor was a day-in, day-out reminder of Ty's betrayal. To have Dee-Dee in the picture as well was almost unbearable, especially this new, apparently improved, classy Dee-Dee.

"Could you honestly say you'd be perfectly calm and rational if some ex of Walter's showed up?" Annie asked her friend.

Sarah grinned. "No, but I am learning to be open to possibilities again with Walter. Don't you think you should do the same with Ty? I'm amazed at how a little change in attitude can make such a huge difference."

"Maybe it's easier for you because you and Walter are actually married. You made a commitment, for better or worse. You have a family you want to save. What do Ty and I have?"

"A love that's lasted for most of your life," Sarah reminded her. "At least since you were old enough to know the meaning of the word. I swear, I think you fell for him in kindergarten. I know I started hearing Ty said this and Ty said that around that time."

Despite her generally foul mood, Annie chuckled. "You can't remember that far back."

"Indeed, I can," Sarah insisted. "The minute the first-graders would come outside for recess, you always headed straight for Ty—much to his disgust, I might add. My point is that the two of you have something worth fighting for. There's history there and friendship, to say nothing of love."

"Letting go of the anger isn't that easy," Annie argued. There were times lately when she'd almost done it, when she'd let herself really feel what was in her heart, but the power of that emotion had scared her right back into her protective shell. "Besides, who says Ty wants to get back together?"

Sarah rolled her eyes. "Please, you can't seriously have doubts about that. Do you imagine he's in Serenity for the heck of it?"

"He's here because he's injured." Okay, she did know better. Even Maddie had told her that Ty was here, at least in part, for her.

"Don't you think most ballplayers stick around the team doctors and trainers after an injury?" Sarah scoffed. "No, Ty is here because you are."

Even as she spoke, Sarah glanced across the spa and her eyes lit up. A smile spread across her face. "I rest my case," she said. "Gotta run."

Annie stared after her, confused by her abrupt decision to go. "Where are you going? Your workout isn't over."

"Oh, yes, it is," Sarah said. "Spend the rest of my time with him."

"Him who?" Annie said, then finally turned around to

see Ty crossing the room in long strides, his gaze on her, an armload of daisies in hand. Her heart climbed into her throat.

As he walked, heads turned. In a spa restricted to women, other than the two male personal trainers who worked there, all that testosterone was a sight worth ogling. Especially since it was so nicely packaged. Annie couldn't seem to tear her gaze away, either.

When Ty stopped in front of her and held out the flowers, she could swear there was a collective sigh around the room.

"You're not due here for hours," she said, because she couldn't think of anything else to say.

"I know. I wanted to see you."

She studied him with suspicion. "Why?"

He grinned as he continued to hold out the bouquet. "To give you these."

"Why?"

He laughed. "So many questions. Why does a man usually bring flowers to a woman?"

"Because he wants something," she retorted.

"Now, there's a cynical response if ever I heard one. Did you consider for even a second that I just wanted to do something nice for you?"

Annie hesitated. She supposed it was a possibility. Still, she once again asked, "Why?"

"Because I love you," he said with simple sincerity.

This time there was no mistaking the sigh, though it only came from those close enough to overhear his quietly spoken declaration.

Annie was so taken aback by the heartfelt reply, she had to sit down. "Oh," she murmured, burying her flaming cheeks in the flowers. Ty sat next to her.

She turned to him, feeling a little frantic. "You're not

supposed to be in here during regular hours. Maybe you should go now."

His lips twitched. "Just when things are getting interesting? I don't think so. You heard me. Don't you have anything you want to say?"

She stared at him blankly. "Like what?"

"Oh, like maybe that you're wildly, passionately in love with me, too?"

She frowned at his teasing, then met his gaze and realized he was serious. "You want me to say that?" she asked in astonishment. "Really? Here and now, in front of an audience?"

He nodded. "But only if it's true."

"Well, it's not," she blurted.

He regarded her with skepticism. "Really?"

"Really," she said, stubbornness and pride kicking in. It wasn't going to be this easy for him, dammit! He wasn't going to waltz in here with his sweet bouquet of flowers and his pretty words and charm her into forgetting everything that had happened or the fact that Dee-Dee was hanging around.

He inched closer to her on the workout bench. "Want me to test that claim?"

Alarm shot through her. They both knew how quickly he could make a liar out of her. One kiss would do it. One kiss with an avid audience and it would be all over town that the two of them were reconciled, or at least on their way. Then the collective pressure of the town would make it all but impossible for her to put some space between them again until she got her equilibrium back.

"You promised," she reminded him, her gaze locked with his. "No more kisses in the spa, remember?"

His gaze never wavered. "It could be a promise that's worth breaking," he suggested.

"You've broken more important ones," she said. "So the track record is there."

He swallowed hard at the harsh words, then nodded and looked away. "So I have," he agreed, suddenly serious. He stood up. "I'll see you tonight, Annie."

For reasons she didn't totally understand, she felt terrible for ruining his good mood and romantic gesture. "Ty," she called out, stopping him.

He stayed where he was, but he didn't turn around, and she realized then that she'd really hurt him. Okay, not the way he'd hurt her, but what did that matter? She wasn't the kind of person who took deliberately mean potshots at people, no matter how deserving they might be.

"I love the flowers," she said softly. "They're beautiful. Thank you."

He faced her then. "No big deal," he said, hands shoved in his pockets.

Annie crossed the room. "It was a big deal," she contradicted. "And I had to go and spoil it. I'm sorry."

Before she could stop herself, she stood on tiptoe and kissed him. She'd aimed for his cheek, but he'd guessed her intention and turned at the last second so the kiss landed squarely on his lips.

And just as he'd taunted, the immediate fire that ran through her blood made a liar of her.

Ty hadn't considered anything beyond giving those flowers to Annie. He certainly hadn't thought about the impact of another of her kisses, not on his composure and not on the women who were watching them as if he and Annie were performing in a live soap opera that was unfolding before their eyes.

"Whoo-ee!" Garnet Rogers said, adding a whistle when Ty finally pulled away from Annie.

The eighty-year-old, who'd worked in the local grocery until a few months ago, spurred similar catcalls and comments from the other members of her seniors jazzercise group.

"I don't know what the man asked," Garnet called out. "My hearing aid's busted. But whatever it was, Annie, you say yes, you hear."

Annie blushed. "Now look what we've done," she muttered, though she sounded more exasperated and amused than angry.

"Hey, you kissed me," Ty reminded her. "I'd backed off and was on my way out the door." He looked around the room. "Right, ladies? You saw that, didn't you?"

"That's the way it looked to me," Garnet confirmed.

Ty gave Annie a perfectly innocent look. "You see? It's not my fault that you couldn't resist me."

"You're dragging a bunch of senior citizens into our drama?" Annie demanded with feigned indignation.

"They don't mind," Ty replied. "Do you, ladies?"

"Not a bit," one of them shouted, a response echoed by several others.

"Better than *The Young and the Restless*," Garnet declared.

Annie shook her head. "You need to go. I doubt their hearts can take much more of this."

"They're taking jazzercise, for goodness' sake. They're fine," Ty said. "How about you and me? Are we okay?"

"If you're asking if I'm likely to drop a fifty-pound weight on your foot when you come back here tonight, you'll just have to take your chances," she said, though her eyes were sparkling. "Go. I have paying clients to see."

"That reminds me," Ty said, turning serious. "What's your going rate for sports injury therapy? I'll bring a check with me tonight."

"It doesn't matter. You're not paying me."

"I was paying Elliott. I'm paying you. This is your profession, Annie. You get paid."

"I don't want your money," she insisted, her jaw set stubbornly.

Ty backed down...for now. He'd see that she got paid, one way or another.

"By the way, Mom told me she ordered that equipment you recommended. It should be here next week."

Annie nodded. "Good. That should help."

The music for the jazzercise group pumped up again. Ty took his cue from that and stroked a finger down Annie's soft-as-silk cheek, enjoying the rise of heat and color that followed in his path. "See you tonight."

He left before she could respond. At the door, he looked back and saw that her hand was on her cheek, her expression vaguely flustered. He gave a little nod of satisfaction. Not a bad afternoon's work at all. He'd have to buy Cal a beer one of these days to thank him.

Helen's cell phone rang just as she stepped into the kitchen at Sullivan's to pick up the dinner Erik had set aside for her to take home. Glancing at the caller ID, she saw that it was Dee-Dee. A feeling of dread settled in her stomach.

Injecting a deliberately cheerful note into her voice, she greeted Trevor's mother. "So, tell me, how did things go during your first meetings with Trevor?"

"It was amazing," Dee-Dee said. "*He's* amazing. I can't believe I thought I could go through life not knowing him."

"You were very young and, I'm sure, scared. We've all made rash decisions we regret."

"I'm glad you understand," Dee-Dee said. "I know I should have had my attorney call you, but you were so sweet when I was there visiting that I felt like I should call you directly."

Helen heard something in her voice that set off an alarm. "Dee-Dee, if this is about the custody situation, then you definitely need to speak to your attorney and have him get in touch with me. I represent Ty."

"I know that, and my attorney will be following up, but I wanted to give you and Ty a heads-up that I'm going ahead and filing for custody. I've discussed it with my fiancé and he supports my decision."

Helen's heart sank.

Dee-Dee went right on. "I've talked it over with Jim, and we've decided that Trevor should have a full-time family. I'm going to ask for sole custody. Ty will have visitation rights, of course, not that I expect Trevor to see much of him with all the traveling he has to do with the team. In fact, Ty's travel schedule during the season is exactly the reason I want Trevor with us."

Helen barely resisted the urge to scream at her that she was being outrageously selfish. This had to be settled in court. It wouldn't be settled on the phone, not when they shouldn't be speaking directly, anyway.

"I'm sorry you've reached that decision," Helen said, struggling to keep her voice calm. "Have your attorney call me."

Dee-Dee didn't have sense enough to quit. "I know Ty's going to be upset by this, but I hope you'll remind him to think about what's best for Trevor," she said.

Upset? Furious was more like it. Ty was going to demand that Helen pull out every stop to halt this scheme of Dee-

Dee's in its tracks. If she'd shown even a modicum of respect for all that Ty had done over the past three years, Helen
could probably have mediated to get Dee-Dee some of what
she wanted. This, however, was like declaring all-out war.

"The court's going to decide what's best for Trevor," Helen
reminded her. "You and I obviously aren't going to see eye
to eye on what that is. I'm sorry about that. I truly am."

She hung up before she said something she'd regret. If
she'd been in her own kitchen, rather than Sullivan's, she
might have picked up the nearest plate and hurled it across
the room. Apparently Erik guessed her agitation, because he
came over and put his arms around her.

"You heard?" she asked.

"Enough to get the idea that Trevor's mom is going
through with a custody suit."

"For full custody," she said. "I don't know why I'm so
shocked. I was just so sure she'd be reasonable. She has to
know she can't win, not after abandoning him on a hotel-
room doorstep. I don't care how much she claims to have
changed, the judge is going to consider that irresponsible
and reckless. Not to mention how bonded Trevor and Ty
have become in these three years that she'd like to conve-
niently erase."

Erik looked as dismayed as she felt. "I'm sorry. Thank
goodness Dana Sue's not here right now. The minute she
hears about this, she's going to start worrying herself sick
about the impact on Annie."

"I know," Helen said. "I'm worried about all of them,
Trevor included, and these aren't my kids who are involved."

"You know you've always thought of both Ty and Annie
as members of your family. Of course, you're worried," Erik
said with the kind of understanding that demonstrated why
she loved him so much.

"I need to see Ty and let him know what's going on," she said, even though she'd prefer to stay right here wrapped in her husband's arms. Of course at some point Erik would have to focus on feeding the restaurant's hungry customers again, so she might as well go.

"You could just call him," Erik suggested.

She shook her head. "Not with news like this. I'll run dinner home to my mother and then try to track him down."

"I'm pretty sure he's working out at the spa with Annie tonight," Erik said. "Dana Sue was pretty upset by that, too. She's afraid those two are getting close and Ty will wind up breaking Annie's heart all over again."

Helen regarded him with dismay. "Well, this news certainly isn't going to help the two of them reconcile."

And being the messenger was going to be the absolute worst part of her day.

"Give me ten more reps and then we're done," Annie said to Ty.

To her amazement, he'd been on his best behavior all evening. There'd been no sly innuendos, no sneaky touches. She had to admit to being a little disappointed, but mostly it had been a relief to have the workout go smoothly without the distraction of him making subtle passes at her. She supposed it proved just how seriously he took rehab, which made him the best possible kind of client.

"How about adding another ten pounds?" Ty asked, even though sweat was already pouring down his chest and soaking the tank top that revealed way too many muscles, to say nothing of the jagged, still-red scars from his shoulder surgery.

"Not yet," she told him.

"I'm telling you this is too easy," he argued.

"If it were easy, you wouldn't be sweating. Ten more at this weight. In here, I'm not your friend. I'm the boss, remember?"

He scowled at her, but he complied with her orders, then set the weights back on their stand.

Annie was about to suggest he head in and take a shower, when she heard the front door open. She frowned. She knew she'd locked it earlier, right after admitting Ty.

"Hey, you guys, it's only me," Helen called out.

Ty's expression froze as he turned to Annie. "This can't be good."

Annie opted for an optimistic spin. "Come on, you don't even know if she's here to see you. She could be stopping by to pick up some paperwork or something."

Ty shook his head. "It's bad. I can feel it. She's heard something from Dee-Dee."

Helen crossed the room, her expression every bit as grim as Ty's. "Hi, sweetie," she said to Annie, giving her a hug. She glanced at Ty's soaked shirt and shook her head. "You'll get a hug later."

"What's up?" Annie asked. "Did you come by to pick up something?"

"I need to speak to Ty," Helen said. "Alone, if you don't mind."

Annie tried not to feel hurt by the dismissal. She smiled brightly. "Of course."

She started away, but Ty called her back. His expression stubborn, he told Helen, "She should probably hear whatever you have to say."

Helen didn't look especially happy about it, but she nodded. "Your call."

As she described her conversation with Dee-Dee, Annie kept her gaze on Ty. His expression ran the gamut of emotions from disbelief to dismay to outrage. Every muscle in his body was visibly tense. Instinctively, Annie walked behind him and rested her hand on his shoulder.

"Helen's going to fix this," she said confidently. "Right, Helen?"

"No question about it," Helen said. "I've already spoken to the P.I., and he's stepping up his investigation. There won't be a thing about Dee-Dee that we won't know by this time next week. Then we'll sit down and decide how we want to use it."

Annie cringed. "You're digging up dirt about her?"

Helen nodded.

"We're going to do whatever it takes to stop her," Ty said, his expression grim. "Surely you can understand why we have to do this. Visitation is one thing. I saw for myself that Trevor loves having a mom in his life. I can reconcile myself to that for his sake, but full custody? I can't let that happen, Annie, no matter what it takes to fight it."

"I suppose," Annie said. "But do you really want to play down and dirty with your son's mother? Someday it could come back to haunt you. Trevor could hate you for publicly humiliating her."

"If it prevents her from taking him from me, I have no choice," Ty said.

"I agree," Helen added, then turned to Annie. "Sweetie, I understand your caution, but in cases like this, sometimes it's necessary to play hardball. I'd hoped we wouldn't have to. I thought by giving Dee-Dee a chance to spend a little time with Trevor, giving her access to him, she'd be reasonable. Instead, she wants it all, and she'll try to cut Ty out of Trevor's life in the process. She said as much on the phone tonight."

"It's just that it's going to get so ugly," Annie said.

"No way around it," Helen said. "Not if we want to win."

"Are you sure compromise is out of the question?" Annie persisted.

Ty regarded her with puzzlement. "Why are you so against me keeping my son?"

She was stunned and dismayed by his interpretation. "I'm not," she insisted. "I just think there ought to be a way to make this a win–win for everyone, especially Trevor." She thought a moment longer, then added, "And much as I hate to say it, I guess I feel kind of bad for Dee-Dee. Trevor is her son, too."

Ty's expression turned to shock. "You feel sorry for Dee-Dee?"

She shrugged. "I never would have believed it myself, but yes, I do." She glanced toward Helen. "I remember how horrible it was when my mom and dad split up. I was a lot older than Trevor, and I didn't understand all the fighting or why my dad ended up leaving town."

Helen frowned. "That was my doing," she admitted. "And, in retrospect, it was a mistake. But, Annie, the situations are not the same. Not even close. Ty's the only parent Trevor's really known. Dee-Dee wants to turn that around, keep him to herself and limit Ty's access to the occasional visit."

"I know," Annie said. "And I certainly don't want to see Ty and Trevor ripped apart. Not at all. I guess I just kind of see Dee-Dee's side, too. I'm sure if they lived in the same town, then shared custody might be an answer, but the way things are, for one of them to win, the other has to lose. Who can pick sides between a mom or a dad, especially when they both love their son?"

Ty had been silent for several minutes, but now his gaze hardened as he met hers. "Are you really able to be that impartial? Or do you want me punished for what happened between us? Do you see this as some kind of karmic justice, me losing my son after the way Dee-Dee's pregnancy and his birth pretty much destroyed our relationship?"

Annie stared at him in shock. "You can't really believe I'd be that petty," she said.

Ty shook his head. "I don't know what I believe. I just know that if you really had any feelings for me at all, now or in the past, you would never be able to suggest I give up my son."

"But that's not what I said," Annie protested.

Ty didn't hear her, though. He'd grabbed his shirt and left the spa without a backward glance.

Annie turned to Helen. "You got what I was saying, right? I was trying to see both sides."

Helen gave her a hug. "I know you thought you were trying to be fair, but right now Ty needs to be surrounded by people he can count on a hundred percent."

"But he can," Annie argued. "I'm always on his side."

"Sorry, sweetie. For a minute there, it didn't sound like it. I need to go after him. We have a lot of plans to make."

"I'll come with you," Annie offered.

"Not tonight. Give Ty some time to cool down, absorb what's going on. Then you can try to explain and he might actually hear what you have to say."

After Helen walked out, Annie went around the spa in a fog, turning out lights and locking up for the night. How had a day that had been so promising turned into such a nightmare? A few innocently spoken words, an attempt at impartiality, and she was the bad guy. It made no sense to her.

But as she walked home, trying to examine the entire conversation from Ty's perspective, she finally saw it as he must have…a betrayal from someone who should have been unconditionally on his side.

Not that they hadn't had disagreements in the past and moved on, but this issue was too huge for them not to be on the same page. His son's future was at stake. And like any parent, Ty was going to fight for what he thought was right. In his view, there was no room for diverging opinions, no room for compromise.

"I messed up," Annie murmured, tears stinging her eyes as she walked.

The only question now was how she was going to make things right.

CHAPTER SEVENTEEN

After storming out of The Corner Spa, Ty headed straight home. He needed to see his son. Trevor would probably be asleep by the time he got there, but he needed to reassure himself that his son was safely tucked in his own bed.

Not that he thought Dee-Dee would do anything as stupid as trying to take him, but right now he didn't trust anyone to do the right thing.

How could Annie have suggested for so much as a second that Dee-Dee was in the right about anything? He knew the disdain she'd felt for the woman who'd come between them, and now she thought that same woman was fit to raise his son? It made no sense to him. All that talk about being fair and objective was nonsense. This was payback. Annie had waited a long time to get it, but, boy, had she picked the one way guaranteed to tear his heart out.

When he walked through the door at home, his mother and Cal called out to him, but Ty merely acknowledged them both with a wave and headed upstairs. The old house that had been in the Townsend family for generations had seemed outrageously big and ostentatious when he was a kid, but now he appreciated the number of rooms that accommodated not only Cal, Maddie and Ty's siblings, but still had room for him and Trevor to have their own suite.

There was the soft glow of a night-light in Trevor's room. Still scared of the dark, he wouldn't go to sleep without it. Turning it on was part of their nighttime ritual, right along with brushing teeth and a bedtime story.

Ty crossed the room to the bed that had been made up with Spider-Man sheets. Trevor had kicked off the covers and lay sprawled in the middle of the bed, his thumb firmly poked in his mouth. Ty's best efforts to stop that habit had yet to succeed.

Looking down on his boy, Ty released the sigh that had been building up ever since Helen had hit him with the news of the likelihood of a full-blown, ugly custody suit. He sat down on the floor beside the bed, pulled up his knees and rested his head against them.

How could this be happening? He'd done everything right. Though he'd initially wanted things to turn out differently, from the moment he'd known the results of the paternity test, he'd accepted responsibility for Trevor. He'd felt a connection to him the first time he'd seen his scrunched-up little face in the hospital nursery, even though he'd been scared spitless about the prospect of being a dad, even though at that time he'd envisioned having only limited contact.

And, from the moment he'd found his son, wrapped in a blue blanket and tucked into a portable carrier, on his hotel doorstep in Denver, Trevor had become the center of his universe. His stupidity had cost him the woman he loved, but he'd gained this, a wonderful little boy whose smile could brighten the worst day. He could have used one of those smiles right now.

As if he sensed his dad's presence, Trevor stirred but didn't wake. Ty reached up and gently brushed his sun-streaked, dark brown hair from his forehead. The emotions that welled up inside him were huge, overwhelming. The only thing that had ever come close were his feelings for Annie.

As he thought about their heated exchange earlier, the accusations he'd leveled at her made him just a little bit ashamed. Deep down, he knew better. He knew she would never take out her anger with him in the way he'd suggested. She would never side with Dee-Dee to get even with him. It simply wasn't in her makeup to be that vindictive.

Of course, acknowledging that forced him to also acknowledge that she might have had a point about the value of compromise, or at least about trying to see Dee-Dee's point of view. He still believed at the very core of his being that none of this was happening because she'd suddenly decided she missed her little boy. There was more to it. He just couldn't imagine what it might be.

What he did know was that he had to find out and there was little time to waste. If the investigator Helen had hired didn't hit some kind of pay dirt in a few days, Ty intended to take matters into his own hands. His teammates, more than likely, knew Dee-Dee's friends. A lot of the women who followed the team formed an alliance of sorts. He suspected they knew one another's secrets.

And, for all he knew, some of the team's other players actually knew Dee-Dee herself. He doubted he was the first professional ballplayer in her life or her last. Somebody was bound to have the insight he needed.

Feeling more at peace now that he'd seen his son and had a plan of action to keep him from feeling powerless, he stood up, kissed Trevor's brow and left the room, closing the door behind him.

When he went downstairs, he found Helen in the living

room with Cal and his mother. Judging from their grim, worried expressions, Helen had filled them in. She met his gaze.

"Any second thoughts?" she asked quietly, her expression somber.

"None," he said at once.

"Okay, then. I'll move forward. I'll send a letter to Dee-Dee's attorney stating our position and reminding him that she has a background that won't bode well for her in court. Maybe he can make her see reason and we'll be able to mediate a settlement. I'm going to check with Tom Bristol, who handled your original case, and see how backed-up the courts are in Atlanta. There's a good chance we can have the case moved over here, once Dee-Dee's filed her papers. A lot of judges are more than happy to move a case, if it'll get it off their docket. That would certainly simplify things."

Ty nodded. The wrangling over jurisdiction mattered less to him than their strategy. "I still think we're missing something important," he said to all of them.

Across the room, his mother, who'd been silent up till now, said, "You mean why, after all this time, Dee-Dee surfaced, in the first place?"

Ty regarded her with surprise. "Exactly."

"I've been wondering the same thing," Maddie said. She turned to Helen. "How do we find out?"

It was Ty, not Helen, who answered. "I thought about trying to get in touch with some of her friends, or maybe asking some of my buddies on the team to ask a few questions. They know the women who hung out with Dee-Dee. Maybe she's kept in touch."

"Good idea," Cal said. "The groupies have always been tight with one another."

Maddie gave him a wry look. "And you know this how?"

Cal grinned at her. "Simmer down, sweetheart. I'm all yours now."

Helen listened to the exchange, her expression thoughtful. Eventually, she nodded. "It's worth a shot."

"Should I make the calls now, or wait until we hear from the investigator?" Ty asked.

"Make the calls," Helen said decisively. "The sooner we can put our case together, the better. I'm also going to want depositions from anyone and everyone who can testify to the kind of father you are."

"I'll have a list for you in the morning," Ty said.

"How about the nanny you have in Georgia? Are you still paying her?"

Ty nodded. "Since I'll need her when I go back to Atlanta, we worked out an agreement."

"Did you do a thorough background check?"

"Of course. She was going to be responsible for my son when I wasn't there. I needed to know everything there was to know about her."

"Perfect," Helen said, standing up. "I need to get home. Flo goes stir-crazy when I'm gone all day and in the evening, too. Sarah Beth's good company for her, and of course the nanny and Mom's caregiver are around, but by this time of night, she's usually driving Mrs. Lowell nuts with her demands."

"How's her hip healing?" Maddie asked.

"Amazingly well, given her age," Helen said. "At least that's what the doctor says. I just know that having her back on her feet and into her own place can't come soon enough. In some ways this has been better than I expected. In others, she can make me crazy faster than anyone else on earth."

"Typical mother-daughter relationship," Maddie assured her.

Ty thought of his visit to his grandmother and what she'd said about Cal helping her and his mom to bond. "Grandma Paula said something like that the other day, too."

Cal groaned. "Oh, boy."

Ty stared at him. "What did I say?"

He realized then that his mother was scowling at him.

"You talked to my mother about me?" she asked, her annoyance plain.

"It wasn't like that," Ty said at once.

"Then she didn't have a litany of complaints about how I'd been neglecting her?" Maddie asked.

"No way," he said, but clearly the damage had been done, because his mother continued to regard him with a disgruntled expression. Heaven save him from touchy women. He didn't understand a one of them, not even the ones he knew best.

It didn't much surprise him when his mom walked Helen to the door and didn't come back. He heard her go directly upstairs. He turned to Cal.

"What did I say that was so terrible?"

Cal laughed. "Haven't you learned by now that the peace between your mom and Paula is fragile? It doesn't take much to upset either one of them."

"All I said was…" He couldn't even recall what he'd said.

"You lumped the two of them in with Helen and Flo, thereby suggesting that theirs, too, is a tense mother-daughter relationship."

"Well, it is," Ty said, still bewildered about why telling the truth had offended Maddie.

"Your mother likes to think their relationship has evolved into something more mature and understanding," Cal explained. "She knows better, of course, but she doesn't like being reminded of it."

Ty shook his head. "This is way too complicated for me. I have my own incomprehensible women to worry about."

Cal regarded him with sympathy. "Dee-Dee?"

"And Annie," he admitted. "It was a helluva lot easier when we were kids. We fought. We got over it."

"The stakes are generally much higher once you're adults," Cal reminded him.

Ty sighed. "Tell me about it." Only his son and his entire future.

Since she'd restricted Ty to working out every other day, Annie spent the evening after their argument at Sarah's. She nibbled at the salad in front of her with disinterest.

Suddenly Sarah set down her own fork and frowned at her. "Okay, what's wrong? You've hardly said two words since you got here. You were just as uncommunicative at the spa earlier. You know how I hate it when you're upset. I especially hate it when you don't touch your food, either."

Annie scowled at her and deliberately forked up a chunk of grilled chicken, stuffed it in her mouth and chewed slowly. She ate a few more bites of the meal, then pushed the bowl aside.

"You're going to finish that before you leave the table," Sarah said.

Her stern tone made Annie smile, despite her sour mood. "You sounded exactly like my mom just then."

"Well, good," Sarah said with a touch of defiance. "Now, either eat or talk. Those are your choices."

Since Annie didn't think she could swallow another bite right at the moment, she asked, "How's Walter?"

Sarah shook her head at the obvious ploy. "He's fine. How's Ty?"

Annie shrugged. "I have no idea."

"You haven't seen him today?"

"Nope."

"Haven't spoken to him?"

"No."

"Is that why you're in this black mood?"

Annie sighed. "No, I'm in this black mood because of the fight we had." She described how the conversation with Ty and Helen had blown up in her face the night before. "I have to fix things, but I have no idea how to do it. I don't think an apology will cut it."

"It would be a good place to start," Sarah suggested.

"But then what?"

They sat there in silence for several minutes before Annie turned to Sarah. "How would you feel about taking a road trip?" she ventured. An idea had formed in her head earlier in the day and while it seemed pretty outrageous, she hadn't been able to shake it.

Her friend regarded her with confusion. "You want to go on a vacation now? Isn't that just running away from the problem?"

Annie grinned. "I was thinking more along the lines of a trip to Cincinnati to track down Dee-Dee."

"Oh, no," Sarah said at once. "That's a really bad idea."

"Why do you say that?" she asked, wondering if Sarah's thoughts were similar to the ones she'd come up with when the voice of reason kicked in.

"Because I doubt Ty or Helen, for that matter, would appreciate you interfering in the situation without their permission." She studied Annie with a penetrating look. "I assume there's no permission involved, right?"

"None," Annie confirmed. She was a tiny bit daunted by

Sarah's strongly negative reaction, but she still thought the plan had merit. At least it meant taking action rather than sitting on the sidelines. "Come on. I'll bet we could get to the bottom of why she's so determined to take Trevor."

"How do you suggest we do that? I'm opposed to kidnapping and torture."

Annie gave her a disgusted look. "So am I," she said. "I haven't worked out all the details. I just think we could snoop around a little, ask some questions, maybe bump into her and become her new best friends."

Sarah continued to look unconvinced. "Do you happen to recall what happened the last time you decided to play Nancy Drew?"

Annie winced. "It was not my fault that branch came down and broke Mrs. Latham's window."

"You were on that branch trying to spy on Bobby Latham," Sarah reminded her.

"I thought he'd stolen my iPod," Annie said. "And that branch was obviously dead. We both know I didn't weigh much then, so clearly anything could have snapped it off. It was a disaster waiting to happen."

"As I recall, Mrs. Latham didn't see it that way. My point is, you don't have a very good track record as a detective. I think this situation is more important than your stolen iPod. You probably shouldn't be meddling in it."

"But if I could figure out what Dee-Dee's up to and give the information to Helen, Ty would see that I'm on his side," Annie argued, even though Sarah's objections were making more sense than she wanted to admit.

"I still say you should just apologize and then ask Ty if there's anything you can do to help." Sarah gave her a pleading look. "You need to drop the idea of getting involved, Annie, at least unless you have Ty or Helen's permission."

"Then you're refusing to go to Cincinnati with me?"

"Yes," Sarah said.

"Okay, then." She was disappointed but not really surprised. She considered several alternatives, then said, "I guess I could go on my own."

Sarah immediately looked alarmed. "Absolutely not."

"Well, you said you won't go. What choice do I have?"

"You could stay here where you belong."

Annie considered it one more time, then shook her head, even though she knew her stubbornness—and her desire to do something to prove her loyalty to Ty—were overruling common sense. "I don't think so."

"Oh, for pity's sake," Sarah mumbled. "When do we leave?"

Annie worked hard to keep a satisfied smirk off her face. "Thank you."

"Don't thank me yet. We'll see how grateful you are when we're both locked up."

"Nobody's going to arrest a couple of women on vacation with their kids."

Sarah blinked at that. "You want to take Tommy and Libby along?"

"Sure. It will be fun. And we'll look totally innocent poking around in Dee-Dee's neighborhood."

"Do you happen to know what neighborhood that is?"

"Not exactly, but I'll bet I can find it online."

"What if she's living with her fiancé? Do you know his name?"

"I don't, but Helen must," Annie admitted, beginning to see that this could be a little more complicated than she'd first envisioned. "Maybe I can get her to spill it."

Still acting as the voice of reason, Sarah asked, "Do you have a plan to entice Dee-Dee to talk to you, a perfect stranger, about one of the most intimate aspects of her life, her custody battle for her child?"

"People spill their guts to strangers all the time," Annie said.

"On airplanes or in train stations, maybe, but on the street?" Sarah asked, her skepticism plain. "First you'd have to get her to stop in the first place."

Annie grinned then. "Thus, Tommy and Libby. She won't be able to resist them, not if she's in this huge maternalistic phase."

For the first time, Sarah actually looked impressed. "You have an incredibly devious mind."

"I do, don't I?" Annie said. "Who knew?"

"I'm not sure it's something to be proud of."

"Probably not, but at the moment, it's coming in very handy, don't you think?"

Sarah heaved a dramatic sigh. "That remains to be seen."

Unfortunately there was only one way Annie could conduct her covert mission. She had to take time off from The Corner Spa, and that would require coming up with some kind of story for Maddie. And since Ty's rehab was also at stake, it seemed unlikely Maddie would approve the impromptu vacation unless Annie took her into her confidence and told her the truth.

The increasingly horrified expression on Maddie's face as Annie explained her plan didn't bode well.

"No, no, no!" Maddie said. "Absolutely not."

"But it's the only way I can think of to help and to prove to Ty that I'm on his side."

"Find another way," Maddie said. "I won't allow you to do this, Annie."

Annie bristled at her words. "You won't *allow* me to do it?"

"That's exactly what I said and exactly what I meant."

"I'm not ten, and I'm not your child."

"No, but you are my employee and my friend. More important, Ty is my son, and he gets to decide how this situation is handled. I know he wants information about Dee-Dee and her motives, but he has his own plan. He also has professionals on his side."

"They don't have what I have," Annie argued. "Motivation."

Maddie sighed in the face of her determination. "Here's the deal, then. You tell Ty this crazy idea of yours, and if he approves, I'll give you the time off with my blessing. I won't even dock your pay for missing all your appointments and having Elliott's workload doubled."

"I can't tell Ty," Annie protested.

"Why not? Because you know he'll disapprove?"

"No, because I don't want to disappoint him if I fail."

"Very considerate, but those are my terms. Ask Ty if this is something he wants you to do." She glanced up and a grim smile settled on her lips. "How convenient! Here he is right now."

She walked past Annie, gave her son a quick peck on the cheek and said, "Talk." She then shut the door firmly behind her.

Ty studied Annie warily. "What was that about? What does she want us to talk about?"

Faced with his distinctly cautious attitude, Annie hesitated. She really thought telling him was a bad idea, but maybe Maddie was correct. He probably had a right to approve the idea or dismiss it, since his future with his son was at stake. Besides, Maddie's fierce reaction, coupled with Sarah's, were beginning to weaken Annie's own belief that this was a good plan.

"I came to your mom to ask for some time off," she began, choosing her words carefully.

"In the middle of my rehab?" he asked incredulously. "Or was that the point? To get away from me?"

Annie ignored the suggestion that she was running away from him. "I wanted to go to Cincinnati."

Ty looked blank. "Cincinnati? Why?" he asked, then stilled. "Oh, no. You weren't thinking of going anywhere near Dee-Dee, were you?"

"I thought maybe I could find out what she's really after," she admitted. "Sarah's going with me. We have a plan."

Ty groaned. "Don't even tell me. I don't want to know. Do you not remember the Bobby Latham incident?"

Geez, did everyone in her life have the memory of an elephant? "I remember. And despite the broken branch and the shattered window, you and Sarah both seem to have forgotten that I saw Bobby with my iPod that day. I proved it, too."

Ty grinned. "And I'm sure you savored your victory every single day while you were grounded."

"Beside the point," Annie said blithely. She gave Ty an earnest look. "Let me do this for you, Ty. Let me try to get Dee-Dee to open up."

He shook his head. "Look, I appreciate the thought. I really do, but you're the last person she'd ever talk to, Annie."

"Why? She doesn't even know me."

"Yes," he said quietly, "she does. When you walked into Wharton's the other day, she took one look at you and knew you were the one I'd been in love with when she got pregnant with Trevor."

Annie was stunned. "She knew about me?"

"Practically from the beginning," he confirmed. "So, you see, she always knew nothing serious was going to happen between the two of us. She chose to sleep with me, anyway. Maybe the pregnancy was an accident, maybe not." He shrugged. "But as soon as she told me, I made it clear that the reason I couldn't marry her was because I was still in love with a girl back home. Apparently she saw that love in my eyes the other day, because she guessed right away that you were the woman."

"And you confirmed it?"

"Of course. I didn't see any reason to lie." He took Annie's hand in his. "So you see, she'll never open up to you of all people."

Annie was torn between disappointment that her one chance to help had been ruined and elation that Ty had acknowledged loving her all those years ago and even as recently as this week.

"I really wanted to do something to make up for the other night," she said.

"I know," he said. "And I can't tell you how much I appreciate the fact that you came up with this crazy scheme, but the truth is, I was wrong the other night. I knew better. I knew you wouldn't go against me. I was just so hurt and angry and terrified, I wound up taking it out on the wrong person."

Annie met his gaze. "Then we're okay?"

He squeezed her hand. "We're more than okay." His gaze held hers. "You want to get out of here?"

Her heart skipped several beats at the heat in his eyes. "And do what?"

"Whatever we feel like doing," he said. "I'll clear it with Mom."

Annie shook her head at that. "I'm capable of asking your mother for time off. How much time were you thinking?"

A slow smile spread across his face. "That depends on how persuasive I am. You'd better ask for the rest of the day."

Annie's blood hummed. "You know she's going to have questions."

"I know," Ty said solemnly. "Don't answer them."

She nodded slowly. "I think we're in total agreement on that one."

As she went to track down Maddie, for the first time in a very long time, Annie threw caution completely to the wind and allowed herself to hope.

CHAPTER EIGHTEEN

As badly as Ty wanted to take Annie straight over to the Serenity Inn, rent a room and make love to her for the rest of the day and into the night, he knew he couldn't do it. If they were going to reconcile at long last, she deserved a whole lot better than a motel room run by a couple who reported directly into the Serenity grapevine. Since he and Annie were both staying with their parents, taking her to either of their homes was out, too.

Standing on the sidewalk in front of the spa, Ty looked into her eyes. "I'm suddenly remembering what it was like when we were first together as a couple."

"You mean all worked up with nowhere to go?" she said, immediately understanding the dilemma.

Ty nodded. "Any ideas?"

"I'm opposed to the backseat of some car," she said.

He laughed. "At my height, so am I, especially since I own a very small hybrid."

"There's always the Serenity Inn. My mom and dad used to sneak away there when they were kids. And before my dad moved back home while he was staying at the inn, I know

my mom used to slip into his room." She grinned mischie-
vously. "They thought I didn't know about it."

Ty regarded her doubtfully. "Seriously? They really believed you didn't know?"

Annie nodded. "Naive, huh?"

"You're not kidding. Everybody in town knew, even me,"
Ty said. "Well, it's not an option for us, anyway. We're not
kids, and way too many people want to get into my business
to make that a viable option. Besides, Helen would shoot me
if some paparazzi caught us. It would not be good for our
case." He met her gaze. "Anyway, you deserve better than
the two of us sneaking around to some hotel room, even if
we thought we could get away with it. I want to get this
right this time, Annie, from the beginning."

"Seems a shame to be playing hooky and not taking advantage of it by doing something spontaneous," Annie said.
She looked as if she'd resigned herself to a dramatic change
of plans from the passionate rendezvous they'd both been
envisioning. "Why don't we pick up Trevor and drive over
to the beach?"

Ty regarded her with surprise. "You want to take my son
along on our romantic tryst?"

"Well, it will definitely change our plans, but it's a surefire
way to keep us from doing anything stupid, don't you think?"

"True. And, to be honest, I love the idea of you spending time with Trevor, as long as you're sure it's not going to
bother you." He leveled a look into her eyes. "Once we're
together—you, me and Trevor, I mean—there's no turning
back, Annie. You can't have a change of heart an hour from
now and insist on coming home. Trevor's a smart kid, even
at three. He'll think it's his fault."

Annie hesitated, and Ty waited silently. Her answer could

change everything between them. They had no future if she couldn't welcome his son into her heart.

"I won't change my mind," she assured Ty eventually. "I want to get to know your son."

Ty's gaze was steady. "You're sure? Because it's okay if you're not. We have to get this right, Annie. It's too important. We're talking about our future here."

She nodded. "I know that. I'm scared, but I'm sure. It's time to do this."

Relief flooded through him. "I'm so glad, Annie. You have no idea how long I've wanted this."

She squeezed his hand. "Then let's go get your boy."

Annie suffered a momentary pang of regret when they got to Ty's house, then drew in a deep breath and walked with Ty to the front door. He glanced down at her.

"Change of heart?" he asked.

"No," she said firmly, and realized it was true. It was time to put the past behind them. She thought she could finally separate the boy from the betrayal.

Before Ty had a chance to unlock the door, it was flung open by Trevor.

"Daddy, Daddy, you're back!" he said, his arms held out to be picked up. "I gots something to show you. Me and Jessie made a tent. We're camping."

"Cool," Ty said. "I can't wait to see it."

Ty lifted Trevor high in the air, earning a giggling reaction of pure delight, then settled him against his chest. Trevor finally turned a shy gaze on Annie. "Hi."

"Remember me? I'm Annie."

Trevor nodded. "I 'member."

"Your dad and I came by because we thought you might want to go to the beach with us," she told him.

Trevor's eyes lit up. "Really?"

"That's the plan," Ty confirmed.

"Can Jessie and Cole come, too?"

"I don't know," Ty began, but Annie shrugged.

"Why not?" she said. "Remember the goal."

"I thought it was for you to get to know Trevor," Ty said.

"And to keep us on our best behavior. Can you think of a better way to do that than having three pint-size chaperones?"

Ty shook his head. "I think you have no idea what you're letting yourself in for, but if you say it's okay, I'll give Mom a call. I'm thinking we'll need to bring the nanny along, too."

"We're two energetic adults. We don't need help. Give her the day off," Annie argued, warming to the idea of having Ty and the kids all to herself. It would give her a taste of what having a family with him would be like. She had a feeling it would add a bittersweet note to the afternoon, for who knew if they would ever have the real thing? There were so many complications to be sorted out.

"Whatever you say," Ty said, though he looked a little skeptical.

In less than an hour, Annie had gone home to put her swimsuit on under her clothes, they had all three kids secured in their car seats, had put a picnic basket in the back, and were on the road across the state toward the ocean. They'd made the same trip a few times with their own families and later, on their own, as teenagers. The drive filled Annie with both nostalgia and anticipation. The aroma of salty sea air tugged at her memory long before they were close enough to actually smell it.

"I'm hungry," Jessie announced less than a half hour out of Serenity.

"I need to go potty," Trevor said. "Now!"

Ty glanced in Annie's direction. "Still think this was a good idea?" he asked as he swerved into a gas station with a market and restrooms.

"Of course," she said gamely. "Jessie, do you need to use the potty, too?"

"No," she replied.

"How about you, Cole?" Ty asked.

Realizing from his silence that Cole was sound asleep, Annie said, "I'll stay in the car with him, if you'll take them inside."

"What do I do with Jessie, while I'm taking Trevor to the restroom?"

Annie regarded him blankly, then realized the problem. He couldn't leave a five-year-old on her own and he couldn't take her to the men's room. "Leave her here," she told him. "Jessie, hon, you stay in the car. Ty will bring you back something to eat."

"I want to choose myself," Jessie protested, looking as if she was about to cry. She'd already unfastened her seat belt and was halfway out of her car seat, eager to go inside.

Annie had been around Jessica Lynn enough to know the disciplinary drill. At one time a holy terror, she'd been tamed by stern parenting. "You can tell Ty what you want, but you stay in the car," she said firmly. "Otherwise, you get nothing until we get to the beach."

Jessie blinked at Annie's tone. For a moment, it looked as if she might launch into a tantrum. Apparently, though, she thought better of it. "I want a candy bar. I love chocolate," she said, sounding a lot like her mother. Maddie had chocolate stashed in her desk at the spa for stressful moments. Clearly, Jessie's desire for a treat outweighed her temptation to argue. With a dramatic sigh to emphasize her unhappiness, she climbed back into her car seat.

"Chocolate it is," Ty said at once, departing with Trevor.

Annie leaned back, exhausted by the very minor test of wills.

"Annie," Jessie called from the backseat.

"Yes?"

"Is Ty your boyfriend?"

How on earth was she supposed to answer that? Annie wondered. She settled for honesty. "We're good friends," she told his little half sister. "We've been friends for a very long time."

"I think he likes you," Jessie confided.

Annie had to fight the temptation to grill her. A five-year-old was hardly an expert at identifying the signs of infatuation. She was certainly no more attuned to Ty's emotions than Annie herself.

And today Annie had come to the conclusion all on her own that Ty really did still have feelings for her, the kind she'd once believed could last a lifetime.

Ty had discovered right after Jessie's birth that a baby could be a real babe magnet. Whenever he'd been home from college, his younger brother Kyle all but begged to take Jessie for a walk in the park. On one occasion, Ty had gone along and realized why Kyle had been so willing to be saddled with his baby sister. Teenage girls flocked around him, cooing over the infant in her stroller.

After Trevor's birth and the absence of Annie, Ty had found that he drew women wherever he went with his son. These weren't the baseball groupies, but the single moms and women who grew starry-eyed at the sight of a man with a baby.

Today, though, with Annie along, the reactions they drew

on the beach were smiles from older women, who obviously assumed they were a family.

In fact, several women walking along the water's edge made it a point to comment on what a lovely picture they made.

"It's so nice to see a young family spending time together," one said, after picking up a beach ball that had blown away and returning it. "Most young people these days are too busy rushing around to enjoy a day at the beach in the middle of the week like this."

Annie blushed at her words, and Ty could tell that she had a denial on the tip of her tongue, so he jumped in to thank the woman.

"We're in the process of reforming," he joked with her. He leaned closer and confided, "In fact, I even talked Annie into playing hooky from work today. I don't think there's nearly enough spontaneity in people's lives these days."

The woman beamed at him. "I couldn't agree more. You all enjoy yourselves, you hear."

When she'd walked on, Annie turned on him with feigned annoyance. "You let her think we're a family."

He shrugged. "Why spoil her illusion? Besides, I kind of enjoy pretending she got it right."

Annie's expression faltered at that. "You do?"

He nodded. "If things had gone differently, you and I would be married by now. I'll bet we'd have at least one baby, too. Didn't you ever imagine that?"

Her expression turned sad. "You know I did. We used to talk about what it would be like once we were married. I'm surprised you remember."

"Just because I behaved like an idiot doesn't mean my memory's gone. I remember everything important we ever discussed."

"Then how could you…" she began, but her voice trailed off. She let the warm sand sift through her fingers, her eyes directed away from him and out to sea.

"How could I cheat with all those other women?" he asked for her, knowing the pain he'd see if he could look into her eyes.

Her chin lifted as she turned to face him. "Okay, yes, how could you do that?"

He hesitated long enough to check that the kids were still engrossed in building a sand castle, then said quietly, "I somehow convinced myself it didn't matter. It was as if that part of my life were completely separate from us."

"Would you have done it if we had been married?"

"Of course not," he said at once.

"There's no *of course* about it," Annie replied heatedly. "Either you were committed to me or you weren't."

"Look, I know it doesn't make any sense, but I convinced myself we had an agreement, that while I was on the road and you were at school, all bets were off. I guess you could say I was sowing my wild oats while I had the chance."

She scowled at him. "Do you hear how immature and self-indulgent that sounds?"

Ty regarded her apologetically. "I do now. God, Annie, if I could take it all back, I would. None of it mattered. It was just what happened on the road, a rite of passage, so to speak. Ask Cal, if you don't believe me. He knows what it's like."

"So, let's say I forget what happened, chalk it up to life experience or whatever," she said. "How do I know you won't revert to the same behavior the second you're back on the road with the team? That's going to happen before we know it, and I don't think I can spend weeks at a time worrying about what you might be doing."

"I know it's going to be hard, because I still haven't earned your trust." He met her gaze. "But I swear to you I will cut off my pitching arm before I will ever hurt you that badly again," he said fiercely. "I mean it, Annie. I had to lose you to realize that you're the only woman who will ever matter to me."

She listened to his declaration and nodded. "You sound sincere."

"Because I am."

They sat side by side on the blanket in silence then, the sun beating on their shoulders, the kids playing beside them.

After a time, Annie turned to him, her lips twitching as she unsuccessfully fought a smile. "You know, Ty, I'd never expect you to cut off your pitching arm," she said. "Maybe some other part of your anatomy, but not your pitching arm."

Ty grinned. "Thanks. That's good to know."

She stood up then. Ty was relieved to see that her body in the sedate one-piece bathing suit was filled out nicely with curves these days. For a moment he flashed back to the early days of her anorexia, when sharp bones protruded and still she thought she was overweight. Thank God she'd found her way back from her eating disorder, though he knew it would be a lifetime struggle.

"Who's hungry?" she asked, directing the question to the kids.

"Me, me, me," they responded eagerly.

"And me," Ty said, his gaze on her and not the sandwiches she was pulling from their picnic basket.

She turned and caught his appreciative gaze, then slowly smiled. "You're gonna have to wait for that," she told him.

"That's okay," he told her. "However long it takes, you're definitely worth it."

★ ★ ★

After the frustrating day she'd had dealing with Dee-Dee's attorney, Helen was in no mood to go home to face an exasperating evening with her mother.

Apparently today hadn't been so hot for her mother, either. Flo had been in too much pain to make her way downstairs, which meant she was more bored and difficult than usual. Within an hour of her arrival home, Helen swore if she heard the ringing of that blasted little bell she'd put beside her mother's bed one more time, she was going to throw it out the window.

During the day Letitia Lowell saw to her mother's needs, took her to her physical therapy appointments, catered to her every whim, in fact. At the end of the day, all the catering fell to Helen, along with looking after Sarah Beth and getting her ready for bed.

She'd managed to get through her daughter's bath, put on her favorite jammies and coax her into bed, when the bell rang yet again.

"Gamma needs us," Sarah Beth said, hearing the bell. She scrambled right back out of her bed and darted past Helen, dragging her favorite stuffed dog behind her.

Helen heaved a sigh and followed. At this rate her daughter was going to be wide-awake when Erik got home from Sullivan's, which would cut into the little bit of time Helen actually got to spend with her husband these days.

By the time she reached her mother's room, Sarah Beth had climbed into bed with her grandmother and was snuggled down beside her. Seeing the two of them like that should have filled her with contentment. Instead, what she felt was a sharp stab of jealousy. She chided herself for the selfish reaction, but the feeling didn't diminish.

"Mom, did you need something?" she asked. "I was trying to get Sarah Beth settled for the night. It's already past her bedtime."

"Now, whose fault is that?" Flo chided. "You were late getting home."

Helen bit back a sharp retort. "Did you need something?" she repeated.

"I need to spend a little more time with my granddaughter," Flo said, brushing a silky strand of hair away from Sarah Beth's cheek. "I'll read her a story while you get me some ginger ale, if it wouldn't be too much trouble." Even as she spoke, she reached for the stack of children's books next to her bed. She let Sarah Beth make her choice and, in the process, left Helen with none.

"No trouble," Helen said tightly. She whirled around and left the room before she could start an argument that would lead nowhere.

As she went downstairs, she tried to recall one single occasion when her mother had ever read to her as a child. She came up blank. In the chaos that had been their life back then, there hadn't been time for cozy moments like the one she'd just witnessed between her daughter and her mother. Even when her mom had been home, she'd been doing the ironing that brought in a few extra dollars. Those dollars had been stashed in an old coffee tin, then eventually deposited in the bank, in the account Helen later learned had been set aside for her college education.

She was standing in the kitchen, thinking about how pathetic it was to resent the growing relationship between these two important people in her life, when Erik walked in. He kissed her distractedly, reached around her to grab the bottle of wine from the counter and poured a glass, then finally really looked at her.

"Uh-oh, I know that expression. What's your mother done now?"

"Nothing," she said. "I'm being petty and ridiculous." The admission was made grudgingly.

"Okay," Erik said carefully. "About what?"

Tears spilled over as she met his gaze. "My mom's reading a story to Sarah Beth."

Erik looked bewildered. "Why is that a problem?"

"She never did that with me. Not once."

He tucked a finger under her chin. "Then isn't it wonderful that she's getting a second chance with Sarah Beth?"

She sighed. "I know you're right. I even realize it wasn't that she didn't want to read to me. There was no time back then. Sometimes she went straight from one job to the next. I was lucky if I saw her for an hour. I knew Mrs. Melrose, the babysitter who lived next door, better than I knew my own mother."

"Then this is a second chance for the two of you, too," he said. "Take advantage of it, Helen. This time is a blessing."

"When I'm being rational, I realize that. It's just that some days it's overwhelming having her here. I come home exhausted. I want time with my daughter and instead I'm interrupted every two seconds by my mother ringing that stupid bell."

"You could hire another caregiver for a couple of hours in the evening," he suggested. "Or have Mrs. Lowell start later. I'm here in the morning. She could come in when I leave for the restaurant and stay for an hour or two after you get home. And the reality is that it's only going to be for a little while longer, anyway. Your mom's making terrific progress."

Helen scowled at him. "Why do you have to be so calm and reasonable? All I need right this second is sympathy."

Wisely, Erik didn't allow the smile on his lips to fully

form. Instead, he reached for her and pulled her into his arms. "I can be sympathetic," he said, holding her close.

Helen rested her head on his shoulder and let herself relax. How had she gotten so lucky? She wasn't an easy woman. She'd been on her own way too long and was far too set in her ways when she and Erik had married, but it worked. He was exactly the man she'd needed in her life. He was strong and patient and mostly knew what she needed before she did. Just as important, he knew when to call her on it when she was being ridiculous, like tonight.

"Have I mentioned lately how much I love you?" she murmured.

"Have I mentioned that I love you more?"

She lifted her face for a kiss, the kind that stole breath and usually led to a frantic dash for their bedroom, only to hear the sound of the maddening little bell.

"I'm going to kill her," she said. "I really am."

Erik merely chuckled and gestured toward the glass of ginger ale. "Is that what she sent you down here for?"

She nodded.

"I'll take it to her and get Sarah Beth into bed. Why don't you take a long bubble bath and meet me in our room." He winked. "We can finish what we almost got started."

"You're a saint," she declared.

"I hope not, darlin', because I surely was hoping to indulge in a little wickedness before the night's over."

Helen laughed at his eagerness and suddenly felt rejuvenated. In just a few minutes he'd set everything right in her world. She knew it might not last past daybreak, but for tonight she intended to enjoy every second.

CHAPTER NINETEEN

The kids had been exhausted on the ride back from the beach. All three of them fell asleep in the car. After helping Ty to carry them inside, Annie decided to walk home.

"Are you sure you don't want to wait until I can give you a ride?" Ty asked. "Mom or Cal should be home soon and they can take over here."

Annie shook her head. She needed to process everything that had happened. Until she'd replayed the wonderful day in her head—even discussed it with Sarah—it wouldn't seem entirely real.

Ty studied her with a frown. "You're not having second thoughts, are you?"

"About us? No," she said truthfully.

"Were the kids too much? I warned you that three of them all at once could be a little daunting."

He looked so genuinely concerned that she stood on tiptoe to press a kiss to his cheek. "Stop fretting. Everything's fine. I had an absolutely fantastic time. It was perfect."

"Perfect, huh? Even though we never..." He winked as he let his voice trail off.

"In a way, that almost made it better," she told him. "It

was real. It wasn't about the two of us not being able to keep our hands off each other. It reminded me how good we are together, how in sync we are."

His expression immediately turned serious. "It's true, you know. What we have, not many people ever find it. There's all that history and being friends and really getting each other. I've missed sleeping with you, don't get me wrong, but I think what I missed just as much is talking. We used to talk every single day, even when we were at separate colleges and even when I first signed with the Braves. Talking things over with you kept me grounded."

"I remember," she said softly, slipping her hand into his, loving the strength of his grip and the feel of the calluses that reminded her of who he was, what he did for a living. Baseball had taken him away from her, but he'd always been so passionate about it. She'd never been able to begrudge him the success, despite its inadvertent role in their breakup. "Sometimes, after we split up, I'd lie awake at night thinking of all the things I wanted to tell you."

"Me, too." He shook his head. "Maybe if I'd just picked up a phone—"

She cut him off. "I wouldn't have listened. You know that. I was too hurt and angry. We finally have a chance now, because enough time has passed. It feels right."

Ty brushed a wisp of hair from her overheated cheek. "It really does feel right," he said before lowering his mouth to claim hers.

Annie could have stood there like that forever with Ty's persuasive lips kissing her like there was no tomorrow, but a cry from inside had them jerking apart.

"Cole's awake," he said unnecessarily. "I have to go."

"Go," she said at once, even though her heart was still

hammering in her chest. "You'll be okay on your own with all three of them?"

He grinned, his attitude cocky. "Piece of cake."

"Okay, then," she said, still not moving, suddenly reluctant to leave, after all.

"I'll call you later, okay?" he said, apparently equally reluctant to end the day.

"Sounds good," she said, recalling too many nights when parting had been unbearable, when weekends together at her college or his had been unsatisfactorily short. It had been so sweetly innocent back then. "Talk to you later."

She forced herself to turn and go and not look back. She made it all the way to the corner before she allowed herself to give a little whoop of pure exhilaration. She and Ty were together again. Really together.

And this time, she was determined to let nothing tear them apart.

Ty actually managed to get all three kids fed and settled in front of the TV in their upstairs playroom before Cal and his mother got home.

"You're late," he noted, then grinned at the immediately guilty flush on their cheeks.

"We played hooky, too," Maddie said.

"Hey," Cal protested. "Don't give away all our secrets."

Maddie chuckled. "We don't have any. Everyone in town knows the comings and goings at the Serenity Inn."

Ty clapped his hands over his ears. "Too much information," he told them emphatically. "And now I really am thankful that Annie and I steered clear of that place."

The comment drew his mother's gaze away from Cal. "You and Annie? You're back together for real?"

"We're getting there," Ty said, a note of caution in his

voice. "Don't go blabbing it around, though, especially not to Dana Sue. Let Annie tell her whatever she wants her to know."

"But—"

Ty cut her off. "I know, you, Dana Sue and Helen tell one another everything," he said. "Not this time, please. And don't go cross-examining Annie at work tomorrow, either."

Maddie regarded him with exasperation. "Now, that's just plain mean. What's the fun of knowing about this if I can't mention it to anyone?"

"How about the satisfaction of knowing a secret?" Cal suggested. "That ought to keep you contented for a day or two, and I imagine that's just about how long it will be before the news leaks out, anyway."

"I suppose," Maddie grumbled, her disappointment plain.

Ty gave her a hug. "Thanks, Mom. And for being so understanding, I will keep what I know about the two of you behaving like teenagers to myself."

Cal gave him a disgruntled look. "According to your mother, everyone already knows about that. Face it, you have no leverage over us."

Ty shrugged. "Too bad."

"Not from where I stand," Cal said. "I'm going up to check on the kids and take a shower. I have to be at school early tomorrow. I scheduled a team meeting before classes begin."

"Uh-oh," Ty said. He knew what that meant. Cal was about to come down hard on somebody for breaking the rules. "What's the problem?"

"Grades," Cal said succinctly. "We're just days from the end of the season and the school year and I've just learned that I have players in danger of flunking some of their core classes."

"It's too late to disqualify them, isn't it?" Ty asked. "You said yourself the season's just about over. How many games are left?"

"Two," Cal said. "But I know about their grades, which means I need to deal with it. And I really need to lay down the law for the benefit of the sophomores and juniors, who don't take this seriously. Otherwise, they won't be eligible next season. Somehow the fact that there's a zero tolerance policy for failing escaped them. It's even worse because a couple of them could be athletic scholarship candidates for college as long as they don't blow it."

"Is there time for them to get their act together?" Ty asked. "The sophomores and juniors, I mean."

"Sure, there's plenty of time, but at the moment they seem to lack the motivation. I need to remind them what's at stake."

"Want me to come in and explain to them why all their classes matter and not just how well they can hit and throw the ball? They might get the importance of a well-rounded education if it comes from me."

Cal looked intrigued. "You could have something there. I've told them that, but let's face it, my pro career was short-lived. They figure I'm revising history. You're a current local hero. Do you mind doing this?"

"I wouldn't have suggested it if I did. I owe you. You dragged me back from the brink of self-destruction more than once." In fact, that out-of-control period after his parents' divorce was the reason his mom and Cal had been thrown together so often. They'd formed a bond while trying to change Ty's unpredictable and moody behavior.

"Indeed, he did," Maddie confirmed. "I think it's a wonderful idea."

"Okay, then," Ty said. "What time do we need to leave? I'll be ready."

"Six-thirty too early? I have the team scheduled to be there at seven."

"I'll be ready," Ty promised. "I guess I should head up, too. Those kids wore me out today."

"Welcome to the joy of parenting multiple preschoolers," Maddie said. "The only thing I have to say to you is that you do survive it. At least I did with you, Kyle and Katie. I'm not so sure yet about Jessie and Cole."

"Hey, those are my little angels you're talking about," Cal protested.

Maddie nodded. "Believe me, I am well aware of that. They have their daddy's energy and wild streak."

"Which you love," Cal said, giving her a kiss on the cheek.

Maddie turned her face up to his. "I do," she admitted.

Ty swallowed hard at the adoration shining in her eyes. He couldn't recall a single time in all the years of her marriage to his dad when she'd looked at Bill Townsend like that. Maybe he'd just been oblivious, but he thought otherwise. He thought Cal Maddox had come along at just the right time and given her back the joy that Ty's father had taken from her. For that, Ty would be forever indebted to him.

He just hoped that someday soon Annie would look at him that way again. They were almost there, but no matter how close they came, he couldn't ignore the faint flicker of caution that came into her eyes from time to time. Nor could he blame her.

"For a woman who just spent an entire day with the man she obviously loves, you don't look very happy," Sarah said to Annie as they sipped margaritas. "And not ten minutes ago, I thought you were going to float away. What changed?"

"I'm wondering if I'm deluding myself that we can work this out," Annie admitted. "Sure, all the elements are there. I love him. He loves me. But what if it's not enough?"

Sarah sighed heavily. "I know just what you mean."

Annie regarded her with surprise. In recent days Sarah had been thoroughly upbeat about her reconciliation with her husband. "I thought everything was going well with you and Walter. You said your first session with Dr. McDaniels was fantastic."

"It was," Sarah said glumly.

"It's not unusual in counseling to hit a rough patch, maybe even to backslide a little," Annie told her.

"I could live with a rough patch," Sarah said.

Annie regarded her with bewilderment. "I'm not following here. Is it the margarita, or am I missing something?"

"Walter refused to go to the last two sessions," she confessed. "I'm at my wit's end, Annie. I don't know what to do next."

Annie was stunned. "But you told me how much you loved Dr. McDaniels, that your sessions had been great."

"They have been, but I was the only one there," Sarah revealed despondently. "Walter had an excuse both times. Bottom line, he figured he was 'cured' after one visit, and that going back was a waste of time and money."

"If you're still going, then the money's still being spent," Annie said.

"I'm taking it out of the money he gives me for groceries. If he knew, he'd give me less money."

"Oh, sweetie, this isn't good," Annie said.

"Tell me about it. I think we're right back to where we started. All Walter can think about is getting us back home to Alabama, where we belong, he says."

"What do you think?"

"That I'm not going back there if we haven't worked out the issues that sent me here in the first place. He still demeans me at every turn, but I'm finally able to see that for what it is, a form of bullying meant to destroy my self-esteem."

Annie was surprised and pleased by Sarah's determination. "Good for you!"

"It probably means the end of my marriage," Sarah said glumly. "I don't see any way around it. We can't fix it if Walter doesn't even think it's broken."

"Is he coming back this weekend?"

Sarah nodded.

"Want me to ask my dad to talk to him again? He seemed to connect with him last time."

Sarah managed a faint smile. "I'm not so sure you could call it a connection. Ronnie scared Walter half to death."

"How? I know he didn't hit him," Annie said. "Did he threaten him?"

"According to Walter, it was a come-to-Jesus talk."

"Well, maybe he needs another one."

Sarah shook her head. "It's like anything else, Annie. Walter's going to have to lose the kids and me before any of this will really sink in. And, I swear, it will be too late. I'm not going to keep trying and trying, when the end result will be the same."

Annie saw the look of resignation on her face and wanted to cry for her. "I'm sorry."

"Me, too." She took another sip of margarita, then lifted it in a mocking toast. "Hey, it could be worse—I could be in denial like Raylene."

Annie regarded her with surprise. "Why do you say that? Have you been in touch with her again?"

"Oh, gosh, I guess I didn't tell you. I felt so bad after you called her that night and she blew you off that I decided to try one more time to plan a get-together. You know, you and me driving over to Charleston for lunch or something."

"And?"

"She pretty much told me what she'd told you, that she was so busy and had so many demands on her time, she couldn't even think about a thing like that until after Christmas. Can you imagine? That's months and months from now, and she doesn't have one single day free for lunch? Whose calendar, except maybe the president's, is that booked up?"

"I suppose if you're all caught up in the Charleston social scene and on a dozen different committees, it's possible," Annie said, though she didn't believe Raylene, either.

"Well, I asked her about that. I asked what committees she's on, just showing an interest, if you know what I mean. She stumbled all over herself trying to think of one. There is something wrong with her. Or with her marriage. Whatever it is, she doesn't want us to know. I'm sure of it."

"I felt the same way," Annie said. She grabbed her cell phone, found Raylene's number and dialed. "My turn to try again."

She waited and waited, but when the phone was eventually answered, the voice was unfamiliar.

"This is Annie Sullivan, an old friend of Raylene's," she told the woman on the other end. "Is she available?"

"Mrs. Hammond isn't home," the voice said stiffly.

"When do you expect her back?" Annie persisted.

There was a discernible hesitation before the woman responded, "I'm not entirely sure. She was called away suddenly. When she returns, I'll tell her you called."

"Raylene was called away? Where? Has something happened to one of her parents?"

"I can't tell you anything. I'm sure when she gets your

message, she'll give you a call and she can answer all your questions herself. Goodbye."

The thump of the phone as it was banged into its cradle, disconnecting the call, filled Annie with dismay and annoyance. "Does everyone in that house just hang up on people?" she grumbled.

"Who was it?" Sarah asked.

"I have no idea. A housekeeper, maybe. Could have been a relative, though it wasn't her mother. She'd have said something when I told her who I was."

"And she said Raylene was called away?" Sarah said. "What does that mean?"

Annie shrugged. "It could mean anything. I suppose there could have been some family emergency."

"Or it was code for Raylene being in trouble."

Annie frowned. "In trouble in what way?"

"I don't know exactly, but it doesn't feel right to me. Raylene sounded so standoffish and secretive, not like she used to be at all. And now this. What if that husband of hers had her locked up in some loony bin?"

Annie regarded her incredulously. "Come on, we don't have any evidence that it's something like that. You're letting your imagination run away with you."

"I'm telling you, something is not right over there," Sarah insisted stubbornly. "We need to find out what's going on."

"Don't you think if Raylene wanted or needed our help, she'd ask for it?" Annie said. "She made it pretty clear she didn't want us to come to Charleston."

"Since when do fledgling Sweet Magnolias pay attention to something like that?" Sarah demanded. "Either we're going to be friends like your mom, Helen and Maddie, or we're not."

Annie nodded eventually, though she had second and even third thoughts about it. "When do we go?"

"When's your next day off?"

"Sunday."

"Then we'll go on Sunday. Walter will be here. He can watch the kids."

"Do you think that's wise?" Annie asked. "Under the circumstances, he could see it as the perfect opportunity to pack them up and take them back to Alabama."

Sarah shook her head confidently. "If he could run off with just Tommy, maybe, but he'll never take both of them, and he certainly won't run off and leave Libby alone."

"Are you so sure about that?"

"I am," Sarah confirmed. "But maybe we'll have your dad come by again, after all, just to make sure."

That was a plan Annie could get behind.

Ty left the high school feeling good about his meeting with the team. He thought he'd gotten through to them about the importance of a well-rounded education. He'd pointed out all the different ways various classes had helped him with his career. It had been a bit of a stretch when it came to chemistry, but he'd even managed to make that sound vital to being a professional athlete.

He was on his way home when his cell phone rang. Caller ID indicated it was Dee-Dee.

"Why are you calling, Dee-Dee? We're only supposed to communicate through our attorneys these days."

"I need to see you, Ty. I drove all night to get here. I'm on Main Street now, in Wharton's. Where can we meet? Can you come here?"

Something told Ty it was a very bad idea for him to be

anywhere alone with Dee-Dee. Who knew what scheme she had in mind?

"How about Helen's office?" he suggested.

"I don't want her involved in this," Dee-Dee said. "Just you and me, in private. I think if we keep the attorneys out of it, maybe we can work things out."

Ty had serious doubts about that, to say nothing of serious reservations about seeing Dee-Dee alone for any reason. "I'm sure Helen will loan us her conference room," he said, more determined than ever not to jeopardize his case by being alone with her so she could claim who-knew-what to the court afterward. It would be just like Dee-Dee to accuse him of trying to bribe her or some such to cast doubt on his suitability as a father to Trevor.

"We'd be more comfortable at your house," she cajoled. "And maybe I could see Trevor."

"Not a chance. It's Helen's office or nothing."

"Fine. Tell me where it is. How soon can you be there?"

He gave her directions, then added, "I'll be there in ten minutes."

And if Helen wasn't around to sit in on the meeting, he'd ask Barb to join them, or at the very least he'd insist on an open door so she could keep her ears attuned to every word that was said.

On his way, he called Helen to fill her in.

"Quick thinking," she told him approvingly. "Any idea what's on her mind?"

"None," he said. "She sounded upset, though, especially when I wouldn't agree to see her in private. I think she has some scheme or other in mind."

"Or maybe she wants to negotiate a way out of this mess, now that we've sent an official letter to her attorney informing her of our position on this. Could be her attorney has finally told her she can't win."

"I doubt she'll listen to reason from anyone," Ty said. "No, she's up to something."

"Well, we'll know soon enough," Helen said. "She just got out of her car in the parking lot. Where are you?"

"Sneaking in the back door right now," he told her. "Thank goodness I know where you hide the spare key."

"Please don't tell Erik about that key. He thinks I stopped leaving it there."

"Our secret," Ty said as he walked around the corner from the hallway and clicked off his cell phone as he entered Helen's office. The intercom buzzed, and Barb announced Dee-Dee's arrival.

"She's not on your calendar," Barb said, a disgruntled note in her voice.

"She's here to see Ty," Helen soothed.

"Well, how was I supposed to know that?" the secretary demanded. "Where is he?"

"In my office," Helen told her.

"How the dickens… Oh, never mind," she said, sounding resigned. "Shall I send her in?"

Ty exchanged a look with Helen, grinning. "I guess I'd better send Barb flowers this afternoon. Otherwise she'll be ticked at me forever."

"Make it chocolates and she'll forget this ever happened," Helen advised, just as the door opened. Dee-Dee stood on the threshold but didn't enter.

"You said we could meet in the conference room," she said, her accusing gaze on Ty.

"Helen turns out to be free, so why don't we chat right here?" Ty suggested. He sat down to emphasize that it was the only option.

For a moment, it looked as if Dee-Dee might balk, but then her expression turned resigned and she came into the room, closed the door and sat down on the edge of the chair next to his. She looked more haggard than she had on her last visit, as if she hadn't been sleeping. Ty couldn't help wondering about that. It was the first time he'd realized that all of this fighting had taken a real toll on her.

Helen sat down behind her desk, in a move deliberately designed to emphasize who was in charge.

"So, this is a surprise," Helen said to Dee-Dee. "It's unusual for a parent involved in a custody dispute to ask to meet without representation present."

Dee-Dee nodded but seemed undaunted by the chiding note in Helen's voice. "I know, but after my attorney got your letter, he sat me down and said he could fight this through to the end for me, but the outcome will probably be the same. I won't wind up with full custody of Trevor." Tears filled her eyes and spilled down her cheeks. "He made me see that the best I can hope for is that Ty and I can work out some kind of arrangement that will give me extended visits with Trevor."

Ty had remained silent up until now, but he couldn't seem to stop himself from muttering, "As if that's going to happen."

Dee-Dee turned to him, her expression forlorn. "Ty, please, can't you be reasonable? Trevor's my son, too. I know I made some terrible mistakes, but I want to make things right. Surely you know how that feels."

Ty wavered. He'd been fighting for a second chance with Annie, but that was hardly the same thing. He saw right through Dee-Dee's tears. She was trying to manipulate him into feeling sorry for her. And on one level he did, but protecting Trevor was more important. He stiffened his resolve.

"You gave up any right to call him your son when you left him, Dee-Dee," he said. "How many times do I need to remind you of that? You're getting married now. You say the man you're marrying is a great guy. Have babies with him."

The moment the words were out of his mouth, Dee-Dee burst into full-blown sobs.

"What the hell?" Ty murmured, casting a worried glance at Helen. Despite his jaded opinion of Dee-Dee, the outburst seemed genuine. He'd never been able to take a woman crying without wanting to rush in to make things better. Before he could stand, though, Dee-Dee turned to him, her expression disconsolate.

"But that's just it, Ty," she said, sounding as if her heart were broken. "I can't. I can't have any more babies. Trevor's the only child I'll ever have."

CHAPTER TWENTY

When Ty didn't show up at The Corner Spa for his rehab session on Friday night, Annie had no idea what to think. She hadn't spoken to him since late the night before, when he'd called to tell her good-night. He hadn't said anything then about canceling their session. Given how dedicated he was to getting back on the ball field, she was mystified.

She couldn't help wondering if he'd had second thoughts about the two of them, but surely he'd tell her if that was the case. If he'd had the guts years ago to tell her about all of his misdeeds—albeit belatedly—coming clean with her about a change of heart after just one afternoon together shouldn't be that difficult.

She tried his cell phone, but the call went straight to voice mail. She glanced at the clock and realized he was now more than thirty minutes late.

"Okay, that's it," she muttered. "I am not waiting around here half the night for him. I'm doing him a favor, and if he can't be more considerate of my time, then to hell with him."

Still grumbling under her breath, she marched around the spa turning off lights and checking locks, then took off for Sullivan's. She was still seething when she got there.

She walked into the bustling kitchen, dodging Erik, Karen and her mother, and settled on a stool out of the way. Eventually her mother actually seemed to notice her.

"Your dad's in the dining room," Dana Sue said. "Why don't you join him? As busy as we are, it's going to be a while before I can take a break. I know he'd love the company."

"Maybe," Annie said. "In a minute. I just need some sulking time."

Dana Sue regarded her with concern. "Problems with Ty?"

Annie nodded.

"I'm sorry, sweetie. I can't listen right this second. Can they wait? Or can your dad help?"

"I don't want to talk about Ty, anyway."

"We have meat loaf on the menu tonight," Dana Sue told her. "How about that with some garlic mashed potatoes? That's good comfort food."

"Not hungry," Annie said, then held up her hand to ward off her mother's protest. "Don't worry. I'll eat in a little while."

"Well, I don't have time to argue with you," Dana Sue said. "But I will be keeping an eye on you, so don't wait too long or I'll get your father in here."

Annie grinned. "He doesn't scare me. Go. Work. I'll be fine." Or at least she would be if she could shake the sick feeling that Ty had been playing her yesterday, that he'd wanted to see if he could get her back, and now that he had, game over. It didn't fit with the Ty she'd once known, but then neither had the serial cheating spree he'd gone on.

When the dark thoughts got to be too much for her, she snagged Erik's attention, since her mom was obviously swamped.

"Meat loaf and mashed potatoes," she pleaded. "I'll be out front with my dad."

"Coming right up," Erik promised.

Annie walked into the dining room. Before she could head toward the booth where her dad could usually be found, though, her gaze was drawn across the room to where Ty sat at a table with Trevor and Dee-Dee. The cozy little family grouping made her want to gag and flee.

Instead, she drew herself up, marched across the restaurant and stood beside the table until Ty looked up.

"Forget something?" she inquired tightly, keeping her voice low in deference to the fact that she was in her mother's restaurant and he was with his son. Anywhere else and in any other company, she might have created a true Sullivan scene, as her mother had after finding out about Ronnie's cheating. Every neighbor on their block had witnessed that spectacle.

Ty shot to his feet at once, his expression dismayed, though there was no way to determine if he was merely embarrassed at having been caught or genuinely contrite for standing her up.

"I'm sorry," he said. "Something came up, and everything else pretty much slipped my mind."

"Hey, it's your career," she said blithely. "Next time you want to blow off a session, though, I suggest you call."

Before he could say another word, she turned and walked away. Her appetite gone, she walked right past her father, through the kitchen and out the back door.

Seconds later, as she was about to turn onto Main Street, she heard footsteps in the alley behind her, but she didn't slow down.

"Annie!"

It turned out to be her dad, not Ty, which made her madder than ever. Still, she stopped and waited. It was hardly her dad's fault that she considered him a poor substitute for the man who should have been chasing her down.

"What happened back there?" Ronnie demanded. "Erik brought your meal to my table while you were speaking to Ty. The next minute you were leaving. Did Ty say something to upset you?"

Now that her worry had been replaced by fury, she was ready to talk. "Let's start with the fact that he never showed up at the spa for his therapy tonight. Add in that I couldn't reach him when I tried to call. Then I find him out with Trevor's mother, having a cozy little family gathering, in my mother's restaurant, of all places!" She met her dad's worried gaze. "I spent most of the day with him yesterday. I let down my defenses. I really started thinking we had a chance, and now this."

"The dinner was probably innocent," Ronnie suggested, though he said it tentatively, as if he didn't quite believe it himself. "I'm sure he's not so insensitive that he'd bring Dee-Dee to Sullivan's otherwise. They probably had some custody issues to work out, or maybe she scheduled another last-minute visit with Trevor."

She scowled at him. "Do you hear yourself? You're making excuses for him. Whose side are you on?"

"Yours, always," her dad said. "I'm just saying that it didn't seem like you gave him even a half a chance to explain."

"Maybe because there was no good explanation," she retorted. "Just excuses. Well, I'm done. I took a chance, and look where it got me." She picked up her pace. She wanted to get home, take a long, soaking bath, go to bed and forget the existence of Tyler Townsend. If Sarah hadn't told her Walter was arriving tonight, she would have gone there and downed a couple of potent margaritas.

Her dad kept pace with her, his expression sympathetic.

"Hey, how would you have felt if I'd given up on your mom the first time there was a bump on our path to reconciliation?"

"That's different," Annie said.

"How? I made the same mistake Ty did. I cheated. Then your mom thought for sure I was about to cheat again with Mary Vaughn."

Annie waved off the comparison. "Everybody knew you'd never look twice at Mary Vaughn."

"Everybody except your mother. She had her doubts, and there I was with Mary Vaughn practically every time she turned around. She had no idea I was thinking of buying the hardware store and seeing Mary Vaughn because she was the Realtor. Trust me, your mother was not happy with either one of us."

"Well, you were destined to be with Mom," Annie said.

"And you've always been convinced you were destined to be with Ty." His look was calculated. "Have you changed your mind?"

Tears stung Annie's eyes. "No," she admitted, her voice choked. "I'm not the problem. He is."

"Because he was out with Dee-Dee?"

She nodded.

"The mother of his child?"

"Yes."

"They're always going to have that bond, Annie. If you can't handle that, then you're probably right to walk away. Otherwise, you'll just be setting yourself up for a lifetime of suspicion and heartache."

"Which is exactly why I'm done," Annie said bitterly.

They'd reached the house now, so she turned to face her dad. "Go on back to Sullivan's and wait for Mom. I'm okay. I'm going to take a bath and head straight to bed."

"You sure? I can hang around if you want to talk some more. Maybe fix you a sandwich."

She managed a faint smile at his ability to slip in a subtle reminder that she hadn't eaten. "There's nothing left to say and I can make my own sandwich."

"Yes, but will you?" he asked, clearly not reassured.

"You're just going to have to trust me, Dad. I know the stakes of not eating."

Ronnie regarded her with dismay. For a moment, it looked as if he might say something more, but then he simply kissed her forehead. "Don't give up on Ty just yet," he said quietly. "I'm still betting on destiny."

Annie watched him walk away and sighed. This was only the second time in her life that she hadn't believed her dad. The last time had been when he'd tried to explain why he had to go away and leave her and her mom. He'd told her it wouldn't change how much he loved her. He'd told her they'd still see each other. It hadn't happened that way.

And Annie had no reason to believe he was right about her future with Ty, either.

Ty's appetite had fled after seeing the misery and barely banked anger in Annie's eyes. He'd wanted to go charging after her, but he hadn't wanted to leave Dee-Dee alone with Trevor. The only reason they were out together in the first place was because he'd felt sorry for Dee-Dee after what she'd revealed in Helen's office. He'd figured giving her some time with Trevor, with him present, was the least he could do.

That didn't mean he was ready to change his stance on any kind of custody, but he wasn't so hardhearted that he could deny Dee-Dee any access at all to the only child she'd ever have.

He'd spoken to Helen privately after the morning meeting, and she'd expressed skepticism about Dee-Dee's story.

"I think she's playing you," Helen said. "She could have brought this up from the beginning. Why now, except to play on your sympathy when she realizes it's the only way to win?"

"At first, I thought the same thing," Ty admitted. "But those tears were real, Helen. I didn't know Dee-Dee all that well, but even when I told her there was no chance for the two of us, she didn't fall apart. She fought to change my mind."

"Maybe, or perhaps she missed her calling. I'm sure there's a role just waiting for her on some soap opera."

Again, Ty had dismissed her doubts.

"Let me at least check into this story," Helen pleaded.

"Doctor-patient records are confidential," Ty reminded her.

Helen lifted a brow. "Who's the lawyer? If she's going to use her inability to have more children as an argument in court, then we're entitled to proof."

Ty had finally relented.

He snapped back to the present when Trevor pulled on his sleeve. "Daddy, is Annie mad at us?"

"Just at me, kiddo."

"Why?"

"Grown-up stuff," he told his son. "I'll fix it."

Dee-Dee listened to the exchange, then said, "I could tell her that you were just being kind, giving me a little time with Trevor."

"I'm not sure she'd believe anything you have to say," Ty said. "No offense."

Dee-Dee shrugged. "None taken. In her place, I guess I

wouldn't believe me, either. Do you want to leave now and try to catch up with her?"

"Our meals just came. I'll talk to Annie later," he said. "It's already past Trevor's bedtime. I need to get him home."

"I could take him back to your house," Dee-Dee offered. Her eyes lit up. "I could read him a bedtime story, maybe hang out till he falls asleep."

"No," Ty said more sharply than he intended.

Trevor's head snapped up at his tone. Ty forced a smile. "Hey, buddy, how are your chicken fingers?"

"'Kay," Trevor said, but he appeared to have lost interest in them. He yawned widely, and his eyes started to drift shut.

Dee-Dee didn't seem hungry, either. Ty finally sighed. "Maybe we should just go."

"Wait," Dee-Dee said, putting her hand on his arm. "I need to ask another favor."

Ty steeled himself against that cajoling tone.

"As long as I've driven back over here, is it okay if I stick around for the weekend? I'd like to spend a little more time with Trevor, if I could."

The request meant that Ty would have to be with the two of them, but once again, he couldn't think of any reasonable way to deny her the opportunity. "Sure, stick around," he said eventually. "Call me first thing in the morning, and we'll figure out a time to get together."

"I could just pick him up, so you wouldn't be tied down all day," she offered.

Ty frowned. "Not going to happen," he said at once, wiping the hopeful expression from her face. "When it comes to your visits with Trevor, where he goes, I go. You might as well accept that."

"I just thought you might need to see Annie or something," she countered defensively. "I was trying to be thoughtful." She regarded him with a frown. "Ty, what do you think is going to happen if I'm alone with Trevor?"

He met her gaze, his own unflinching. "I'm not willing to find out," he said succinctly. "We do this my way or you might as well go back to Cincinnati first thing in the morning."

She gave him a sad look, but she nodded in agreement. "We'll do it your way," she said quietly.

Of course, that was only partially true, because if Ty *really* had his way, she'd go back to Ohio and never see Trevor again. Lately, though, seeing how good she was with Trevor and how much his son was starting to love his mom, it was getting harder and harder to justify keeping the two of them apart.

Four different people reported to Annie that they'd seen Ty with Trevor and an unfamiliar woman on Saturday. With each sighting, Annie's mood grew increasingly grim. By the end of the day she was ready to stuff a sweaty old towel into the mouth of anyone who mentioned Ty's name to her.

Unfortunately, Maddie chose that precise moment to summon Annie to her office.

"Close the door," Maddie ordered. "We need to talk."

"If this is about Ty, then we don't need to talk," Annie said, still standing in the doorway.

"It is and it isn't," Maddie said, making herself as clear as mud. "Close the door."

Reluctantly, Annie stepped inside and shut the door, but she didn't sit down.

"Do you realize you've been growling at your clients all day long?" Maddie asked, her tone surprisingly gentle. "I'm pretty sure I know what's on your mind, but you can't take it out on the people paying us for our services. We're supposed to be a place women come to relieve stress and get pampered, not a military camp where people get yelled at by a drill sergeant."

Annie winced. "Have I been that bad?" Not that she really needed to ask. She knew she had been.

Maddie's expression softened. "Depends on who you ask. Mindy Laughlin left in tears, but then she cries if someone says boo to her."

Mindy Laughlin had been the last person to mention having seen Ty, Trevor and Dee-Dee. Annie might have been less than receptive to her observations.

"I'm sorry. I'll apologize to Mindy and everyone else."

"That would be good," Maddie said. "In the meantime, though, is there something you'd like to get off your chest? I'm a good listener, as you well know."

"You're Ty's mother. You'll take his side."

"Not automatically," Maddie said, then grinned, "though I might be a little bit prejudiced in his behalf."

"I don't need to hear you defending him," Annie declared. "Did you know he blew off his rehab appointment last night?"

"Because Dee-Dee showed up unexpectedly," Maddie said. "I don't know the details, but something happened. Ty said he'd explain later."

"Is that more important these days than his career?"

Maddie gave her a chiding look. "You know Ty puts Trevor before his career."

"Trevor, certainly, but Dee-Dee?" Annie scoffed. "I didn't know she figured into the equation."

"She's Trevor's mother. None of us have to be crazy about that, but it's a fact. And right now—well, things are a bit uncertain about what role she'll play in Trevor's life. Ty's trying to juggle all that, along with his need to rehabilitate his shoulder and get back to playing ball. You could cut him a little slack."

"I would if he'd just been straight with me. He didn't call. He didn't answer my calls. For all I knew, he could have been run over by a bus."

"In Serenity?" Maddie said.

"It was an expression. I know there are no buses in Serenity," Annie said impatiently. "I just meant I was sitting around here worrying about him, and what do I find when I stop by Sullivan's? There he is with Dee-Dee and Trevor, looking like the perfect little family."

"You know better," Maddie said.

"Do I? Do I really?"

"Of course."

"No," Annie told her. "I thought I did, but now what I know is that the same old pattern of lies and evasions is starting all over again. Been there, done that. It's not happening again. Now, I need to go before I say something I'll regret. Good night, Maddie."

Maddie regarded her with disappointment as she walked out and closed the door. Out of respect for their long history, she closed it gently, but what she'd really wanted to do was slam it hard enough to rattle its hinges.

Not that any of this was Maddie's fault, but right this second she was the only person in the vicinity whom Annie could hold accountable for Ty's actions. He was certainly nowhere to be found. And why not? Because he was spending the day with Dee-Dee and his son again. Just the thought of it was enough to have her grinding her teeth.

It was a good thing she and Sarah were going to Charleston tomorrow. Because as difficult and unrewarding as their mission to check on Raylene might turn out to be, it had to be a huge improvement over sitting around and wondering what Ty and Dee-Dee were up to.

After spending most of the weekend around Dee-Dee, observing her with Trevor and feeling the knot in his stomach finally lessen, Ty actually listened when she requested on Saturday that Trevor be allowed to go home with her to Cincinnati for a brief visit.

"Just a few days, Ty, please. I want Jim to meet him. We'll fly up, stay a couple of nights and come back Tuesday. You can come along if you want to."

He silenced all of the instincts that told him to say no, and after conferring with Helen finally said yes. He also took a huge leap of faith and decided not to go along. He needed to see Annie, and sooner or later he was going to have to learn to trust Dee-Dee to do as she'd promised. If she passed this test, well, then he'd have to see whether he could live with more liberal visitation terms.

Still, it was the hardest decision he'd ever made in his life. Letting go of his son, even for twenty-four hours, just about killed him.

"You'll have him back here Tuesday night," he said again as he drove them to the airport. "I swear, if you don't, Dee-Dee, I'll make sure you never set eyes on him again."

"I understand," she said. "I won't break my promise, Ty. There's too much at stake. Don't you think I know that?"

"Just making sure," he said grimly.

Inside the airport, he hugged Trevor fiercely, then watched as his son walked onto the plane with Dee-Dee. All the way Trevor babbled excitedly about everything he saw. In the doorway, he turned and waved happily at Ty. The expression of sheer joy on Dee-Dee's face was almost enough to convince Ty he'd done the right thing.

Fear, however, settled in the pit of his stomach. He knew it would still be there until the moment Trevor returned.

By the time he'd gotten home from the airport on Saturday, it was too late to see Annie, but first thing on Sunday morning, Ty went straight over to her house to try to set the record straight. He had his apology all ready, along with an explanation that would win her over, no matter how mad she was. He even stopped at his grandmother's to pick a bouquet of flowers.

When Ronnie opened the door, his expression was daunting.

"Is Annie here?" Ty asked.

"No."

Ty began to see that his problem went beyond Annie. The whole family was now furious with him. Justifiably so, he was forced to admit.

"Where is she?"

"She's gone for the day," Ronnie said, his expression still forbidding.

Ty resigned himself to getting information one tidbit at a time. "When are you expecting her home?"

"I have no idea."

"Okay, then," he said, giving up. "Just tell her I stopped by and ask her to call me."

He started to go when Ronnie said, "Not so fast. I think you need to come inside, so the two of us can have a little chat."

Ty winced, but he knew there was no choice. He followed Annie's dad into the kitchen. Ronnie poured a second cup of coffee and set it in front of Ty, then picked up his own cup and refilled it.

"Mind telling me what the devil you were thinking the other day?" Ronnie asked.

"If this is about me and Dee-Dee, I can explain, but I think I should be explaining to Annie."

"Start with me and let's see if I agree with you," Ronnie said.

Ty filled him in on the custody dispute, Dee-Dee's big announcement, all of it. "I was just trying to cut her a break, let her spend a little time with Trevor. Since I didn't want to leave her alone with him, I had to be there every second."

"And yet you allowed him to go to Cincinnati with her," Ronnie observed.

"Reluctantly," Ty admitted. "But these visits are going to happen, and after spending time with her on Friday and yesterday, I decided it was time to take a chance. Helen agreed it was the right thing to do."

"Okay, let's say I get that," Ronnie said grudgingly. "Couldn't you take five seconds to call and explain all that to Annie?"

"I should have, no question about it," Ty admitted.

Ronnie leveled a look straight into his eyes. "Are you really serious about getting back together with her? Because if you're not, you need to back off right now."

"I've never been more serious about anything in my life," Ty swore. "I love her, Ronnie. I've always loved her. I'd marry her tomorrow if she'd have me."

"Well, good luck with that," Ronnie said sarcastically. "Right now, I wouldn't give you two cents for your odds."

"She's that furious?"

"She's hurt and angry, yes, but worse, she's questioning every bit of progress you've made. She doesn't trust anything that's happened. Just when she was ready to forgive you and move on, you start hanging out with the very woman who came between you in the first place. Take it from someone who's been there, it's not smart, and I don't care how logical your reasons may be."

"I didn't think I could risk leaving Dee-Dee alone with Trevor, not at first," Ty said. "Surely Annie understands that?"

"And there's not another soul in this town you could have trusted to supervise their visits?" Ronnie asked skeptically. "How about now? You've let Trevor leave town with her. Does that mean you won't need to supervise every visit from here on out?"

"I honestly don't know."

"Well, how about this? If you're still worried, I'll hang out with Trevor and Dee-Dee, if that's really the only reason you're spending all this time with them. You know nothing's going to happen on my watch."

Ty saw the point he was trying to make. "You're right. I should have asked someone else to keep an eye on Dee-Dee when she's with Trevor. And I may take you up on your offer the next time she's in town. Right now, though, I need to make things right with Annie. Do you really not know what time she'll be back?"

"She didn't say," Ronnie confirmed. "But I will tell her you were here."

Ty gave him a rueful look. "And we both know that'll be the end of it. She won't call me."

"Probably not," Ronnie agreed. "She's a stubborn one." He seemed proud of the fact.

"Then maybe you could just call me and I'll come back," Ty suggested. "I might get the door slammed in my face, but that's a whole lot better than just letting her hang up on me or, worse, refuse to take my call at all."

Ronnie studied Ty and apparently saw whatever he'd

hoped to see, because he nodded. "I'll call you, but after that, you're on your own."

"Fair enough," Ty said. "Thanks."

"Don't thank me. And, if I were you, I wouldn't try to stick your foot in the door so she can't slam it. You'll just have another serious injury to recover from before you can go back to playing ball."

Ty chuckled. "I'll definitely keep that in mind."

The truth was, though, that he'd risk an injury if it meant getting through to Annie.

CHAPTER TWENTY-ONE

On the drive to Charleston, Annie filled Sarah in on what had happened with Ty.

"You realize that Ty being with Dee-Dee could have been perfectly innocent," Sarah said.

"It was," Annie admitted. "At least according to Maddie, but that's not the point. I should have heard about it from Ty. I shouldn't have stumbled across them at Sullivan's, especially not when he'd blown off his rehab session with me to be with her."

"I can't deny that had to look bad," Sarah conceded.

Annie held up her hand when Sarah would have gone on. "Never mind. Enough about me. I've already talked this to death. I'm sick of even thinking about it. How's Walter been this weekend? On good behavior?"

Sarah sighed. "Exactly the way he's been every other weekend. Sweet and attentive and full of all sorts of pretty words, but when it comes down to actually making some real progress by seeing Dr. McDaniels, he refuses to do it. I give up. I told him today before we left that I don't want him coming back next week, that I'm going to have Helen file the divorce papers."

Annie stared at her in surprise. "You're sure? It's only been a couple of months since you decided to give him another chance."

"I'm a hundred percent sure," Sarah said, sounding surprisingly at peace with the decision. "Why wait? The handwriting is on the wall. And so you know, your dad's going to my house right now. He'll be staying put till we get back."

She met Annie's worried gaze. "I swear, I don't think I could have left today if he hadn't agreed to go over there. Walter was mad enough to take *both* kids and go home to Alabama just to get even with me. He was still yelling and carrying on when I walked out to come pick you up."

Annie pondered the mess both of their lives were in. How on earth did anyone ever get married and stay that way? Ironically, of the Sweet Magnolias, only Helen's marriage had yet to hit any obvious bumps. Maybe it was because, as a divorce attorney and the most cynical of them all, she'd been forty when she'd finally married Erik. She'd been witness to way too many bad marriages not to make sure hers had a good foundation.

Maddie and Cal's marriage appeared solid enough, but she'd had her share of ups and downs with Bill Townsend, Ty's dad. Of course, Cal was a saint compared to Bill, and openly counted his lucky stars that Maddie had agreed to marry him. Annie suspected it would be years, if not forever, before their honeymoon phase was over.

As for her own parents' marriage, though their love had lasted since they were teens, they'd had to split up before they'd found their way back to the kind of enviable marriage that Annie had once expected to have with Ty.

Perhaps she and Ty had already faced their toughest challenges, she thought wistfully. Maybe if they could weather this rough patch, it would finally be smooth sailing. She had her doubts, though. Dee-Dee's continued presence was an irritant she was going to have to learn to handle.

She glanced up and realized they were on the outskirts of Charleston. "Do you need directions yet?" she asked Sarah. "I did an online search, so we should be able to go straight to Raylene's house."

"I put the address into the GPS system," Sarah told her. "Can you imagine? I never used that back in Alabama or in Serenity, but I bought one just because I knew it would come in handy someday."

Following the automated directions, they turned onto Raylene's street on the fringes of the downtown historic district. When they pulled up in front of the large, well-kept home with its fancy wrought-iron gate and climbing rose bushes still in full bloom, both Annie and Sarah sucked in a deep breath. The sweet scent of the roses reached them even on the street.

"Impressive," Sarah murmured as she looked over the three-story house and well-tended grounds.

"Obviously orthopedic surgery pays well," Annie added. "Looks to me like they recently renovated and were meticulous about historical detail. That doesn't come cheap."

"Hard to believe Raylene grew up in a little house just like ours in Serenity. No wonder her mother was always denigrating everything in town and was chomping at the bit to get back to the world she knew in Charleston."

Annie drew her rapt gaze away from the house and faced Sarah. "But we both suspect that a spectacular home and society marriage haven't made Raylene happy."

"I guess we'll find out for sure soon enough," Sarah said.

Annie glanced at her watch. "It's not quite noon. Do you suppose church services have ended?"

Sarah looked blank. "Why?"

"Because in this world, Sunday-morning church is part of the routine. It's as much a social obligation as going to the right charity events. I'm sure her grandparents and her husband's family insist on it."

Sarah shrugged. "Raylene was always a bit of a rebel. Maybe she stays home to spite them."

"I suppose it's possible," Annie said, though she had her doubts. "Let's ring the doorbell and see if anyone's around."

"What do we do if she takes one look at us and slams the door in our faces?" Sarah asked.

"Let's not get ahead of ourselves," Annie said, though truthfully she had no idea how they could force Raylene to confide in them if she didn't want to.

When they walked up onto the sweeping porch from which it was possible to glimpse the harbor, the door swung open, but it was Raylene's husband who emerged. He regarded them with immediate suspicion.

"May I help you?" His Southern drawl managed to sound welcoming and haughty at the same time.

Annie stepped forward. "Hi. I'm Annie Sullivan, Dr. Hammond. We met at a medical conference here in Charleston a couple of years ago. I'm a sports injury therapist."

His expression remained suspicious. "And?"

"I'm also a childhood friend of Raylene's. Sarah is, as well," she said, gesturing toward Sarah, who was eyeing Raylene's husband with distrust. Annie injected a cheery note into her voice. "Is she here? We drove over to have lunch today in Charleston and decided to stop by. I know we should have called first, but this was an impulsive decision, and we were hoping she could join us."

"Raylene's not here," he said, still without an ounce of warmth in his tone. "And I don't recall her ever mentioning you. She doesn't say much about her time in Serenity."

He said it as if she'd been sentenced to a term in a particularly odious prison.

Annie controlled her desire to make some sarcastic retort. After all, they were here for information, not to raise his hackles. "Has she gone to church? Will she be back soon?"

"She's away," he said with unmistakable reluctance.

Sarah finally found her tongue. "On vacation?"

He frowned at the question as if she'd crossed the bounds of propriety by asking. "The point is, she's not here. I'll let her know you stopped by."

It was clearly a dismissal, but Annie had passed the point of annoyance. She was sick of being treated like pond scum. At the very least he owed her a smidgen of professional courtesy.

"Actually, I'd really like to speak to Raylene today," she said stubbornly. "How about a phone number where she can be reached?"

"Impossible," he said.

"She's in some Third World country where phones aren't available?" she asked, not even trying to mask her sarcasm. Sarah glanced at her in surprise.

He tried to stare Annie down, but she didn't flinch.

"Why are you pushing this?" he asked finally. "She hasn't heard from you in years. What's so important that you need to speak to her today?"

"We *have* spoken recently," Annie said, catching the unmistakable flicker of surprise in his eyes. The next bit was a stretch, but she wanted to see how he reacted. "We told her we'd be stopping by."

Sarah obviously caught on to her tactic. She jumped in. "So, you see it is odd that she would go out of town without letting us know."

"Not two minutes ago, you said this was an impulsive visit," he countered, clearly not buying their story. Before they could invent more fibs, he added, "Look, I have no idea what goes on in Raylene's head half the time. She's gone. Deal with it. I will let her know you stopped by, but that's the best I can do. Now, if you don't mind, I have an appointment I must keep."

He went back inside and shut the door in their faces.

"What was it my grandma used to say?" Sarah asked. "Handsome is as handsome does. Obviously his good looks weren't accompanied by the first clue about good manners."

"You know what surprises me?" Annie asked. "Most doctors would not go out of their way to be rude to someone in the same profession. I may not be a physician, but I get referrals from a lot of them. I network in some of the same circles he does. I could really harm his reputation if I set out to do it. Why would he take that kind of chance?"

"So we can rule out good breeding and common sense," Sarah concluded as they walked back to the car.

A moment later, a large white SUV emerged from the alley behind the house and drove off, with the doctor at the wheel.

"So, what do you think? Golf? Or a date?" Annie asked.

Sarah pulled away from the curb, made a U-turn and set off right behind him. "Why don't we find out?"

Unfortunately, when they reached the gated entry of a large, exclusive country club, they could go no farther.

"I guess we'll never know," Sarah said glumly.

Annie shot her a look of disbelief. "Keep driving," she ordered. At the guardhouse, she put on her most brilliant smile. "We're with Dr. Hammond," she said.

The guard looked puzzled. "He didn't mention guests."

"Isn't that just like him?" Annie said to Sarah. Again, she beamed at the guard. "You could check with the dining room, see if he's expecting guests."

"Of course," he said agreeably. He made the call, hung up

an instant later and opened the gate. "Go right on in. Sorry about the mix-up."

As they drove onto the lush country club grounds, Sarah turned to Annie with approval. "You're good."

"I told you I was going to master the whole Nancy Drew thing sooner or later."

"Now what?"

Annie pondered their next step. She wasn't sure what else they needed to accomplish. They'd already proved that Paul Hammond was here to meet another woman. Beyond that, what really mattered?

Except discovering where Raylene had gone, and that answer wasn't here.

"We might as well leave," she told Sarah. "We know he's a cheating jerk, or at least we have a very strong suspicion that he is. Maybe we can track down Raylene's parents. They might be able to tell us where she is, and that's all I really care about."

Unfortunately, a search of the Charleston phone directory didn't provide any clues about Raylene's parents, which left them exactly nowhere.

"Do you remember her grandparents' names?" Annie asked.

"Not really. We might as well head home," Sarah said in defeat.

"I suppose you're right," Annie agreed. "But to tell you the truth, I'm more worried about Raylene than ever."

"Me, too, but what can we do beyond checking every day or so to see if she's back?"

Annie wasn't satisfied to sit by passively. It went against her nature. Besides, if she channeled her need for answers into focusing on Raylene, maybe she wouldn't be quite so obsessed with finding out what Ty and Dee-Dee were doing.

Right this second, those were answers she was almost afraid to discover.

"Let's not leave just yet. Why don't we have lunch and make a plan?" she suggested to Sarah. "I have a few contacts around Charleston, people who know our friend Dr. Hammond. They might be happy to spill the beans on his personal life, especially if he treats them as arrogantly as he treated us."

Sarah nodded. "I like the way you think, Nancy Drew."

"Wait until you see if we turn up any information before you get too excited," Annie told her. "My P.I. credentials are a little shaky."

But something told her that a powerful motivation could make up for a lack of professional-caliber skills.

Ty was thoroughly frustrated by his inability to reach Annie. When he'd heard nothing from Ronnie by dinnertime, he'd walked back over to the house, only to find it pitch-dark. There was no sign of Ronnie's car, though Annie's was sitting in the driveway.

From there he walked to Sullivan's, but Ronnie wasn't in his usual booth. Nor was there any sign of Annie.

That left Sarah's. When he arrived there, he hit pay dirt. Ronnie's car was out front, and every light in the house was on. He walked around to the kitchen, but spotted no one. He could hear childish squeals and laughter coming from upstairs, though.

Returning to the front door, he rang the bell. Through the side panels of glass he saw Ronnie jog lightly down the stairs, Libby wrapped in a towel in his arms and a buck naked, soaking-wet Tommy running alongside.

When Ronnie opened the door, he regarded Ty with impatience. "I don't have time for this now," he said. His shirt was soaked, as were his jeans.

"I can see that," Ty said, barely containing his amusement. "Need some help?"

Ronnie shrugged. "Why not?" He headed back up the stairs with Libby, while Ty rounded up Tommy and herded him along behind.

"Have they actually had their baths yet?" Ty inquired.

"Are you kidding me?" Ronnie asked. "They're like slippery little eels in the tub. They keep getting away from me. I don't remember Annie being like this."

"There was only one of her," Ty reminded him. "Why don't you get Libby ready for bed? She looks clean enough. I'll finish up with Tommy."

A half hour later, both kids were tucked in and asleep. They looked like little angels, but Ty knew from his own experiences with Trevor, Jessica Lynn and Cole that appearances could be deceiving. Awake and teamed up, they could be holy terrors.

Downstairs he grabbed a couple of beers from the fridge and handed one to Ronnie, who looked exhausted.

"How'd you wind up babysitting, anyway?" Ty asked him.

"Like I told you this morning, Annie and Sarah had someplace to go. Sarah didn't want Walter here alone with the kids, because she'd just told him their marriage was over. She was afraid he'd run off with the kids. Instead, he gave me an earful about what an ungrateful woman she was, then took off. I've been on my own ever since. I've got to tell you, I'd rather build a house single-handedly than wrestle with those two for an entire day."

Ty chuckled. "I could take over if you want to get home and get some sleep."

Ronnie shook his head. "No offense, but they were left

with me. I can't go off and abandon them, even with you here in my place. Besides, Sarah should be home any minute. She called a half hour ago."

"Will Annie be with her?"

"Hard to tell. Sarah may drop her off at home, or she could come here and hitch a ride home with me."

"Mind if I hang around to find out? I need to see her, Ronnie. The longer she carries around this anger she's feeling, the harder it's going to be for me to make things right."

"You deserve hard," Ronnie reminded him.

Ty didn't even try to deny it. "Yes, I do."

Ronnie gave a little nod of satisfaction. "As long as you know that, I suppose you might as well stay."

But ten minutes later when Sarah arrived, Annie wasn't with her.

Sarah regarded Ty with a narrowed gaze. "She went home to bed," she said pointedly. "She's not very happy with you, by the way."

"I'm well aware of that."

"After the day we've had, her mood's not good. I think we're both pretty much thinking all men are scum." She glanced at Ronnie. "Not you, of course. You're a saint to have stayed with my kids all day."

"Not a problem," Ronnie told her.

"You didn't have any trouble with Walter, did you?"

"None I couldn't handle," Ronnie said. "But he's on the warpath, Sarah. Make sure you get to Helen first thing in the morning, okay?"

"Already planning on it," Sarah assured him. She turned to Ty. "You going to beat me there?"

"Meaning?"

"Until you settle this mess with Trevor's mother once and for all, maybe you should give Annie some space," Sarah told him. "Drawing her into all that drama isn't fair. The way it stands now, she doesn't know what she has to deal with from one minute to the next."

"I'm not always so clear on that myself," Ty said, "But I want Annie to know she comes first with me."

"Does she really?" Sarah inquired, her skepticism plain. "Seems to me, Trevor needs to be your top priority right now, and that's as it should be. He is your son, after all."

"I hear what you're saying," Ty told her. "But Annie needs to know she has a place in my life. I didn't make that clear when this mess started three years ago. I can't make the same mistake again."

Sarah didn't look entirely convinced, but she shrugged. "Your choice, of course."

Ronnie, however, gave him a hard look. "Be sure, Ty. Because if you're not in this for the long haul, Sarah's right, you need to let Annie go now."

Ty stared down both of them. "How many times do I have to say it? Annie's the only woman I've ever loved. I'm going to find a way to make this work."

Unfortunately, right this second, he had no idea what that strategy was going to be. He had a feeling he was long since past the point when a bouquet of daisies would do the trick.

Helen was enjoying a rare moment of alone time with her husband over morning coffee when she heard the thump of her mother's cane approaching the kitchen. She barely resisted the desire to groan. Erik gave her a commiserating look.

"Be nice," he said quietly. "Imagine what being cooped up here all this time has been like for her. Flo's a social creature. The only real company she's had has been Barb and our friends."

"I know," Helen said. "But is a half hour alone with you too much to ask?"

"It won't be much longer now," he consoled her. "You've seen how much better she's getting around. I'm sure she's just as impatient to be on her own as you are to have her settled in her own place. Talk to her about that. It'll give you both something to look forward to."

"I don't want her to feel like I'm anxious to shove her out the door," Helen said, though that was exactly how she felt, especially on the days when Flo spent an hour telling her how she was mismanaging her household.

Just as Flo reached the doorway to the kitchen, Erik stood and gave Helen a kiss. "I'm going to catch a little more sleep. I don't have prep duty at the restaurant this morning."

Flo walked into the kitchen clutching the morning paper in one hand. She beamed at Erik, but the look she reserved for Helen was more tentative. "Good morning," she said. "Is there coffee made?"

"I'll pour you a cup before I go," Erik said, getting a cup from the cabinet and setting it in front of her. "There are freshly baked cinnamon rolls, if you're interested."

Flo immediately shook her head. "Not for me. I have to start watching my girlish figure. After going without exercise for so long and your excellent cooking, I've put on a few pounds. My clothes are starting to get tight. Now that I'm moving better, it's time to get serious about taking the weight off."

Helen regarded her with surprise. "Mom, you look great. In fact, you look even healthier than you did when I came to get you in Florida. You don't have anything to worry about."

Erik slipped off as Flo countered with a litany of all the things she thought were wrong with her appearance. Helen finally lost patience.

"Mom, you're seventy-two. You're never again going to look like you did at fifty."

"Maybe not, but I can try," Flo said. "You'd be wise to take care of yourself, too. Years ago, when I was your age, I thought my looks would last forever, but of course they never do."

Helen refused to admit that she'd already started to worry about the fine lines at the corners of her eyes and around her mouth. The latter, she was sure, had deepened because she so often pursed her lips to keep from saying the wrong thing to her mother.

When Helen remained silent, her mother tapped the paper on the table. "I thought maybe we could check the classifieds for apartments or houses for rent."

Though she was delighted Flo had raised the subject, Helen had reservations about her plan. "I don't want you wasting money on rent," she told her. "Once we've sold the condo in Florida, you'll be able to buy whatever you want. I spoke to the Realtor yesterday and she tells me she's just about certain she's going to have a contract on the condo by the end of the week. It won't be quite what we were hoping for, given the slow turnaround in the real estate market, but it will even give you some money to put into savings after you buy something here."

Flo's eyes lit up. "Really? What perfect timing! Then we definitely have to start looking. Shall we call that nice young woman, the one who was in school with you? She's in real estate now, as I recall."

"You mean Mary Vaughn Lewis?"

"That's the one. I'd forgotten that she was married to Sonny Lewis." She frowned. "Or did they get divorced?"

"They did, but they're remarried now," Helen told her.

Flo shook her head. "I don't understand these on-again,

off-again, on-again marriages. I swear I don't. People need to fight harder to stay married in the first place."

"Amen to that," Helen said in a rare moment of agreement with her mother. "Unfortunately, that's not the advice most people want to hear from their divorce lawyer."

Flo chuckled. "No, I suppose not. So, shall I call Mary Vaughn or will you?"

"I'll call her," Helen said with some reluctance. Mary Vaughn's determined attempts to get her claws into Ronnie on a few occasions had made her less than a favorite with the Sweet Magnolias, but Jeanette had coaxed them all into giving her a second chance. And now that she was happily remarried to Sonny, the concerns about her going after Ronnie were pretty much averted. Still, Helen was cautious. Once burned, twice shy. Even though Mary Vaughn had never done anything to her, if something affected one of the Sweet Magnolias, it affected them all.

"Would you rather speak to someone else?" Flo asked, picking up on her lack of enthusiasm.

"No, Mary Vaughn is the best. I'll have her start looking around for some possibilities and we can schedule an evening next week to meet her. By then we should know more about whether the condo's sold."

Flo regarded her with excitement. "I can't tell you how I'm looking forward to this," she said. "It'll be fantastic to have my own space again. Not that you and Erik haven't been wonderful, because you have been, but you two need your privacy and so do I."

In a typically perverse way, Helen took offense at Flo's eagerness to be gone. What, Helen reflected, did it say about her that one second she couldn't wait to get her mother out from underfoot, and the next she was upset because Flo wanted the same thing?

It said her conflicted feelings about her mom ran as deep as ever, she realized with dismay. All these weeks under one roof and they'd only rarely found any common ground. How was that possible?

Maybe some mothers and daughters just weren't meant to outgrow the old parent-child relationship and find a deeper connection as adults. Then, again, she thought, maybe some just had to work a little harder at it. She resolved then and there to do just that…before it was too late. These days, seventy-two wasn't old, but it was an age when no one should take anything for granted.

CHAPTER TWENTY-TWO

Annie had successfully dodged every one of Ty's attempts to reach her during the day on Monday. He'd thought they ought to have at least some kind of conversation to start the peace process before his therapy session that night, assuming she even planned to show up for that. He'd made it clear in all of his messages that he intended to be there on time, so hopefully she wouldn't blow that off, too. He could only keep his fingers crossed that her professionalism would win over her temper.

When he arrived at The Corner Spa, the lights were on and the door was unlocked. Ty considered those good signs.

But when he walked inside, he was greeted by Elliott, not Annie. His heart sank.

"Where's Annie?" he asked at once.

"In the office, actually."

"So, she's determined to avoid me?"

Elliott shrugged. "No idea. I'm on my way out."

Ty's spirits immediately brightened. It appeared she hadn't ditched him, after all.

"Good luck," Elliott said, regarding him with a man-to-man, commiserating look. "She's not in a particularly good mood. I'm pretty sure that has something to do with you."

"Yeah, I'm prepared for that," Ty told him.

He walked into the hallway leading to his mother's office, Jeanette's and the one shared by the personal trainers. There was a light burning only under the door at the end of the hall. He knocked and walked in without waiting for a response.

Annie was behind her desk making notes in a client folder. She glanced up and regarded him warily, holding tight to the pen in her hand.

"I wasn't sure you were coming," she said.

"Not even after the half-dozen messages I left for you today?"

"Things with you have a way of changing without notice."

"Fair enough," he said. "I'm trying to reform."

"Well, good luck with that," she said, her expression still forbidding.

Ty had had years to get used to the way Annie closed in on herself when she was hurt, like a turtle retreating into its shell. He knew patience and persistence were the only ways to coax her back out. Reverse psychology might help, as well, especially under these circumstances.

"I guess I could work out on my own tonight, if you're too busy to coach me," he said casually. "It'll give me a chance to bump up those reps the way I've been wanting to." He turned and headed out the door.

He took several steps down the hall before he heard her mutter a curse under her breath and shove back her chair.

"Don't even think about it," she said, catching up with him. "I'm in charge here."

"Hard to be in charge if you won't speak to me," he commented.

"I'll speak, but strictly on a professional basis, are we clear about that?"

He hid a smile. "If you say so."

"I say so," she confirmed, pointing toward the first piece of equipment. "That came today. Have you ever used one like it before?"

He nodded.

"I'll set the weights, then let me see ten reps."

"Ten?" he scoffed. "How about thirty, and bump up the weight by at least ten pounds?"

"Did I or did I not say ten reps and that I'd set the weights?"

This time he did grin. "Yes, ma'am."

"Oh, don't you dare *yes, ma'am* me," she groused. "I'm not your mother."

"No, but you are the boss, am I right?"

"As a matter of fact, I am," she said, looking pleased that he'd accepted it.

They were a half hour into an increasingly strenuous workout, with her giving orders and Ty dutifully following them, before she finally turned a plaintive look on him and asked, "Why'd you do it, Ty? Why'd you blow me off for Dee-Dee?"

"That's not the way it happened," he told her. He met her gaze. "Will you actually listen, let me explain from start to finish without interrupting?"

She sat down on the bench across from his. "Talk."

He explained about everything that had happened the week before, from Dee-Dee's unexpected announcement to her decision to stay in town and his very reluctant agreement to let her take Trevor to Cincinnati for a few days.

He'd spoken to Trevor half a dozen times since they'd left, and the little boy seemed to be loving every minute of his time with Dee-Dee. Ty was grateful for that, but it still gave him a pang to know his son was now sharing his affections with his mother and prospective stepdad. He had no idea what to do with all these conflicting emotions. It would be nice to share them with Annie. First, though, he had to make peace with her.

"I should have called you immediately," he admitted. "I should have filled you in, but things started happening so fast, she was so emotional and Helen was so skeptical of her story, I felt like I was being pulled in different directions. I never meant to shut you out. First thing yesterday morning I came looking for you to explain everything, but your dad said you were gone for the day. I even tried to catch up with you again at Sarah's last night."

Annie met his gaze. "If you and I are going to be together, we have to start facing things like this as a team, Ty. At the very least I can listen, even if you don't want to hear my opinion."

He shook his head. "You have a right to do more than listen. You do have a stake in how all this turns out. At least that's what I want."

He hesitated, then added, "I suppose I keep remembering how it was before. Once I told you about Dee-Dee, about her being pregnant, you closed down. You didn't want to hear anything. You said you were done with me, that it was none of your business what we decided. I guess some of that is still in my head. As if things weren't awful enough, I was cut off from my best friend, the person I counted on to be straight with me."

Annie regarded him with sorrow. "I guess we're going to have to work at learning to communicate better, especially when it comes to Trevor and Dee-Dee."

"And I'll do that," Ty promised. "Will you?"

"I'll do my best," she agreed.

"So, how about going to Wharton's for a burger?" Ty suggested, seizing on their newfound rapport. "I missed dinner and I'm starved. We can really talk all this through. I'd like to know what you think."

Despite her very recent vow to be more open and improve communications, she hesitated.

"I don't know if Wharton's is a good idea," she said.

"Too many onlookers?" he guessed at once.

She nodded. "It adds to the pressure. It's going to be difficult enough for us to finally get this right without everyone in town watching every move we make."

"Then we'll take a drive, get dinner somewhere else. You choose."

"How about my house?" she suggested, surprising him. "My dad's playing basketball with Cal, Erik and Jeanette's husband, Tom. They always go out for pizza and beer after. Mom's at the restaurant. No one will be home for hours."

Ty held her gaze, saw the flush that rose to tint her cheeks pink. "You and me alone in an empty house?" he said slowly. "Suddenly food's the last thing on my mind."

"Nutrition is as important as exercise in your recovery," she reminded him, though she sounded a little breathless.

"I know, but maybe we could get a different kind of exercise before we worry about that burger."

"How about we discuss that after we get to my house?" she suggested. "Who knows how annoyed I might get with you between here and there?"

Ty grinned at the response. "Not to worry. I'm suddenly highly motivated to stay on your good side."

Annie laughed, the first genuine laugh he'd heard from her in ages.

"Yes," she taunted. "I imagine you are."

Suddenly, Ty realized something he should have learned about Annie years ago. When she had the upper hand, she was in her element. Her self-confidence soared. It was a good reminder to him that he should never again let her suffer any doubts about how amazing she was, how important she was to him.

Satisfied that they were finally on the same page and moving forward, Ty hid a triumphant smile and held the door for her, then waited while she locked up. "It's a nice night. Want to walk?"

"Sure."

It was only a few blocks, but it seemed to take an eternity to get to Annie's. Her sudden silence disconcerted him. He was at a loss for a safely neutral topic. This didn't bode well for how things were likely to go once they reached Annie's.

Inside the door, though, Ty decided to go for broke. As soon as it closed behind them, he stopped her and backed her against the wall.

"Have I mentioned how beautiful you are?" he asked, his mouth hovering over hers. "And how it drives me crazy being so close to you and keeping my hands to myself? The other day at the beach I wanted to rip off your bathing suit and have my way with you right there on the beach, the way we used to do."

"We were stupid kids back then, Ty," she said, a hitch in her voice. "And it would have been totally inappropriate for you to make a pass at me with Trevor, Jessie and Cole right there with us."

"Really?" he said with feigned surprise. "I had no idea you were so straitlaced."

She frowned at the accusation. "I'm mature, not straitlaced," she informed him, her voice huffy.

"There aren't any kids around now," he noted, running

a finger along her cheek. "No other adults, either. In fact, there's not a soul around to stop us from doing whatever we want to do." He held her gaze. "Except you, of course. You can stop this."

She shivered. "I don't want to. I should, because I'm still mad at you, but I don't want to."

He smiled at her obvious frustration with herself. "Do you need to wrestle with yourself a little longer over this?"

"No, I need you to get me into my room before I have time to come to my senses," she told him. She wrapped her arms around his neck, her legs around his hips, and held his gaze. "Step on it, Ty. Prove to me all those workouts are paying off."

"You don't have to ask me twice," he told her. "I've waited too damn long for this."

In her room, which still had the white eyelet ruffled spread and curtains from her teen years, he set her gently on top of the covers, then drank in the incongruous sight. Annie, all woman and eagerly awaiting him, atop a bedspread that reminded him of her innocence when he'd first made love to her so long ago. He had to shake off the crazy thought that in a way he was about to take her virginity all over again… and might be risking getting caught in the process. Though the former was hardly possible, the latter added a surprising edge of danger and excitement to the moment. Recently he'd made peace with Ronnie, but he had no idea how Ronnie would feel if he found the two of them together in Annie's bed.

"I feel like I did the first time I made love to you," he said as he settled on the bed beside her. "I'm scared to death I'm going to do something wrong."

She touched his cheek. "You couldn't possibly. We always got this right, from the very beginning."

They really had, Ty recalled, which made him question himself again. Why on earth had he ever looked at another woman? Stupidity? Immaturity? Availability? Maybe a combination of all three, he decided.

Pushing that thought from his mind and concentrating on the second chance right in front of him, he slowly, deliberately rediscovered Annie's body, from the curve of her shoulder to the gentle swell of her stomach, from her now perfectly rounded hips to the pink-tinted tips of her toes. He took his time with the journey, lingering where he drew low moans of pleasure, increasing the intensity of his touches when she writhed beneath him.

Every uninhibited response made him want to do more to show her how much he loved her. He wanted to make this last an eternity, or at least to be the start of forever.

When he entered her at last, he kept his eyes on hers, his gaze steady. He wanted her to have no doubts that he knew exactly whom he held in his arms, exactly who was driving him wild with passion.

"Only you, Annie," he murmured as his body reached its climax. "Always, only you."

She shuddered with her own release then, and when he again looked into her eyes, they were filled with tears. Touching a finger to the dampness on her cheeks, he studied her with a worried frown.

"I thought I knew what it was like to be with you," she whispered, obviously trying to explain the tears, "but I was wrong. This was better than anything I let myself remember. If I'd remembered this, I could never have let you go."

Annie was terrified to leave her bed, to leave this room where she and Ty had found their way back to each other's arms. Outside there were so many things that could still tear them apart—Dee-Dee, Trevor, even his career.

Ty glanced at the clock on her nightstand. "I think we need to get out of this bed. Either your mom or your dad could be home any minute."

She clung to him when he would have stood up. "If we're really quiet, they'll never know you're in here. It's not as if I'm five. They don't look in on me when they come home at night."

Ty grinned. "Is that really a chance you want to take?"

"The risk I don't want to take is leaving this room," she admitted. "I feel safe right here, as if nothing can harm us or come between us. We know how to communicate in here."

"Nothing is going to come between us again," Ty assured her. "I promise."

"How can you? Dee-Dee's still out there."

"She's not a threat to us. She's not even a threat to me and Trevor anymore. Helen's got that covered. I have complete faith in her. I may have to make more compromises than I'd like, but I'll keep my son. I believe that with all my heart."

"I'm not sure I'll ever be able to see you with Dee-Dee and Trevor without feeling a twinge of panic deep inside," Annie admitted. "The bond you have with her because of Trevor—"

"Is just that," he said. "Because of Trevor. There's nothing else between us."

"I want to believe that," Annie said.

"Then do. Just take a leap of faith and believe in me, in us. Dee-Dee has a fiancé herself. She doesn't want me any more than I want her."

Annie held his gaze and slowly nodded. After all, what choice did she have, really? She loved him. Nothing that had happened had changed that. After the hell of the past three years, she couldn't imagine anything worse that could. And sometimes, she'd learned, the only thing to do was take a deep breath and then listen to her heart.

While Ty was in the shower, Annie whipped up a meal of scrambled eggs with chive cream cheese, toast and turkey sausage for the two of them. She was whistling as she worked, when the back door opened and her mom walked in. Naturally Dana Sue immediately took note of the two places set at the kitchen table.

"Is your dad home from his night with the guys already?" she asked Annie.

"Uh, no," Annie hedged, uneasy about how her mom was going to react to the truth.

"Then who's using the shower?" Even as Dana Sue asked the question, understanding dawned and her eyes widened. "Ty's here? Upstairs?"

Annie felt heat climbing into her cheeks. "Afraid so."

Dana Sue studied her for a full minute and then a grin slowly spread across her face. "Well, hallelujah! Where's the phone? I need to call Maddie."

"Don't you dare," Annie said, horrified. "You're going to be totally discreet about this."

"You're in my house," Dana Sue reminded her, her expression smug. Sounding like she had when Annie had been a teenager, she added, "I get to decide who knows what goes on under my roof."

Annie stared at her. "You can't be serious."

Her mom chuckled. "Okay, no, but the look on your face when I said that was priceless."

"You could be even more discreet and disappear before Ty comes down here," Annie suggested. "Otherwise, he's going to be totally embarrassed that we got caught."

Instead, her mother went to the other end of the table, pulled out a chair and sat. "He deserves a little embarrassment. If I'm going to be his mother-in-law, he needs to get used to it."

"Hold on," Annie said, dismayed. "Nobody's said anything about a wedding."

"Well, why on earth not?" Dana Sue demanded.

"We're barely back together, for one thing."

"And for another?" her mom asked.

"His life is pretty complicated at the moment," Annie said, defending Ty.

"Life's always complicated. You make time for the things that matter."

"Mom, I do not want you to start bullying him about marriage the second he walks into this kitchen. If that's your plan, I'm going upstairs right now and telling him to sneak out my bedroom window."

"I'll just be outside waiting for him when he hits the ground," Dana Sue said, though her lips were twitching with amusement.

Still, Annie thought she sounded serious. "Mom, please, you and Maddie have to stay out of this," she pleaded.

"Stay out of what?" Ty asked, walking into the kitchen without the slightest hint of embarrassment. He even walked directly to Dana Sue and dropped a quick kiss on her cheek, as if this were a perfectly normal encounter.

"She needs to stay out of our lives," Annie told him.

"They're mothers. It comes with the territory," he said with a shrug. He grinned at Dana Sue. "I guess we're busted, huh?"

"And how," Dana Sue confirmed. "So, when's the wedding?"

Annie groaned. Ty merely reached for her hand and held tight. "We haven't discussed it yet," he said. "But we will."

Apparently something in his tone, the hint of certainty, convinced her mom, because she stood up, kissed him on his forehead, then kissed Annie. "I am so telling Maddie about this," she said, her eyes alight with excitement. "Things are finally going to be right between the two of us again."

"Hey, it's not about the two of you," Annie reminded her as she left the room. Her mom didn't reply.

Annie turned to Ty in exasperation. "You realize we won't have a moment's peace from now until we announce our engagement," she told him. "Assuming we do."

"Why wouldn't we?" he asked.

She frowned at the question. "Well, you haven't asked me to marry you, for starters. And I haven't said yes. Let's not start taking anything for granted, okay?"

"You want me to court you, make a big production out of the proposal?"

She thought about it, then nodded. "Yes, I think I do."

"Okay, then, not a problem."

"Just like that?"

"Why not? You deserve romance and a whole lot more. I can do that."

"You are a constant surprise," she said.

"That's the goal," he told her. "I have it on very good authority that surprises and a touch of romance keep things fresh."

"What authority?"

"Cal," he said.

"Your stepfather has been giving you advice on romance?"

"Hey, my mom seems happy, so who better to give me some tips? Of course, he claims to have learned a few things from my grandma Paula."

Annie regarded him with amazement and more than a little distress. "So courting me is going to be kind of like a big family project?"

"Don't worry. The execution is all up to me."

"I'm relieved."

He pulled her into his lap. "Never fear. I have a few surprises of my own."

"Such as?"

"Now, they wouldn't be surprises if I told you, would they?"

"I'm not that fond of surprises," she said grumpily. Most of the major ones in her life had fallen more into the shock category. They hadn't been good.

"I'll turn that around," he told her. "I promise. Now, I should probably get out of here before your dad gets home. He might not be quite as enthusiastic about what went on here tonight as your mom was."

"I think that's a given," Annie said. She snuggled against his chest, his arms tight around her. "Though, I'm not anxious to let you go. My offer still stands. You can sneak back into my room and spend the night."

"Your mom's already onto us, and she'll tell your dad," Ty reminded her. "It's okay, though. I'll be back."

"Promise?"

"Again and again, for the rest of our lives."

Annie looked deep into his eyes and saw something she'd once taken for granted: commitment. And, for the first time in a very long time, she let herself believe in Ty and the future he was promising.

CHAPTER TWENTY-THREE

Ty wasn't all that surprised to find his mother waiting up for him when he got back to the house. He'd known she would have questions about whatever Dana Sue had reported to her earlier tonight. What did surprise him, though, was finding Helen with her. Her grim expression suggested they weren't waiting here to congratulate him for reconciling with Annie.

He sat on the sofa and looked from one to the other. "Okay, what's wrong?"

Helen handed him some kind of official-looking document.

"What is it?" Ty asked, too impatient to look over the pages. "Just cut to the chase."

"Dee-Dee found herself a sympathetic judge in Ohio," Helen said. "I haven't figured out how she pulled it off, but that's a court order demanding that she be given temporary custody of Trevor until further details of a custody arrangement can be worked out."

Feeling the worst sense of betrayal he'd ever felt in his life, Ty shot to his feet. "You have to be kidding me! Come on, Helen, how can this be happening? How could Dee-Dee pull this off? She promised me she'd have Trevor back here tomorrow, dammit! She promised!"

"Well, apparently she doesn't intend to honor that promise, and now things are going to get really complicated, Ty," Helen said, her tone calm, but her eyes sparking with her own sense of outrage. "We're going to wind up with courts in two states warring over who has jurisdiction in the case. Because Trevor's in Ohio, the Ohio court will claim it should hear the case. And the court here, which has taken over jurisdiction from Georgia, will argue that any further proceedings be held right here."

"Why did I let myself get talked into this visit?" Ty moaned. "I trusted her. I felt sorry for her." He raked his fingers through his hair. "And this is what I get for it? Well, it's not going down this way, I can tell you that right now. I'll go up there and get Trevor." He gave Helen a hard look. "We can use this against her, right? The fact that she broke the terms on which I allowed the visit."

"We can try," Helen said. "It certainly won't reflect well on her that she lied to you, but it's going to be a while before it even gets to that stage. It could take some time for the courts to settle the whole jurisdictional dispute."

"This is crazy!" Ty exploded, pacing furiously. "Dee-Dee is not going to lay claim to my son. She's just proved every opinion I ever had about how reckless and irresponsible she is."

Helen regarded him with sympathy. "Remember what she told us, Ty, about not being able to have kids. She's desperate for a family, and she sees this as her only chance."

Ty stopped pacing and sat down. "What do I do?" he asked Helen.

"I go into court tomorrow and file papers to restore full custody to you. We're going to fight this, Ty."

"And in the meantime, what? I just leave him up there? Not going to happen."

His mother spoke for the first time. "Maybe you should go up there and reason with her, Ty. If everything you and Helen have said is true, then Dee-Dee is probably scared. It sounds to me as if she's so desperate for a child that she felt this was the only way. Get her fiancé involved. If he's the kind of upright man Dee-Dee claims he is, he's not going to want to be part of some messy custody battle. He'll be anxious to settle this."

"How do I even know they're where Dee-Dee said they'd be?" Ty asked wearily. "She could have taken Trevor anywhere."

"The papers have a Cincinnati address listed," Helen told him. "I compared it to the one she'd given to you, and they match."

"You really think she'll stick around there?" Ty asked, not buying it. "This guy's supposedly rich. He could send them anywhere in the world."

"The fact that she filed papers in court tells me she wants this to be legal," Helen said.

Ty wanted to believe her, but panic triumphed over reason. This couldn't be happening, not now when his life was coming back together, when he and Annie had a real shot at finally becoming the family he'd always dreamed of. Now every ounce of his energy had to be focused on getting Trevor back. Annie would have to take a backseat. She'd have to understand.

"Ty, try not to overreact," his mother urged. "Let Helen handle this through proper channels."

"That could take forever. I told Dee-Dee I wanted my son back here on Tuesday, and by God he's going to be back here," he declared fiercely, heading for the door.

"Where are you going?" Maddie asked, coming after him.

"To Cincinnati, and so help me God, I'd better find Dee-Dee there with my son, or all hell is going to break loose."

Blinded by rage, he sat behind the wheel of his car for a few minutes, drawing in deep, supposedly calming breaths, but they didn't do any good. This was all his fault. He'd let Dee-Dee get to him. And, face it, he'd wanted some time to work things out with Annie, so he'd let his guard down and okayed this trip. He was an idiot, and now his son was paying the price.

Even as he sat there berating himself, Ty was wise enough to know he shouldn't be driving in this condition. He pulled out his cell phone and hit the speed dial for Annie. Maybe it was selfish, but he needed her now more than he ever had.

As soon as she answered, he explained what had happened. "I need to go after my son, but I'm too furious to be behind the wheel of a car right now."

"I'll be there in ten minutes," she said without hesitation. "Sit tight. And, Ty, try not to worry. Trevor's just fine. Dee-Dee loves him. That's the whole point of this. She's not going to let anything happen to him."

"I know, I know," he said. "Just hurry, please."

Because right now, every second that passed felt like an eternity.

The two of them drove all night in alternating shifts to reach Cincinnati by daybreak. Ty located the address that Dee-Dee had given him, but when they reached the house, it was obviously deserted. There was no car in the driveway, no evidence of anyone around, no lights, not even a night-light in whatever room was intended for Trevor. That was when Ty nearly lost it.

"How could she keep him when she doesn't even know

that Trevor can't sleep without a night-light on?" he asked, choking back a sob. "She doesn't know what books he likes to read before bed or what his favorite pajamas are."

Annie reached out and laid her hand over his white-knuckled grip on the steering wheel. "Don't," she pleaded. "I might not know much, but I do know she'll get him whatever he needs. You have to stop thinking the worst. You'll make yourself crazy. Now, let's sit here and try to come up with a plan."

Her calm, reasonable attitude made him want to snap at her, too, but she was right. The situation called for logic, not hysteria.

"Why don't we get some breakfast?" she suggested. "You'll feel better once you've eaten."

He regarded her incredulously. "I'm not budging from this driveway."

"Okay, then. I saw a fast-food place on the corner when we turned onto this street. I'll walk there and bring something back. It's only a couple of blocks."

"You shouldn't be walking around alone at this time of night," he argued.

"It'll be daylight any second now," she assured him. "And it looks like a perfectly respectable, safe neighborhood."

"You have no idea whether it's safe or not," Ty said. "I'll take you and we'll order at the drive-through. It'll be faster."

Annie nodded. "If it would make you feel better, you could go and I could keep an eye on the house. I can sit right there on the front stoop."

Ty was torn. He hated to leave the house unattended for even five minutes, but he didn't want to risk Annie's safety. "No, we're sticking together. This won't take long."

At the drive-through, they ordered breakfast sandwiches, hash browns, juice and giant containers of coffee. Annie's dis-

gruntled complaints about the grease in their order brought
the first smile to his lips in what seemed like forever.

"Hey, it was your idea to come here," he reminded her.
"You can eat salads and oatmeal for a week to make up for it."

"I'll have to," she said.

Back at Dee-Dee's they took their food and went to sit on
the front steps. The air had the crisp bite of fall in it. Leaves
on the huge old trees that lined the street were starting to
turn. In South Carolina it was easy to forget how dramatically the seasons changed further north.

"The neighbors will probably call the cops on us," Annie
said.

"Let 'em," Ty said belligerently. "I wouldn't mind filling
the local police in on what Dee-Dee's up to."

"Can I ask you something?" Annie said eventually.

"Sure."

"Why are we waiting around here if you're so convinced
that Dee-Dee's fiancé is mixed up in this and will give them
whatever money they need to take off?"

"Because my mom and Helen are convinced that Dee-
Dee wants this to be handled in court."

"Could Dee-Dee have Trevor at her fiancé's place?"

"I suppose it's possible," he admitted. "I know his name's
Jim Foster, but I don't have an address or phone number for
him."

"I'll try Information," Annie said.

Unfortunately, the list of potential James Fosters was too
long to be much help. Even so, she said, "I'll start calling, if
you want me to."

Ty nodded. It was better than sitting around waiting for
daylight and doing nothing.

Before she could start dialing, Ty reached for her hand.
"Thanks for coming with me."

She met his gaze. "I'm glad you asked me," she said quietly. "It means a lot that you didn't take off alone and leave me in the dark about what was going on."

"I guess we're making progress."

She smiled at that. "I guess we are."

He held her gaze then. "Marry me, Annie. When this is over, marry me." Before she could answer, he rushed on. "I know I promised you all sorts of romance and serious courting, but right this second I need to know that, no matter what, we're going to be together forever."

For a moment, he thought she might hold out for the promised romance, but instead, she slid a little closer to him and slipped her hand into his. "Yes," she said quietly. "Whenever the time is right and Trevor's back where he belongs, I'll marry you."

Ty's heart turned over in his chest. "I love you, Annie Sullivan."

She nudged him in the ribs. "Good thing, because now that I've said yes, you're stuck with me."

With one last smile for him, she turned her attention to the list of numbers she'd managed to get from Information and started to make the calls, wincing when more than one of the recipients made a rude comment about the early hour. Each one turned out to be a dead end.

"The right one must have an unlisted number," she finally said in defeat.

"It's okay. We'll find them," Ty said with grim determination. "Maybe one of the neighbors will have a number for him. People should be getting up soon."

They sat there, side by side, until after daybreak. Ty felt the oddest sense of contentment steal through him, even under these awful circumstances. He could almost believe that with Annie by his side, everything would turn out okay.

He glanced down and saw that her eyes were closed as she leaned against him. Little wonder, after driving all night herself before he finally convinced her he was calm enough to take the wheel. He figured they could sit here a little longer before stirring things up with the neighbors.

To his shock, though, a few minutes later he heard the front door of Dee-Dee's house open. He shook Annie even as he shot to his feet. The woman standing in the doorway was vaguely familiar somehow, but it most definitely wasn't Dee-Dee. His heart sank.

"You might as well come inside," she said. "The neighbors will start to talk if you hang around out here much longer."

Ty stared at her incredulously. "You're inviting two perfect strangers into your house? Are you nuts?"

She grinned at him then. "You don't remember me, do you? I don't know why I'm surprised. Back then, you only had eyes for Dee-Dee. I'm Andrea."

A faint memory stirred. "You were going out with…" His voice trailed off.

She laughed. "I'm not surprised you can't remember. I could hardly remember myself from one week to the next. These days, however, I'm living a perfectly respectable life." She gave him a pointed look. "Just like Dee-Dee." She finally turned her attention to Annie.

"And you're the girl who got away," she said. "Ty talked about you a lot back then. In fact, he talked about you so much, I have no idea why Dee-Dee ever thought she had a chance with him."

Her humor and candor finally struck a chord with Ty. She'd been the voice of reason years ago, clear-headed, a little bit cynical, when so many of the other girls had been starry-eyed romantics.

"So you and Dee-Dee are roommates now?" he said.

She nodded. "I gave her a place to stay when she first came back from Wyoming. Neither one of us has been near a ball park in years. And, of course, she's about to marry Jim, who's about as respectable as they come. The only thing missing from her life is her little boy."

"She can't just take him from me," Ty said.

"She went to the court," Andrea reminded him. "She has permission for him to be here until custody is settled."

"Then if she's doing all this by the book, where is she?" Ty demanded.

"At Jim's, about a half hour out of town," Andrea said. "She called and told me to keep an eye out for you. She had a feeling you'd come tearing up here the second you got the court documents. I've already called her. She should be here soon."

Annie squeezed his hand. "I told you it was going to be all right."

Ty wasn't going to be convinced of that until he held Trevor in his arms again, but at least he could almost believe that would happen sooner, rather than later.

Annie felt as if she were caught up in some kind of a nightmare, though it was finally taking a turn for the better. Once Trevor walked through the door and Ty released the breath it seemed like he'd been holding most of the night, the nightmare truly would end.

In the meantime, she couldn't help looking around at the cozy little house where Dee-Dee lived, marveling at how ordinary it seemed. The furniture was comfortably shabby. There were plants on every windowsill. The art on the wall was cheerful and bright. When she commented on it, Andrea said casually, "Oh, yeah, Dee-Dee painted most of them."

"She's an artist?" Annie asked in amazement.

"I say she is. She says she's just dabbling."

"She's good."

"Tell her that. Maybe your opinion will count more than mine. Of course, she hasn't listened to Jim, and he collects masterpieces. Can you imagine?" She seemed awed by the idea of it. So, to be honest, was Annie.

Ty said nothing, his gaze firmly fixed on the front door. When they finally heard a car turn into the driveway, he was off the sofa and outside before Annie could blink.

She followed slowly behind him, just in time to see Dee-Dee emerge slowly from behind the wheel. She walked around to the passenger side and reached for the door, but Ty was there before her, yanking it open and releasing Trevor from his car seat.

"Hey, buddy," he said, clinging to him so hard Trevor finally complained. With obvious reluctance, Ty set him down.

"Daddy, guess what?" Trevor said, bouncing on the balls of his feet. "Me and Mommy had a 'venture."

"I know that," Ty said.

Andrea crossed the yard and hunkered down in front of him. "Hi, Trevor, I'm your mom's friend Andrea. Know what? When I found out you were coming, I baked a ton of cookies. Want to come inside and have one while the grown-ups talk?"

"Uh-huh," Trevor said at once. He looked first to his dad, then his mom. "'Kay?"

"It's fine," Ty said, then glanced to Annie.

"I'll go with them," she said at once.

They left Ty to have it out with Dee-Dee. From time to time their voices escalated, but they immediately reined them in, whether out of concern for the neighbors or to keep Trevor from hearing the argument.

Sitting with cookies and a glass of milk, Trevor talked

about the excitement of the trip, about the big house where he was staying and the swing set in the yard. He was clearly unaware of how much tension there was over it.

Andrea ruffled his hair as she took a seat at the kitchen table. "She's a good person," she said to Annie. "And this thing about not being able to have any more kids, it's really hit her hard. Maybe you could convince Ty to give her a break."

"Ty's the only one who can decide how he wants to handle this," Annie said. "He's been there for his son from the beginning."

"Not the very beginning," Andrea corrected. "I was there when she was puking her guts out with morning sickness. I was there when she lost her job because she couldn't be on her feet long enough to wait tables. Ty was trying to pretend it was all going to go away, so he could be with you."

Annie winced at the picture she was painting. "The point is, the minute he knew Trevor was his son, he took responsibility for him. He's raised him."

"Only because Dee-Dee gave him that chance. She recognized that Trevor would have a better life with Ty. Isn't that what a mom's supposed to do, what's best for her kid? She was barely more than a kid herself, but she did the right thing."

"It's still the right thing," Annie said.

"Haven't you ever done anything you wanted to take back?" Andrea asked. "Hasn't someone ever given you a second chance?"

Despite her desire not to hear what Andrea was saying, her words resonated with Annie. "I understand what you're saying, but it's not up to me," she repeated.

"Just do what you can, what feels right to you, that's all I'm asking," Andrea said.

Annie merely nodded. What else could she do? The request wasn't unreasonable. It just meant that she and Ty might be at odds on the most important issue they'd ever have to face.

When Ty finally walked inside, he was more at peace, but he still didn't entirely trust Dee-Dee. As they'd talked, though, he'd seen for himself how scared Dee-Dee had been that he would cut Trevor out of her life forever. He also saw how attached Trevor was to her. As much as he might want it, he knew he couldn't go back to the way things had been.

Reluctantly, he'd come to a decision. He'd give the visit a few more days. Maybe by then he'd be able to reason with Dee-Dee. Perhaps there was a compromise they could both live with, one that would prevent the need for a lengthy court battle. Of course, he didn't intend to let Trevor or Dee-Dee out of his sight in the meantime.

In the kitchen, he explained his decision to Annie. "If you can stay, I want you here, but I understand if you need to get back. I'll arrange for a flight to Atlanta or Columbia, whichever we can get first, and then have a car pick you up to drive you from the airport to Serenity."

Annie nodded, her expression neutral. "I think that would be best."

"Then I'll make the arrangements." He made the necessary calls, but his gaze never left Annie's face. She looked unbearably sad. When he'd hung up from the last call, he said, "I'll take you to the airport. There's a flight leaving in ninety minutes."

"You stay here with Trevor," she said. "I can take a cab."

Ty wasn't always attuned to the moods of other people, but there was no mistaking the fact that Annie was withdrawing from him right before his eyes. He made the call for a taxi, then walked with her to the porch to wait.

"You understand why I have to stay, right?"

"Of course."

"And you know I want you here?"

"Sure," she said, though she sounded oddly defeated.

"Okay, then tell me why you look as if I've just stolen something precious from you."

Before she could reply—if she'd even intended to—a cab pulled to the curb. She pressed a quick, impersonal kiss to his cheek. "I'll see you at home."

And then, before he could get to the bottom of what was going on in her head, she was gone. And he had a sinking sensation in the pit of his stomach that unless he figured things out in a hurry, she might be leaving him for good.

Two days after she'd returned from Cincinnati, Annie was just finishing up with a client when Elliott came to her, his expression filled with barely contained fury. "There's someone in your office. You need to see her right now."

"Who is it?"

"She wouldn't give me a name. She said she was an old friend."

Annie shrugged. She couldn't imagine any reason for the big mystery, but she had a few minutes before her next client was due. "Okay, I'll see her. Let me know when Phyllis gets here, okay?"

"I'll take Phyllis's session today," Elliott said. "You're going to need more than a few minutes," he said, his tone as grim as his expression.

Annie studied him. "What's going on? Something about this woman upset you?"

He nodded. "She had bruises, Annie. Ugly ones. Some look fresh to me. Others look as if they're fading. I'd lay money that she's been abused. If I'm right, the first call you need to make is to the police."

"Maybe she was in an accident," she said, unable to imagine who she knew who was likely to have been abused.

Elliott shook his head. "You'll see. Just go before she changes her mind about coming here and takes off. She's awfully skittish. For all I know the person who did this to her is right on her heels."

Annie practically ran to her office. When she opened the door, she took one look at the woman huddled in a chair, her face turned away. But even before the woman turned to face her, even before she saw the extent of the damage, she knew.

"Raylene," she whispered. "Oh, my God, Raylene, who did this to you?"

It had been four months since Helen's mother had moved in. She was getting around well now and no longer needed Mrs. Lowell to help her beyond driving her to physical therapy, but Helen still didn't believe she was ready to live on her own. As much as she'd griped about Flo's presence, she was reluctant to see her move out. She kept thinking about the lost opportunity to finally make a real connection with her mother. Time was slipping away, and the bond was no stronger than it had ever been.

Unfortunately, now that the condo in Florida had sold and the money would soon be in the bank, her mother seemed determined to start looking for her own apartment. Mary Vaughn had set aside time to take them around tonight.

However, when Helen came in from work expecting to find her mother ready and filled with exuberance, she found Flo sitting on the sofa, all dressed except for her shoes. She was wearing a pair of slippers. She was also verging on tears.

Helen immediately went to her. "Mom, what's wrong? Are you hurt? Did you fall again?"

Her mother shook her head.

"Then what's going on? Why do you look as if you're about to cry?"

Flo gave her a plaintive look. "I wanted to be all dressed when you got here, so we could go out and look at apartments. I even spoke to Mary Vaughn myself this afternoon, and she says she has some perfect ones for us to see."

Helen still wasn't getting the problem. "It looks to me as if you're ready to go. If you're not feeling up to it, though, we can do it another day. There's no rush. In fact, I think it would be better to wait another week or two, at least."

Her mother shook her head. "I feel fine, but we won't be able to go another day, either."

Helen regarded her blankly. "Mom, I'm not following this. What's the problem?"

Flo gestured across the room to a suitcase. "I had the nanny bring that down. I wanted to put on a pair of my favorite shoes."

"Okay," Helen said slowly. "Were they missing? Did you forget to pack them?"

Flo looked up at her with a dismayed expression. "I can't wear them. None of them. Not one single pair of shoes I own."

"Why on earth not? Are your feet swollen?"

"Just look at them," her mother said.

Helen opened the suitcase that had apparently been stuck in the back of the closet since they'd driven up from Florida in the car she'd rented for the trip. At least she assumed it had been there, because she couldn't recall seeing it before. She knelt down and examined the shoes, a dozen or more pairs of the kind of high-heeled sandals she might have chosen.

Oh, these weren't the expensive Jimmy Choos or Manolo Blahniks that filled her closet, but the styles were similar, sexy shoes meant for a woman who was steady on her feet. These were indulgence shoes, the kind Helen knew better than anyone, because she had a wardrobe of them.

"If I put those on, I'll break my neck next time," her mother said despondently. "I'm just too old and unsteady to take that chance."

Helen couldn't help it, she started to chuckle.

Her mother regarded her indignantly. "It's not funny."

"It is a little bit funny," Helen said, grinning. "All these years I've wondered why you and I were nothing alike. Oh, we're both workaholics, but that's because you had to be and I love it. These shoes..." She picked them up one by one and held them in the air. "*These* are what we have in common."

Her mother stared at her for a moment, then started to chuckle right along with her. "Well, it is a starting point, isn't it? Not everyone can claim an addiction to amazing shoes."

Helen stood up and announced decisively, "Let's forget about looking at apartments tonight. I'll call Mary Vaughn and reschedule. I saw in the paper that there's a shoe sale going on at the mall. And there were some fantastic flats I've had my eye on. Even I can't walk around in three-inch spike heels all the time anymore. I certainly can't chase after Sarah Beth wearing them."

Her mother's eyes lit up. "Flats? I could wear flats. Anything to get out of those horrible sneakers I've been wearing. For so many years that's all I could wear when I was working as a waitress. The minute I could start wearing something prettier and more feminine, I went a little crazy."

"Then let's get Sarah Beth, who's a shoe diva in training, and go shopping. The Decatur-Whitney women need to splurge."

For all these months—years, in fact—Helen had been try-ing to find a way to bond with her mother. Who knew it had been underfoot, literally, all along.

CHAPTER TWENTY-FOUR

It took Annie an hour to persuade Raylene to leave her office at the spa and go to Sarah's.

"I don't want to see anyone else," Raylene whispered, a flush of embarrassment behind the bruises and cuts on her face. "I only came to you because I didn't know where else to go."

"Sarah's not just anyone. We're friends, Raylene, all three of us. We'll deal with this together."

Raylene finally nodded. She looked as if she was simply too tired to fight anymore. Annie bit back all the questions she had, determined to save them until Raylene would only have to answer them once. Given how secretive she'd become in recent years, once was going to be difficult enough.

"I'll call and tell her we're on our way," Annie said.

She left her office to make the call, filling Sarah in as succinctly as possible. "It's okay if she stays with you, isn't it? I think that would be better than my house."

"Of course she can stay here, assuming she can tolerate having the kids around. It might be too much for her."

Annie hadn't considered that. "I guess we'll just have to play it by ear."

After she'd hung up, she went to Elliott. Before she said a word, he merely said, "I've got you covered. If you need any kind of backup, let me know. I'd like to get my hands on whoever did that to her."

Annie nodded. "I think there will be a waiting line for that. Thanks, Elliott."

Back in her office, Raylene needed help just to stand. Once she was on her feet, she arranged a scarf to hide most of the damage to her face, then walked gingerly down the hallway and out the back entrance to the parking lot where Annie had left her car. They made the five-minute drive in silence.

At Sarah's, she turned to Annie. "Thank you for not asking any questions."

"Oh, I have plenty of them," Annie said. "So will Sarah, but you can answer them when you're ready."

"Right now, I just need a safe place to hide out for a little bit. Then I'll go back home."

Annie stared at her incredulously. "I can't believe you're even considering going back home! Are you crazy? Look, I know you said no questions, but Paul is the one who did this to you, right?"

"He never meant to lose his temper the way he did," Raylene said, near tears. "Honest. And it was because of you and Sarah. He was upset that you'd come to Charleston. And he knew you followed him to the country club. He accused me of asking you to spy on him."

"I'm sorry if he got mad at us and took it out on you," Annie said contritely. "But that was just the excuse this time, wasn't it?" She didn't even try to hide her contempt. "What did he tell you the last time? And the time before that? I'm sure he has a fresh excuse every single time."

"Don't, please don't," Raylene begged. "He's not a bad person. He's given me everything I could possibly want."

"Except the ability to feel safe in your own home," Annie said more calmly. "Nothing is worth more than that, sweetie. Nothing! Not the fancy house, not the country club. None of it."

She stopped the lecture, because it was evident that Raylene wasn't ready to hear it yet. Once she'd rested, once she'd had her injuries checked out, once she'd had time to think things through, she would see that she couldn't go back home. And if she still didn't get it, then Annie and Sarah would talk until she understood that her life shouldn't be like this. She deserved better.

Sarah was waiting for them at the front door. Because Annie had prepared her, she managed to keep her shock out of her expression. Instead, she simply opened her arms and welcomed Raylene into them.

"I've sent the kids next door for an hour or so," she told them. "That'll give us time to get you settled, Raylene. I have a room all ready for you. Did you bring anything with you?"

Raylene shook her head. "All I could think about was getting away."

"That's okay. You can borrow some of my clothes until we have a chance to shop. They'll be too big for you, but they'll do."

"Or I can get you some things from my house," Annie offered. "I'll run over there right now."

She needed a few minutes to herself, anyway. Because seeing Raylene had reminded her that no matter how terrible things had gotten between her and Ty, she'd never had to endure anything like this, being abused by a man who was supposed to love and protect her. The quick drive to her house would offer her a chance to give thanks for that.

★ ★ ★

Ty was almost at his wit's end. Ever since Annie had left Cincinnati, she'd stopped taking his calls. He'd managed to catch her once or twice at the spa, but mostly because he'd asked the receptionist to simply tell her it was a client on the line. Those occasions had been awkward and unsatisfactory. No matter how he tried to engage her in conversation, she responded with yes-or-no answers in a monotone.

He knew from talking to his mom that Annie was spending a lot of her spare time these days trying to help Raylene, who'd turned up in town in bad shape. He also knew that had nothing to do with her refusal to talk to him. Something had happened in Cincinnati, something he'd obviously missed, to make her pull away yet again.

Thankfully, he and Trevor would be back in Serenity in a few hours, thanks to a hastily negotiated settlement between the attorneys that would give Dee-Dee limited visitations for now and more generous ones once she'd proved to Ty and the court that she was completely reliable.

After spending some time with Jim Foster, there was no longer any question in Ty's mind that his son would be safe spending at least some time with them. Ty would come along with Trevor, at least until after the wedding. He'd admitted he would feel more comfortable about extending the visits once Dee-Dee and Jim were married. They'd both understood. Helen and Dee-Dee's attorney were working out the details now.

Amazingly, it had been Andrea who'd convinced him to open his heart and his mind to what Dee-Dee was asking. As the person who'd spent the most time with Dee-Dee over the years, she'd enabled him to see Dee-Dee for the person she'd become, rather than the reckless young woman she'd once been. And Dee-Dee herself had convinced him she'd only acted so rashly out of fear.

With the custody arrangements all but completed, he could turn his full attention to making plans with Annie. He just had to get her attention long enough to resolve whatever had caused her to pull away just when everything should have been perfect.

He glanced into the rearview mirror and saw that Trevor was sound asleep in the back of the car. That was too bad, because he'd be reenergized and ready to play once they got to the house.

Sure enough, the instant he pulled to a stop in the driveway, Trevor woke up, bright-eyed and eager to see his grandma, Cal, Jessie and Cole. He'd even insisted on picking out presents for them when they'd stopped on the road for lunch. Ty wasn't sure what his mom and Cal were supposed to do with a battery-operated hamster, but Trevor had insisted they needed it.

As soon as they were inside, his mom pulled him aside. "Go to Annie. I know she's been on your mind. I'll get Trevor to bed."

He regarded her with gratitude. "Are you sure?"

"Of course."

He hesitated, then turned back to her. "Mom, I'm sorry for how crazy I was acting the night I found out Dee-Dee had filed for custody. None of that was your fault or Helen's, but I acted as if it were."

Maddie gave him a fierce hug. "Who could blame you? I can't imagine what I'd do if someone came along and took any one of my kids away from me. I suspect my vocabulary would be a lot worse than yours and I'd mow down anyone who stood between me and getting them back."

"But you were on my side. I forgot that for a minute."

"And now you've remembered. Go. Fix things with Annie. She's been too quiet since she got back from Cincinnati. Some of that's worry about Raylene, but I know the rest has to do with you."

"I asked her to marry me," Ty told her. "And she said yes."

His mom's eyes brightened, then filled with tears. "Oh, Ty, I am so happy for you."

"I'm just scared she's already thinking of reasons to take it back."

"You won't let her, and that's all there is to it. You could always talk that girl into just about anything."

"She's not a girl anymore. She's a woman and stubborn as a mule."

"I have faith in you."

Ty carried that faith with him as he went to find Annie.

Annie was having a margarita with Sarah and Raylene when her cell phone rang. She glanced at the caller ID and saw it was her mom.

"Hey, Mom, what's up?"

"Ty's here at Sullivan's and he's looking for you. Should I tell him you're at Sarah's?"

Annie wanted to say no, but what was the point? If he was determined to find her, he'd eventually track her down.

"Don't tell him I'm at Sarah's. Tell him I'll meet him at our house." She might as well get this conversation over with, and she didn't want an audience.

When she hung up, she drank the last of her margarita and stood up. "I have to go," she announced.

"Ty's back?" Sarah asked.

Annie nodded.

Raylene gaze her a quizzical look. "You don't look happy about that. How come?"

Sarah's gaze narrowed. "She's right. You don't look happy."

"I'm going to tell him that this isn't going to work, after all." She'd made up her mind to that on the flight back from Cincinnati. Even with Ty's proposal ringing in her ears, she couldn't get beyond the fact that there would always be drama in their lives over Trevor and Dee-Dee.

Ironically, if she and Ty had no history, she might have been able to accept that. Lots of couples dealt with baggage from the past. In this case, though, that baggage had ripped her relationship with Ty apart. She'd begun to see that she would always be afraid it could happen again. Why set herself up for that kind of heartache?

Sarah and Raylene were both staring at her incredulously.

"You can't break up with Ty," Sarah said. "You've loved him forever."

"And he's even asked you to marry him," Raylene said. "You told him you would."

"I've had time to think about it," Annie told them. In fact, that was all she'd had since leaving Ty with Dee-Dee in Ohio, time to reconsider.

"Hold on," Sarah said. "Let's talk about this before you go and ruin your life."

"No time," Annie said. "He'll be at the house in a few minutes."

"I'm sure he won't mind having to wait," Sarah said determinedly, "especially when he finds out what's at stake."

"Yeah, you two have the relationship that Sarah and I both want," Raylene said. "You're with someone who's loved you forever, someone who respects you and listens to you."

"Someone who has a son with another woman," Annie added pointedly. "I adore Trevor and I think I could be a good stepmother to him, but he would be a constant reminder of the past. And Dee-Dee's going to be popping in and out of our lives."

Sarah scowled at her. "What you're really saying is that you don't trust Ty enough, that you don't love him enough."

Annie started to argue, but then fell silent. In fact, Sarah had gotten it exactly right. She simply didn't have enough faith in what she and Ty had. Recognizing that broke her heart.

Ty sat on the front steps at Annie's. She'd refused to let him inside, probably because she knew if she did, it was a very short trip straight to her bedroom. He'd listened with increasing dismay to her litany of reasons for breaking up with him.

"So, you see, this is for the best," she said, winding up. "You'll be free to move on, and so will I."

"That's not how it's going to work," he said flatly. "I proposed. You said yes. I'm not letting you back out now, especially when I haven't heard even one reason that makes a lick of sense."

She was about to launch into a repetition of her reasons, when he pulled her into his arms and kissed her until she all but melted against him. He released her and sat back.

"My reason for staying together trumps yours for breaking up," he said.

She blinked a couple of times, as if trying to get her bearings. "Sex isn't the issue."

"No, but love is," he said. "I love you. I've said that. I've done everything I can think of to prove it to you. I'm here, for heaven's sake. I could have done my rehab in Atlanta or anywhere else, but I came home because of you. This was our chance to get it right."

"It was our chance," she agreed. "But it didn't work out."

He stared at her incredulously. "How can you say that? You agreed to marry me just a few days ago."

She looked flustered by his vehemence. "Okay, maybe it almost worked out, but then I came to my senses."

"When, exactly, did you come to your senses?"

"In Cincinnati," she said. "Or on the flight home, to be more precise."

"Let me guess," he said. "It was because you'd left me behind with Dee-Dee."

She nodded. "She's always going to be there, Ty. She's Trevor's mom, so that's as it should be. I guess I'm just not broad-minded enough to want her reminding me all the time that the two of you cheated on me."

Ty raked a hand through his hair in frustration. "Years ago," he reminded her. "Other than Trevor, there is nothing between us now. Dee-Dee's in my past. There's no other woman in my life except you. Why can't you accept that?"

The look she gave him was bleak. "I don't know," she said ruefully. "I just know I can't."

"Do you believe I love you?"

She hesitated, then said, "I want to."

He could have stood up right then and walked away. Maybe that was what he should have done, but he couldn't. Instead, he clasped her hands and waited until she met his gaze. "Then I'm going to spend as long as it takes, do whatever it takes until you do. Because I am not giving up on us, Annie Sullivan. Not ever."

Then he did stand up and walk away, leaving her to wrestle with the certainty that he *would* be back, again and again, for as long as it took.

Annie had to give credit to Ty for persistence. He'd told her he wasn't giving up easily and he hadn't. She didn't know

what to make of his determination in the face of her conviction that they'd be better off apart.

When it came to his rehab, she'd never known anyone to
work harder or with more grit and determination. When it
came to trying to win her back, he was no slouch, either.
Her resolve had been wavering for a while now, though she
was doing her best not to let him figure that out.

She was reminding herself yet again that she had to be
strong, when her cell phone rang.

"Where are you?" she asked when she heard Ty's voice.
"Here I was just thinking about how dedicated you've been,
and you don't show up tonight."

"I'm here," he said. "Upstairs."

She glanced overhead, as if she could spot him through
the ceiling. "What are you doing up there?"

"Come up and find out."

The spa's hot tub and private massage rooms were upstairs.
She wasn't sure she had any business going close to either one
with Ty, not when it was getting harder and harder to remember all the reasons why she needed to stay clear of him.

"I think you'd better get back down here, so you can work
with the weights."

"Later," he insisted. "After you come up here."

"I am not climbing into the hot tub with you," she warned
him.

"Okay."

"Or giving you a massage. You'll need to talk to Jeanette
to schedule that."

"Not an issue."

She snapped her phone shut, then climbed the stairs…and
walked into a candlelit, flower-filled fantasy. The armloads
of daisies he'd brought her were nothing compared to this
sea of flowers in every color of the rainbow.

"Oh," she whispered on a gasp. "Ty, what have you done?"

"I knew I'd never talk you into a romantic dinner in Charleston. You still seem to be under the misguided impression that you and I aren't meant to be together. I decided it was time to prove you wrong."

Tall tapers, chunky white candles and tea lights were everywhere. Bouquets of flowers filled every kind of vase or container imaginable. And it all surrounded a table set for two.

"I suppose my mother provided dinner," she said with a sense of wonder.

He nodded. "It's your favorite. Chateaubriand for two."

She blinked hard. "I haven't had that since..."

"Since we had dinner in Atlanta right after I signed with the Braves."

It was also the night they'd made love for the first time after years of waiting for it to be just right, to be sure it was going to last forever. The frenzied lovemaking on the beach had followed, along with too many other places to count.

She nodded, suddenly speechless.

"There's apple pie with Erik's homemade cinnamon ice cream for dessert," Ty added.

He crossed the room and hit a switch on a CD player. Soft music filled the room.

"Are you trying to charm the socks off me?" she asked, looking into his eyes. The love she saw there nearly staggered her. She wondered how she could ever have questioned it.

"Socks, shoes, anything else you'd care to shed," he said, drawing her into his arms. "I love you, Annie Sullivan. I could live with never again walking onto a ball field, but I can't live without you. Please don't ask me to do that."

She swallowed hard. "What are you saying?"

"The same thing I've been saying over and over. Marry

me, Annie. Be a mom to Trevor. Have more babies with me. I can't change the past, but I can promise to make the future everything you deserve."

"And Dee-Dee?"

"You'll never have to see her. I'll make sure Trevor visits her as scheduled, but she won't set foot in our home ever again."

"That may not be entirely practical," she admitted. "I suppose I could tolerate seeing her once in a while." Especially if she had Ty's ring on her finger and her house filled with their kids.

"I'll do whatever it takes to make you comfortable with the situation. Let's not forget she's marrying Jim next week."

Annie was surprised. She'd feared they would drag it out, maybe never marry. "That soon?"

Ty grinned as if he'd read her mind. "The church is booked, the wedding cost a fortune. She won't be backing out."

The news was reassuring, but she tried to cling to one last shred of sanity. How could they possibly make it work, make it last, if he was going back to Atlanta any day now, and she wanted to stay right here in Serenity? She didn't want to be one of those baseball wives who followed their husbands from city to city during the season. Nor did she like the idea of waiting patiently in Atlanta, when her life was here.

He grinned at her. "I can practically hear those wheels grinding away in your head. You're overthinking it. You're worrying about me being in Atlanta, when you want to make Serenity your home."

"It's not a ridiculous consideration," she told him.

"Of course it's not. We can live here. When the team's on the road, it hardly matters where home is. We can keep my place in Atlanta for the rest of the time. We'll work it out. It doesn't have to be either one or the other. We can do it all, Annie. This is the way it was always supposed to be."

He touched her cheek, then kissed her until she could almost believe in the future he was describing. "You're sure," she whispered when she could gather her thoughts again. "This is really what you want, that *I'm* the one you want, because I won't share you, Ty. I can't do it. I love you too much."

"You and me," he swore. "Not just husband and wife, but best friends...forever."

★ ★ ★ ★ ★

Turn the page for a special preview of
MENDING FENCES
by #1 New York Times *bestselling author*
Sherryl Woods,
available soon in trade paperback from
MIRA Books.

CHAPTER ONE

Present

Grady Rodriguez had been a police officer for nearly twenty years, but he'd never gotten used to interviewing young women who'd been the victims of date rape. It wasn't quite the same as talking to those who'd been assaulted by strangers. For those women, there was little ambiguity about the attack. It was usually random, unexpected, violent and degrading. It could happen to any woman at any age who happened to be in the wrong place at the wrong time.

Date rape tended to happen to young, often inexperienced women who knew their attacker. They were left with a million and one questions about what they might have done differently, how their judgment about the guy could have been so wrong, why saying no hadn't been enough. He'd responded to too damn many of those calls, listened to too many brokenhearted sobs, seen too many injuries.

In either case, the women questioned everything about themselves. They dealt with unwarranted shame, sometimes made a thousand times worse by the well-meaning reactions of the people who loved them. In all instances, it changed who they were, made them more cautious, less trusting. Sometimes it destroyed relationships or even marriages.

From everything he could see as he and his partner, Naomi Lansing, walked into the off-campus Coral Gables apartment where tonight's attack had happened, Lauren Brown was typical. A pretty college student with shiny, long blond hair, she barely looked old enough to date. A kid that young shouldn't have had her innocence stripped away in a manner that left her eyes glazed with pain and disillusionment. Seeing her huddled in a corner of the bed in her room in tears, Grady wanted to punch his fist through a wall, but Naomi was cool and calm, the kind of soothing presence the situation required.

Naomi's compassion allowed him to remain in the background, to study the scene in a coldly analytical way. They were the perfect team for this kind of investigation, something he'd never have predicted back when they'd first been assigned to work together and every encounter had been a test of wills.

"She was like that when I came in," Lauren's roommate, Jenny Ryan, told them in an undertone. "Just rocking back and forth and crying. She said her date had hurt her, but she wouldn't say anything else. She asked me not to, but I called nine-one-one anyway. The creep shouldn't get away with this. I don't care who he is."

Something in her words gave Grady a chill, the hint that Lauren's attacker was well known, perhaps well-respected in the University of Miami campus community.

"You did the right thing," Naomi assured her. "We'll take it from here. Could you wait in the other room?"

For a moment, Jenny hesitated. "I'm not sure I should leave her."

Naomi sat on the edge of the bed, careful not to crowd Lauren. "You'll be okay, right? You're up to talking to me?"

Lauren's head bobbed once, but she didn't look up.

As Naomi began murmuring the most intrusive questions in her quiet, matter-of-fact voice, Grady studied the bedroom. Painted and carpeted in the bland beige of inexpensive rentals, it was decorated in a style that was too shabby to be chic. There were mismatched pieces of furniture, a few snapshots—family pictures, it looked like—stuck into the dresser mirror, a laptop computer next to a stack of textbooks and an antique rocker he would bet had been a prized possession from home.

Other than the tangled spread and sheets on the bed and a few pieces of clothing that had been tossed on the floor, the room was neater than most coed rooms he'd seen. Carefully gathering the clothes she'd apparently been wearing, he noted the buttons missing from her blouse, the torn strap of her bra and a rip in her panties, all consistent with someone intent on having sex, perhaps with an unwilling partner. He found three buttons scattered around the carpet and added those to the evidence.

Leaving it to Naomi to retrieve the sheets and spread and whatever trace evidence they might contain, Grady walked into the living room to join the roommate. "Any idea who Lauren was out with tonight?" he asked her.

"Evan Carter," she said without hesitation. "You know who he is, right?"

"Yeah, I've heard of him," he said, struggling to maintain a neutral expression.

Carter was a star football player at the University of Miami. Only a sophomore, there was already speculation about him becoming a top NFL draft choice before graduation. News reports, however, also cited his excellent grades, good enough for the career he hoped to have in the legal field representing professional athletes. He had brains, talent and charm—the kind of trifecta that made it easy for people to miss any hints of a darker side, the sense of entitlement and immunity that came with being a celebrity of sorts.

A local boy, Carter was already used to the spotlight by the time he entered UM. He'd been courted by both the Florida Gators and by Florida State Seminoles, top UM rivals. When he'd opted to stay close to home, there'd been a sigh of relief from the Miami fans, who'd followed his stellar high school career.

"Is that the crowd Lauren hangs out with—the jocks?" he asked Jenny.

"No way. To tell you the truth, Lauren's never dated much. She's basically pretty shy and quiet. She's here on a scholarship, so she studies a lot. Evan's the first guy she's really talked much about. They're in the same biology class—I'm in it, too—and they've been working on this project together for a couple of weeks now. When he suggested dinner and a movie, she couldn't believe this superjock had asked her out. She was so excited." Her lower lip quivered and her expressive dark eyes filled with anger. "Damn him for doing this to her!"

"Were you here when they left? Did you see them together?"

Jenny shook her head. "I had to go to the library to do some research for a paper that's due on Monday. I didn't get back till about two minutes before I called you."

"So you can't be sure they actually got together tonight," he suggested.

Jenny practically quivered with indignation. "Are you trying to say she made it all up or something?" she demanded.

"Lauren would *never* lie about who she had a date with or about what happened. Lauren doesn't lie. Period."

"Maybe a girl who doesn't date much developed a crush on this unattainable guy, built herself a whole fantasy scenario," he suggested.

"No, absolutely not!" Jenny said emphatically. "She's the most honest, grounded person I know. Her dad's a minister, for goodness' sake. She has this whole moral code she lives by. Most of the time the rest of us fall way short of meeting her standards, but she never judges any of us for that."

Satisfied, Grady backed off on any suggestion that Lauren could have exaggerated anything that happened with the Carter kid. Instead, he focused on what Jenny herself knew firsthand. "But you yourself didn't witness any part of the date, correct?"

She sighed. "No. I never saw them together, but I imagine there are plenty of witnesses in the building or on the block. It's mostly college kids living in this area, so there's always somebody going in or out, especially on a Friday night. And Evan's the kind of guy who attracts attention. He makes sure of it."

Grady knew the type. They thrived on being the center of attention, being recognized. They also thought they were above the law. Maybe tonight Grady would get lucky and that tendency would seal the case against Evan Carter.

"If Detective Lansing looks for me, tell her I'm going to knock on a few doors, see what I can find out from the neighbors," he told Jenny. "I'll be back in a few minutes. You'll stay put, right?"

"Of course. I'm not leaving Lauren."

The white stucco building on the fringe of the UM campus only had four units, two upstairs, two down. He tried the downstairs doors to no avail, then loped back upstairs and knocked on the door across the hall from Lauren's. When it swung open, the sound of classic jazz flowed through the air. The long-haired kid wearing boxers, a T-shirt and flip-flops stared at him with blurry eyes and a bewildered expression.

"Is the music too loud or something?" he asked Grady. "I try to keep it low."

"The music's not a problem," Grady assured him. He showed him his ID. "Mind if I ask you a couple of questions?"

"Am I in trouble?"

The kid sounded nervous, which made Grady wonder what he was up to. Then he caught a whiff of marijuana and knew. That, however, was a problem for another night.

"No, no trouble," he assured him. "This is your apartment?"

"I have a roommate, but he's out on a date."

Grady made a note. "What's your name?"

"Joe Haas."

"And your roommate's?"

"Dante Mitchell."

"He plays football, doesn't he?" Grady asked, trying to envision the huge defensive tackle sharing a place with this skinny, unassuming kid.

"We're from the same hometown. His folks think I'm a good influence on him." He shrugged, his grin self-deprecating. "As if he'd ever listen to me. Still, we get along okay."

"Have you been home all night?"

"It's Friday night," he said as if that was answer enough. "I've been here just chilling out."

"Seen anybody? Heard anything unusual?"

He stared at Grady with a blank expression. "Like what?"

"Anything that seemed out of the ordinary?"

"Did one of the apartments get robbed? Is that why you're asking all these questions?"

"No. I'm just trying to get a feel for what was going on around here tonight."

"I think everybody's out, except me. Dante left around seven. Jenny headed out about the same time with a bunch of books. She always goes to the library on Friday night. She says it's quieter then. The guys downstairs, they always head straight for happy hour after their last class on Friday. I don't think they've come in yet. They're usually pretty noisy, so I would have heard them if they'd come back."

"What about Lauren? Have you seen her?"

He shook his head. "I know she had a date with some jock, a friend of Dante's."

"Did she tell you that?"

"No, Dante mentioned it. He thought it was pretty hilarious for some reason."

"Why was that?"

"I guess because Lauren's really shy and this guy thinks he's some big hotshot."

"You know a name?"

Joe shook his head. "I'm not that into football. Dante probably said, but it didn't stick."

"And you never saw Lauren with this guy?"

He shook his head, then frowned. "Lauren's okay, isn't she? Nothing happened to her tonight, did it?"

Grady ignored the questions. "Thanks. If you think of anything else, give me a call." He handed him his business card.

Joe followed him back into the hall, his expression filled with concern. He bypassed Grady and headed straight for Lauren's door. Grady intercepted him. "Not tonight."

Alarm shadowed the boy's eyes. "I just want to check on Lauren. She's a sweet kid, you know?"

"Talk to her tomorrow, okay? She'll need a friend then."

He leveled a look at the kid. "And you might want to lose the weed before I come around again. Next time I won't look the other way."

"Shit!" Joe said, his expression immediately guilt ridden. He all but ran back to his own apartment and shut the door.

Grady shook his head. For a fraction of an instant he was grateful he didn't have teenagers, but then he thought of his beautiful little Megan and his heart ached. She would have been sixteen now and he would give every last breath in his body to have his daughter back, no matter what sort of foolish mistakes she might make.

Tonight wasn't the night to travel down that dark path, though. Another young girl needed him.

Inside Lauren's apartment, Jenny was exactly where he'd left her, blindly thumbing through a magazine, her attention directed toward the room where Naomi was still questioning Lauren.

"Did anybody see anything?" she asked when she realized he was back.

"The kid across the hall was the only one home, and he confirmed she was supposed to go out with some jock tonight, but he didn't see him and didn't have a name. He says his roommate had told him that."

Jenny smiled. "Joe's a little spacey most of the time, but he's a good guy. It might not seem like it, but he's practically a genius. He's studying physics, but most of the time he's bored, because he knows as much as the professors. He puts up with a lot from Dante, who thinks he's God's gift to the universe. Will it help that Dante knew about the date, too?"

"It might," Grady conceded.

"What happens next?"

"We'll need to get Lauren to the hospital, get her checked

out," he said. "Can you come along? It might make her feel better to have a familiar face around."

"If she needs me, I'm there," Jenny told him.

A few minutes later, Naomi emerged with Lauren and the four of them made the trip to the Rape Treatment Center at Jackson Memorial Hospital for the necessary indignity of a physical examination.

As they waited outside while a physician gathered evidence and offered counseling to Lauren with Jenny at her side, Grady sat beside Naomi and compared notes. "You think she'll go through with this? Will she press charges against the Carter kid?" he asked. "It's a tough road, especially with his high profile. The publicity could be pretty devastating, even if her name's kept out of it."

"She's scared," Naomi said. "But she's starting to get angry. If she weakens, something tells me her roommate will make sure she fights back."

He nodded. "Jenny's mad enough for both of them. I wish all the girls we come across had someone in their corner like that."

Naomi nodded. "Me, too."

"We need to do this one by the book," Grady said wearily. "I want an arrest warrant in hand before we go anywhere near that kid."

"That could take time," Naomi warned. "It's almost morning now and half the judges are going to be on the golf course and the rest are probably out on their boats."

"We'll call the state attorney's office and leave that problem up to them. I don't care how long it takes, I want that warrant before we say boo to that kid. The media's going to be all over this case and I'm not losing it because we didn't cross every *t* and dot every *i*."

Just then the weary-looking physician who handled far too many of these cases emerged from the treatment area.

"How's it going, Doc?" Grady asked Amanda Benitez.

"I'm starting to have a very jaded outlook on life in general and men in particular," Amanda said. "This guy roughed her up pretty good. He was smart about it, almost as if he knew how to go about it without leaving the kind of obvious visible marks that would call attention to what he'd done. Her stomach, her upper thighs have some nasty bruises, though. He was strong and he was mean."

Grady read between the lines. "He's done this before?"

"I'd say yes. You know the pattern as well as I do. It's not just about the sex. This is a guy who gets off on hurting women, the more innocent and defenseless the better. You have a name?"

Grady nodded. "And when this goes public, the shit is going to hit the fan."

It was well past midnight on Saturday and Marcie had just finished cleaning up the kitchen, putting every dish and glass back into place, polishing every piece of chrome and mopping the floor for the second time that day, when the doorbell rang.

Worried that it would wake Ken and the kids, she hurried into the living room to answer the door. Startled to see two uniformed officers and two other people in plain clothes outside at this hour of the night, she was tempted not to open the door, but weighed her caution against the possibility that they'd wind up waking her family by continuing to ring the bell. She finally opened the door a crack, the security chain still in place.

"Can I help you?"

"Pinecrest police, ma'am," one of the uniformed officers

said. "We have two detectives from Coral Gables who'd like to speak to your son. Since they're out of their jurisdiction, we came along."

"I don't understand," Marcie said.

"You're Mrs. Carter?" the female detective asked. "Evan Carter's mother?"

Marcie's breath lodged in her throat. "Yes, why?"

"We need to speak to your son," she repeated. "Is he here?"

"He's asleep. What is this about?"

"I'm Detective Lansing," the woman told her. "And this is Detective Rodriguez. We need to talk to Evan. Would you get him, please?"

Though it was phrased as a question, Marcie recognized a command when she heard one. She tried to think what Ken would do. He'd probably tell them to go away and come back at a civilized hour, but Marcie had been brought up to respect authority. Four very somber police officers from two jurisdictions were more than enough to intimidate her.

"You'll have to give me a few minutes," she said at last. "He's a sound sleeper."

"No problem. We'll wait," the woman told her.

Reluctantly Marcie let them inside, then started to climb the stairs. After only a couple of steps, she turned back. "Maybe I should…" she began, her tone apologetic. "Could I see some identification?" She'd read stories about fake police officers, even in uniform, and home-invasion robberies. Even though she recognized the Pinecrest logo on the uniform and saw the marked car in the driveway, it was smart to be absolutely sure.

Without comment all four of them held out badges and ID, removing any doubt that they were exactly who they'd said they were. She almost wished she hadn't asked. Until that instant, she'd been able to hold out a slim hope that this was all some hoax or maybe a case of mistaken identity.

Evan was a good kid. He always had been. Oh, he had a mouth on him. He was like his father that way, but he'd never given them any trouble. He'd never so much as put a ding or dent in the car, never gotten into mischief the way some of the other boys in the neighborhood had. His dad had seen to that. Ken was a stern disciplinarian and both her kids showed him a healthy amount of respect.

Thinking about that made this whole scene feel surreal. Once again she hesitated. "Why do you need to see Evan at this hour? Is he in trouble?"

For the first time, Detective Rodriguez spoke. "Ma'am, could you just get him? We'll explain everything then."

Filled with a sense of dread, she climbed the stairs. At the top she debated waking Ken but decided against it. Who knew what he would do or say? He had a quick temper and a sharp tongue. He tended to act first and think later. He might wind up making a bad situation worse. If Evan needed him, there would be time enough to wake him then.

Inside Evan's room, she found him sprawled face-down across his bed with a sheet barely covering him. Sometimes when she saw him like this, it caught her by surprise. In her heart, he was still her little boy, not a full-grown man with broad shoulders and muscles toned by hours of training at the gym. His cheeks were stubbled with a day's growth of beard and his blond hair, usually so carefully groomed, stuck out every which way. Seeing him reminded her of the way Ken had looked when they'd first met, way too handsome for his own good.

"Evan," she murmured, her hand on his shoulder. "Wake up! Evan!"

He only moaned and buried his head under the pillow, just as he had for years when she'd tried to wake him for school. Marcie knew the routine. She yanked the pillow away and then the sheet, averting her gaze from his naked body as she did so.

"Wake up!" she commanded, shaking him.

"Wha…? Go 'way."

"Get up now," she said urgently. "There's someone here to see you."

He blinked up at her. "What? Who?"

"They're police officers, four of them. Two local and two from the Gables."

"Shit, oh shit," he muttered, raking his hand through his hair.

Something in the panicked expression that flitted across his face terrified Marcie. Had there been an accident? Had he left the scene? Or drugs? She knew there were kids at college who used them, but Evan had always been smart enough to steer clear. He'd wanted his football career too much to risk messing it up by experimenting with drugs or steroids. Ken had hammered that lesson home years ago.

"Do you know what this is about?" she asked. "Should I get your dad?"

"I'll handle it," he said, grabbing a pair of jeans and yanking them on, then snatching up a T-shirt from the end of the bed and pulling it over his head. "Don't come downstairs, Mom, okay? I'll take care of this."

Marcie fought to stay calm. "I don't like the sound of this, Evan. I think someone should be with you. Do I need to call a lawyer?"

"I said I'd handle it," he snapped. "Go to bed."

Marcie winced at his tone. She should have been used to it by now. Ken used that exact same tone when he spoke to her, but it was relatively new coming from Evan.

"You're not going down there alone," she insisted. "Now either I come with you or I get your father."

"Whatever," he said belligerently.

Marcie followed him downstairs. At the bottom of the steps, the two detectives stood in his path.

"Evan Carter?" Detective Rodriguez asked.

"Yes. What the hell is this about?" he demanded, his voice radiating antagonism.

Again, he sounded so much like his father, it gave Marcie goose bumps. Instinct kicked in. She was about to try to smooth things over with the detectives, but realized they were oblivious to his attitude and totally focused on their own mission.

"You're under arrest for the rape of Lauren Brown," the woman said quietly. "Anything you say can and will be used against you..."

Rape! Marcie was incredulous. This simply couldn't be happening. As the detective read Evan his rights, Marcie fought back the bile rising in her throat and ran upstairs to wake her husband. She couldn't shake the sound of the word *rape*. It kept echoing in her head.

"Ken, get up now! The police are arresting Evan. They say he raped somebody."

She didn't have to say it twice. Ken bolted out of bed with a curse and ran for the stairs, Marcie right on his heels. She heard Caitlyn's door open and knew that her daughter had been wakened by the commotion as well.

"Mom, what's going on? Why is there a police car outside?"

Marcie couldn't bring herself to explain. "It's all a terrible misunderstanding," she said. "I'm sure that's all it is. Your father will straighten everything out, but I need to go with him."

"Go with him where?" Caitlyn asked, her eyes wide. "It's the middle of the night."

"To the police station. I'm going to call Emily and see if

you can go over and spend the night at their house, okay? I don't want you here alone."

"Who's been arrested? Is it Dad?"

"No, sweetie, it's your brother, but like I said, it has to be a mistake." Her hand shook as she picked up the phone and hit the number on the speed dial for Emily.

Her friend and neighbor answered on the first ring, instantly wide awake. "Marcie, is everything okay? I saw the flashing lights on a police car turning onto your street, but I never heard a siren. What's going on?"

"I can't explain now. Can Caitlyn stay with you?"

"Of course," she said at once. "Send her over. Is there anything else I can do?"

"Pray," Marcie said, her voice catching on a sob. "Pray that the police have made some horrible mistake. My boy…" She couldn't even finish the sentence.

"They came for Evan?" Emily said, sounding as shocked as Marcie felt.

"Yes. Please, just watch out for Caitlyn. She's on her way. I don't know how long we'll be gone. I'll tell you everything tomorrow."

"Go. Don't worry about anything here. Just promise that you'll call me if there's anything else I can do."

Marcie sighed as she hung up. She wondered if Emily would sound half as supportive once she found out what Evan had been accused of doing. There were some things even a best friend could never understand or forgive.

And if there was any truth, any truth at all to the charges, Marcie wasn't entirely certain she'd ever understand it, either.